BERA
THE ONE-HEADED
TROLL

Eric Orchard

:01

First Second
New York

For my mother

Copyright © 2016 by Eric Orchard
Published by First Second
First Second is an imprint of Roaring Brook Press,
a division of Holtzbrinck Publishing Holdings Limited Partnership
175 Fifth Avenue, New York, New York 10010
All rights reserved

Library of Congress Control Number: 2015944380

ISBN: 978-1-62672-106-7

Our books may be purchased in bulk for promotional, educational, or business use. Please
contact your local bookseller or the Macmillan Corporate and Premium Sales Department at
(800) 221-7945 ext. 5442 or by e-mail at MacmillanSpecialMarkets@macmillan.com.

With special thanks to Andrew Arnold

First edition 2016
Book design by Gordon Whiteside
Printed in China by RR Donnelley Asia Printing Solutions Ltd, Dongguan City, Guangdong Province
1 3 5 7 9 10 8 6 4 2

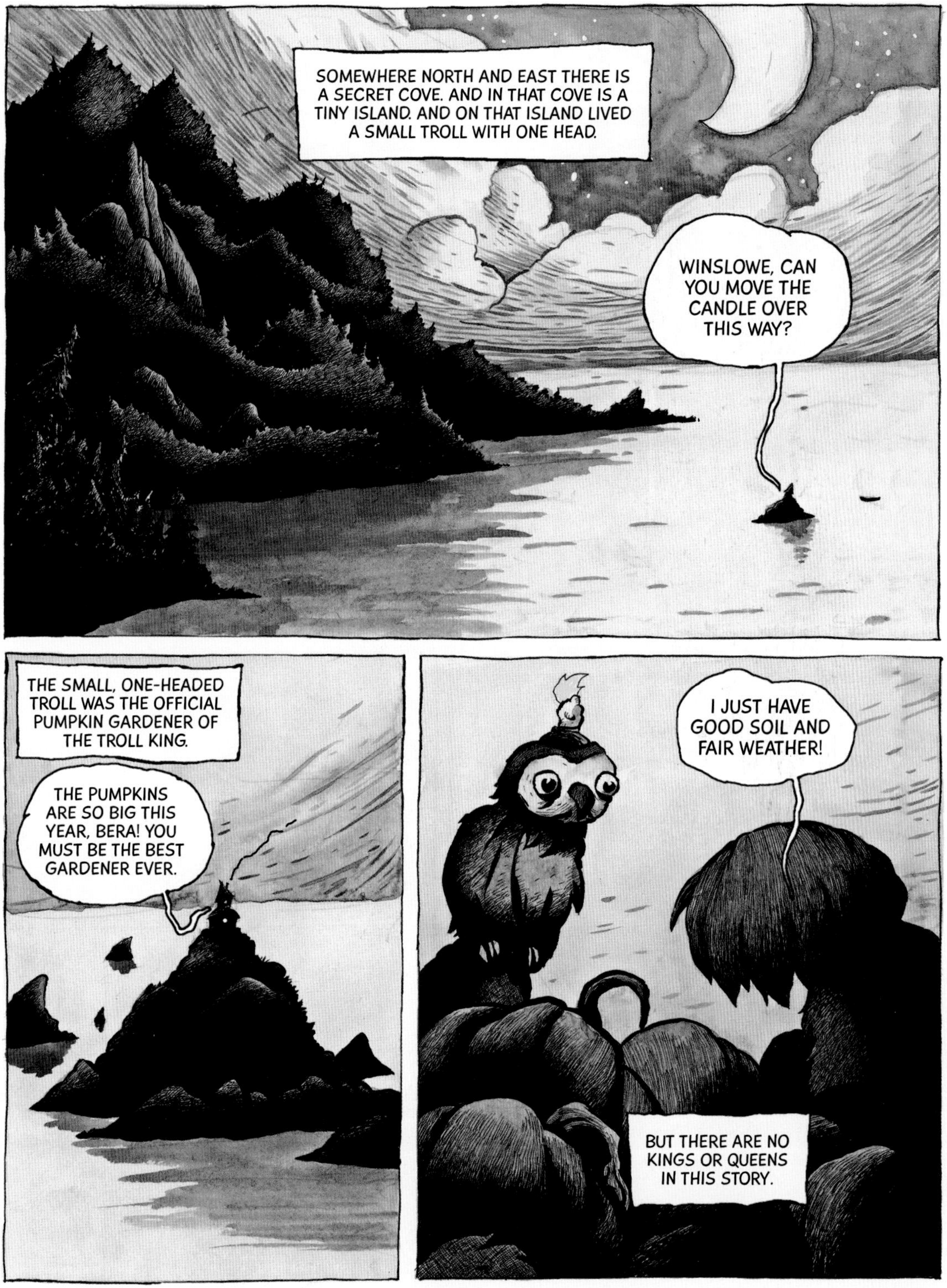
SOMEWHERE NORTH AND EAST THERE IS A SECRET COVE. AND IN THAT COVE IS A TINY ISLAND. AND ON THAT ISLAND LIVED A SMALL TROLL WITH ONE HEAD.
WINSLOWE, CAN YOU MOVE THE CANDLE OVER THIS WAY?
THE SMALL, ONE-HEADED TROLL WAS THE OFFICIAL PUMPKIN GARDENER OF THE TROLL KING.
THE PUMPKINS ARE SO BIG THIS YEAR, BERA! YOU MUST BE THE BEST GARDENER EVER.
I JUST HAVE GOOD SOIL AND FAIR WEATHER!
BUT THERE ARE NO KINGS OR QUEENS IN THIS STORY.

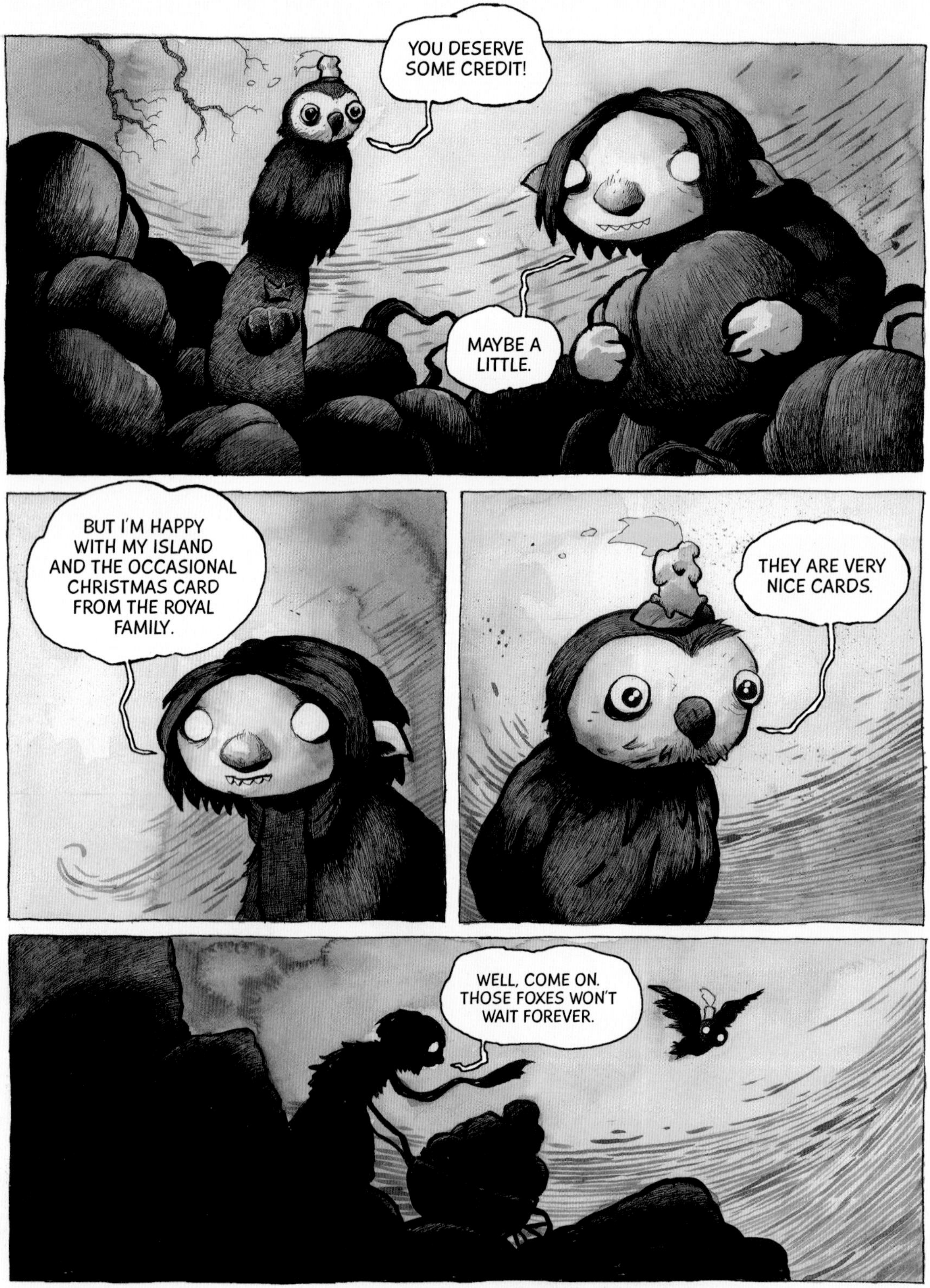
YOU DESERVE SOME CREDIT!
MAYBE A LITTLE.
BUT I'M HAPPY WITH MY ISLAND AND THE OCCASIONAL CHRISTMAS CARD FROM THE ROYAL FAMILY.
THEY ARE VERY NICE CARDS.
WELL, COME ON. THOSE FOXES WON'T WAIT FOREVER.

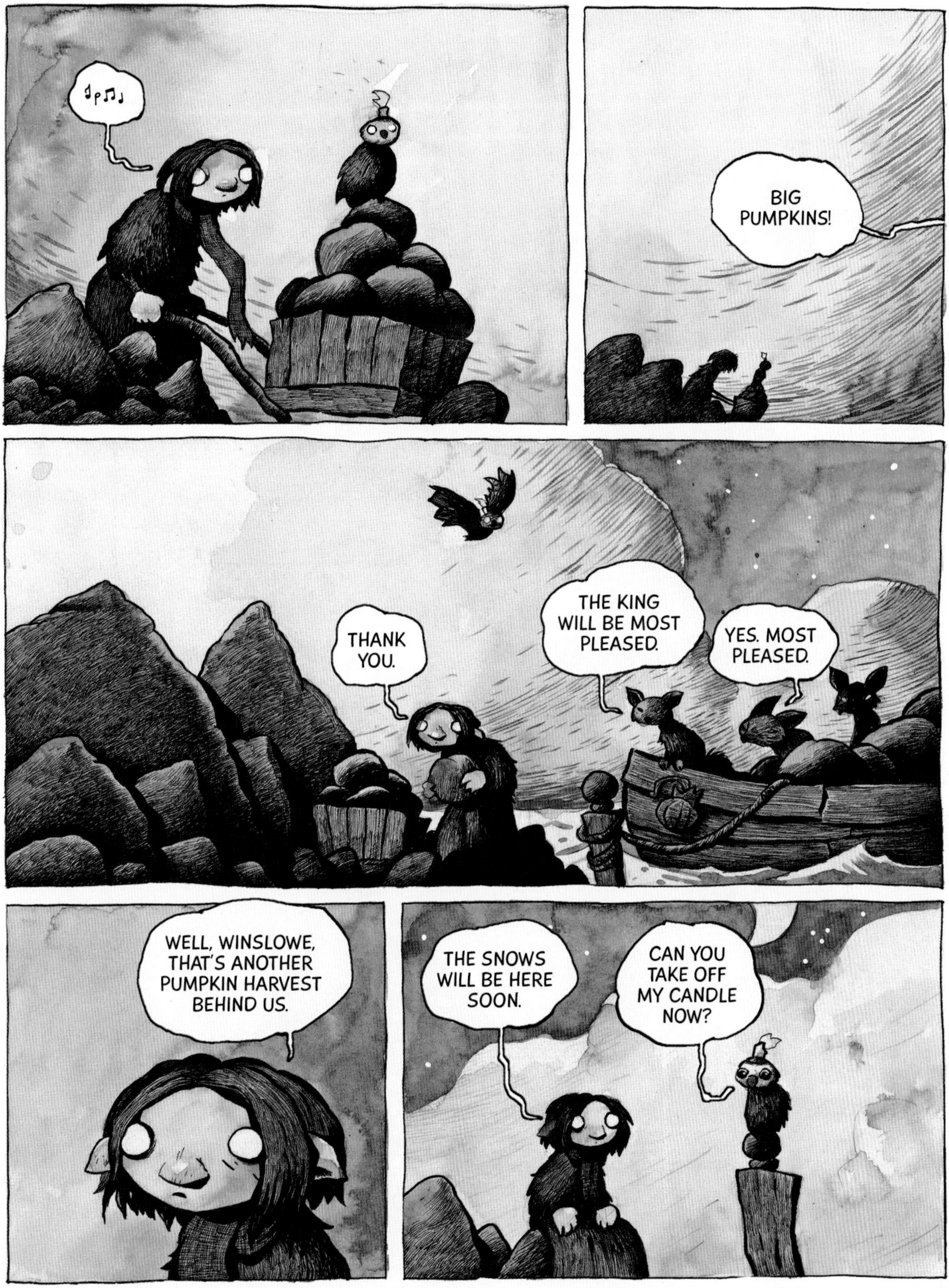

♪♪♫♩
BIG PUMPKINS!
THANK YOU.
THE KING WILL BE MOST PLEASED.
YES. MOST PLEASED.
WELL, WINSLOWE, THAT'S ANOTHER PUMPKIN HARVEST BEHIND US.
THE SNOWS WILL BE HERE SOON.
CAN YOU TAKE OFF MY CANDLE NOW?

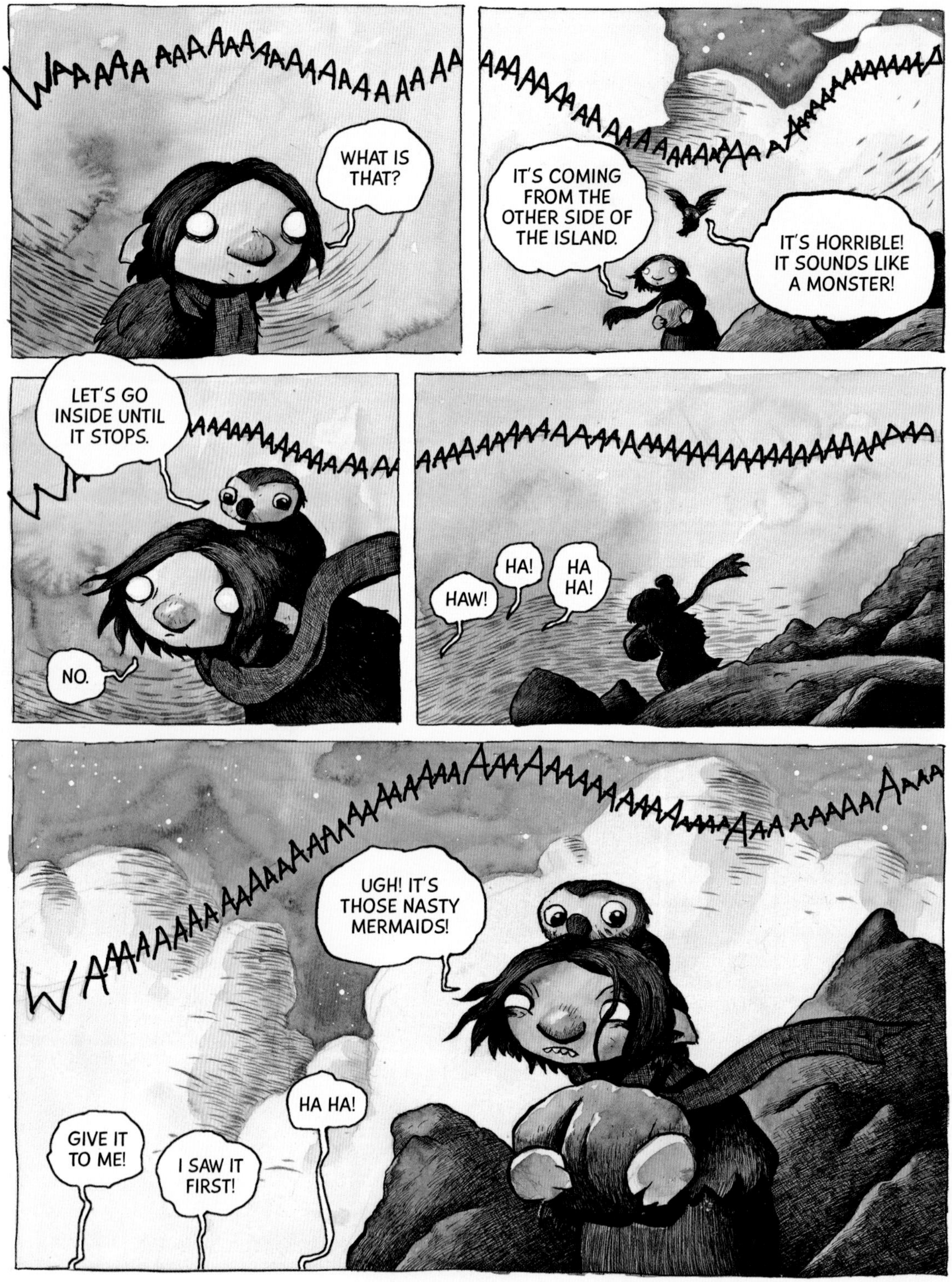
WHAT IS THAT?
IT'S COMING FROM THE OTHER SIDE OF THE ISLAND.
IT'S HORRIBLE! IT SOUNDS LIKE A MONSTER!
LET'S GO INSIDE UNTIL IT STOPS.
NO.
HAW!
HA!
HA HA!
UGH! IT'S THOSE NASTY MERMAIDS!
GIVE IT TO ME!
I SAW IT FIRST!
HA HA!

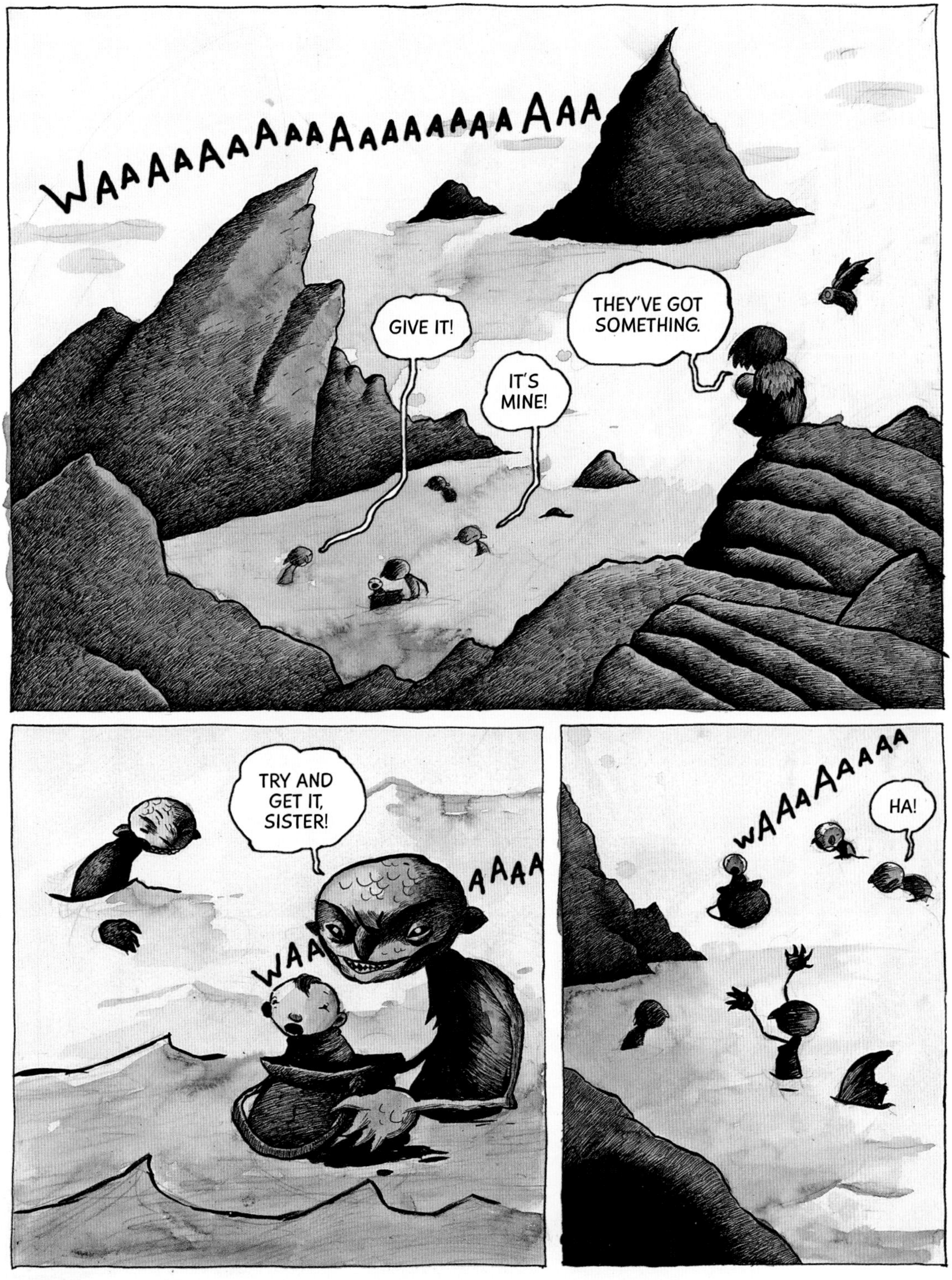
WAAAAAAAAAAAAAAAAAAAA
GIVE IT!
IT'S MINE!
THEY'VE GOT SOMETHING.
TRY AND GET IT, SISTER!
WAA
AAAA
WAAAAAAAAA
HA!

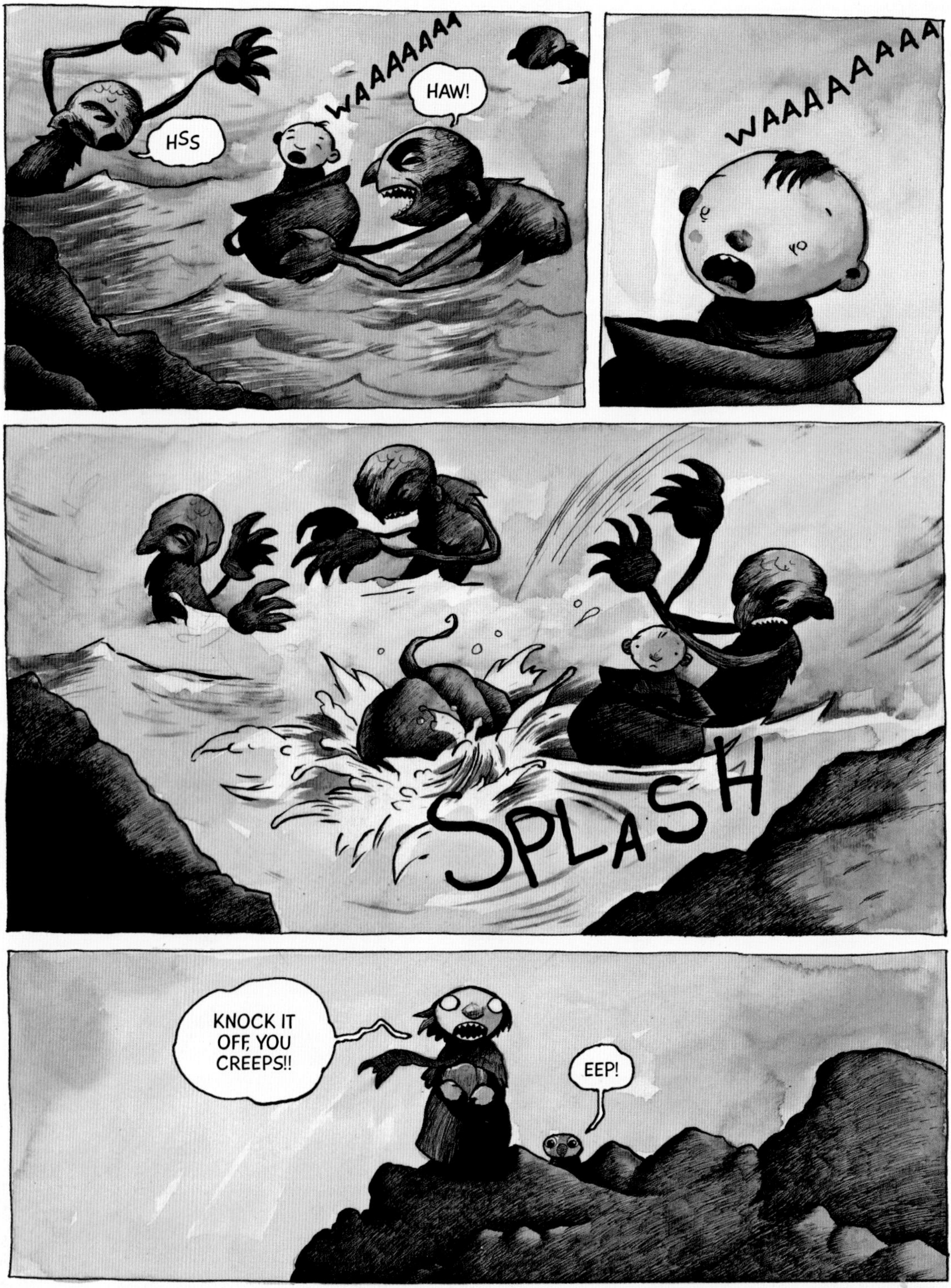
HSS
WAAAAAAA
HAW!
WAAAAAAAAA
SPLASH
KNOCK IT OFF, YOU CREEPS!!
EEP!

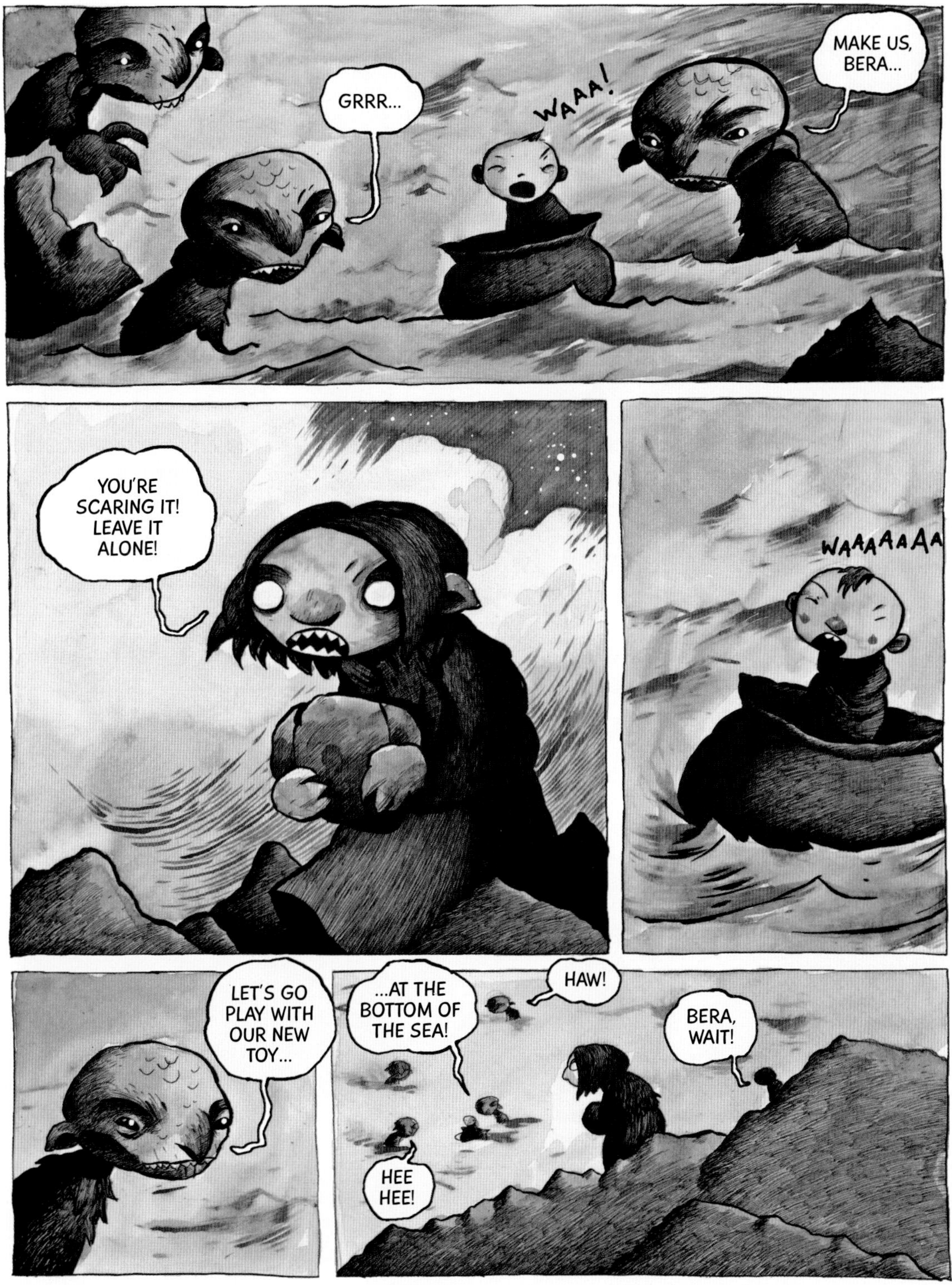
GRRR...
WAAA!
MAKE US, BERA...
YOU'RE SCARING IT! LEAVE IT ALONE!
WAAAAAAA
LET'S GO PLAY WITH OUR NEW TOY...
...AT THE BOTTOM OF THE SEA!
HAW!
HEE HEE!
BERA, WAIT!

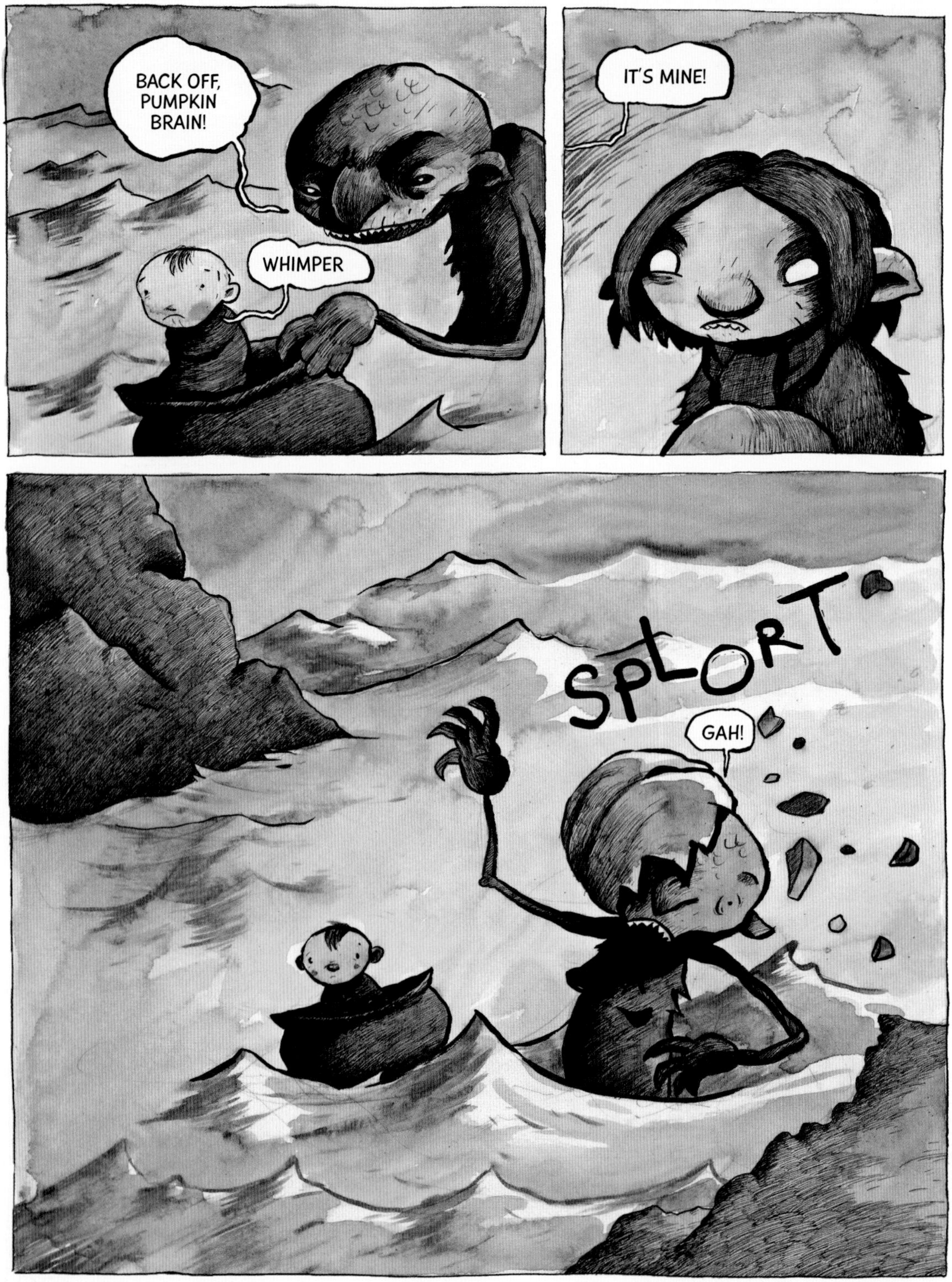
BACK OFF, PUMPKIN BRAIN!
WHIMPER
IT'S MINE!
SPLORT
GAH!

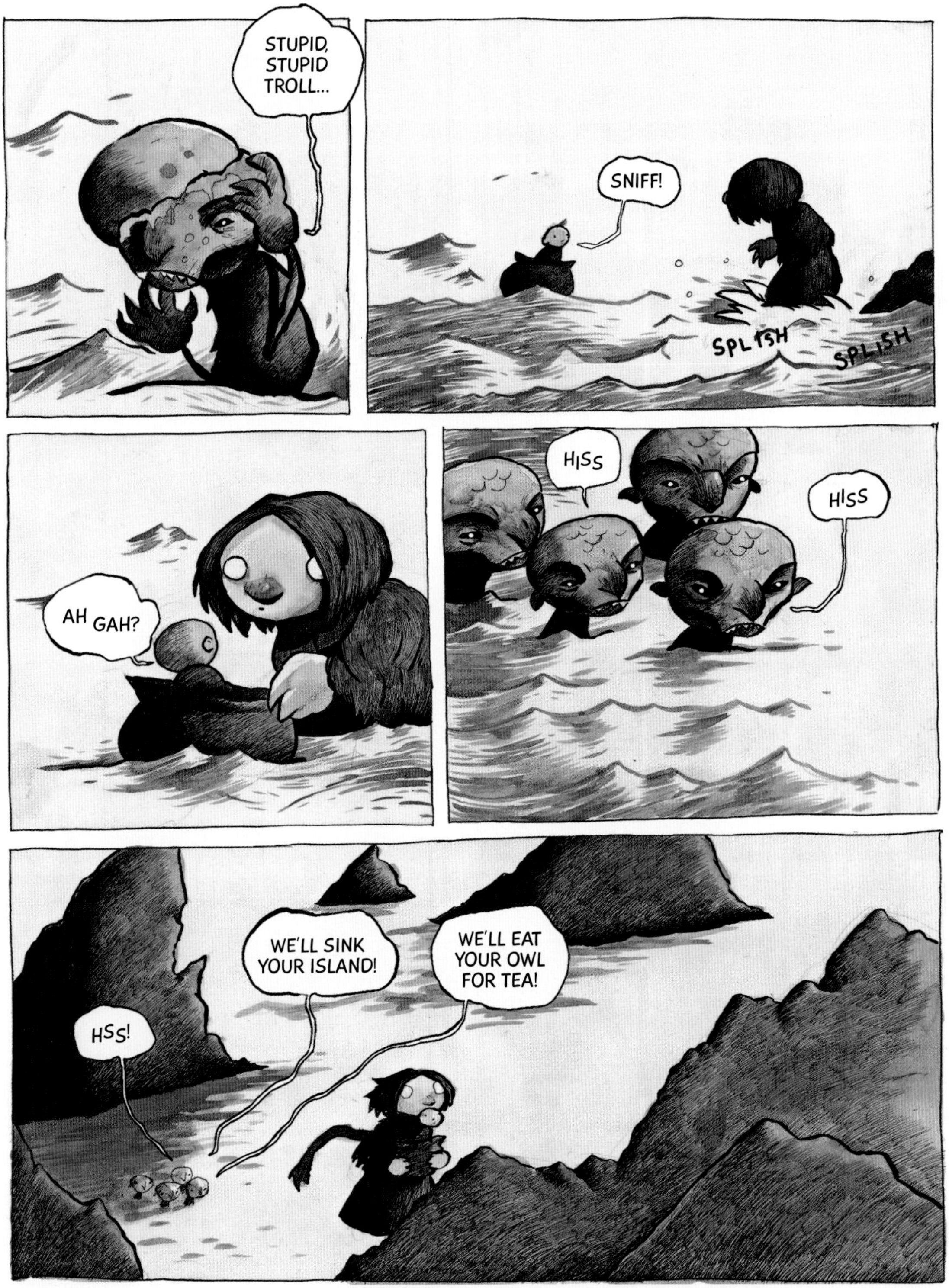
STUPID, STUPID TROLL...
SNIFF!
SPLISH
SPLISH
AH GAH?
HISS
HISS
HSS!
WE'LL SINK YOUR ISLAND!
WE'LL EAT YOUR OWL FOR TEA!

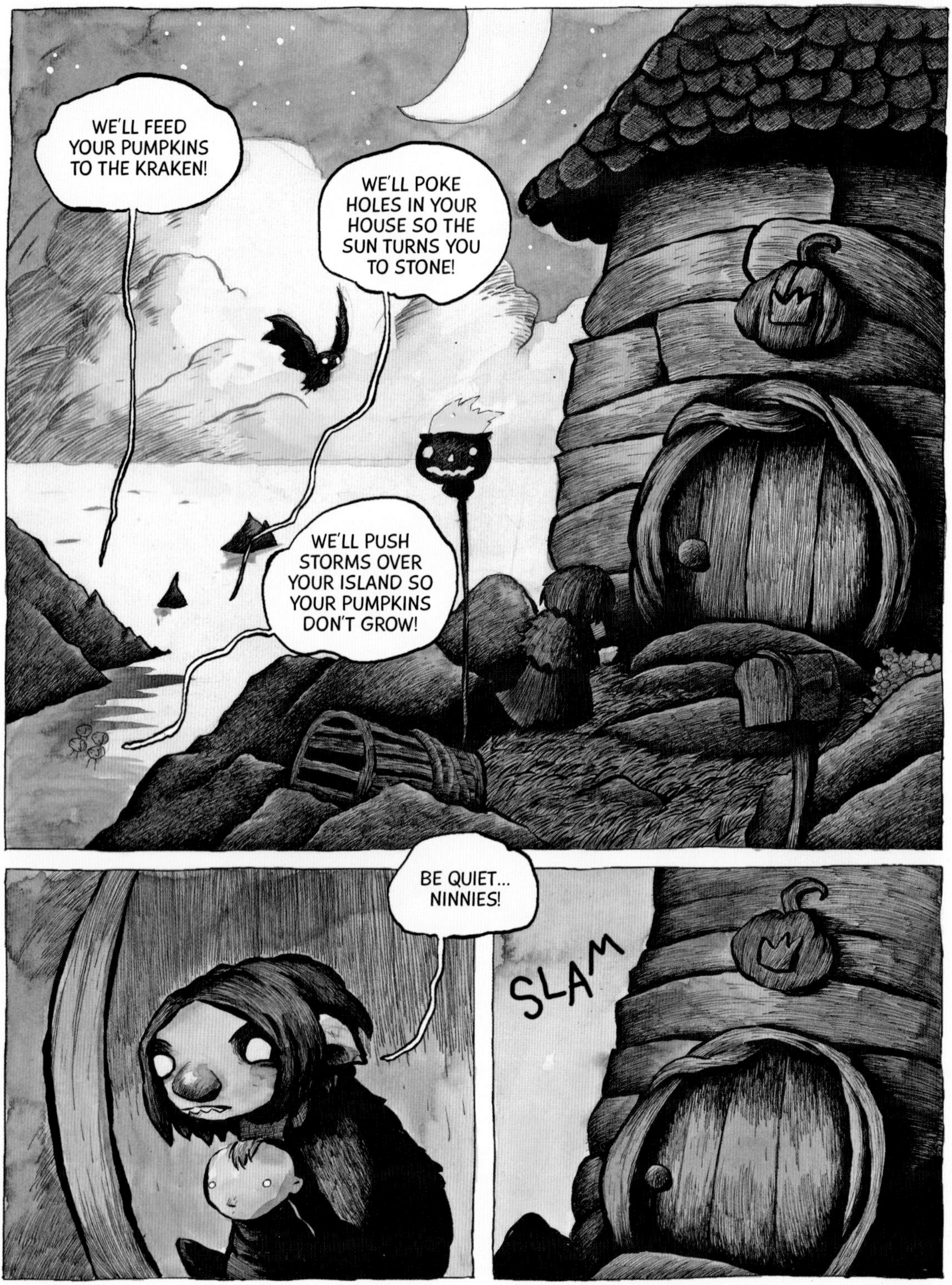
WE'LL FEED YOUR PUMPKINS TO THE KRAKEN!
WE'LL POKE HOLES IN YOUR HOUSE SO THE SUN TURNS YOU TO STONE!
WE'LL PUSH STORMS OVER YOUR ISLAND SO YOUR PUMPKINS DON'T GROW!
BE QUIET... NINNIES!
SLAM

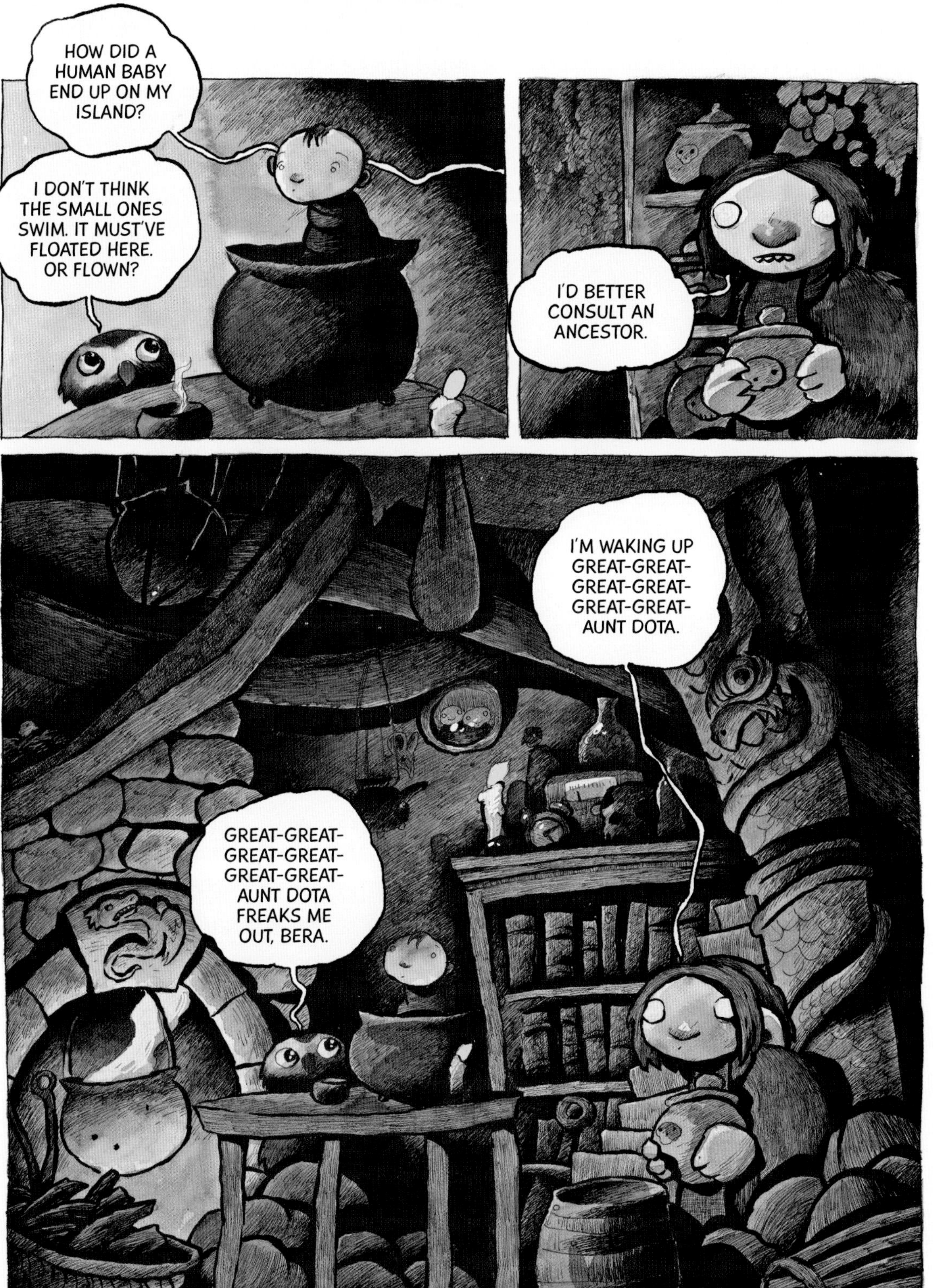
HOW DID A HUMAN BABY END UP ON MY ISLAND?
I DON'T THINK THE SMALL ONES SWIM. IT MUST'VE FLOATED HERE. OR FLOWN?
I'D BETTER CONSULT AN ANCESTOR.
I'M WAKING UP GREAT-GREAT-GREAT-GREAT-GREAT-GREAT-AUNT DOTA.
GREAT-GREAT-GREAT-GREAT-GREAT-GREAT-AUNT DOTA FREAKS ME OUT, BERA.

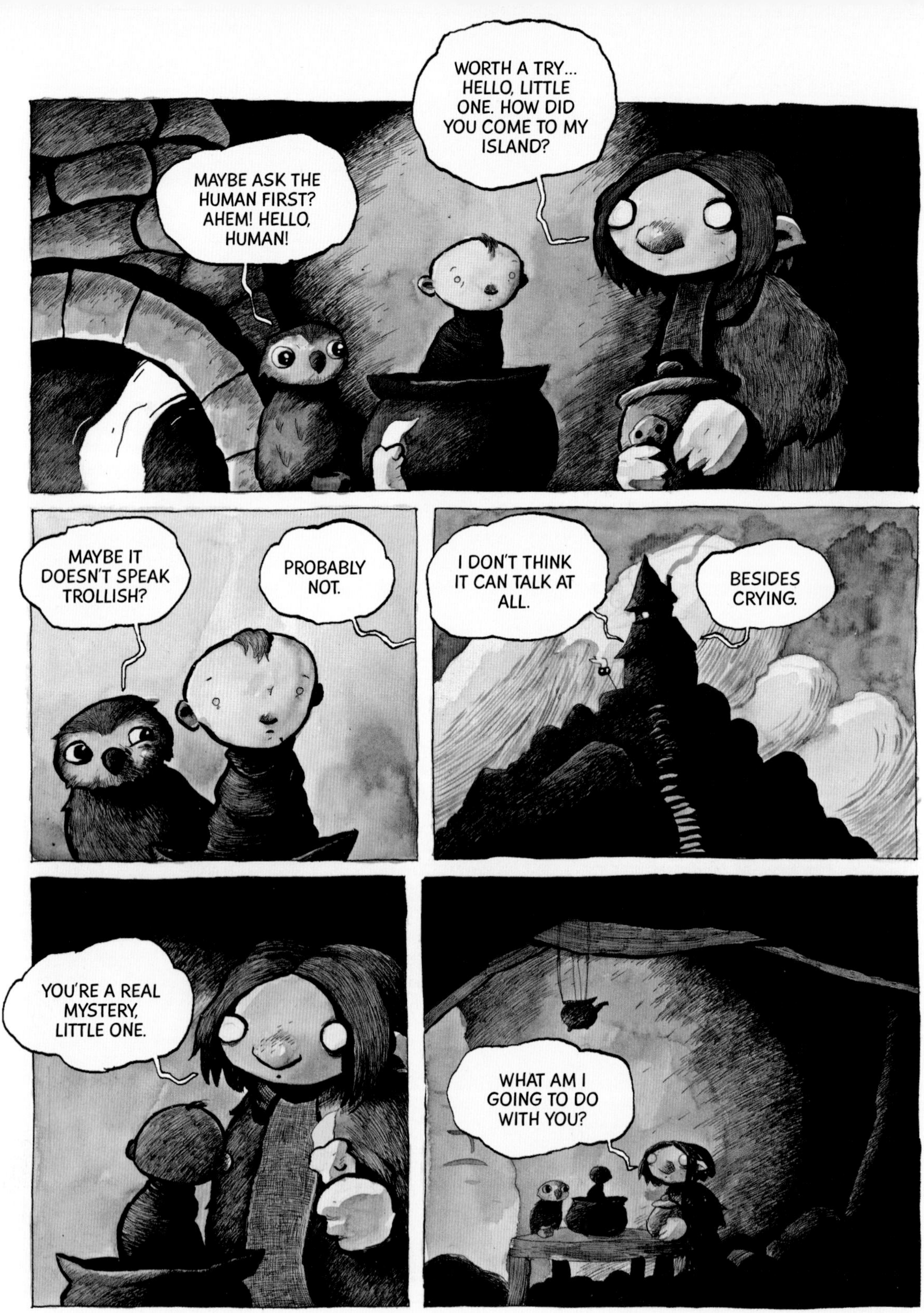
MAYBE ASK THE HUMAN FIRST? AHEM! HELLO, HUMAN!
WORTH A TRY... HELLO, LITTLE ONE. HOW DID YOU COME TO MY ISLAND?
MAYBE IT DOESN'T SPEAK TROLLISH?
PROBABLY NOT.
I DON'T THINK IT CAN TALK AT ALL.
BESIDES CRYING.
YOU'RE A REAL MYSTERY, LITTLE ONE.
WHAT AM I GOING TO DO WITH YOU?

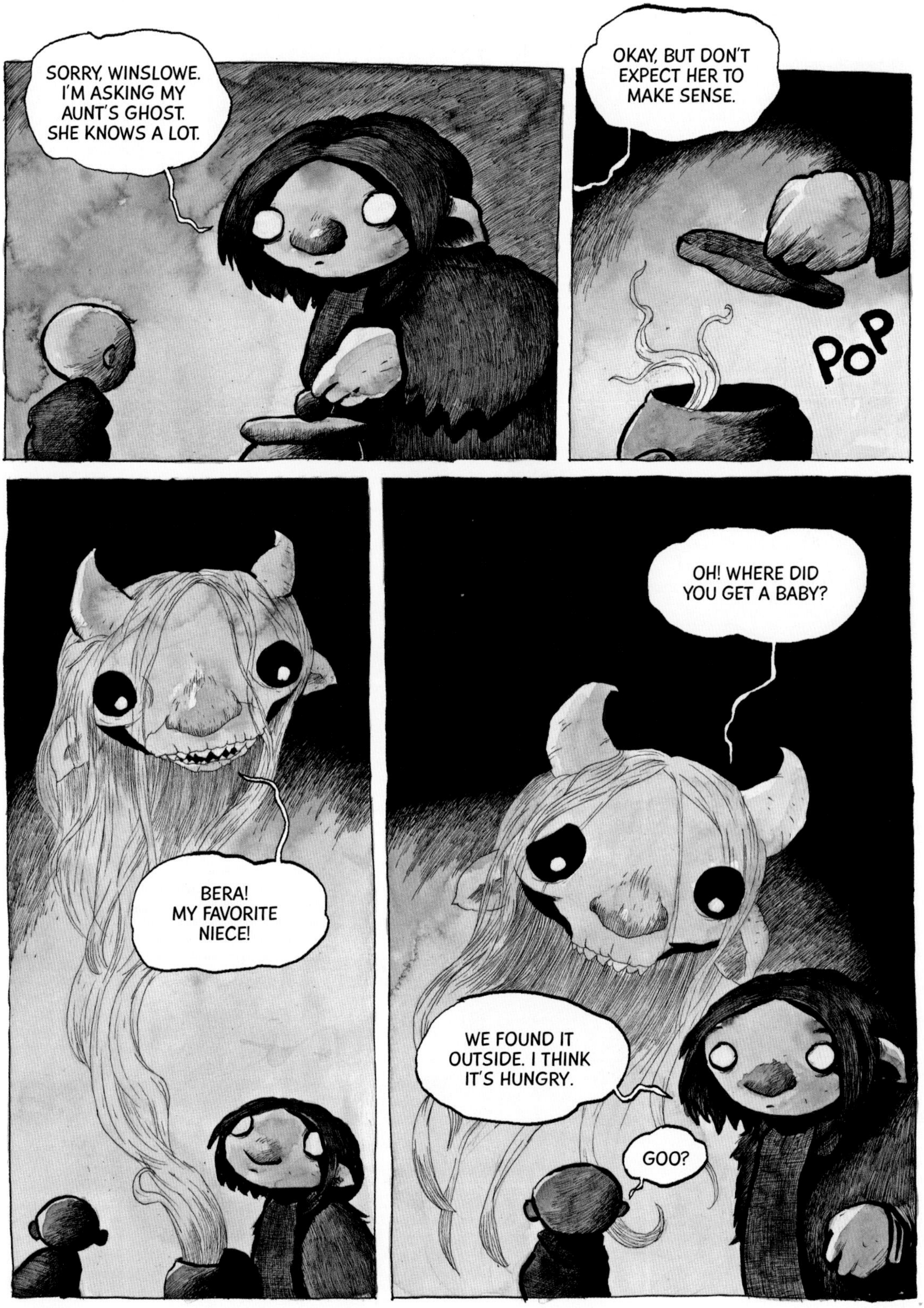
SORRY, WINSLOWE. I'M ASKING MY AUNT'S GHOST. SHE KNOWS A LOT.
OKAY, BUT DON'T EXPECT HER TO MAKE SENSE.
POP
BERA! MY FAVORITE NIECE!
OH! WHERE DID YOU GET A BABY?
WE FOUND IT OUTSIDE. I THINK IT'S HUNGRY.
GOO?

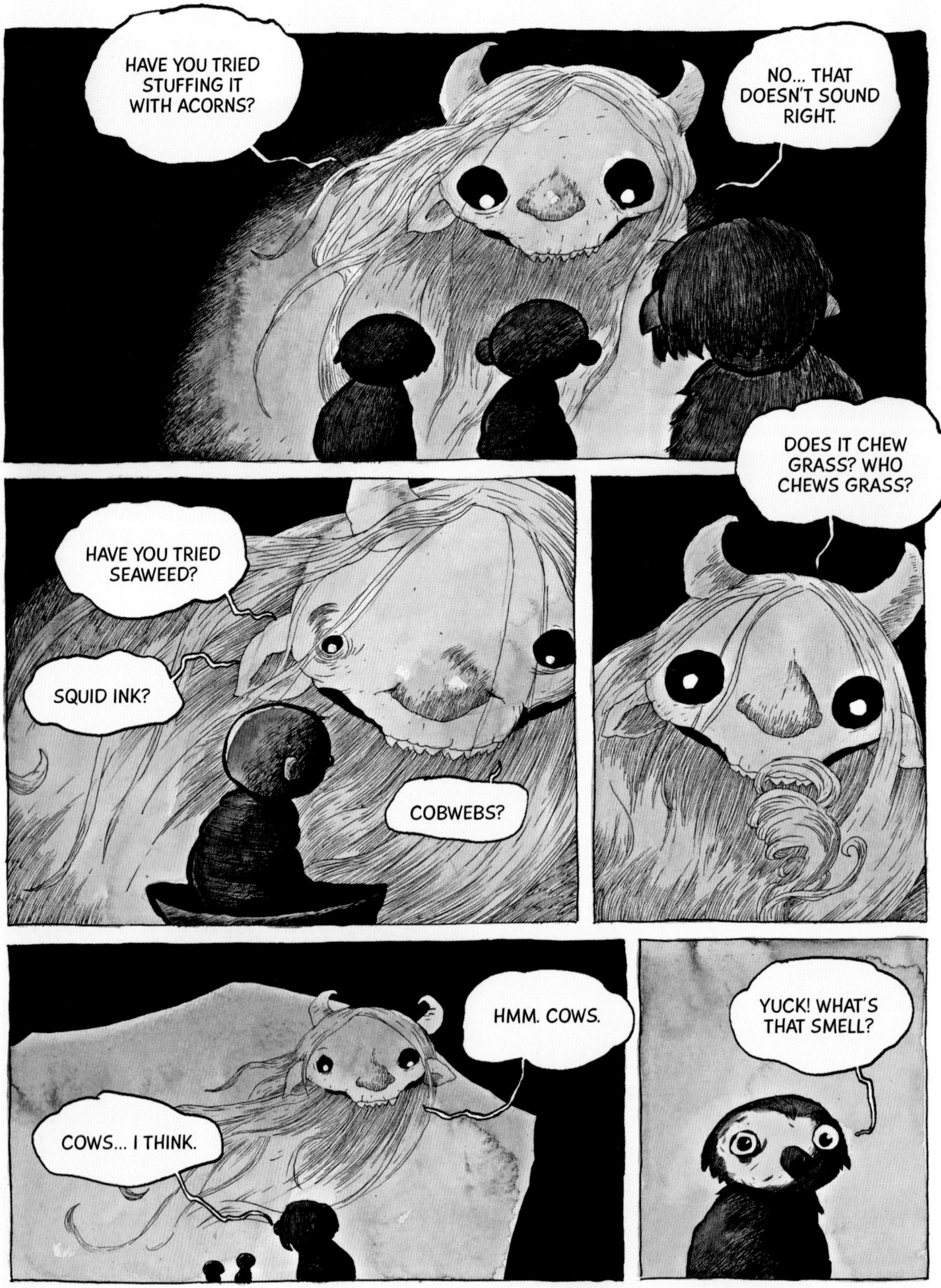
HAVE YOU TRIED STUFFING IT WITH ACORNS?
NO... THAT DOESN'T SOUND RIGHT.
HAVE YOU TRIED SEAWEED?
SQUID INK?
COBWEBS?
DOES IT CHEW GRASS? WHO CHEWS GRASS?
HMM. COWS.
COWS... I THINK.
YUCK! WHAT'S THAT SMELL?

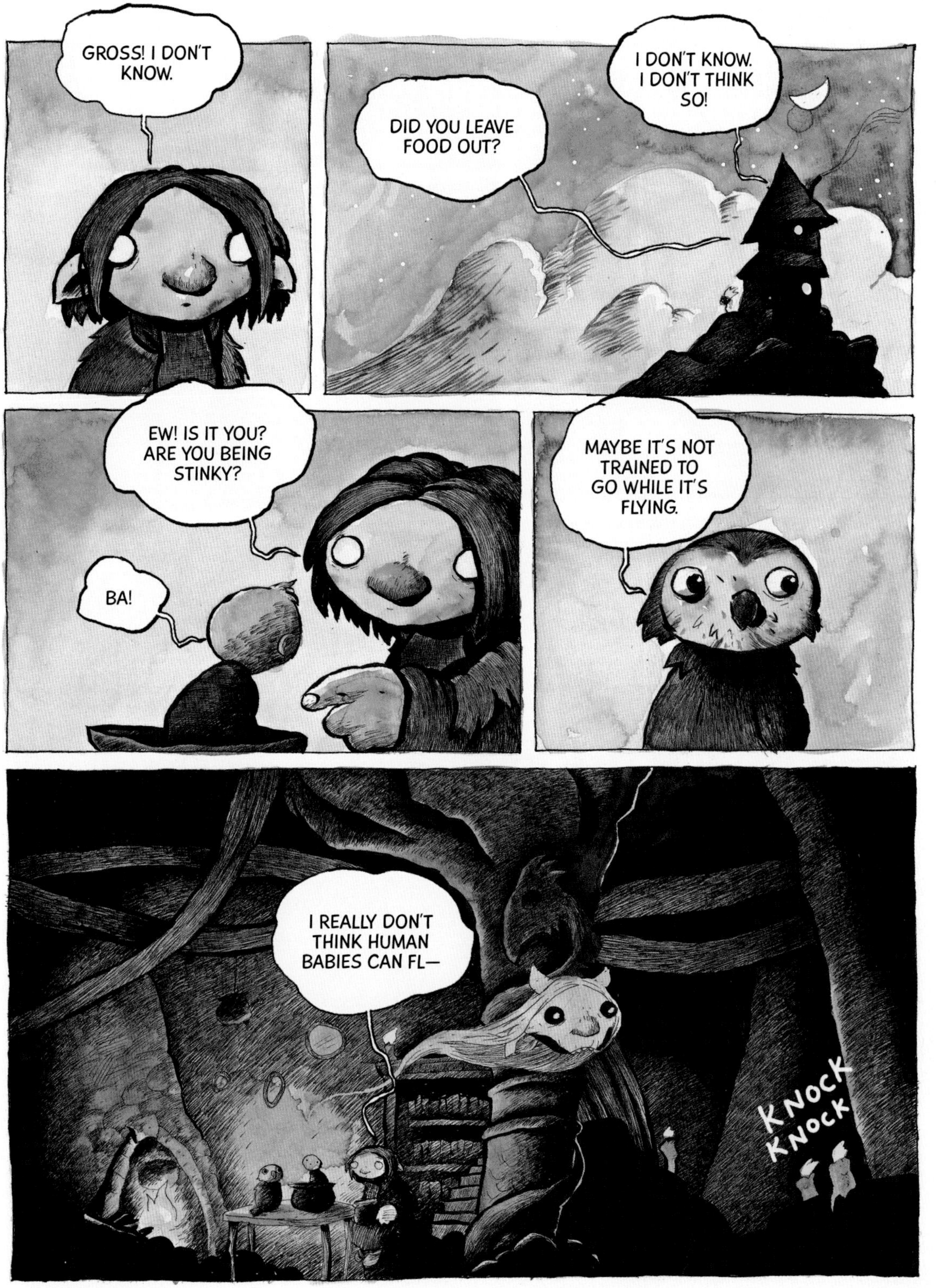
GROSS! I DON'T KNOW.
DID YOU LEAVE FOOD OUT?
I DON'T KNOW. I DON'T THINK SO!
EW! IS IT YOU? ARE YOU BEING STINKY?
BA!
MAYBE IT'S NOT TRAINED TO GO WHILE IT'S FLYING.
I REALLY DON'T THINK HUMAN BABIES CAN FL—
KNOCK KNOCK

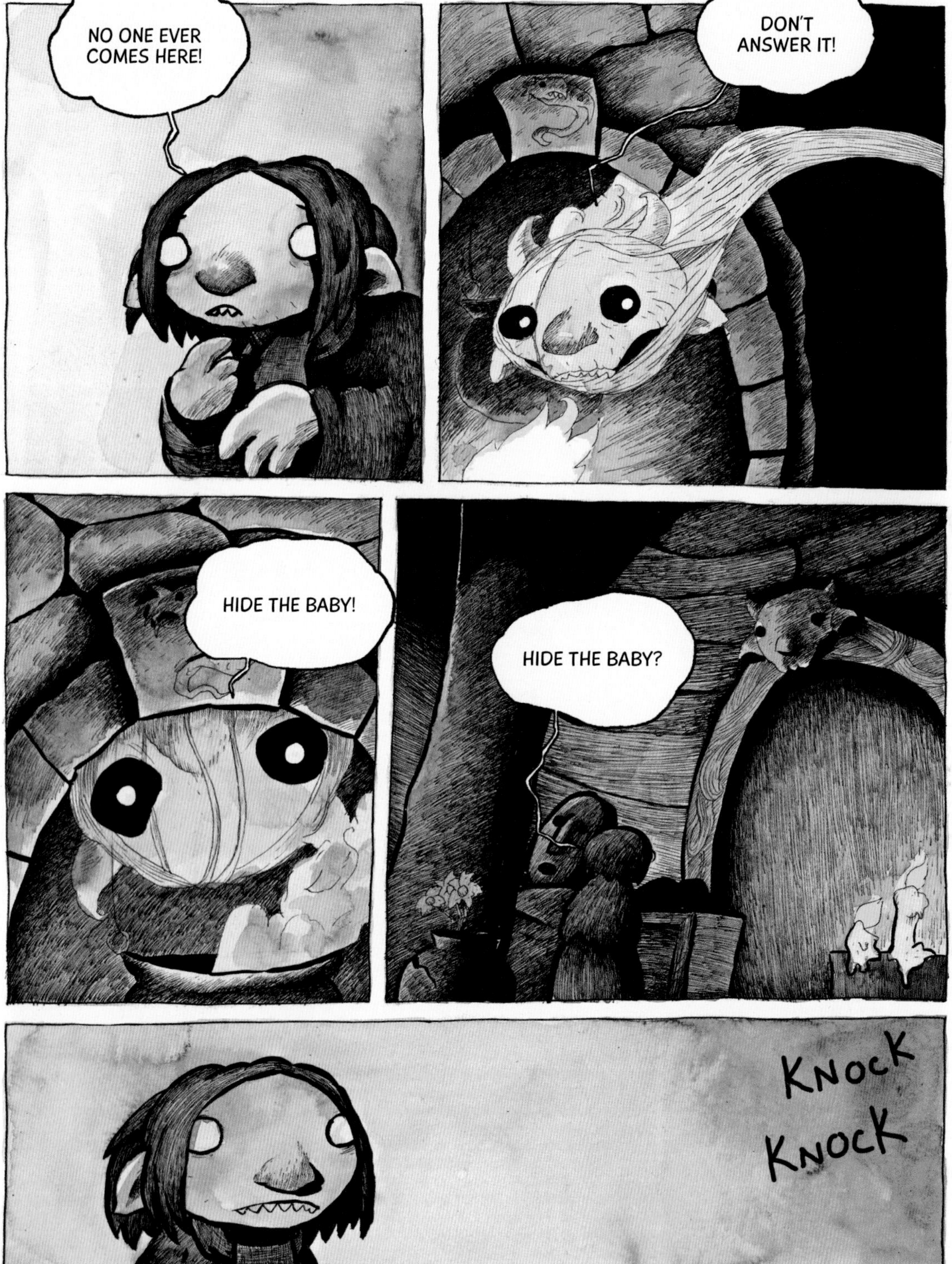
NO ONE EVER COMES HERE!
DON'T ANSWER IT!
HIDE THE BABY!
HIDE THE BABY?
KNOCK KNOCK

THE FORCE AT THE DOOR IS MALIGNANT AND EVIL!

IT IS?

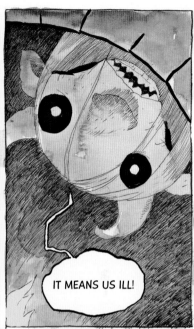

IT MEANS US ILL!

MAYBE WE'D BETTER HIDE THE BABY.

SH-SHOULD I GET MY SWORD?

NO! IT WON'T DO ANY GOOD!

KNOCK KNOCK!

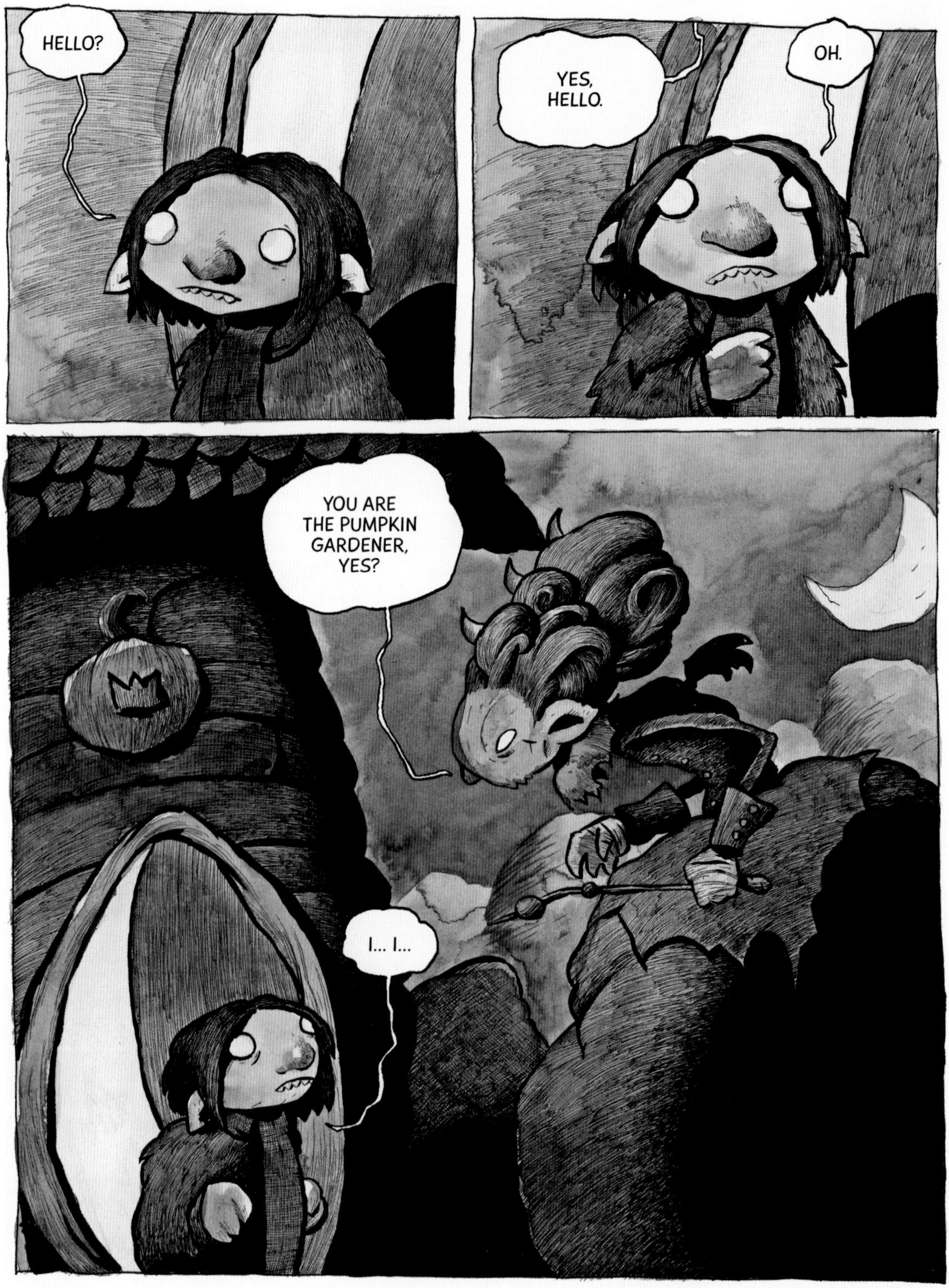
HELLO?
YES, HELLO.
OH.
YOU ARE THE PUMPKIN GARDENER, YES?
I... I...

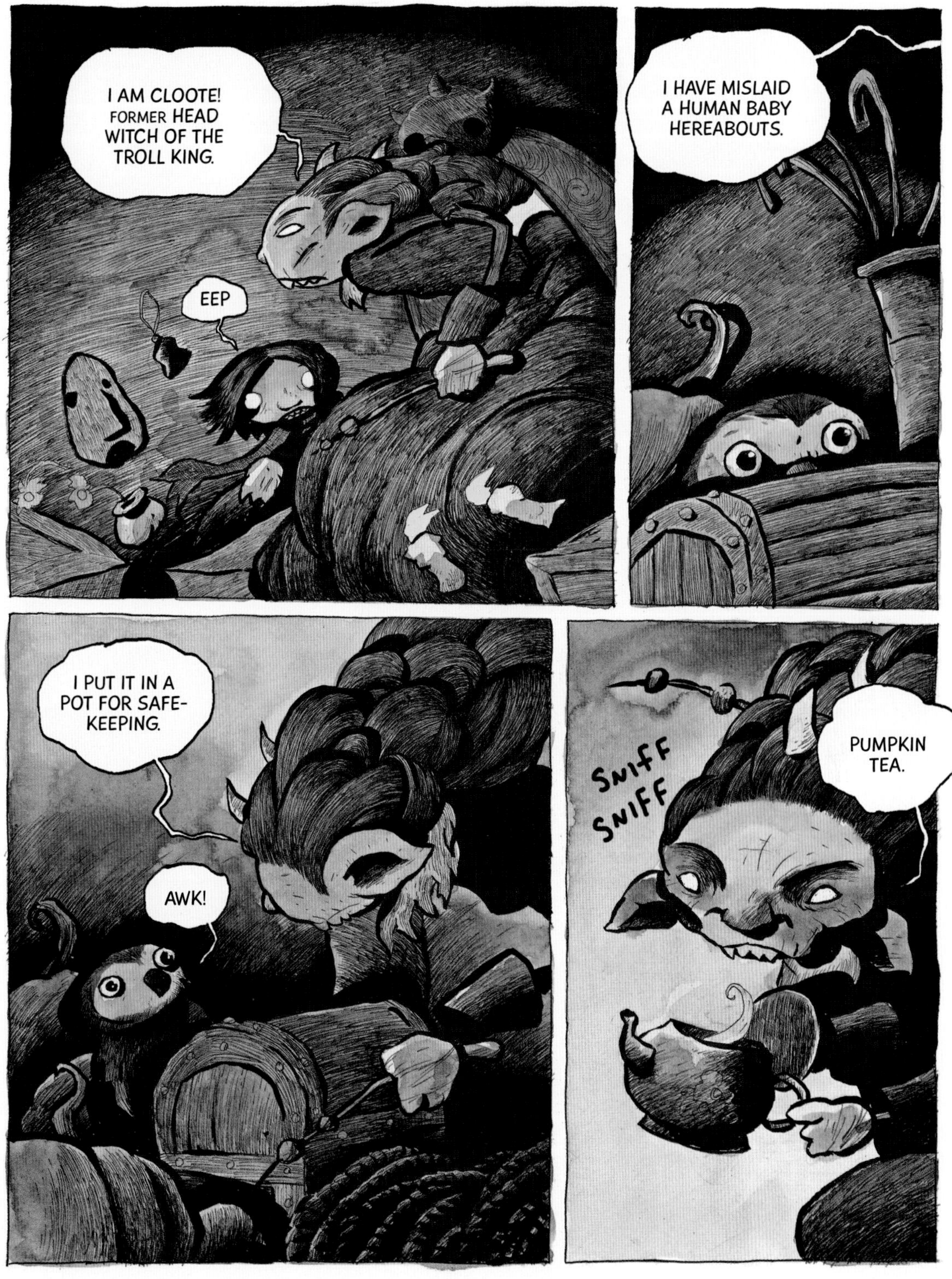
I AM CLOOTE! FORMER HEAD WITCH OF THE TROLL KING.
EEP
I HAVE MISLAID A HUMAN BABY HEREABOUTS.
I PUT IT IN A POT FOR SAFE-KEEPING.
AWK!
SNIFF SNIFF
PUMPKIN TEA.

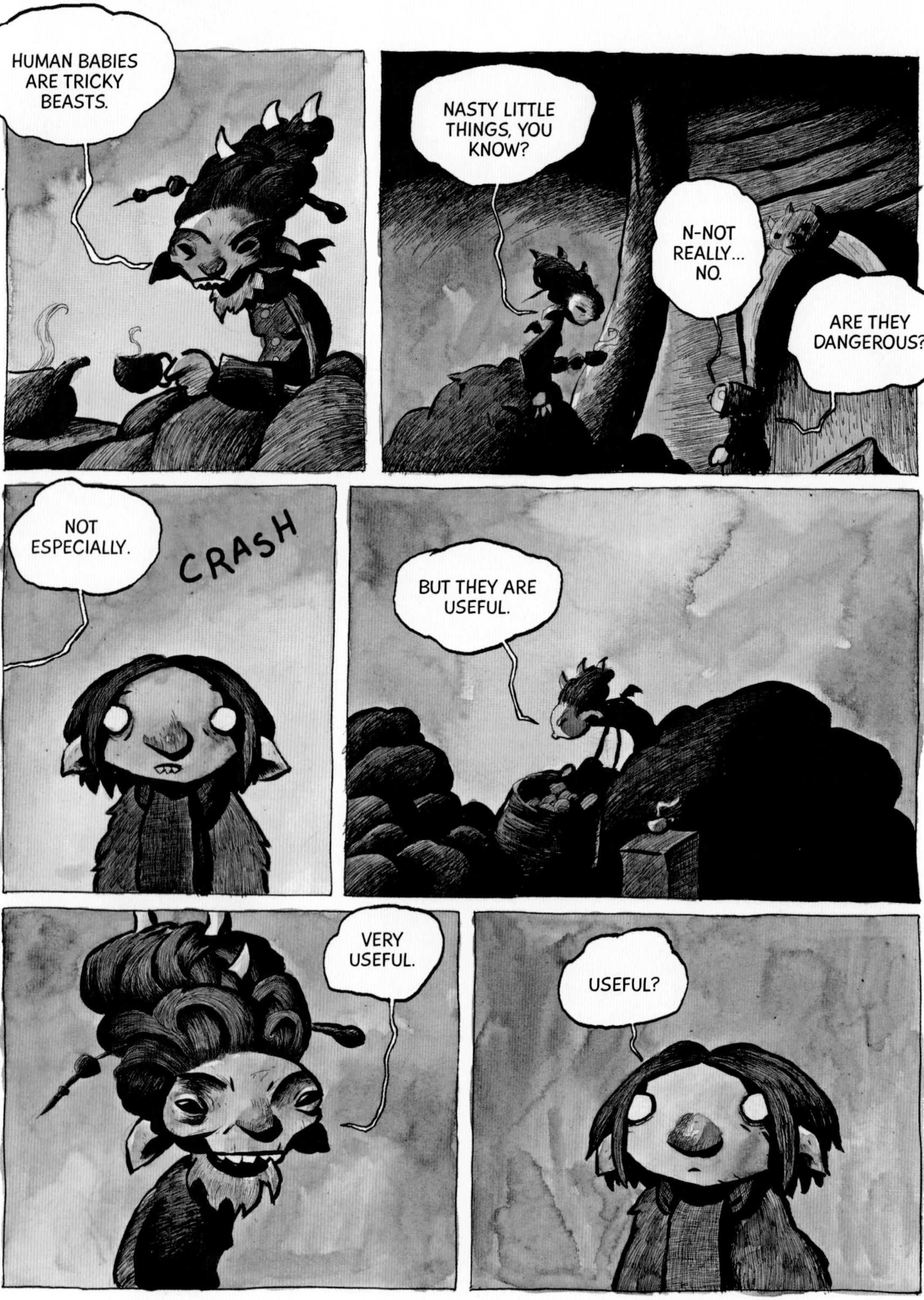
HUMAN BABIES ARE TRICKY BEASTS.
NASTY LITTLE THINGS, YOU KNOW?
N-NOT REALLY... NO.
ARE THEY DANGEROUS?
NOT ESPECIALLY.
CRASH
BUT THEY ARE USEFUL.
VERY USEFUL.
USEFUL?

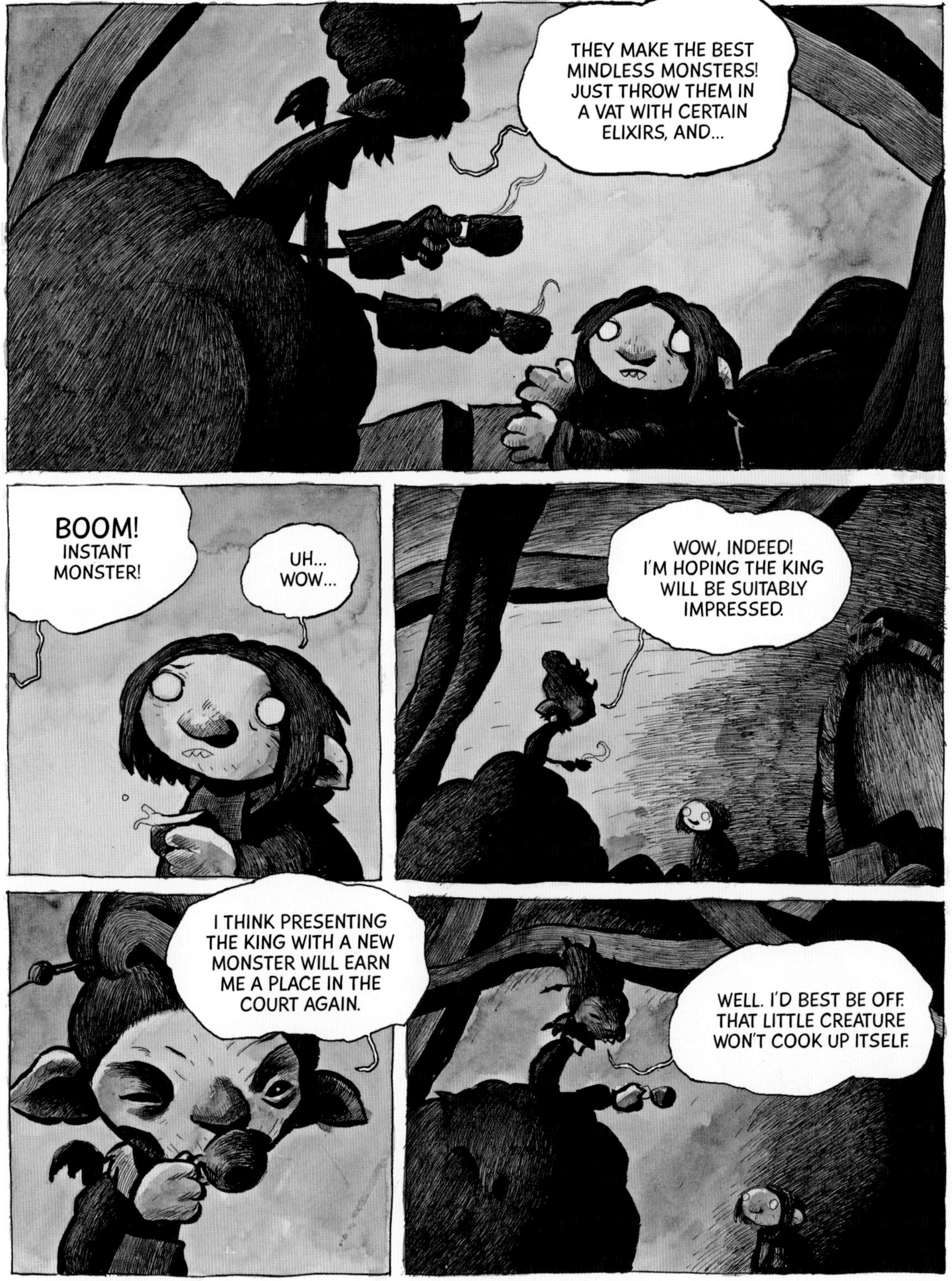
THEY MAKE THE BEST MINDLESS MONSTERS! JUST THROW THEM IN A VAT WITH CERTAIN ELIXIRS, AND...
BOOM! INSTANT MONSTER!
UH... WOW...
WOW, INDEED! I'M HOPING THE KING WILL BE SUITABLY IMPRESSED.
I THINK PRESENTING THE KING WITH A NEW MONSTER WILL EARN ME A PLACE IN THE COURT AGAIN.
WELL. I'D BEST BE OFF. THAT LITTLE CREATURE WON'T COOK UP ITSELF.

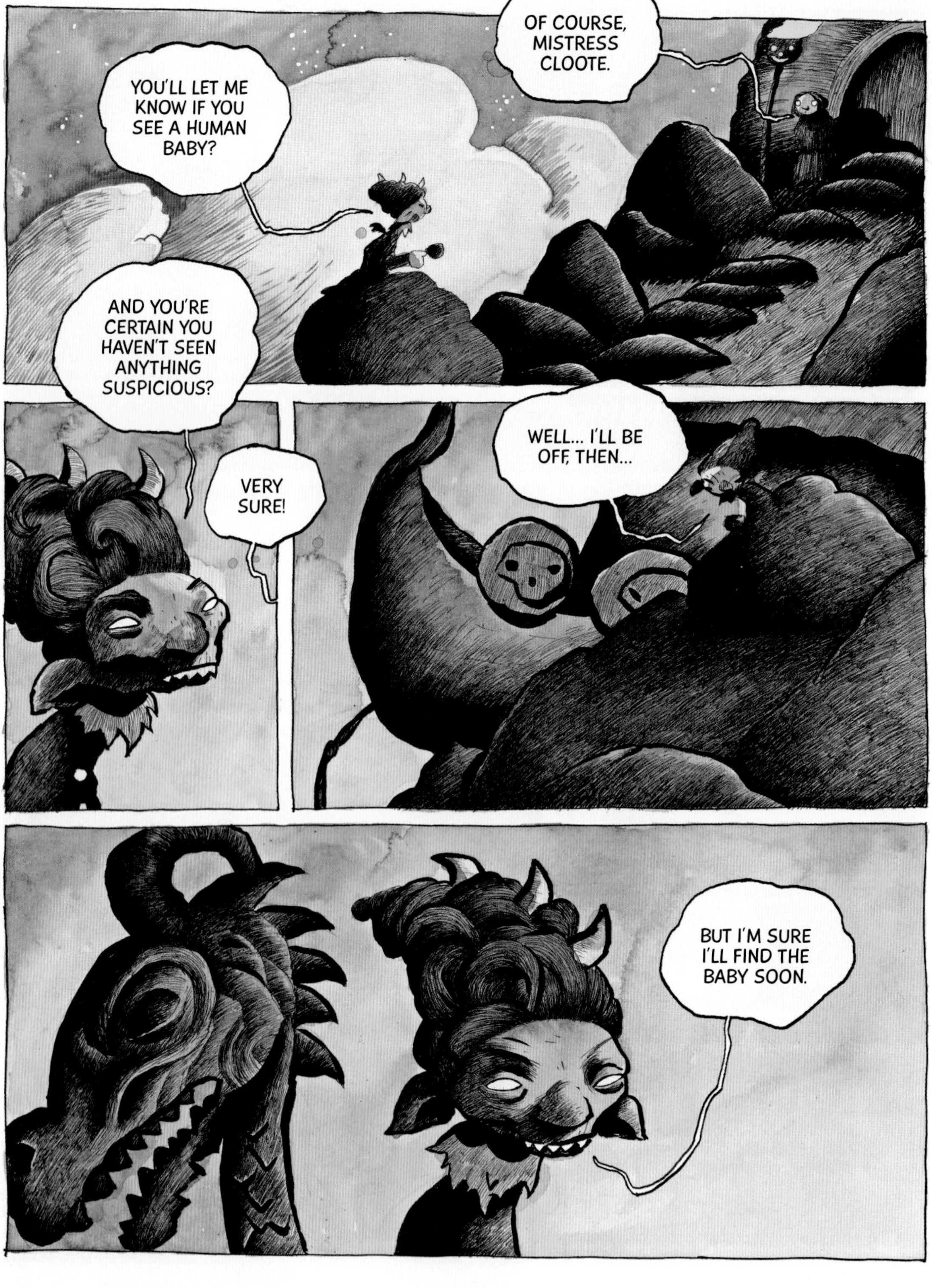
YOU'LL LET ME KNOW IF YOU SEE A HUMAN BABY?
OF COURSE, MISTRESS CLOOTE.
AND YOU'RE CERTAIN YOU HAVEN'T SEEN ANYTHING SUSPICIOUS?
VERY SURE!
WELL... I'LL BE OFF, THEN...
BUT I'M SURE I'LL FIND THE BABY SOON.

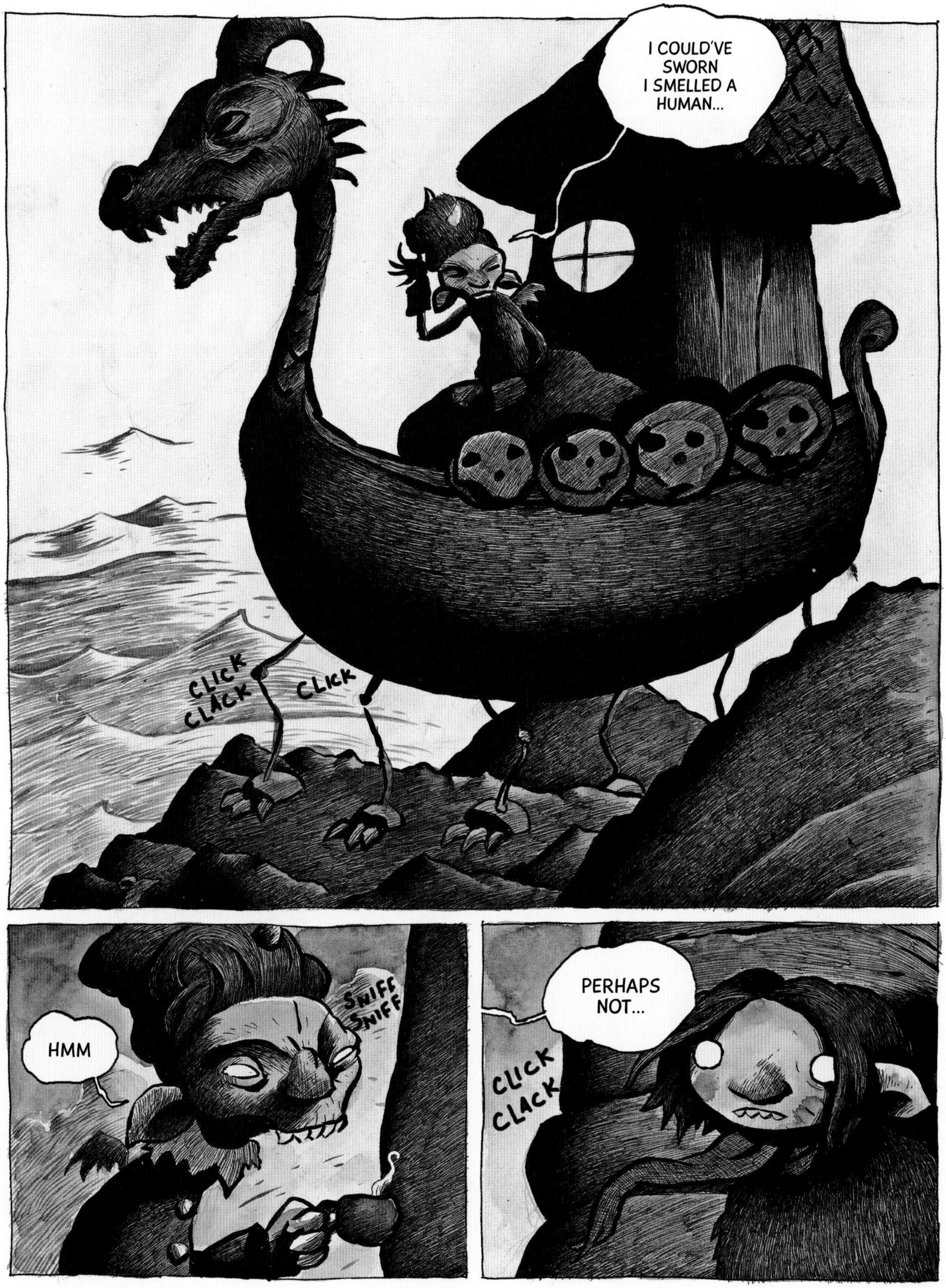
I COULD'VE SWORN I SMELLED A HUMAN...
CLICK CLACK
CLICK
HMM
SNIFF SNIFF
PERHAPS NOT...
CLICK CLACK

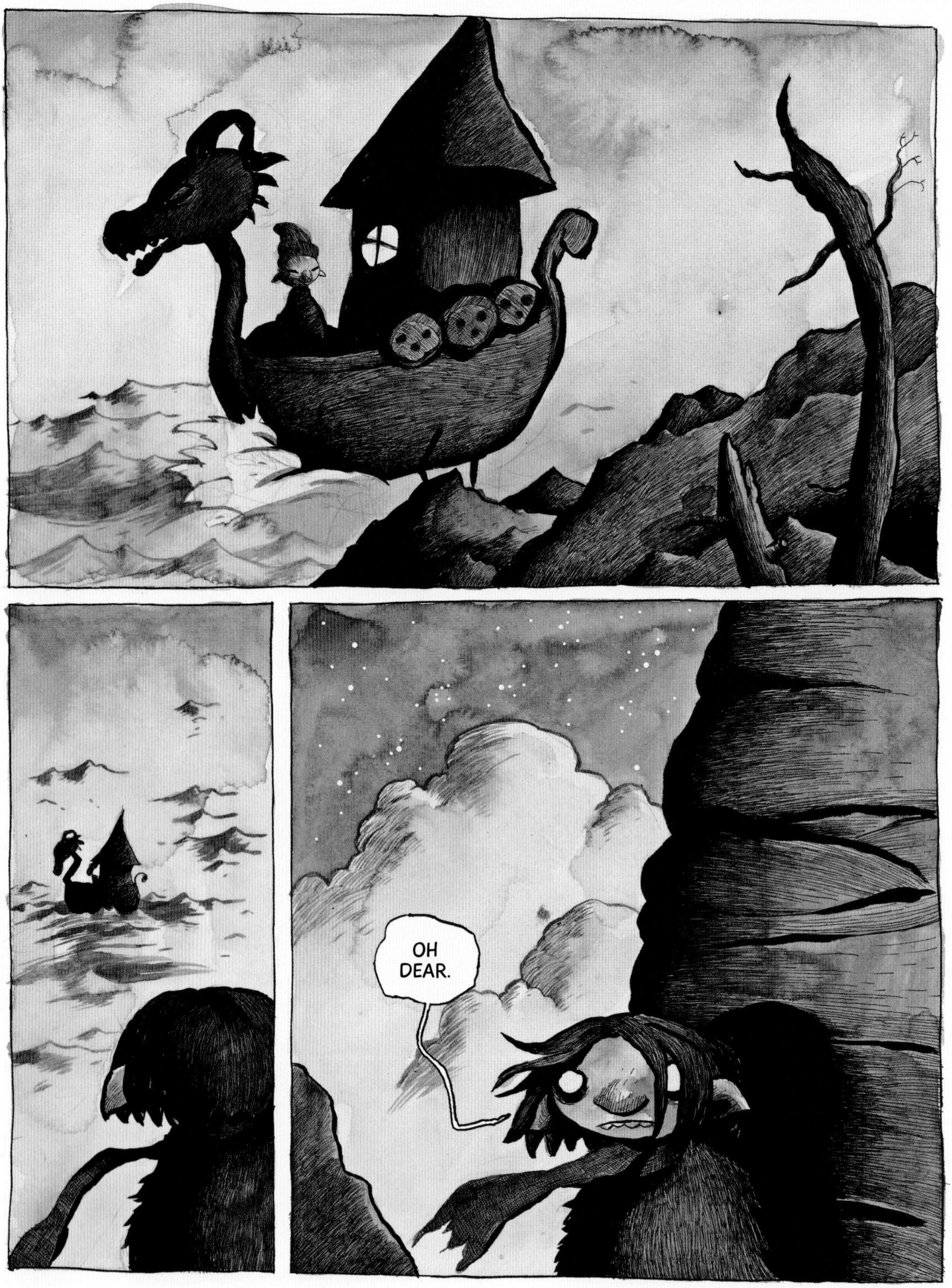
OH DEAR.

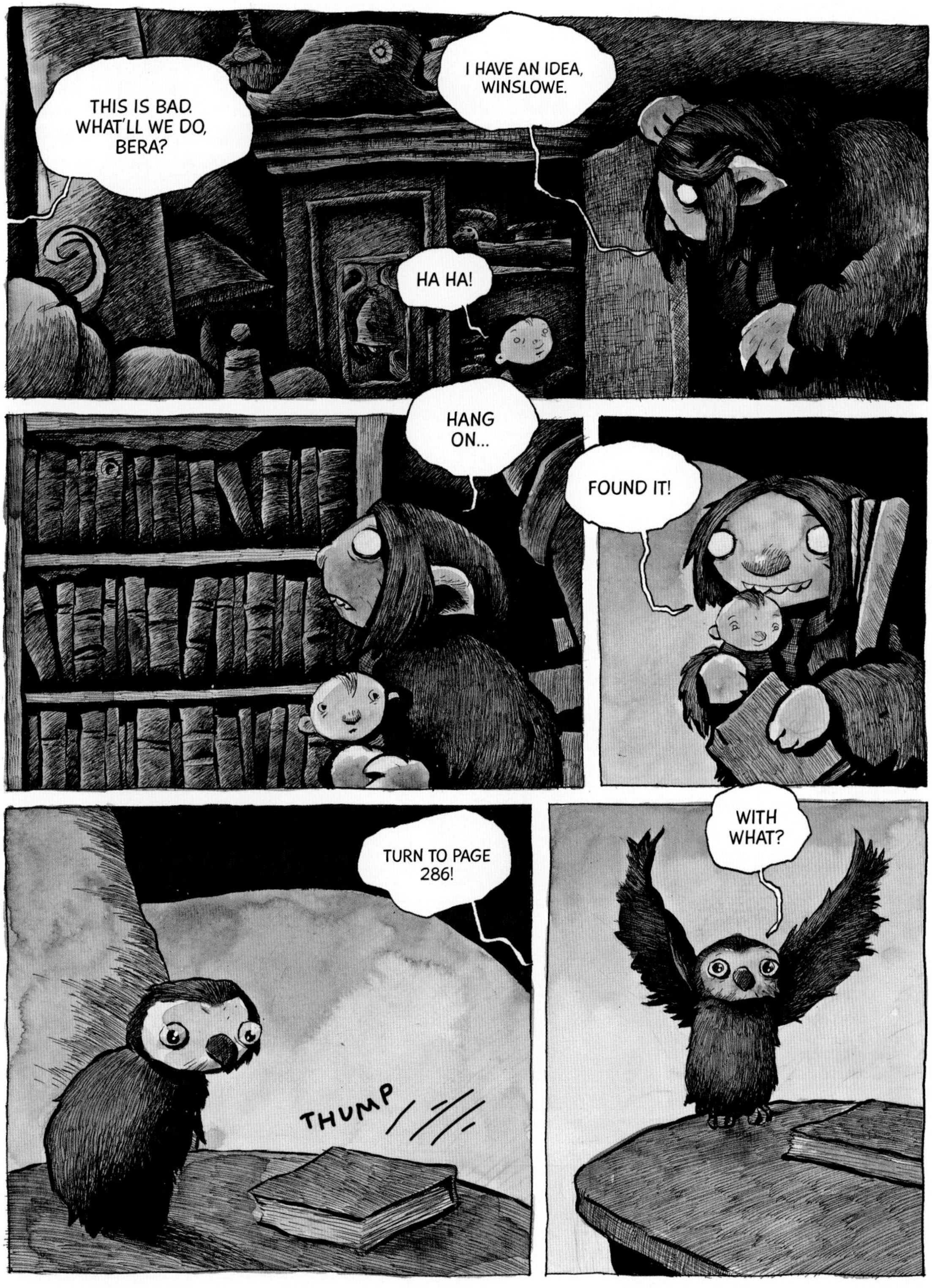
THIS IS BAD. WHAT'LL WE DO, BERA?
I HAVE AN IDEA, WINSLOWE.
HA HA!
HANG ON...
FOUND IT!
TURN TO PAGE 286!
WITH WHAT?
THUMP

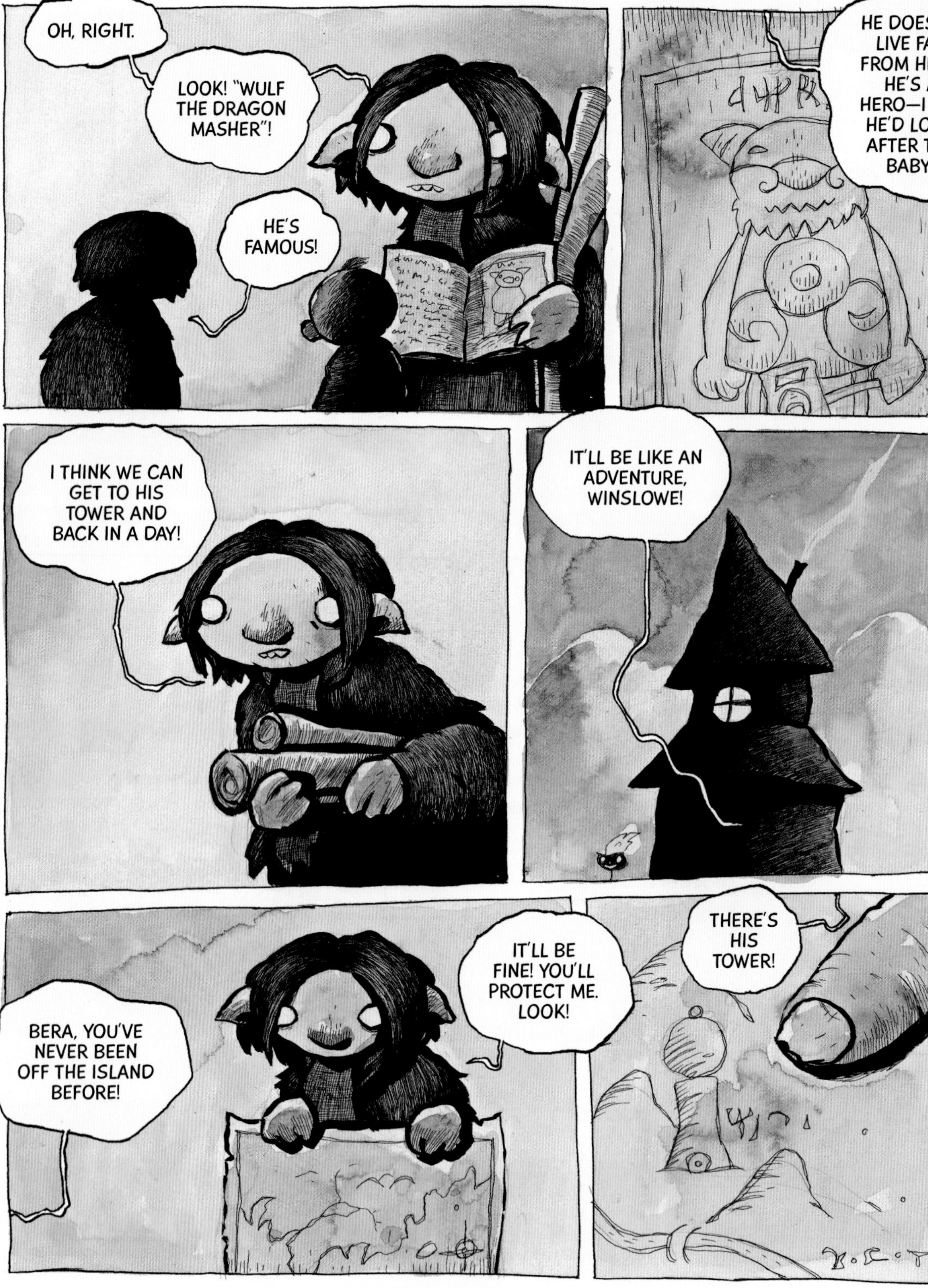
OH, RIGHT.
LOOK! "WULF THE DRAGON MASHER"!
HE'S FAMOUS!
HE DOESN'T LIVE FAR FROM HERE. HE'S A HERO—I BET HE'D LOOK AFTER THE BABY!
I THINK WE CAN GET TO HIS TOWER AND BACK IN A DAY!
IT'LL BE LIKE AN ADVENTURE, WINSLOWE!
BERA, YOU'VE NEVER BEEN OFF THE ISLAND BEFORE!
IT'LL BE FINE! YOU'LL PROTECT ME. LOOK!
THERE'S HIS TOWER!

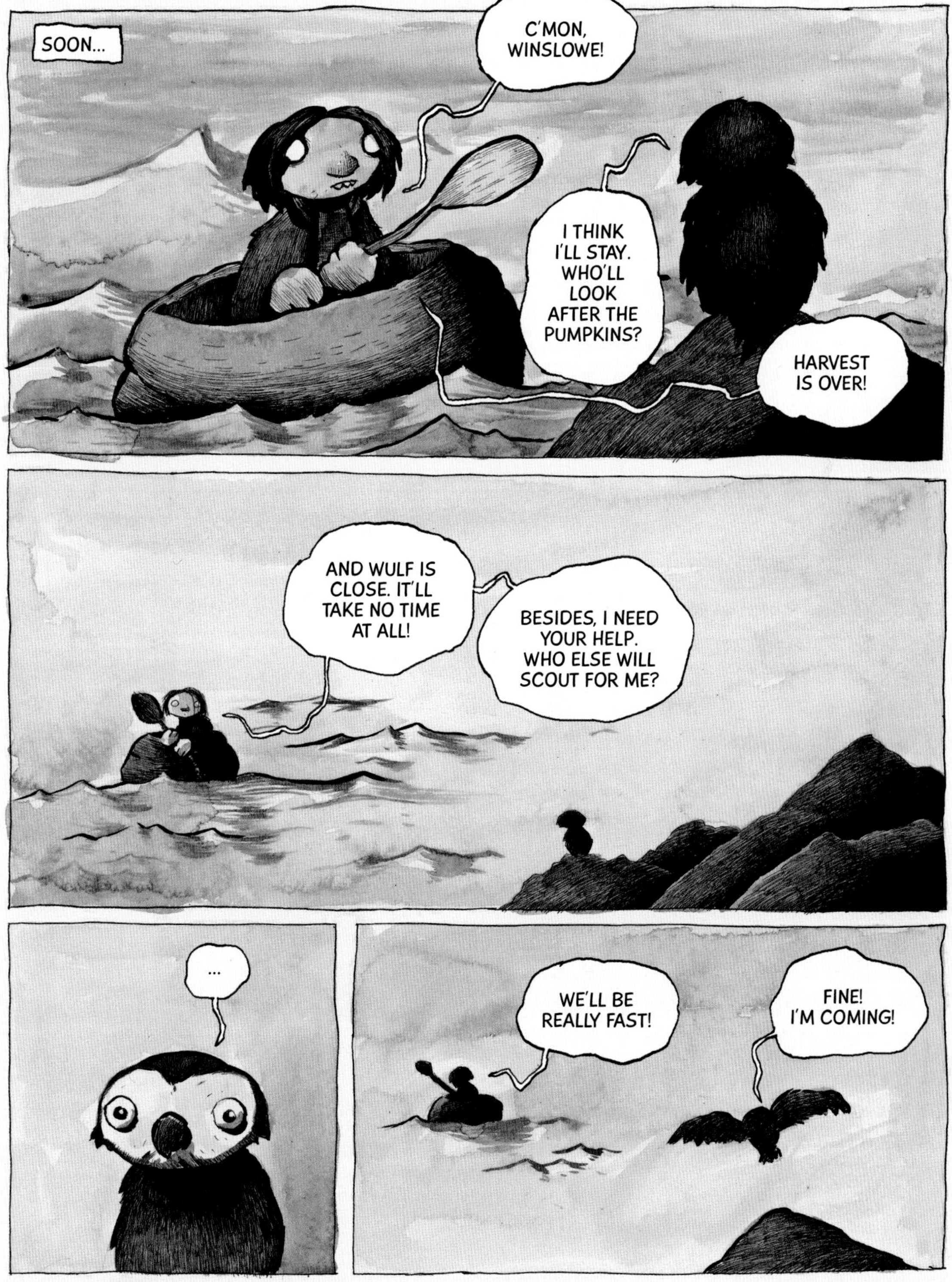
SOON...
C'MON, WINSLOWE!
I THINK I'LL STAY. WHO'LL LOOK AFTER THE PUMPKINS?
HARVEST IS OVER!
AND WULF IS CLOSE. IT'LL TAKE NO TIME AT ALL!
BESIDES, I NEED YOUR HELP. WHO ELSE WILL SCOUT FOR ME?
...
WE'LL BE REALLY FAST!
FINE! I'M COMING!

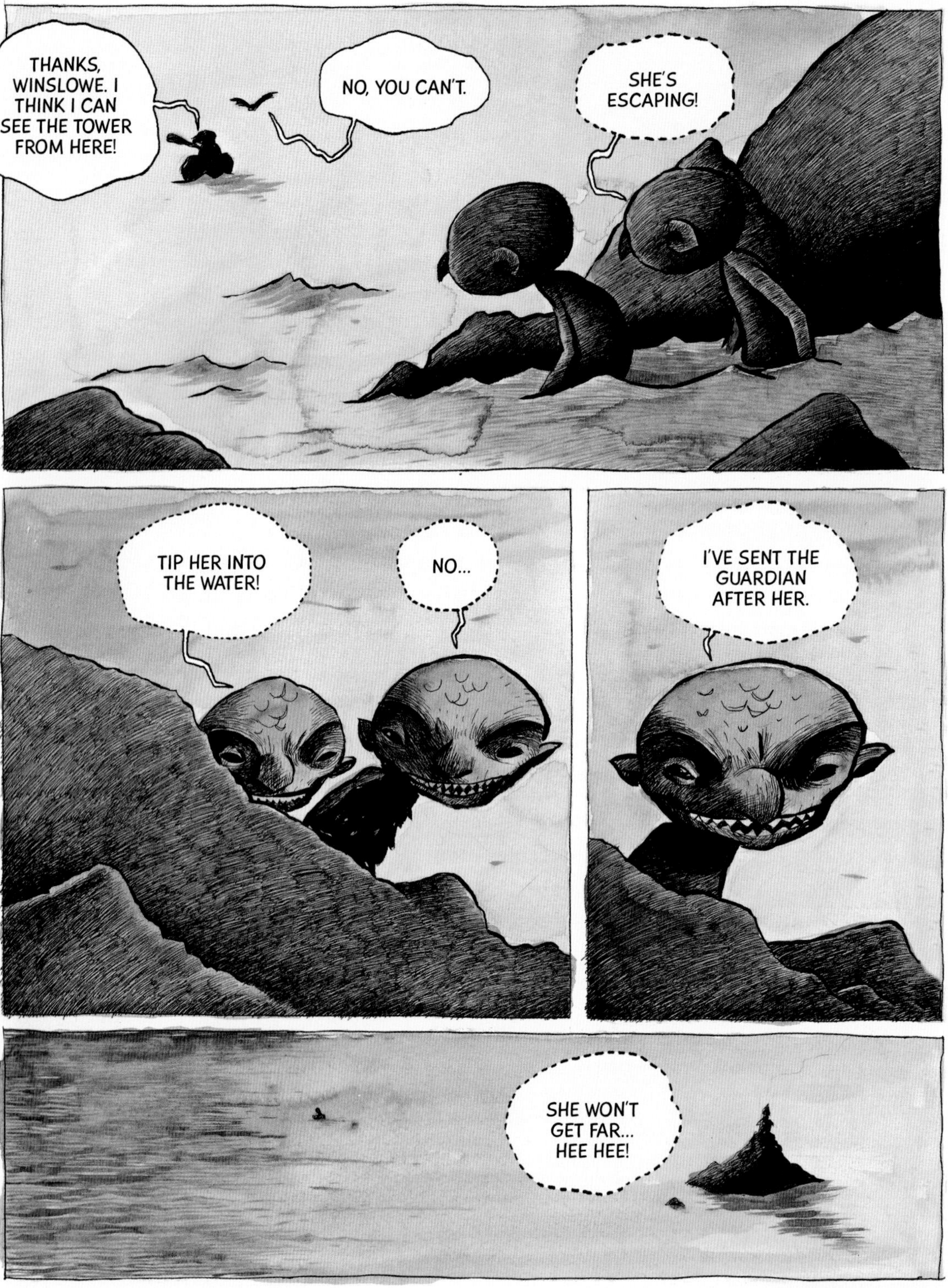
THANKS, WINSLOWE. I THINK I CAN SEE THE TOWER FROM HERE!
NO, YOU CAN'T.
SHE'S ESCAPING!
TIP HER INTO THE WATER!
NO...
I'VE SENT THE GUARDIAN AFTER HER.
SHE WON'T GET FAR... HEE HEE!

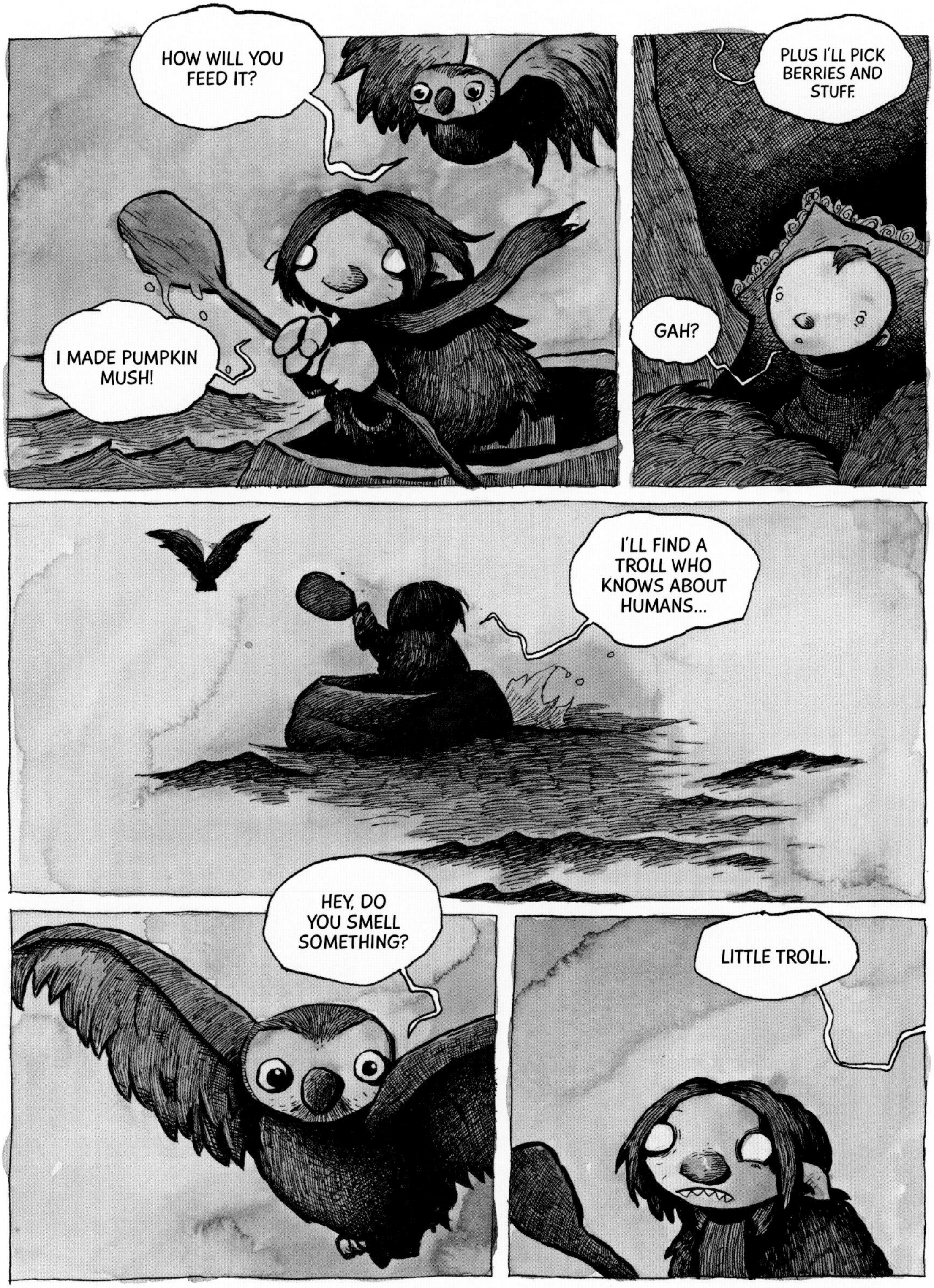
HOW WILL YOU FEED IT?
I MADE PUMPKIN MUSH!
PLUS I'LL PICK BERRIES AND STUFF.
GAH?
I'LL FIND A TROLL WHO KNOWS ABOUT HUMANS...
HEY, DO YOU SMELL SOMETHING?
LITTLE TROLL.

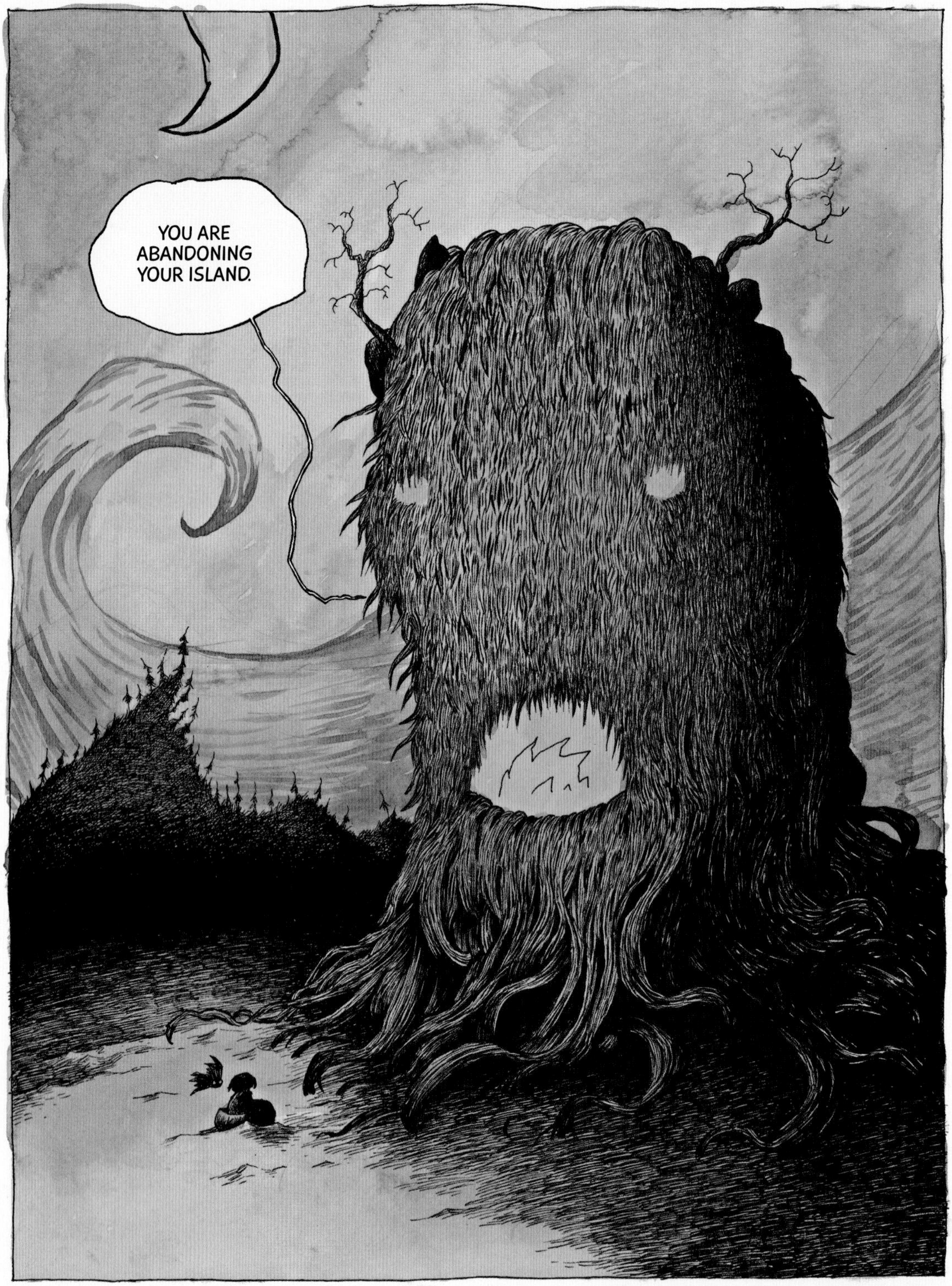
YOU ARE ABANDONING YOUR ISLAND.

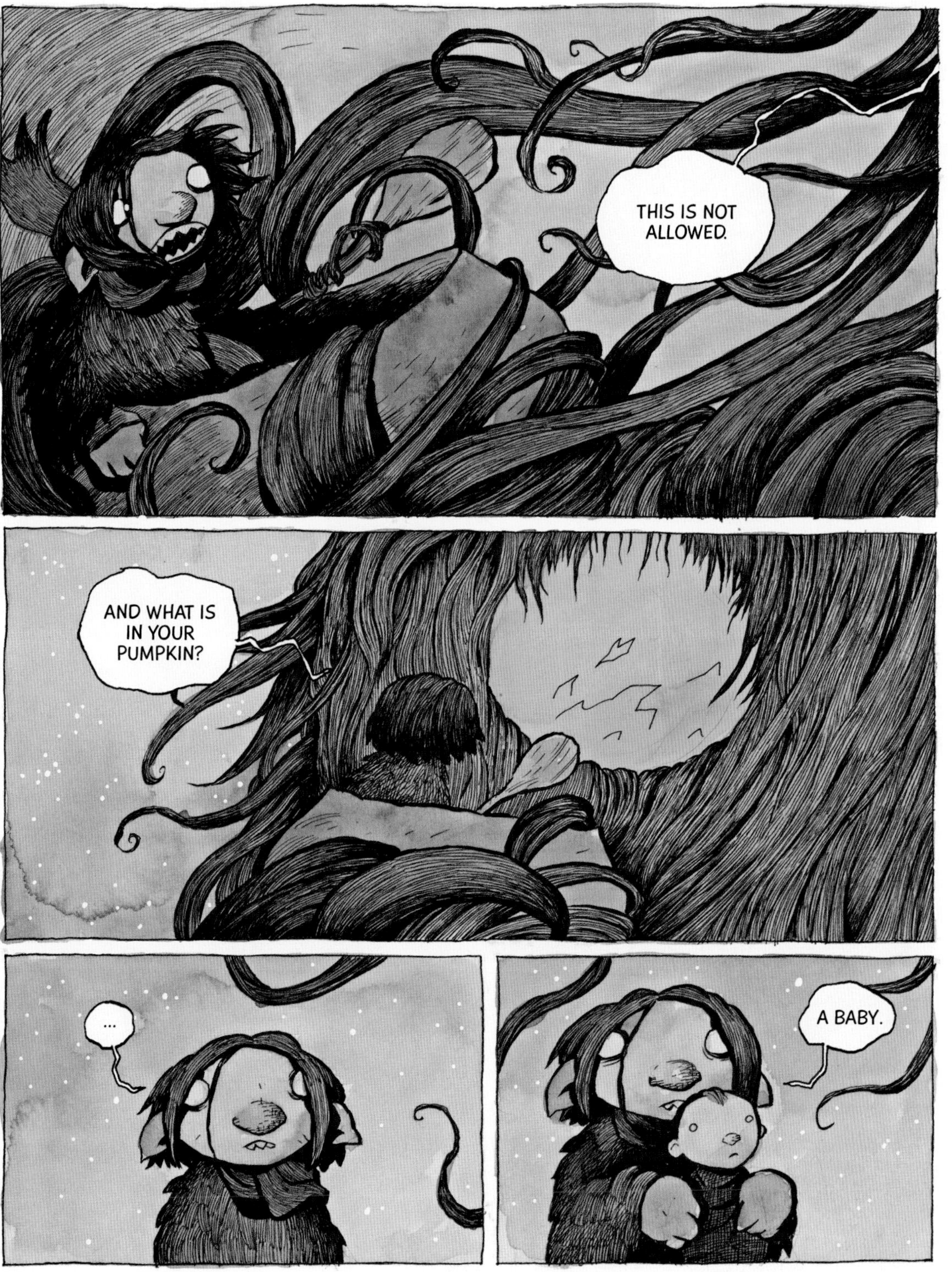
THIS IS NOT ALLOWED.
AND WHAT IS IN YOUR PUMPKIN?
...
A BABY.

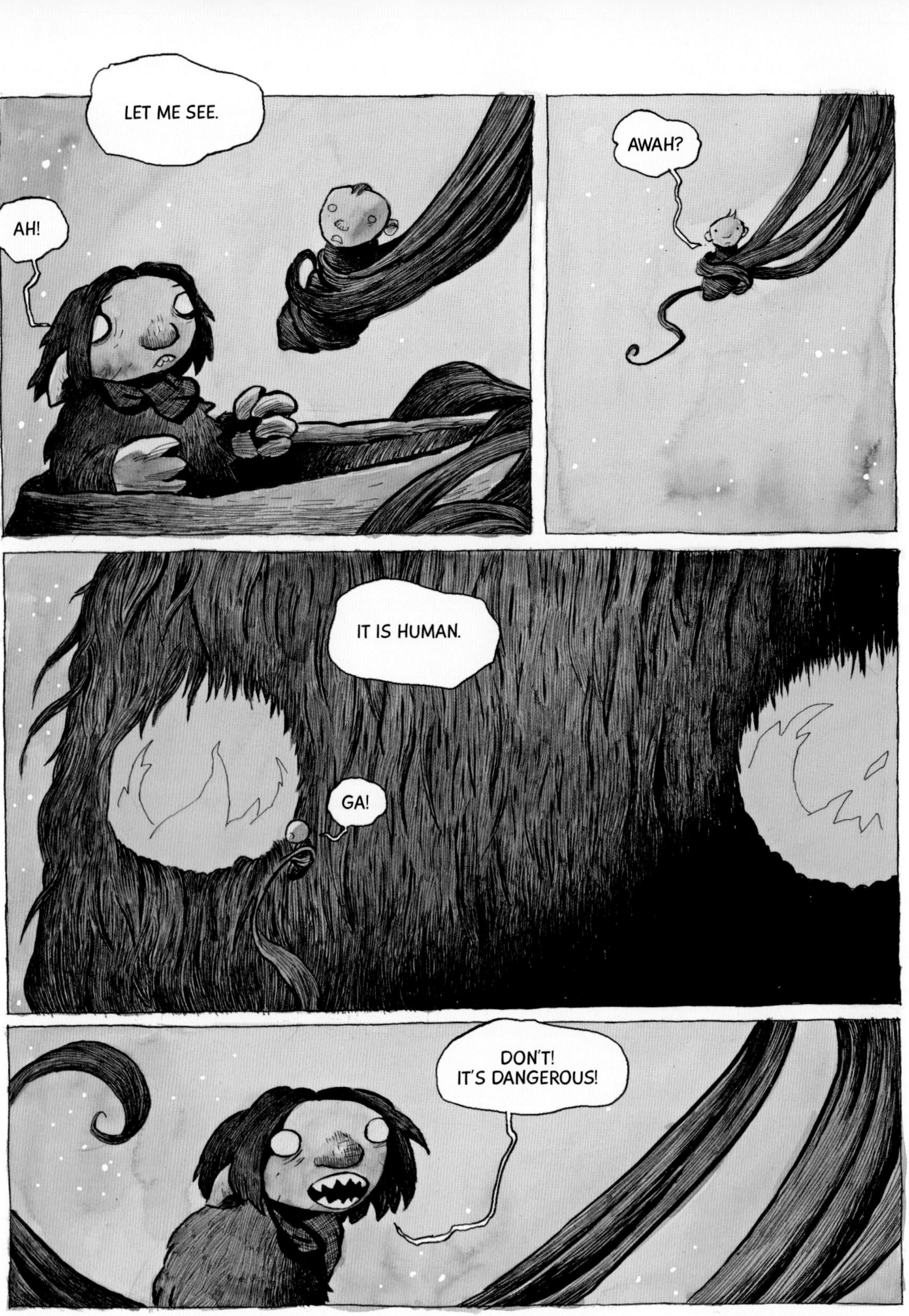
LET ME SEE.
AH!
AWAH?
IT IS HUMAN.
GA!
DON'T!
IT'S DANGEROUS!

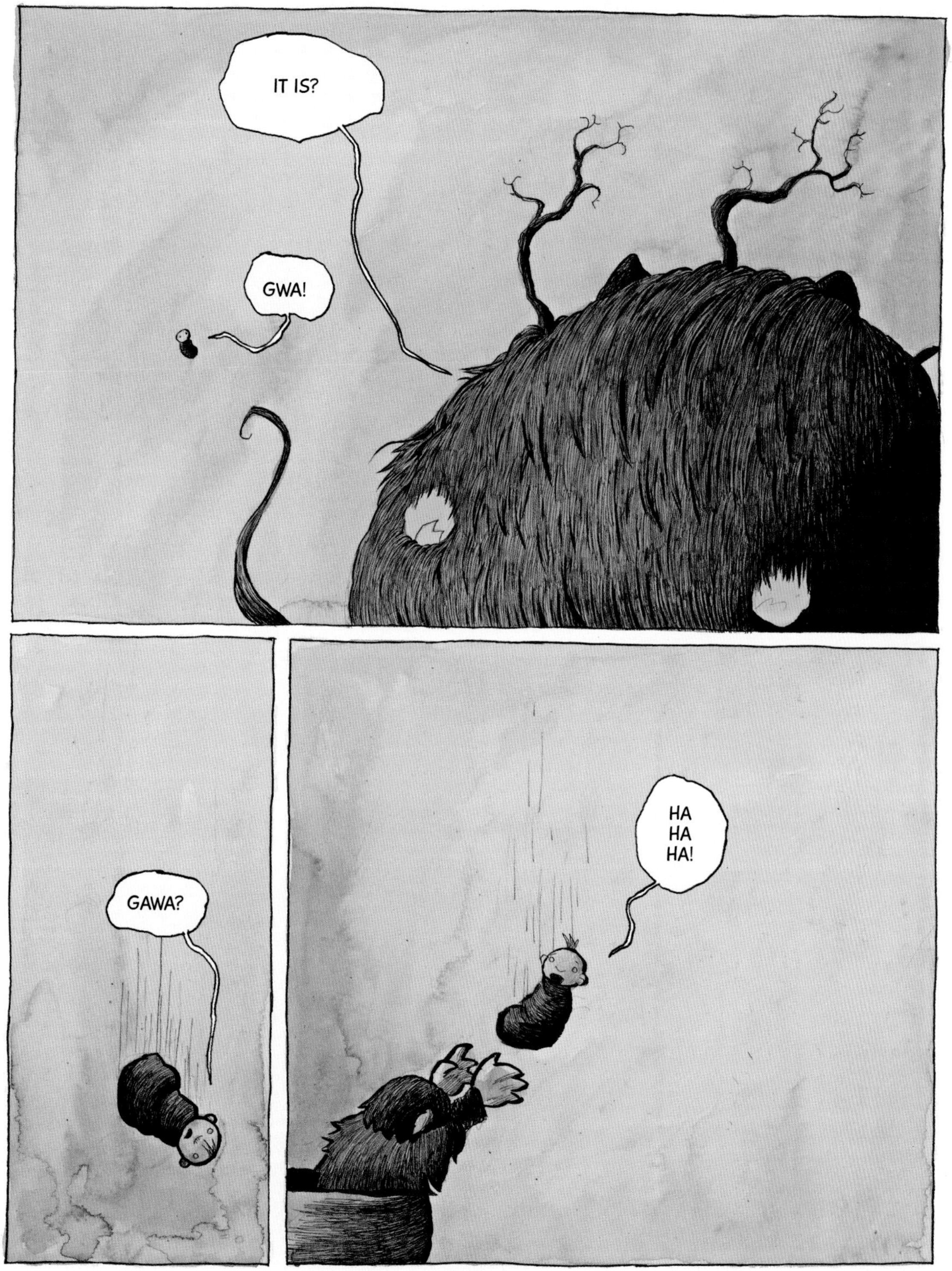
IT IS?
GWA!
GAWA?
HA HA HA!

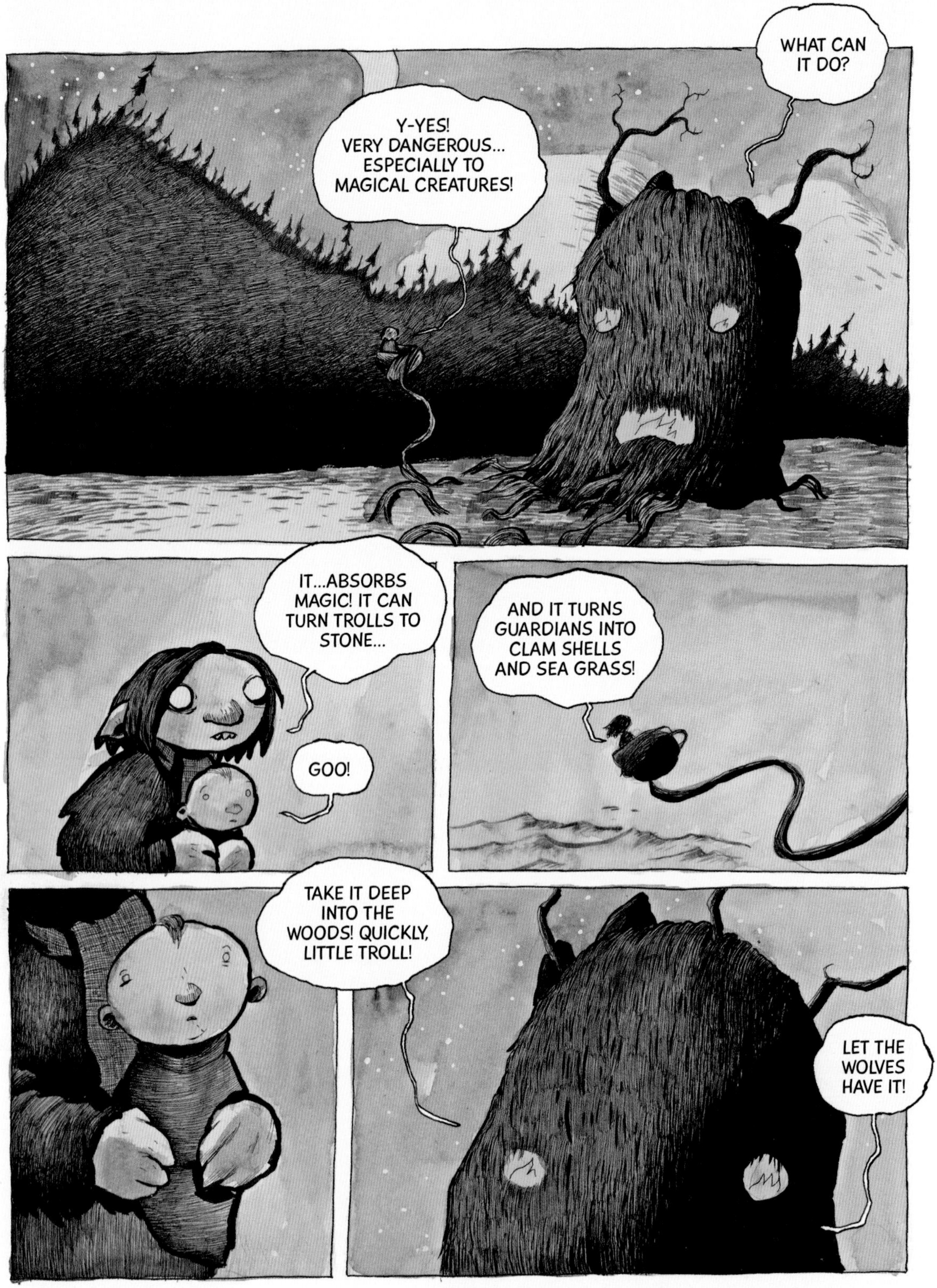
WHAT CAN IT DO?
Y-YES! VERY DANGEROUS... ESPECIALLY TO MAGICAL CREATURES!
IT...ABSORBS MAGIC! IT CAN TURN TROLLS TO STONE...
GOO!
AND IT TURNS GUARDIANS INTO CLAM SHELLS AND SEA GRASS!
TAKE IT DEEP INTO THE WOODS! QUICKLY, LITTLE TROLL!
LET THE WOLVES HAVE IT!

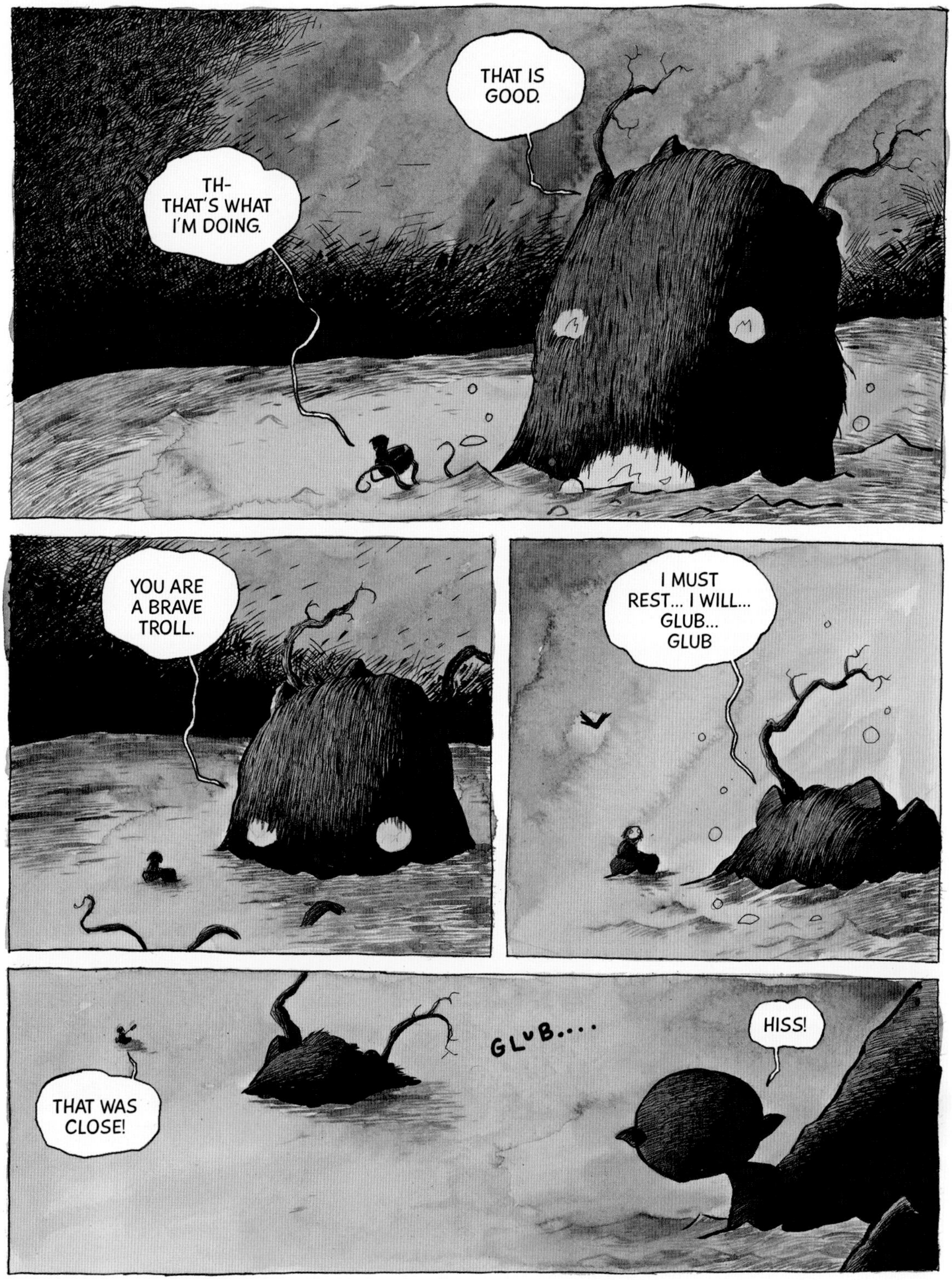
TH- THAT'S WHAT I'M DOING.
THAT IS GOOD.
YOU ARE A BRAVE TROLL.
I MUST REST... I WILL... GLUB... GLUB
THAT WAS CLOSE!
GLUB....
HISS!

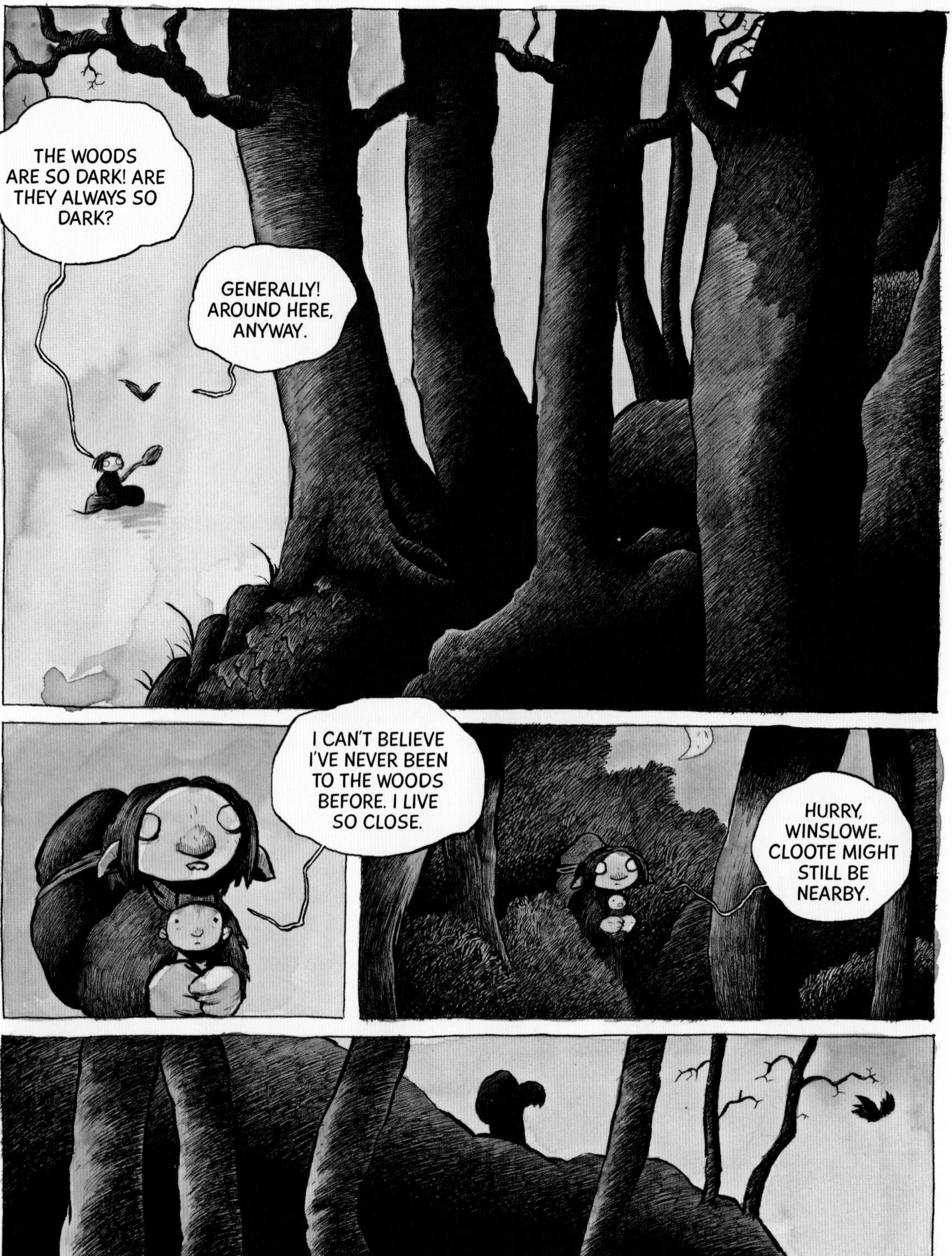
THE WOODS ARE SO DARK! ARE THEY ALWAYS SO DARK?
GENERALLY! AROUND HERE, ANYWAY.
I CAN'T BELIEVE I'VE NEVER BEEN TO THE WOODS BEFORE. I LIVE SO CLOSE.
HURRY, WINSLOWE. CLOOTE MIGHT STILL BE NEARBY.

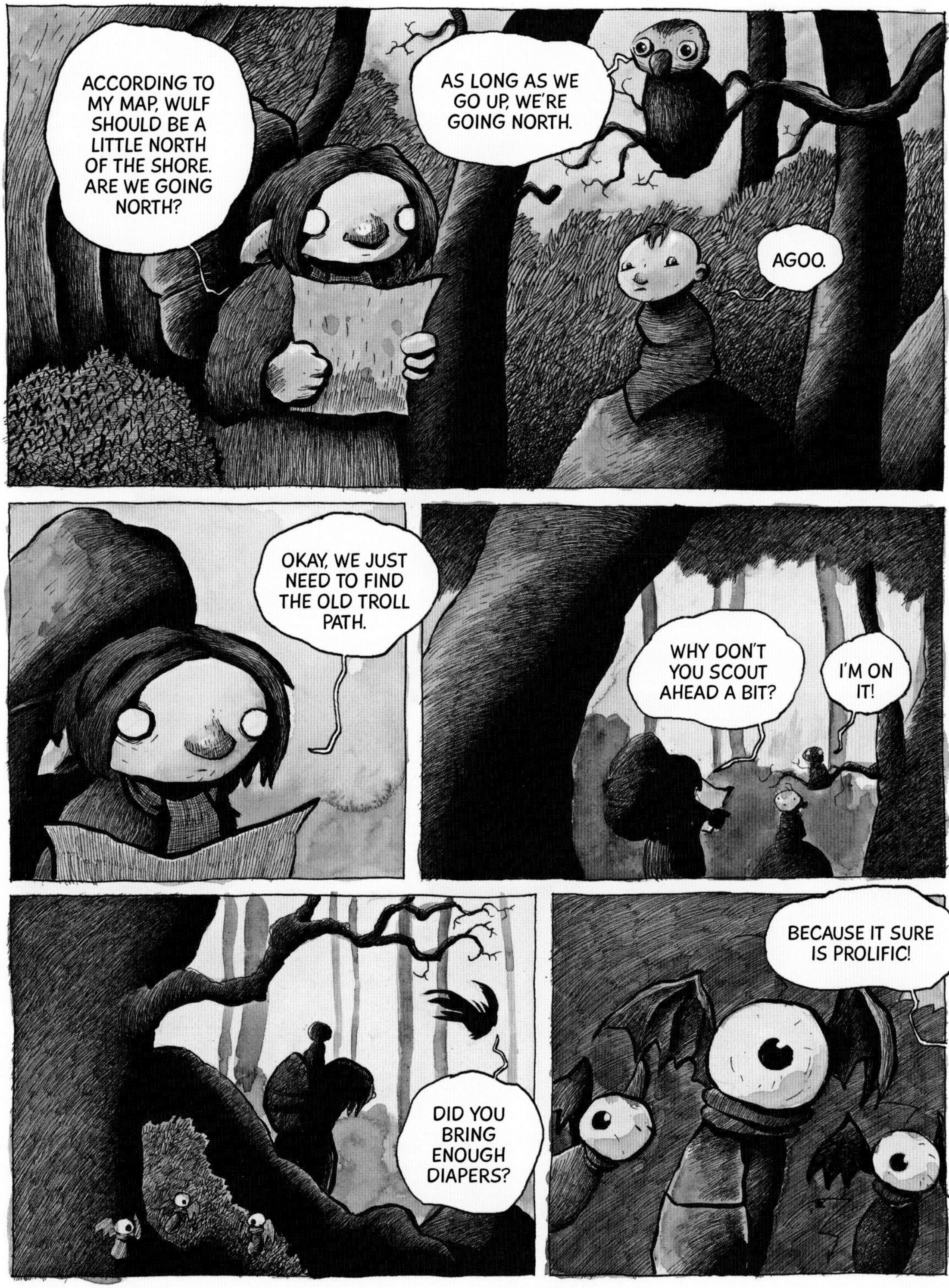
ACCORDING TO MY MAP, WULF SHOULD BE A LITTLE NORTH OF THE SHORE. ARE WE GOING NORTH?
AS LONG AS WE GO UP, WE'RE GOING NORTH.
AGOO.
OKAY, WE JUST NEED TO FIND THE OLD TROLL PATH.
WHY DON'T YOU SCOUT AHEAD A BIT?
I'M ON IT!
DID YOU BRING ENOUGH DIAPERS?
BECAUSE IT SURE IS PROLIFIC!

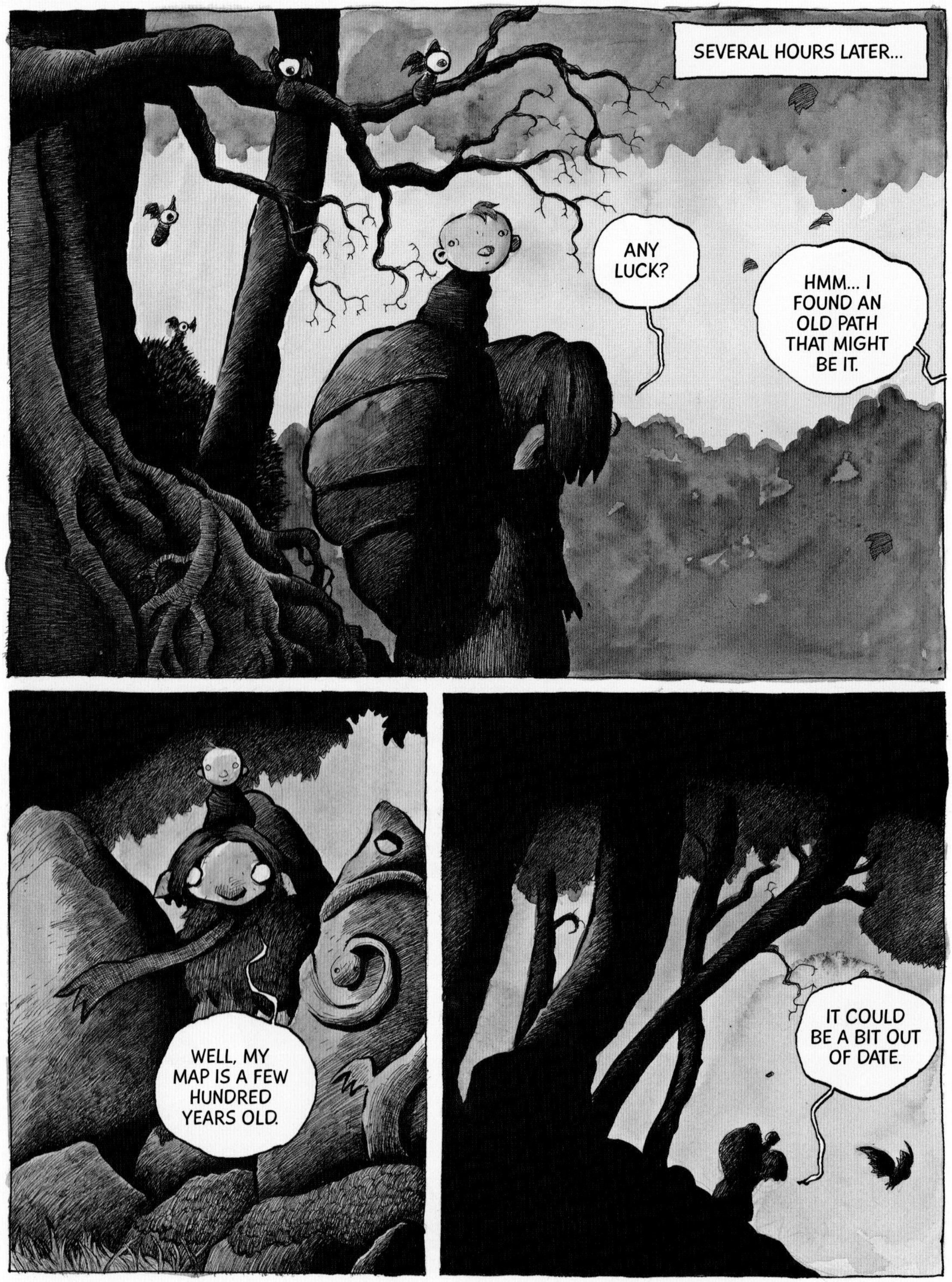
SEVERAL HOURS LATER...
ANY LUCK?
HMM... I FOUND AN OLD PATH THAT MIGHT BE IT.
WELL, MY MAP IS A FEW HUNDRED YEARS OLD.
IT COULD BE A BIT OUT OF DATE.

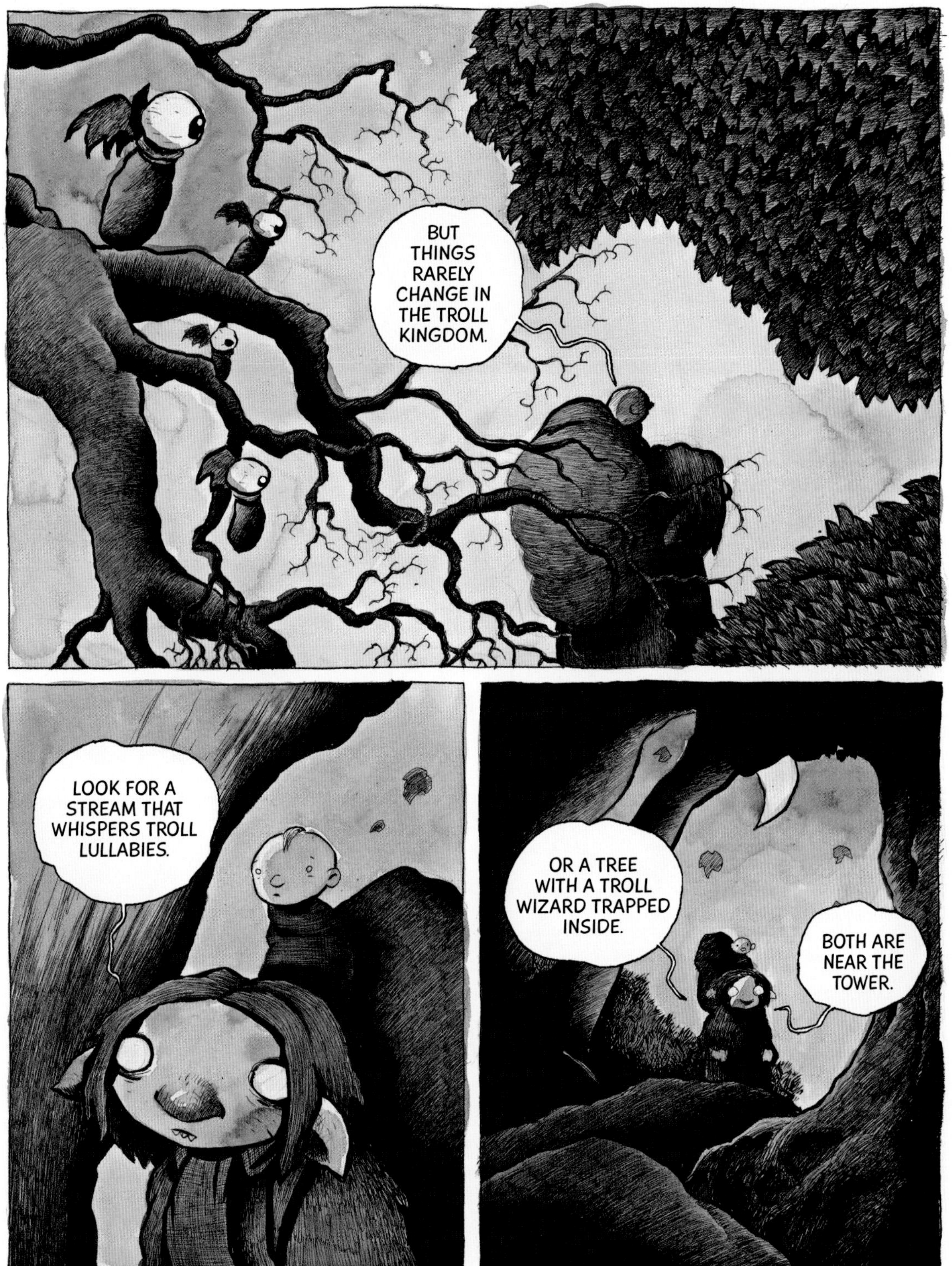
BUT THINGS RARELY CHANGE IN THE TROLL KINGDOM.
LOOK FOR A STREAM THAT WHISPERS TROLL LULLABIES.
OR A TREE WITH A TROLL WIZARD TRAPPED INSIDE.
BOTH ARE NEAR THE TOWER.

WAAAAAA AAAA AA AAA AA AAAAAAA AAAAA AA AAAAA AA AA AAAAAAA AAAA AA

MUCH LATER...

WHAT'S WRONG WITH THE BABY, BERA? IS IT SICK?

I DON'T KNOW.

WAAAAAAAA

MAYBE IT'S TIRED. I KNOW I AM.

AAA A A AAA

AA AA AAA

ME TOO.

AND I'M WORRIED ABOUT THE SUN COMING UP. A FEW MORE HOURS, AND I'LL BE A LAWN ORNAMENT.

BERA, LOOK. IS THAT A LIGHT THROUGH THOSE TREES?

WAAAAAAAAAAAAAA AA AAA AAAAAAAA

IT MUST BE WULF'S TOWER...

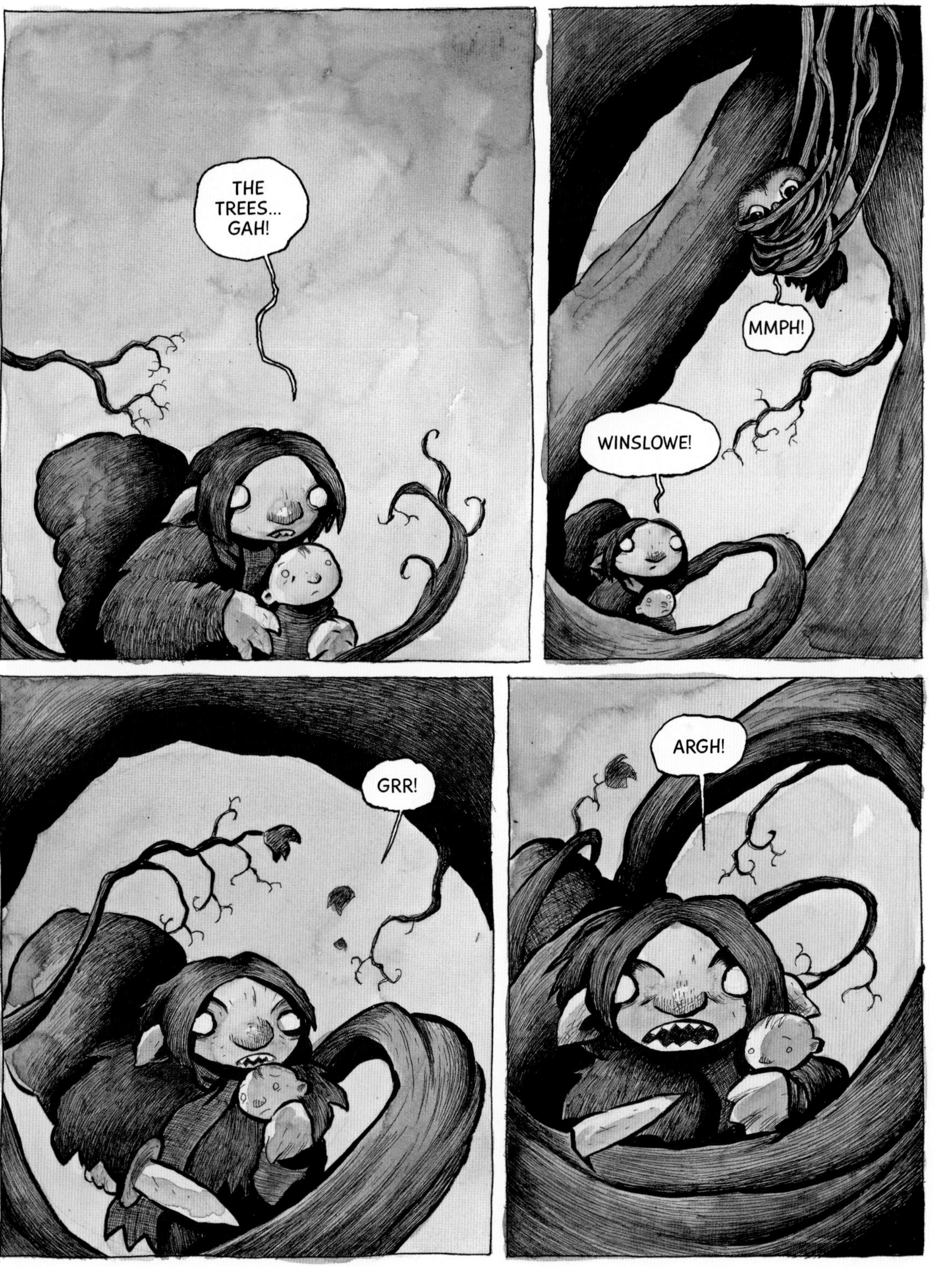
THE TREES... GAH!
MMPH!
WINSLOWE!
GRR!
ARGH!

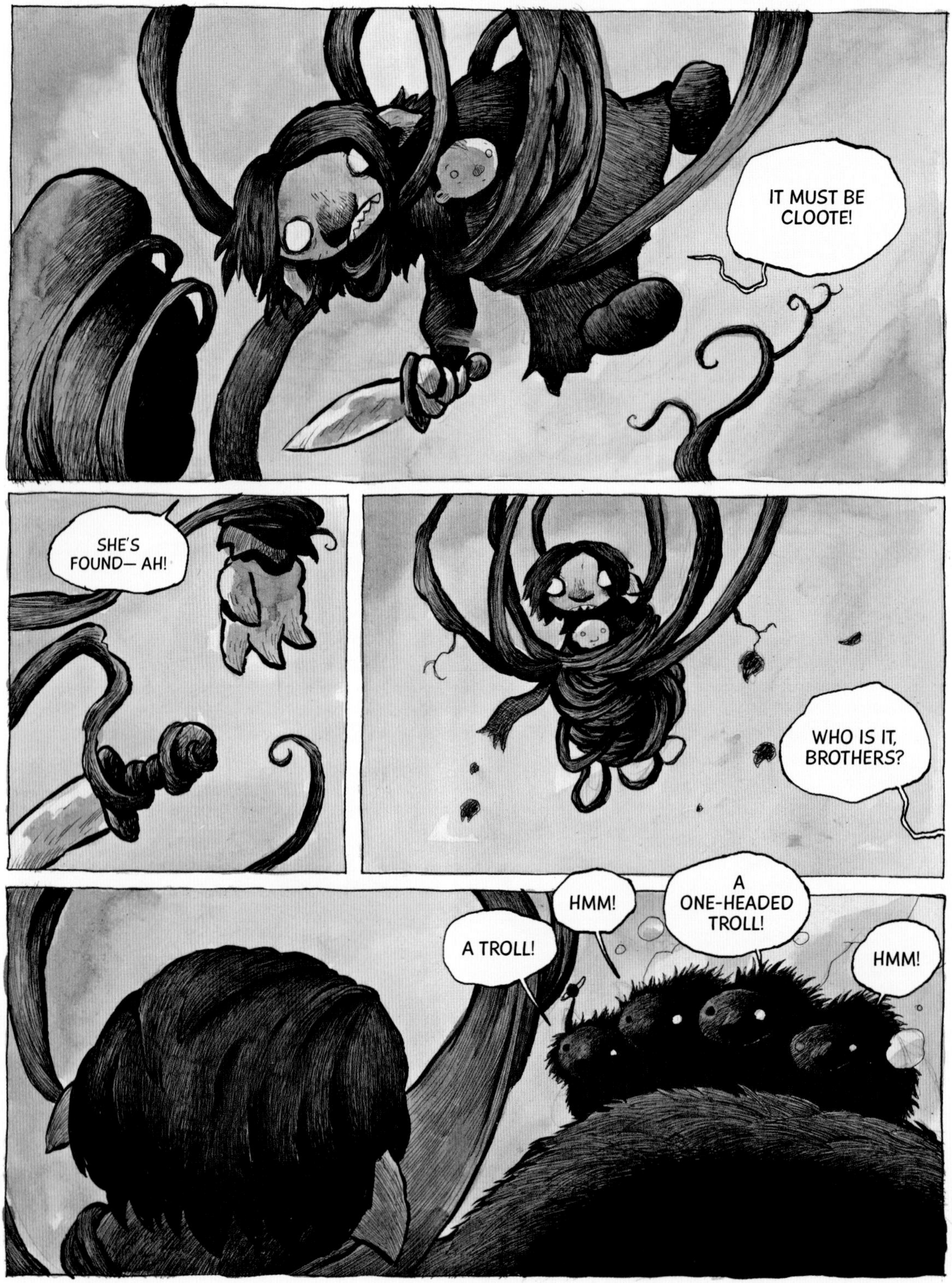
IT MUST BE CLOOTE!
SHE'S FOUND— AH!
WHO IS IT, BROTHERS?
A TROLL!
HMM!
A ONE-HEADED TROLL!
HMM!

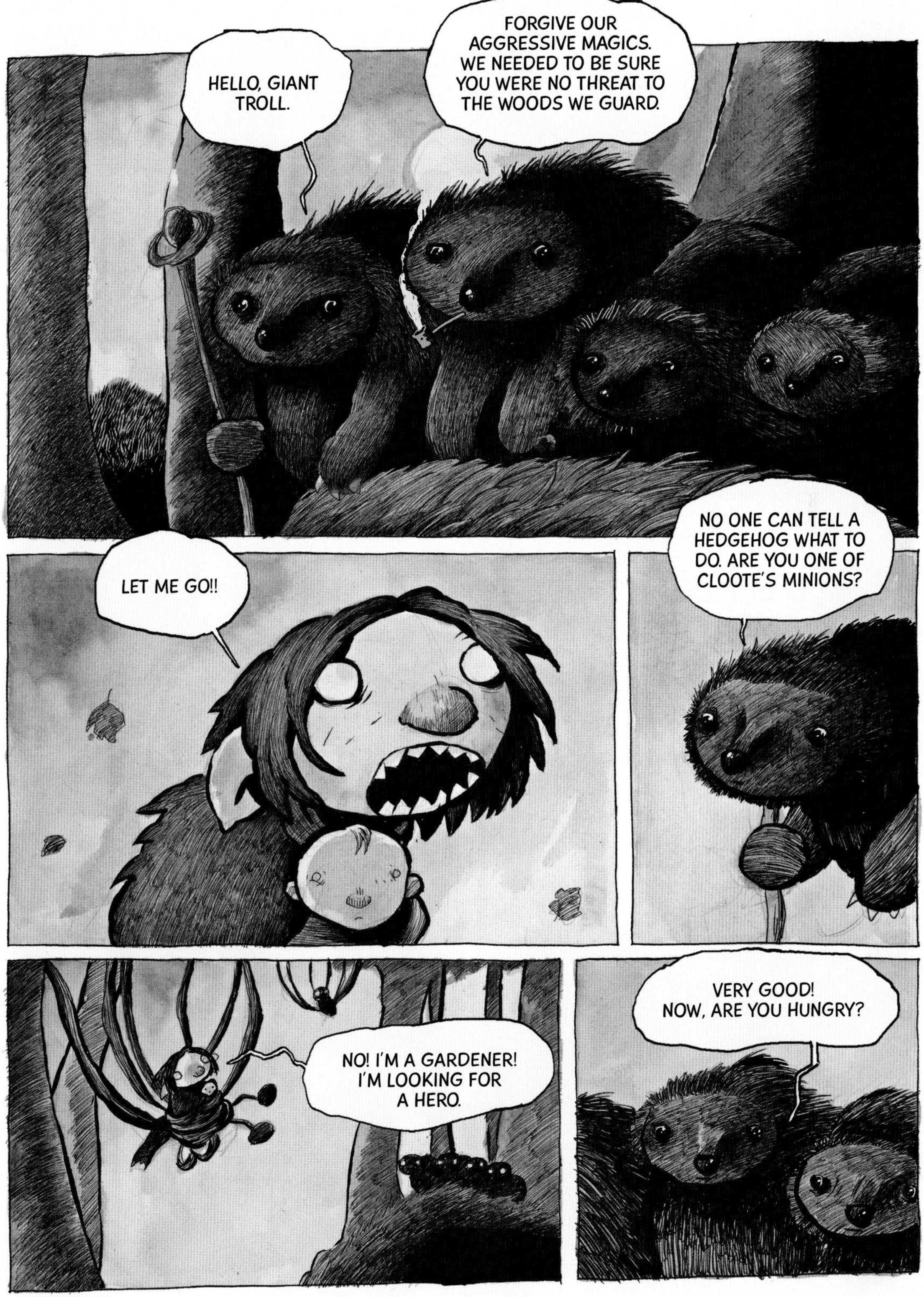
HELLO, GIANT TROLL.
FORGIVE OUR AGGRESSIVE MAGICS. WE NEEDED TO BE SURE YOU WERE NO THREAT TO THE WOODS WE GUARD.
LET ME GO!!
NO ONE CAN TELL A HEDGEHOG WHAT TO DO. ARE YOU ONE OF CLOOTE'S MINIONS?
NO! I'M A GARDENER! I'M LOOKING FOR A HERO.
VERY GOOD! NOW, ARE YOU HUNGRY?

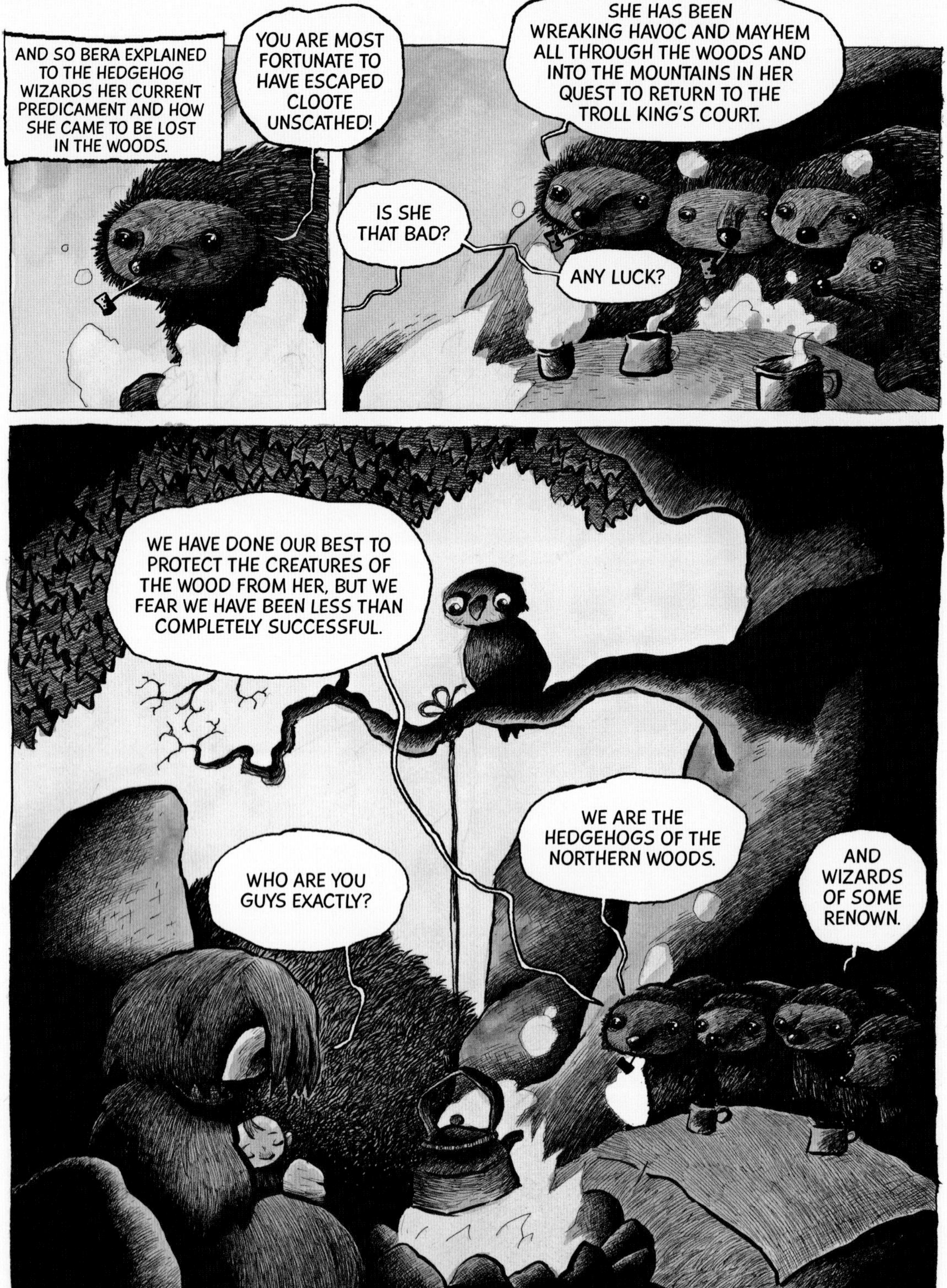
AND SO BERA EXPLAINED TO THE HEDGEHOG WIZARDS HER CURRENT PREDICAMENT AND HOW SHE CAME TO BE LOST IN THE WOODS.
YOU ARE MOST FORTUNATE TO HAVE ESCAPED CLOOTE UNSCATHED!
SHE HAS BEEN WREAKING HAVOC AND MAYHEM ALL THROUGH THE WOODS AND INTO THE MOUNTAINS IN HER QUEST TO RETURN TO THE TROLL KING'S COURT.
IS SHE THAT BAD?
ANY LUCK?
WE HAVE DONE OUR BEST TO PROTECT THE CREATURES OF THE WOOD FROM HER, BUT WE FEAR WE HAVE BEEN LESS THAN COMPLETELY SUCCESSFUL.
WHO ARE YOU GUYS EXACTLY?
WE ARE THE HEDGEHOGS OF THE NORTHERN WOODS.
AND WIZARDS OF SOME RENOWN.

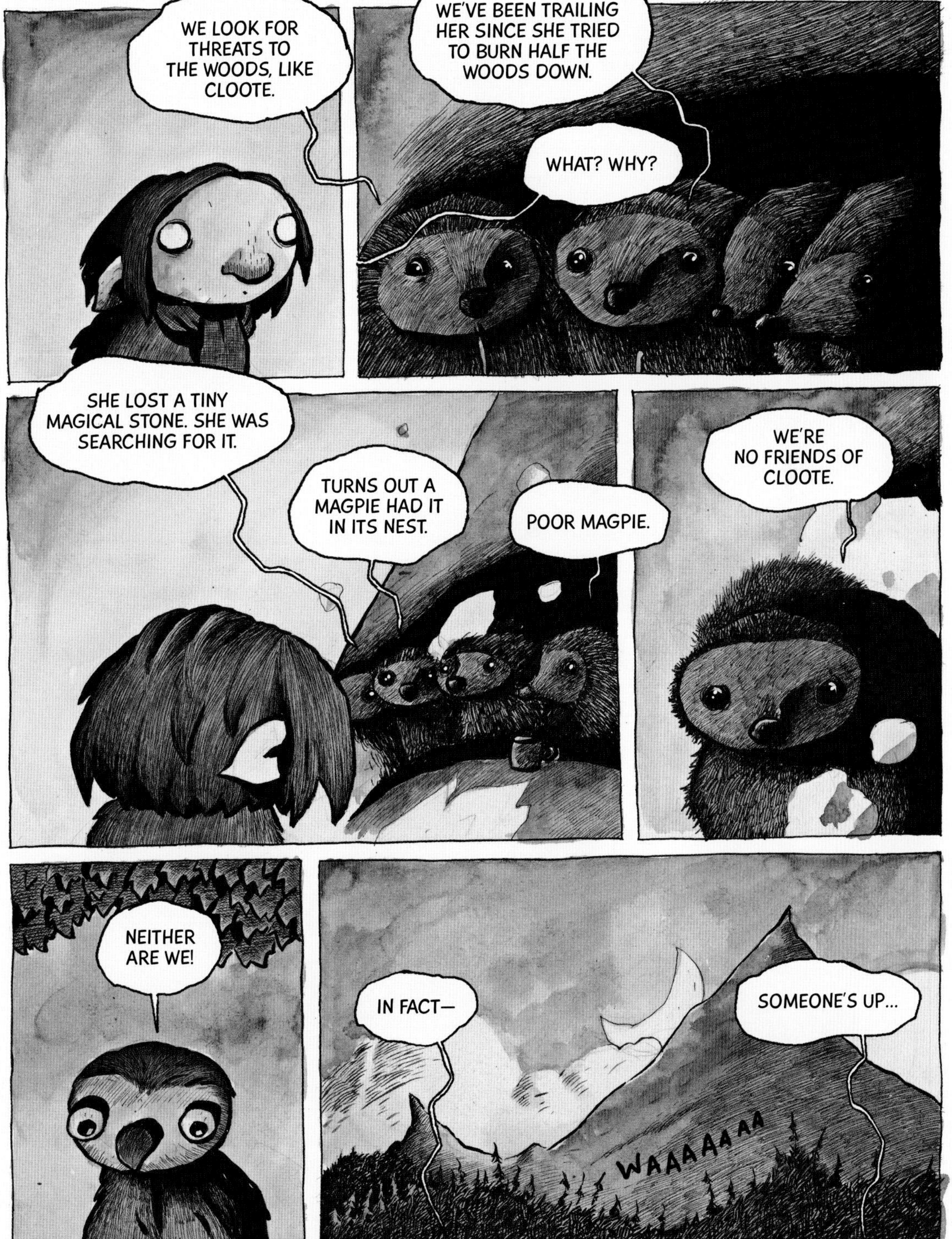
WE LOOK FOR THREATS TO THE WOODS, LIKE CLOOTE.
WE'VE BEEN TRAILING HER SINCE SHE TRIED TO BURN HALF THE WOODS DOWN.
WHAT? WHY?
SHE LOST A TINY MAGICAL STONE. SHE WAS SEARCHING FOR IT.
TURNS OUT A MAGPIE HAD IT IN ITS NEST.
POOR MAGPIE.
WE'RE NO FRIENDS OF CLOOTE.
NEITHER ARE WE!
IN FACT—
SOMEONE'S UP...
WAAAAAAA

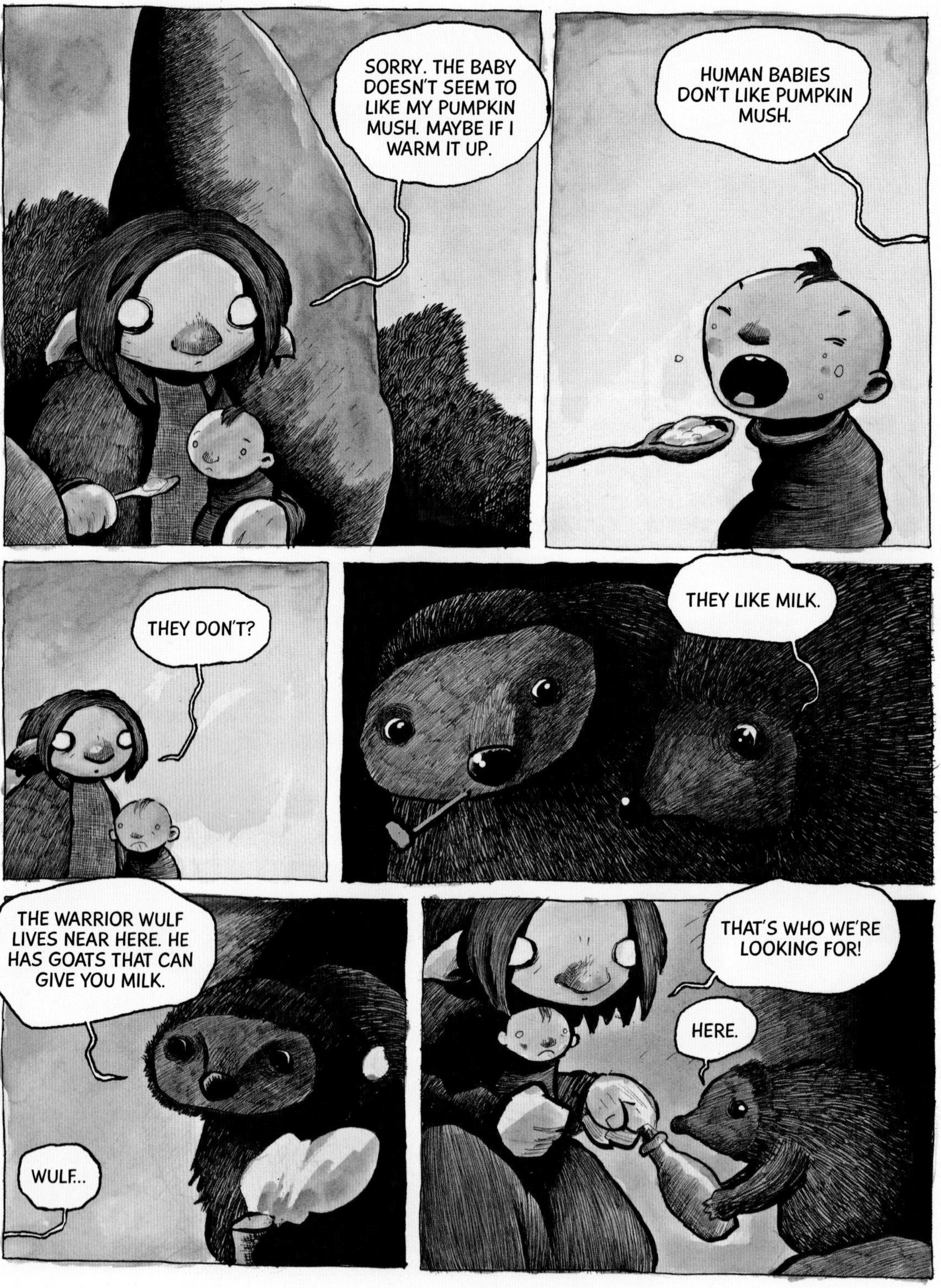
SORRY. THE BABY DOESN'T SEEM TO LIKE MY PUMPKIN MUSH. MAYBE IF I WARM IT UP.
HUMAN BABIES DON'T LIKE PUMPKIN MUSH.
THEY DON'T?
THEY LIKE MILK.
THE WARRIOR WULF LIVES NEAR HERE. HE HAS GOATS THAT CAN GIVE YOU MILK.
WULF...
THAT'S WHO WE'RE LOOKING FOR!
HERE.

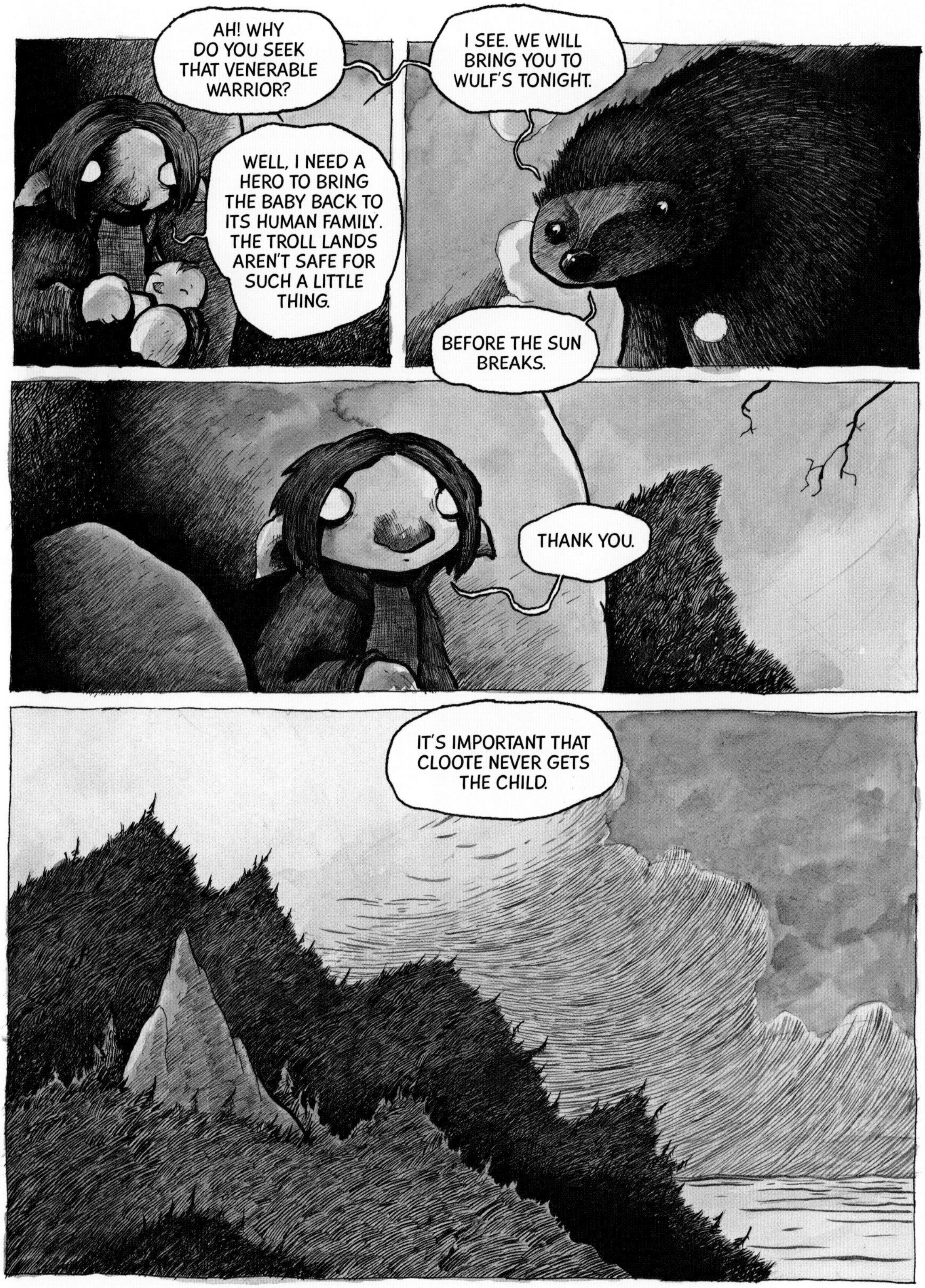
AH! WHY DO YOU SEEK THAT VENERABLE WARRIOR?
WELL, I NEED A HERO TO BRING THE BABY BACK TO ITS HUMAN FAMILY. THE TROLL LANDS AREN'T SAFE FOR SUCH A LITTLE THING.
I SEE. WE WILL BRING YOU TO WULF'S TONIGHT.
BEFORE THE SUN BREAKS.
THANK YOU.
IT'S IMPORTANT THAT CLOOTE NEVER GETS THE CHILD.

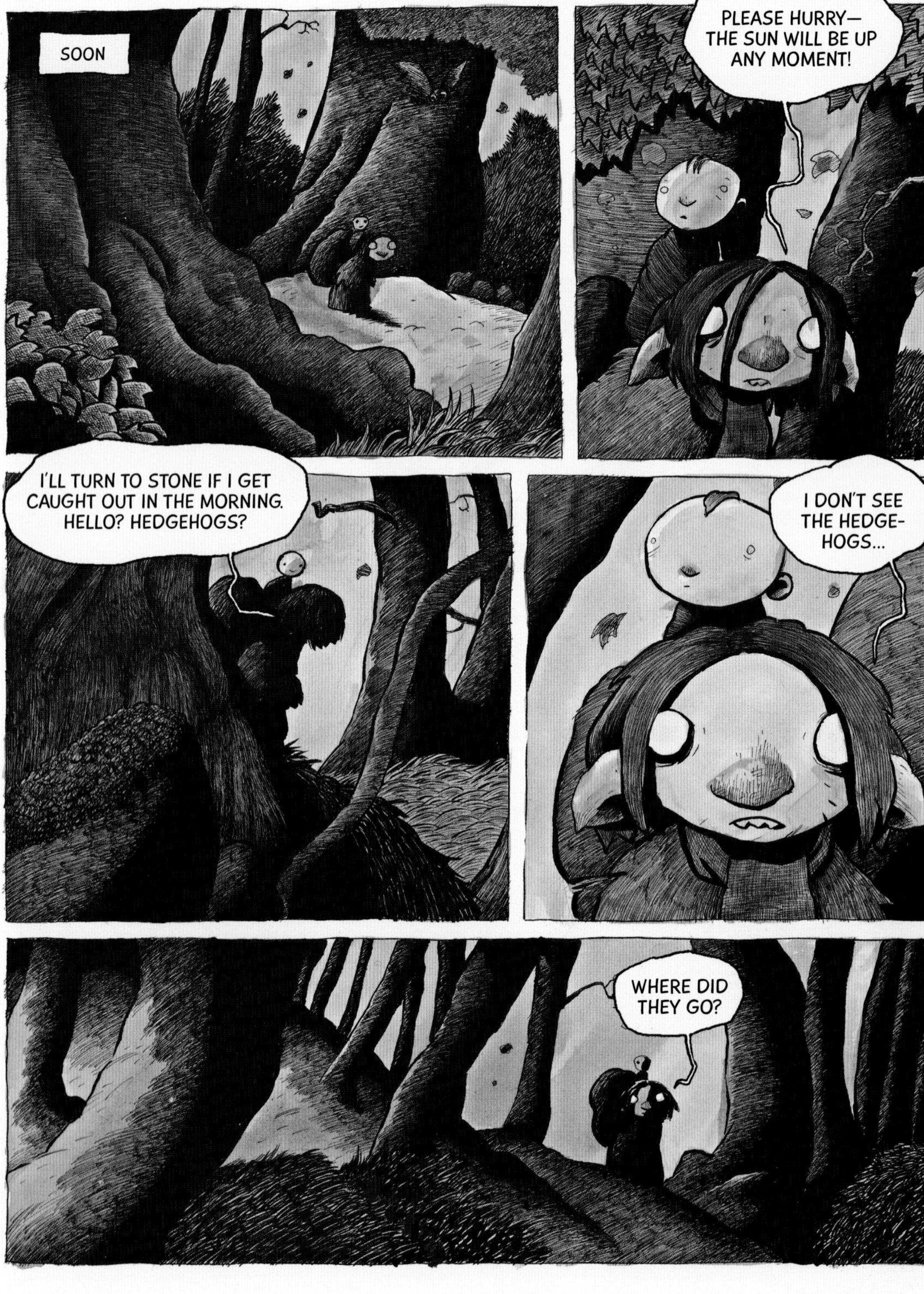
SOON
PLEASE HURRY— THE SUN WILL BE UP ANY MOMENT!
I'LL TURN TO STONE IF I GET CAUGHT OUT IN THE MORNING. HELLO? HEDGEHOGS?
I DON'T SEE THE HEDGE- HOGS...
WHERE DID THEY GO?

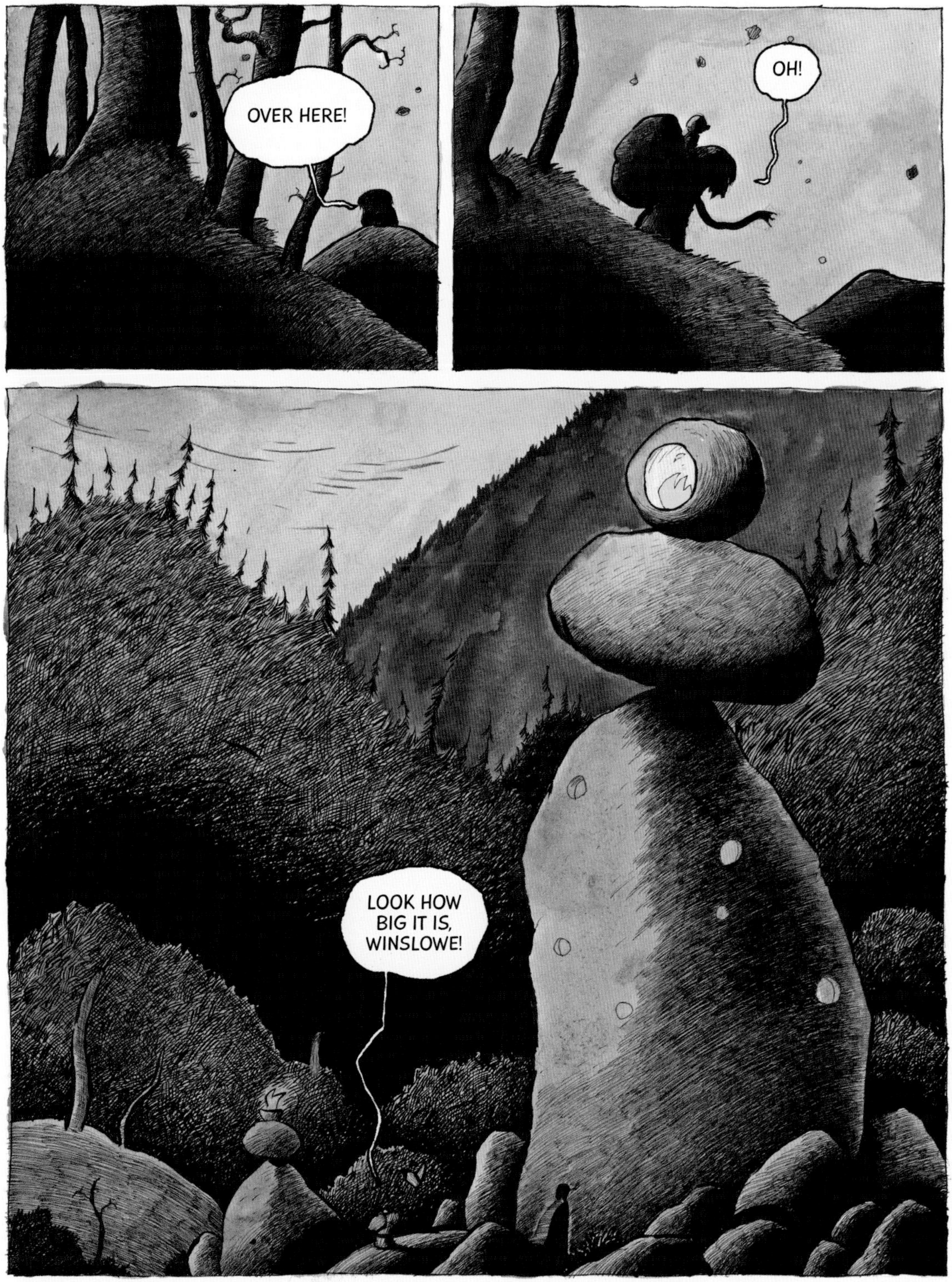
OVER HERE!
OH!
LOOK HOW BIG IT IS, WINSLOWE!

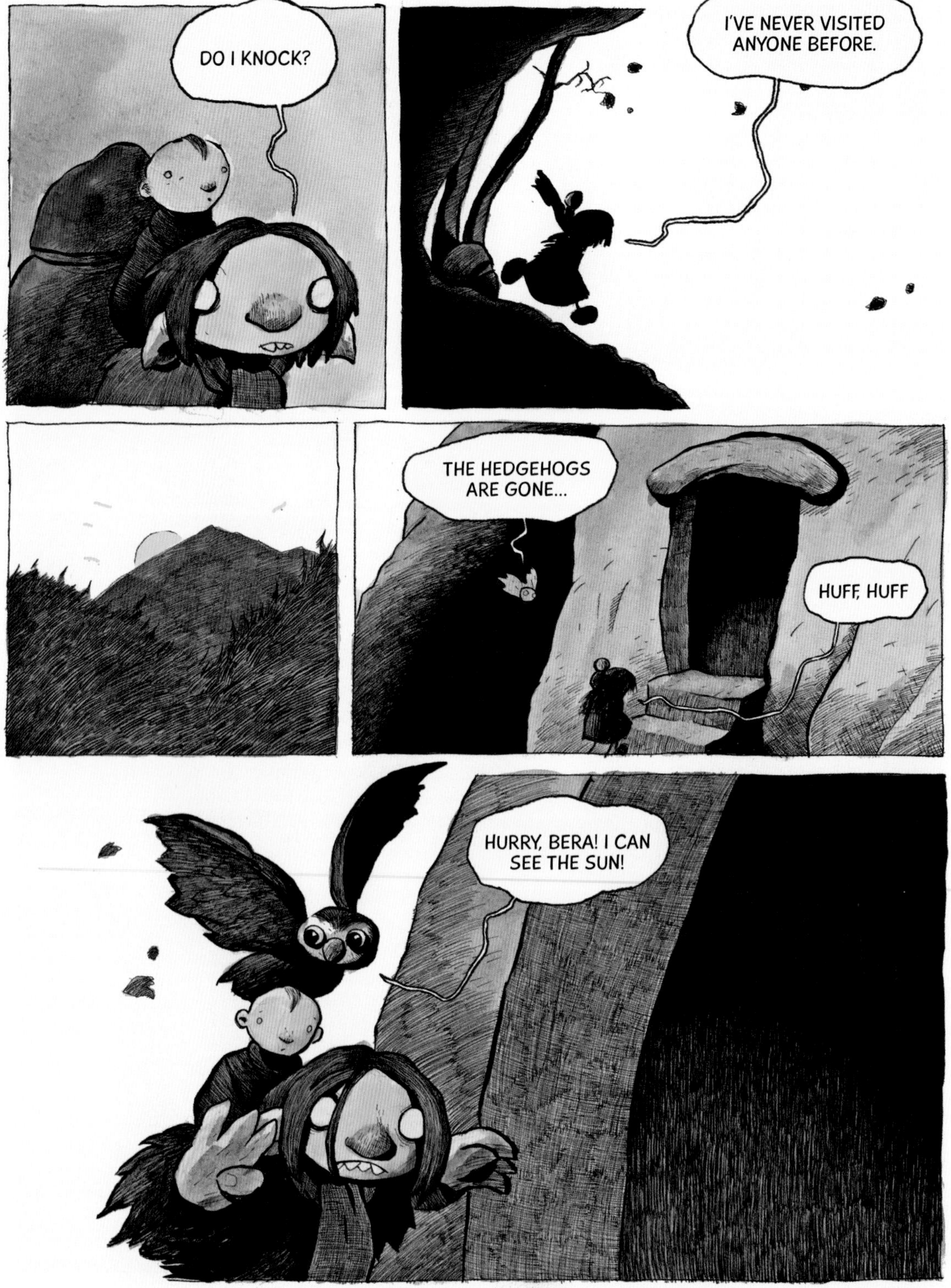
DO I KNOCK?
I'VE NEVER VISITED ANYONE BEFORE.
THE HEDGEHOGS ARE GONE...
HUFF, HUFF
HURRY, BERA! I CAN SEE THE SUN!

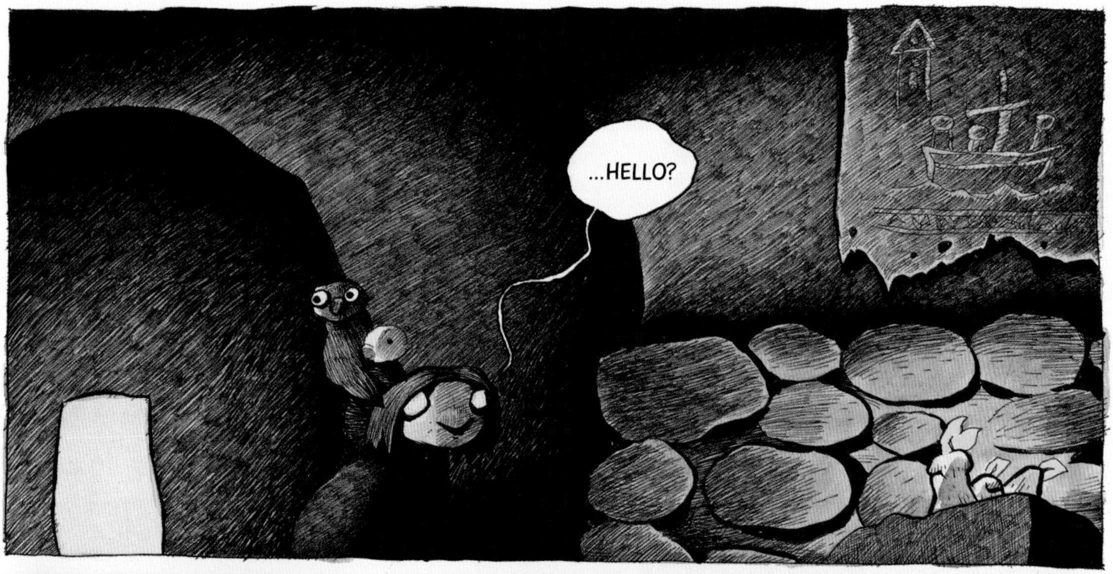
...HELLO?

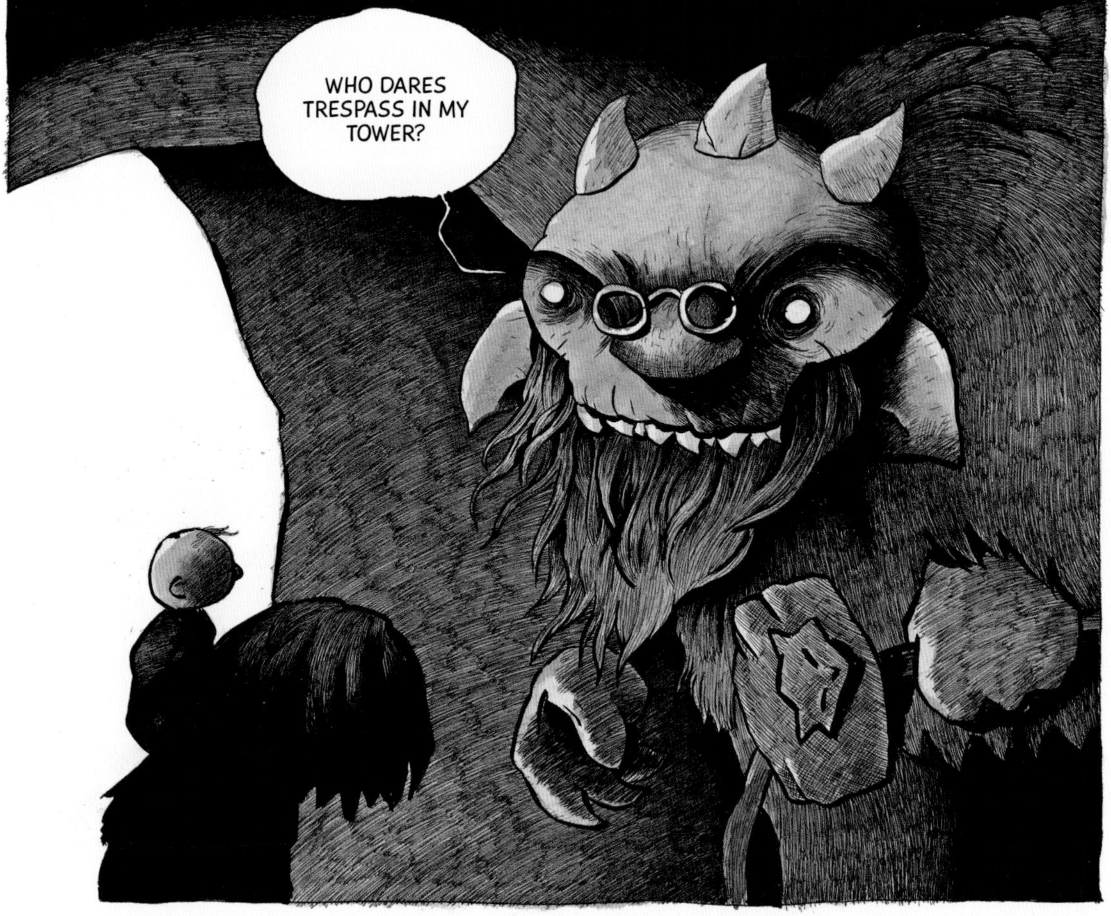
WHO DARES TRESPASS IN MY TOWER?

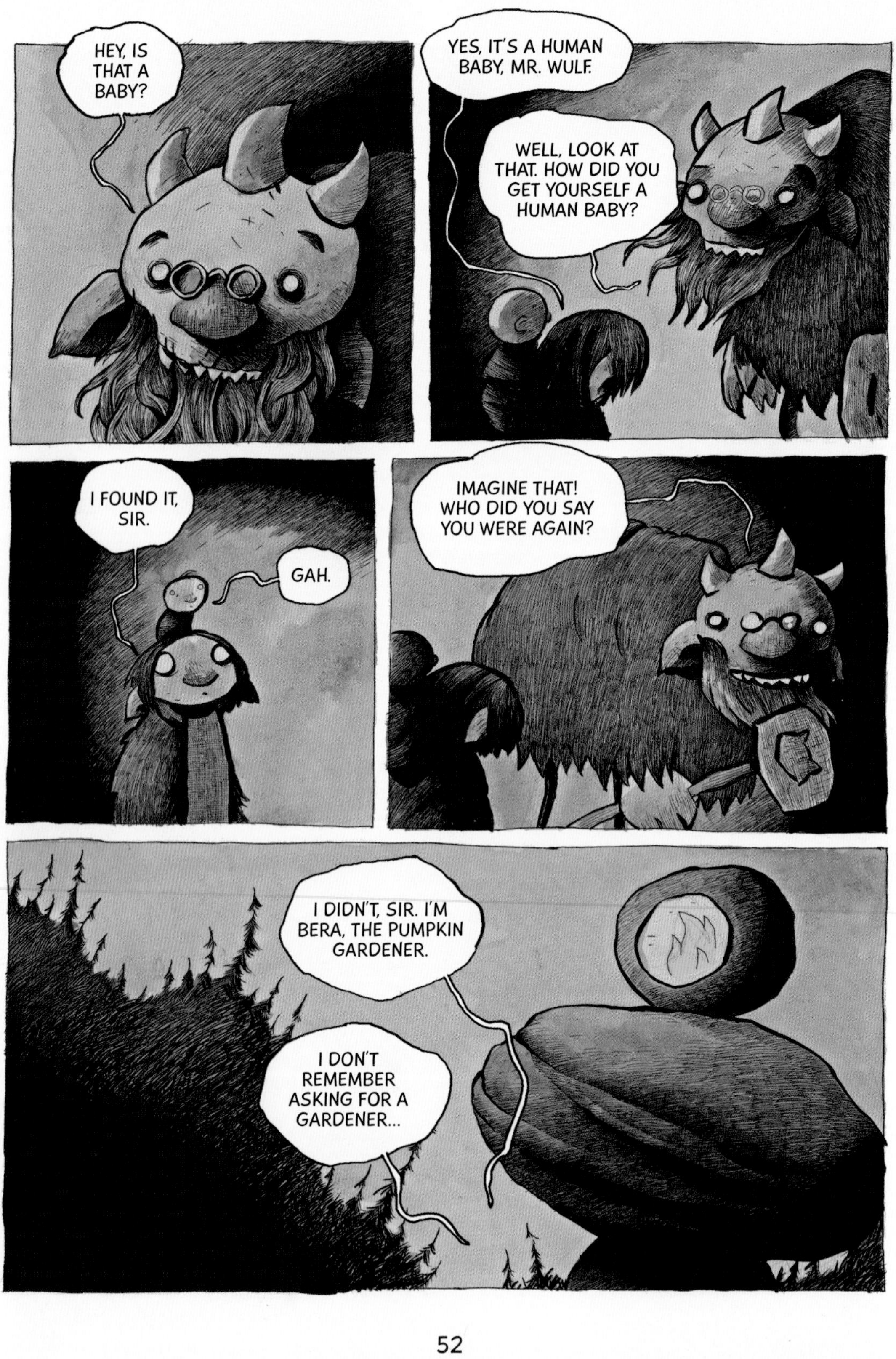
HEY, IS THAT A BABY?
YES, IT'S A HUMAN BABY, MR. WULF.
WELL, LOOK AT THAT. HOW DID YOU GET YOURSELF A HUMAN BABY?
I FOUND IT, SIR.
GAH.
IMAGINE THAT! WHO DID YOU SAY YOU WERE AGAIN?
I DIDN'T, SIR. I'M BERA, THE PUMPKIN GARDENER.
I DON'T REMEMBER ASKING FOR A GARDENER...

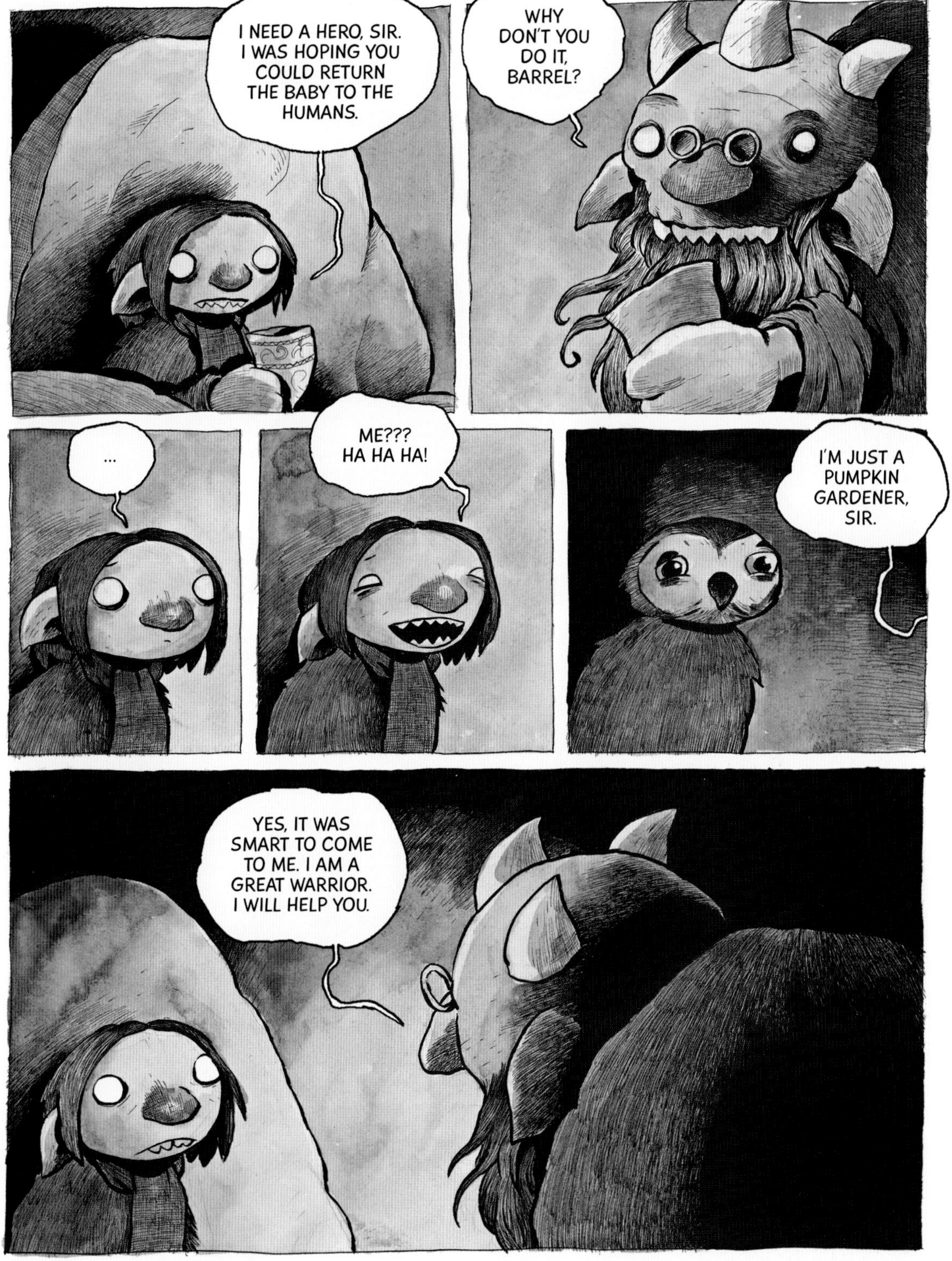
I NEED A HERO, SIR. I WAS HOPING YOU COULD RETURN THE BABY TO THE HUMANS.
WHY DON'T YOU DO IT, BARREL?
...
ME??? HA HA HA!
I'M JUST A PUMPKIN GARDENER, SIR.
YES, IT WAS SMART TO COME TO ME. I AM A GREAT WARRIOR. I WILL HELP YOU.

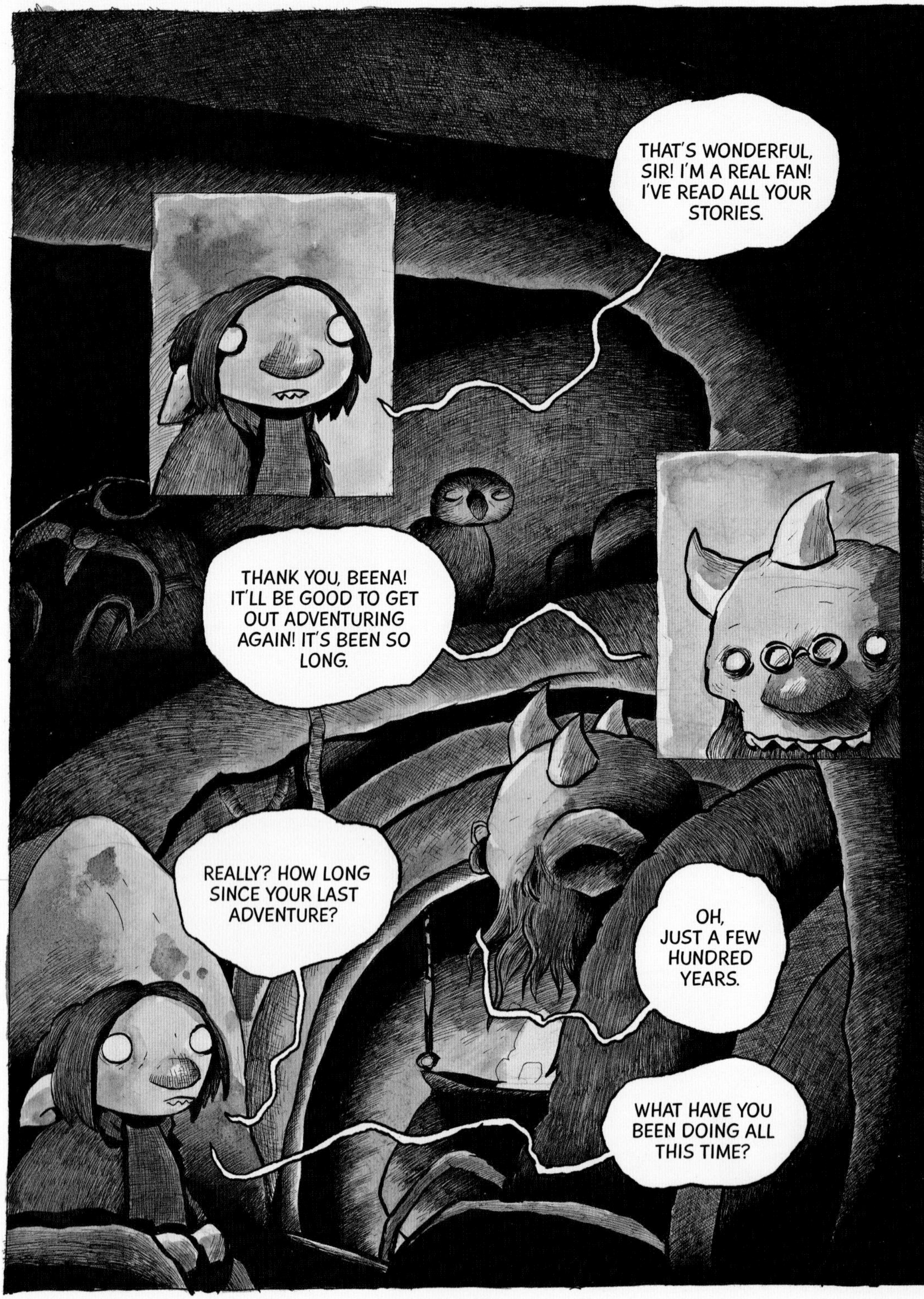
THAT'S WONDERFUL, SIR! I'M A REAL FAN! I'VE READ ALL YOUR STORIES.
THANK YOU, BEENA! IT'LL BE GOOD TO GET OUT ADVENTURING AGAIN! IT'S BEEN SO LONG.
REALLY? HOW LONG SINCE YOUR LAST ADVENTURE?
OH, JUST A FEW HUNDRED YEARS.
WHAT HAVE YOU BEEN DOING ALL THIS TIME?

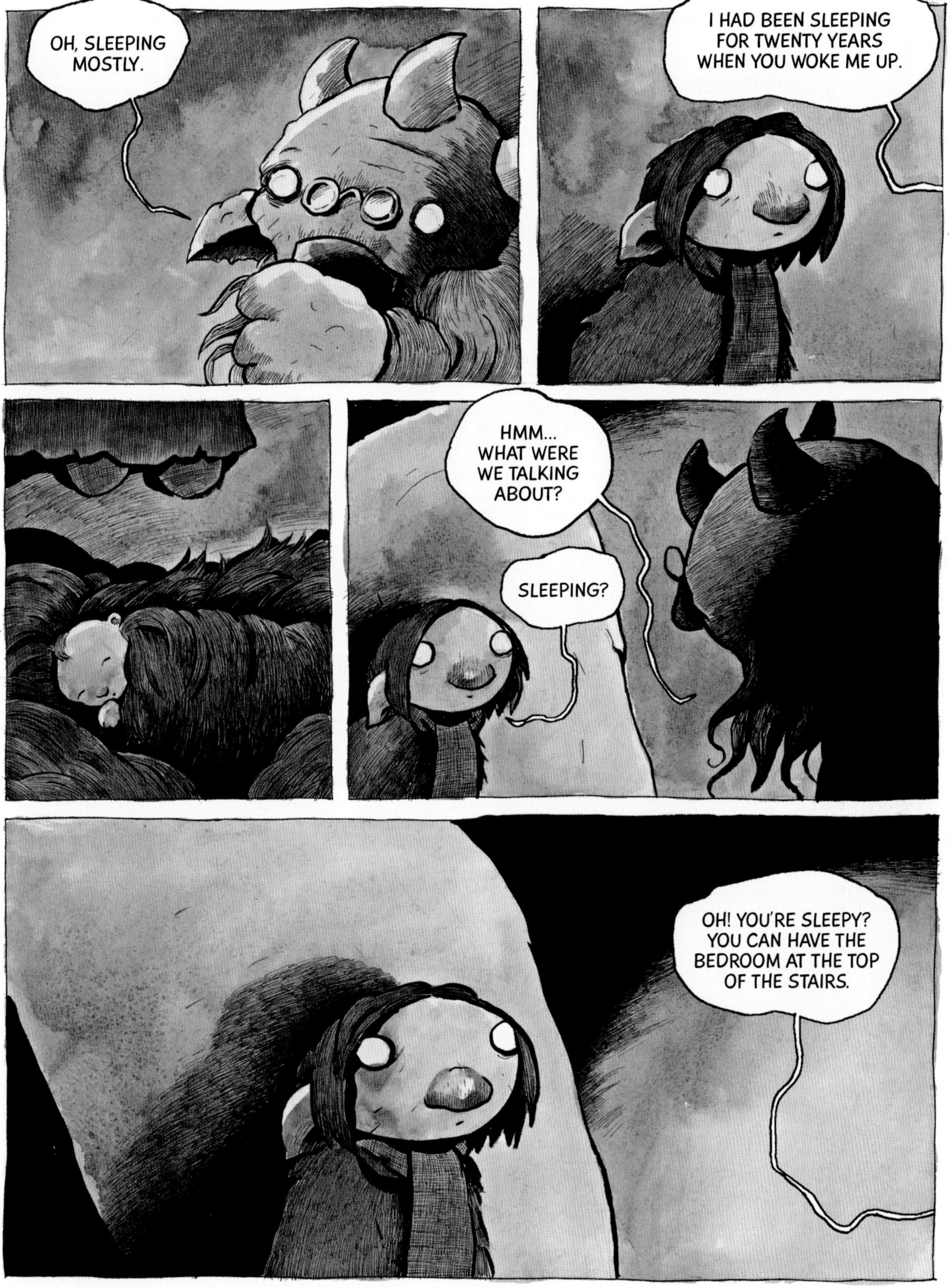
OH, SLEEPING MOSTLY.
I HAD BEEN SLEEPING FOR TWENTY YEARS WHEN YOU WOKE ME UP.
HMM... WHAT WERE WE TALKING ABOUT?
SLEEPING?
OH! YOU'RE SLEEPY? YOU CAN HAVE THE BEDROOM AT THE TOP OF THE STAIRS.

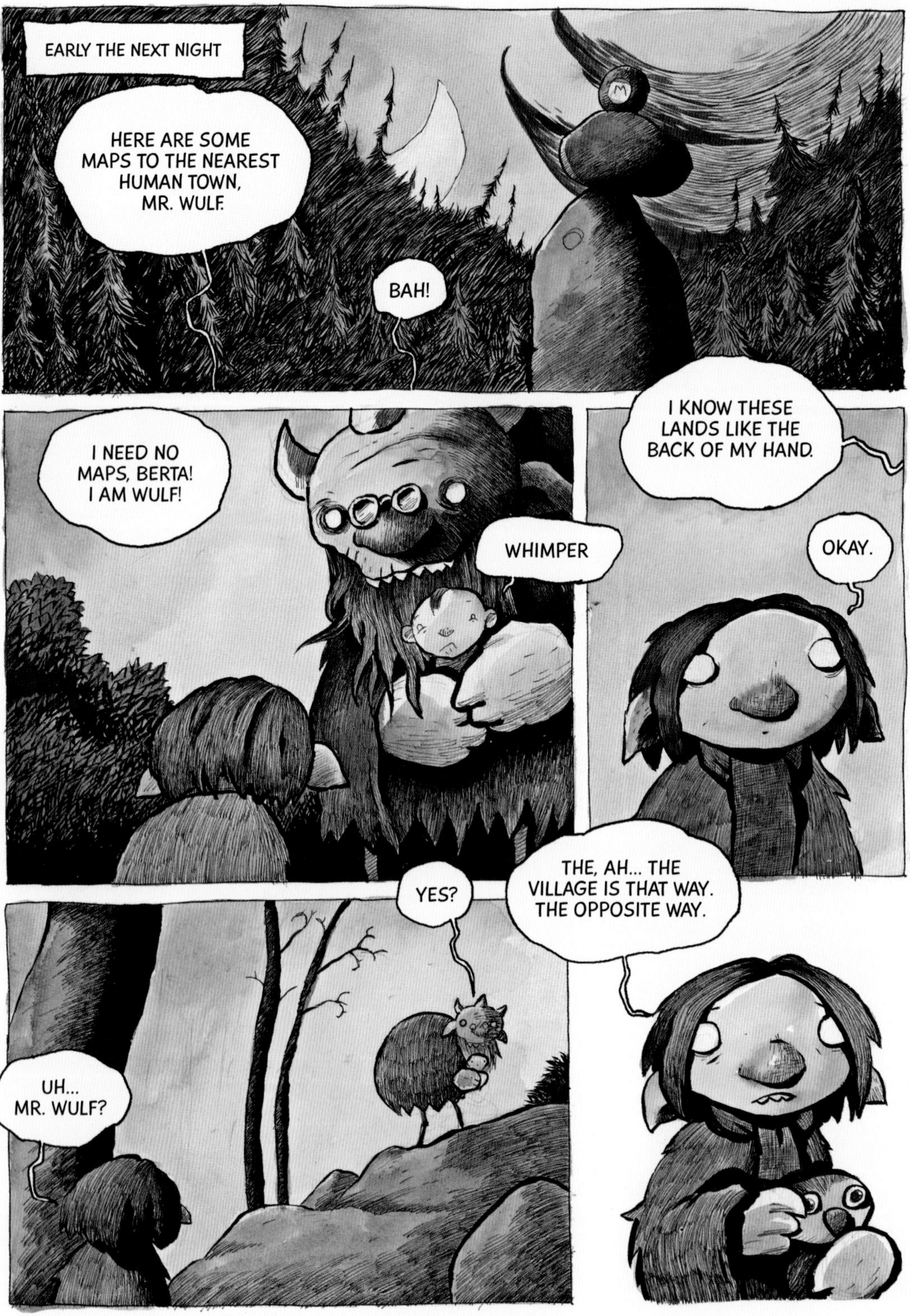
EARLY THE NEXT NIGHT
HERE ARE SOME MAPS TO THE NEAREST HUMAN TOWN, MR. WULF.
BAH!
I NEED NO MAPS, BERTA! I AM WULF!
WHIMPER
I KNOW THESE LANDS LIKE THE BACK OF MY HAND.
OKAY.
UH... MR. WULF?
YES?
THE, AH... THE VILLAGE IS THAT WAY. THE OPPOSITE WAY.

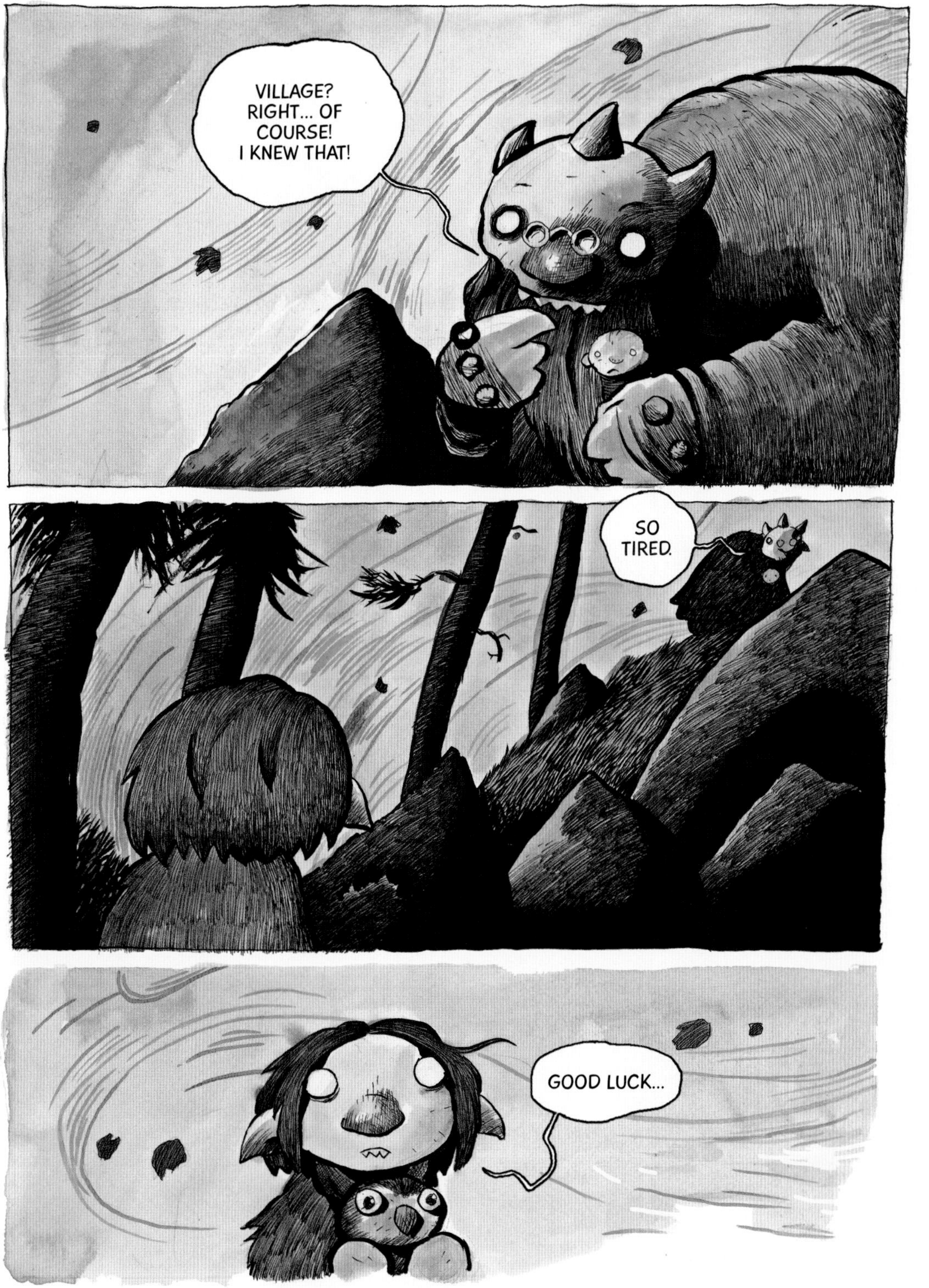
VILLAGE? RIGHT... OF COURSE! I KNEW THAT!
SO TIRED.
GOOD LUCK...

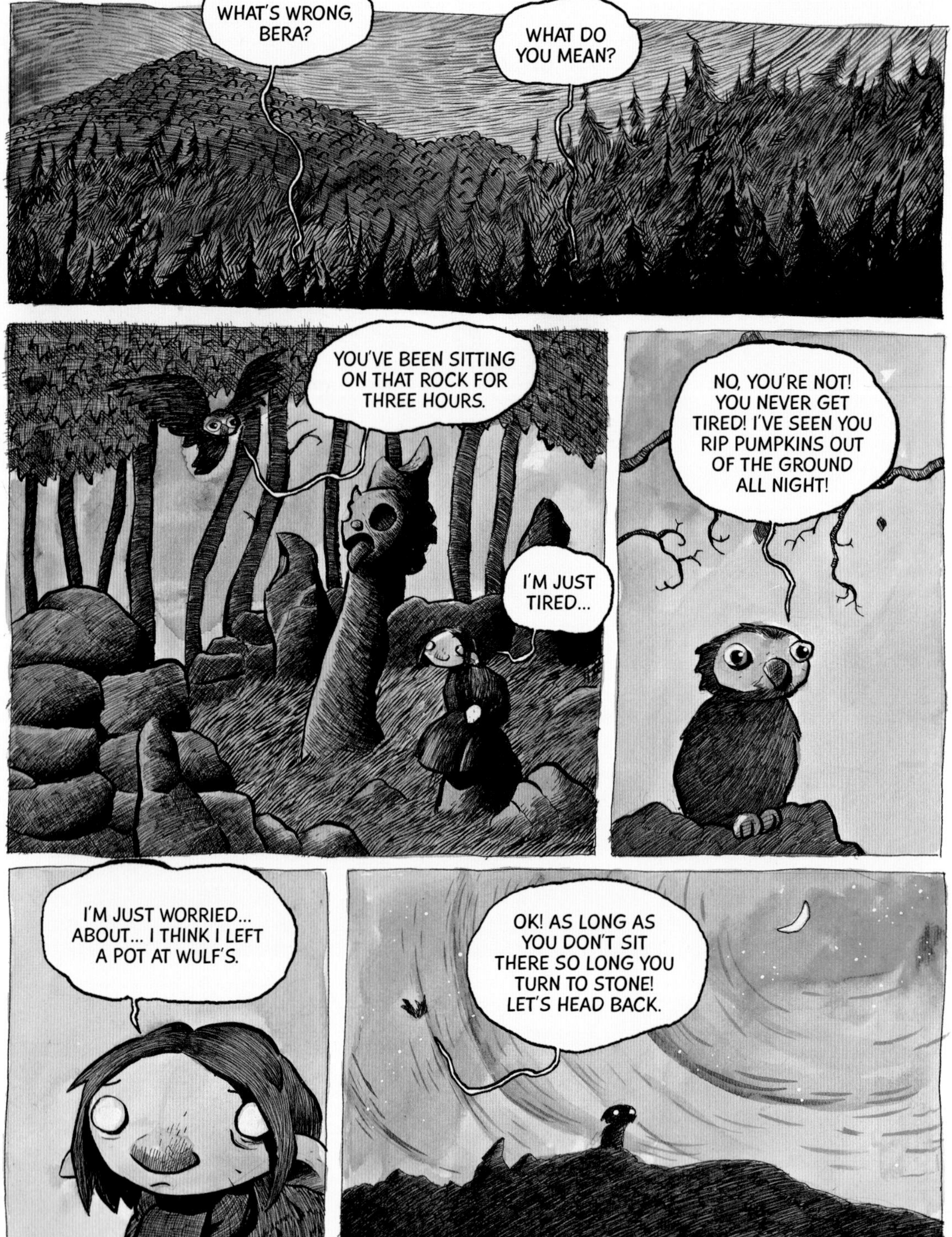
WHAT'S WRONG, BERA?
WHAT DO YOU MEAN?
YOU'VE BEEN SITTING ON THAT ROCK FOR THREE HOURS.
I'M JUST TIRED...
NO, YOU'RE NOT! YOU NEVER GET TIRED! I'VE SEEN YOU RIP PUMPKINS OUT OF THE GROUND ALL NIGHT!
I'M JUST WORRIED... ABOUT... I THINK I LEFT A POT AT WULF'S.
OK! AS LONG AS YOU DON'T SIT THERE SO LONG YOU TURN TO STONE! LET'S HEAD BACK.

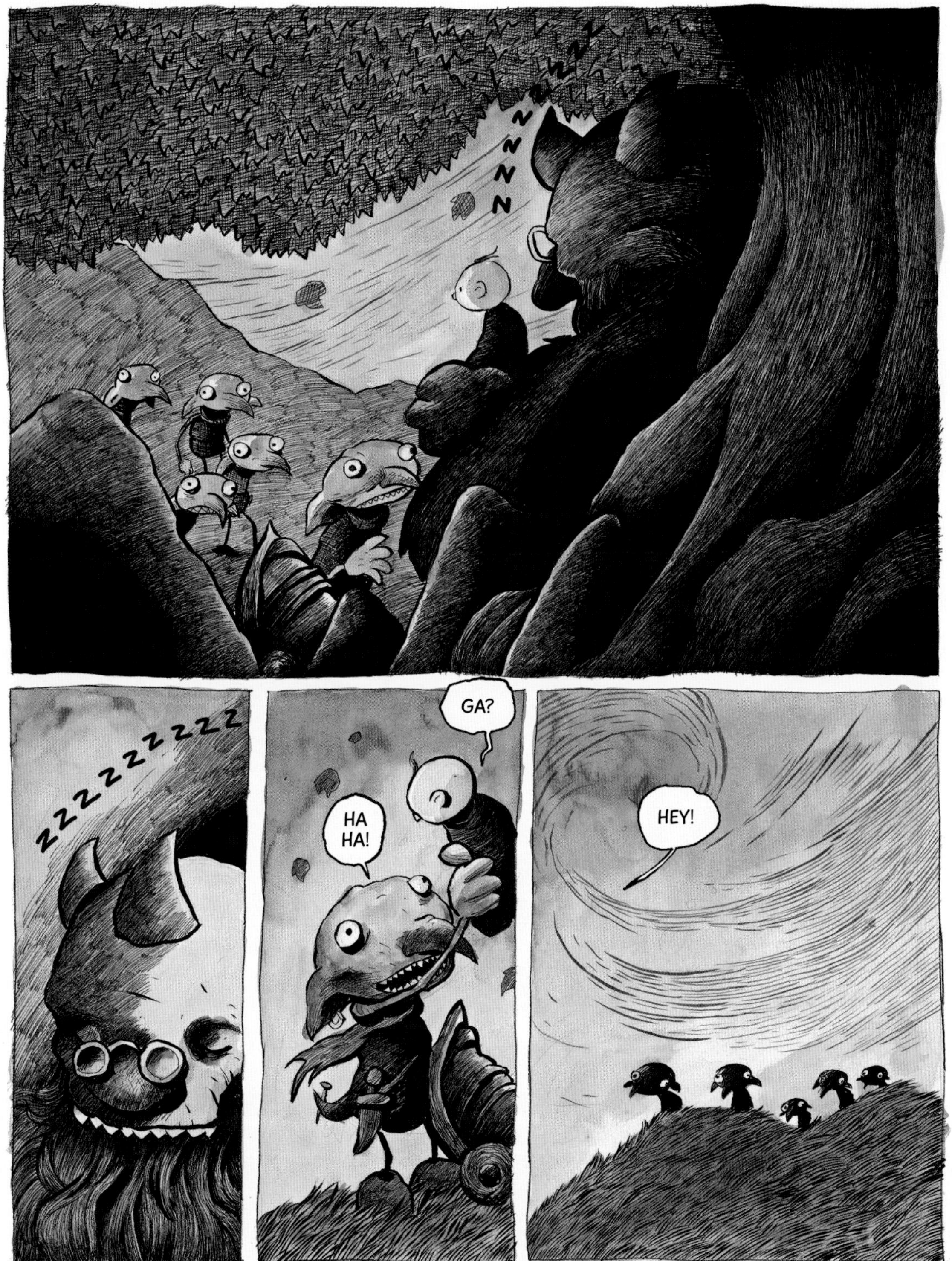
NNNN
ZZZZZZZZZ
GA?
HA HA!
HEY!

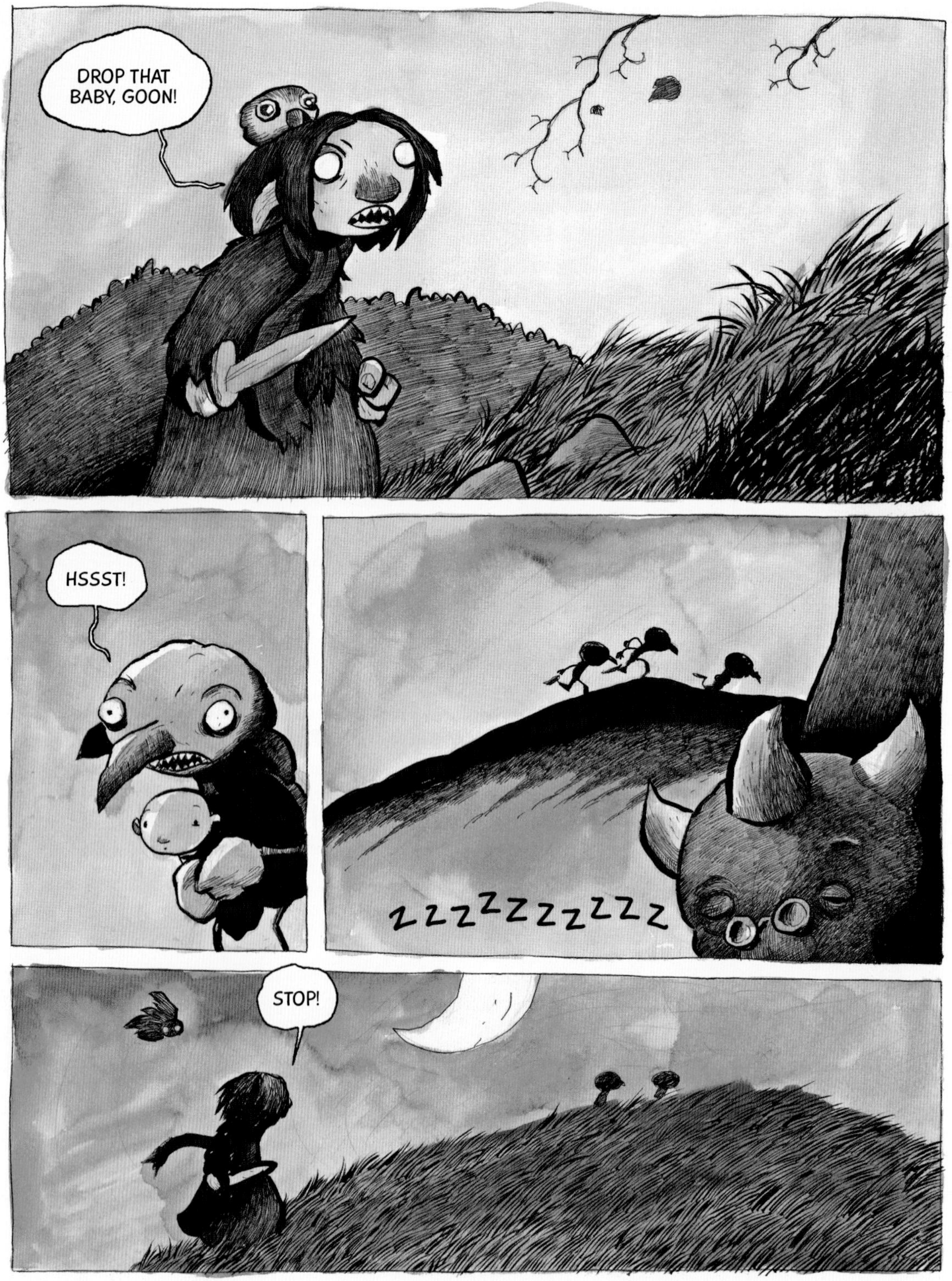
DROP THAT BABY, GOON!
HSSST!
ZZZZZZZZZZZ
STOP!

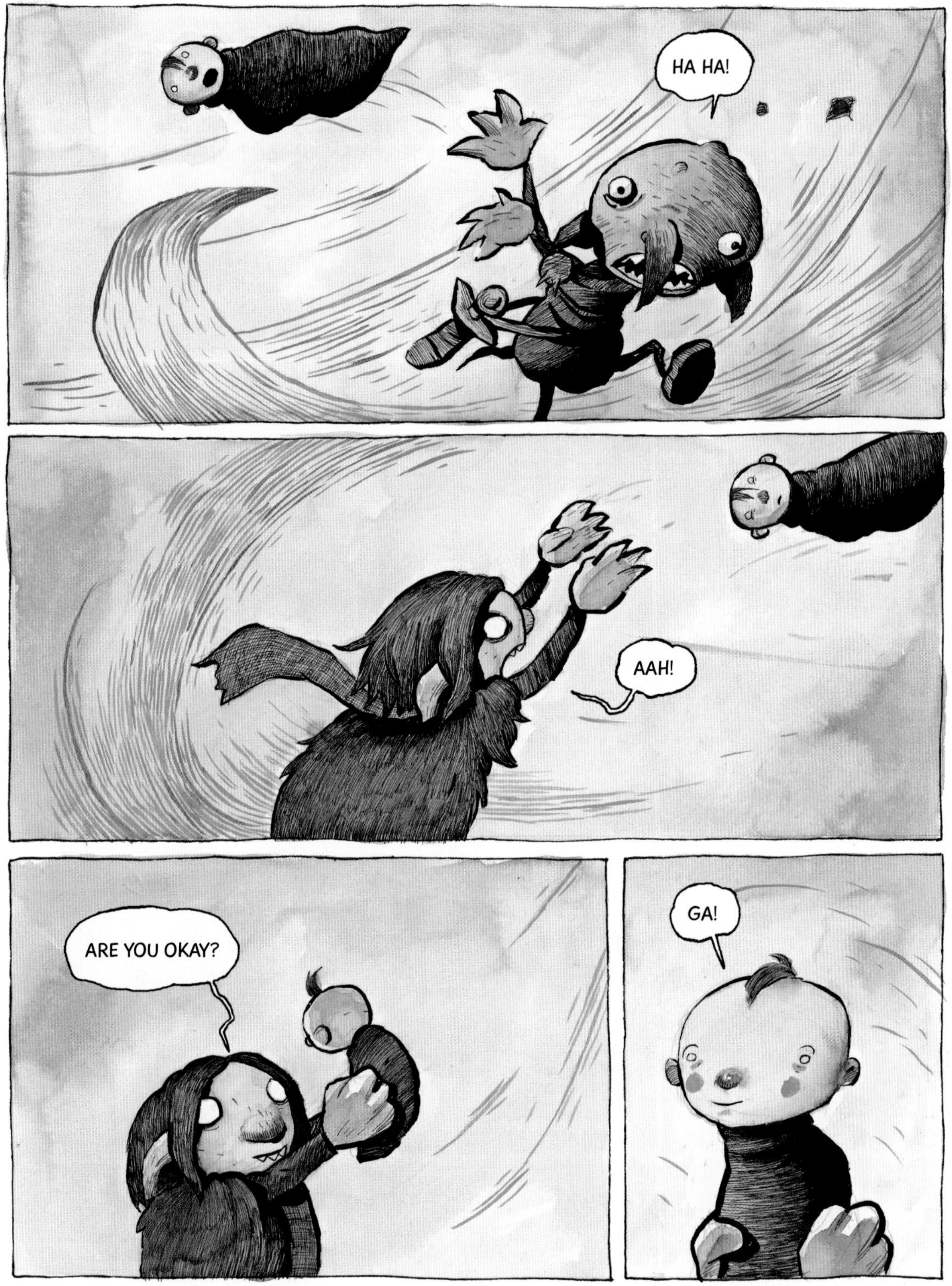
HA HA!
AAH!
ARE YOU OKAY?
GA!

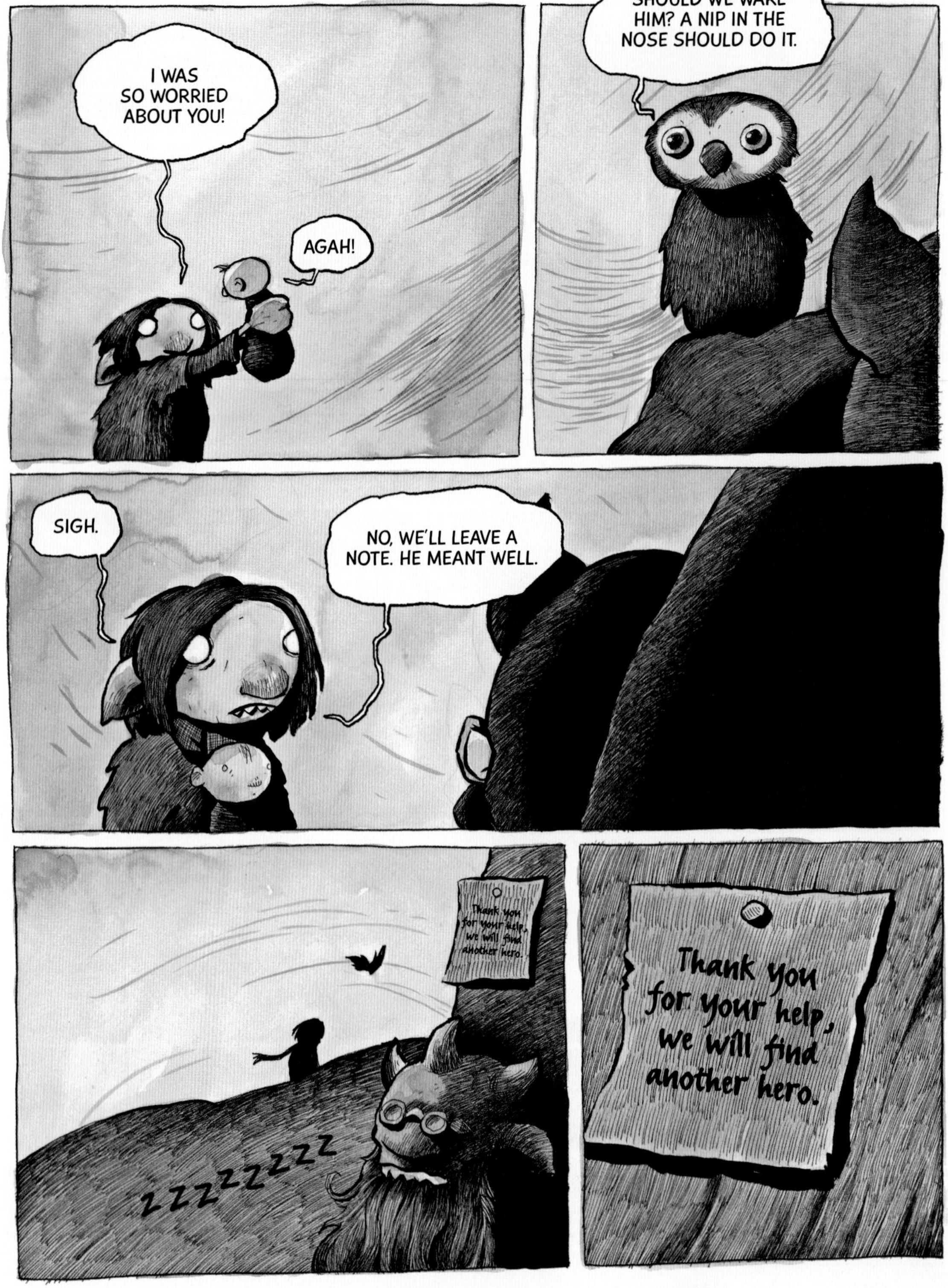
I WAS SO WORRIED ABOUT YOU!
AGAH!
SHOULD WE WAKE HIM? A NIP IN THE NOSE SHOULD DO IT.
SIGH.
NO, WE'LL LEAVE A NOTE. HE MEANT WELL.
Thank you for your help, we will find another hero.
ZZZZZZZZZ
Thank you for your help, we will find another hero.

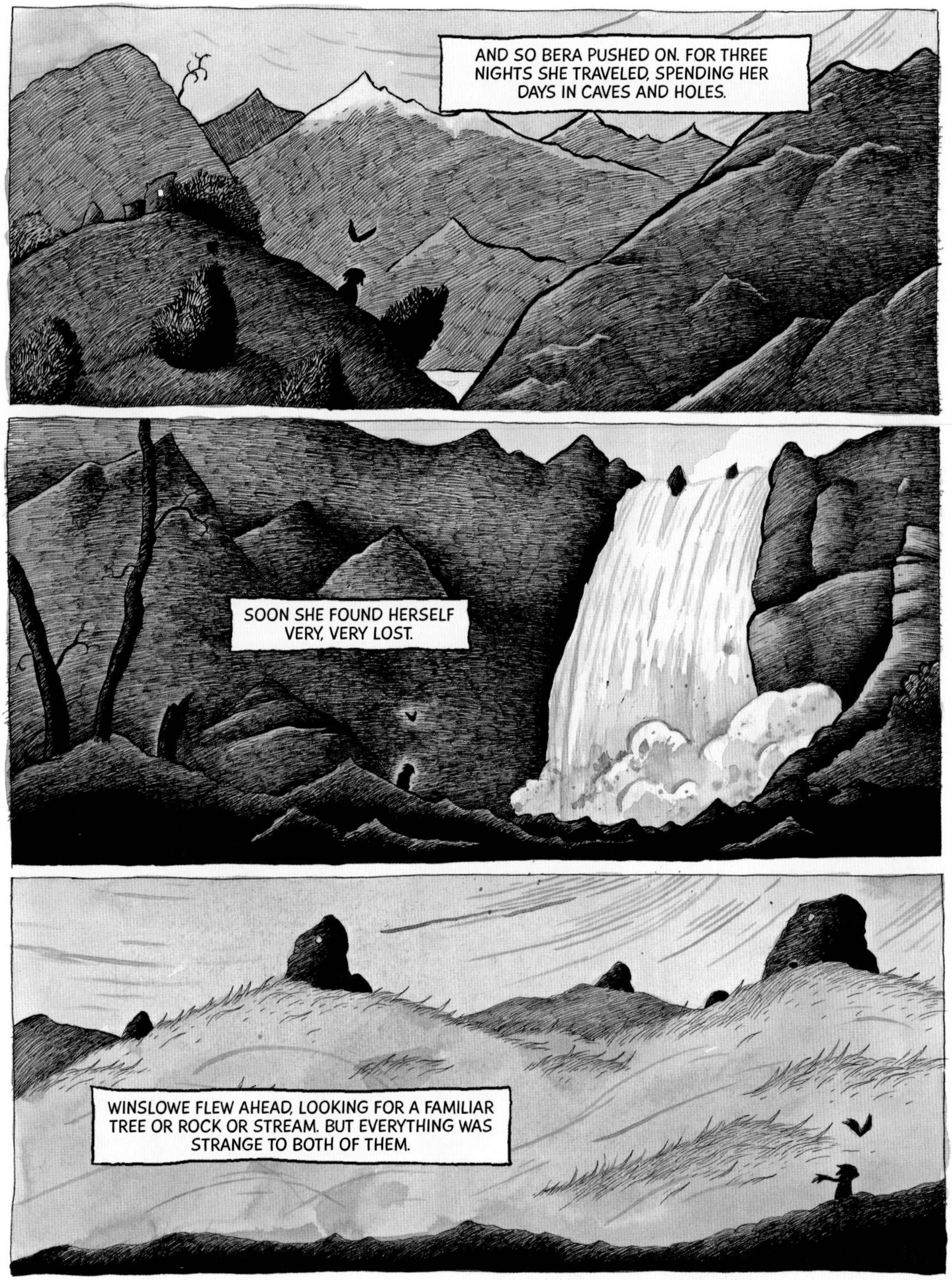
AND SO BERA PUSHED ON. FOR THREE NIGHTS SHE TRAVELED, SPENDING HER DAYS IN CAVES AND HOLES.
SOON SHE FOUND HERSELF VERY, VERY LOST.
WINSLOWE FLEW AHEAD, LOOKING FOR A FAMILIAR TREE OR ROCK OR STREAM. BUT EVERYTHING WAS STRANGE TO BOTH OF THEM.

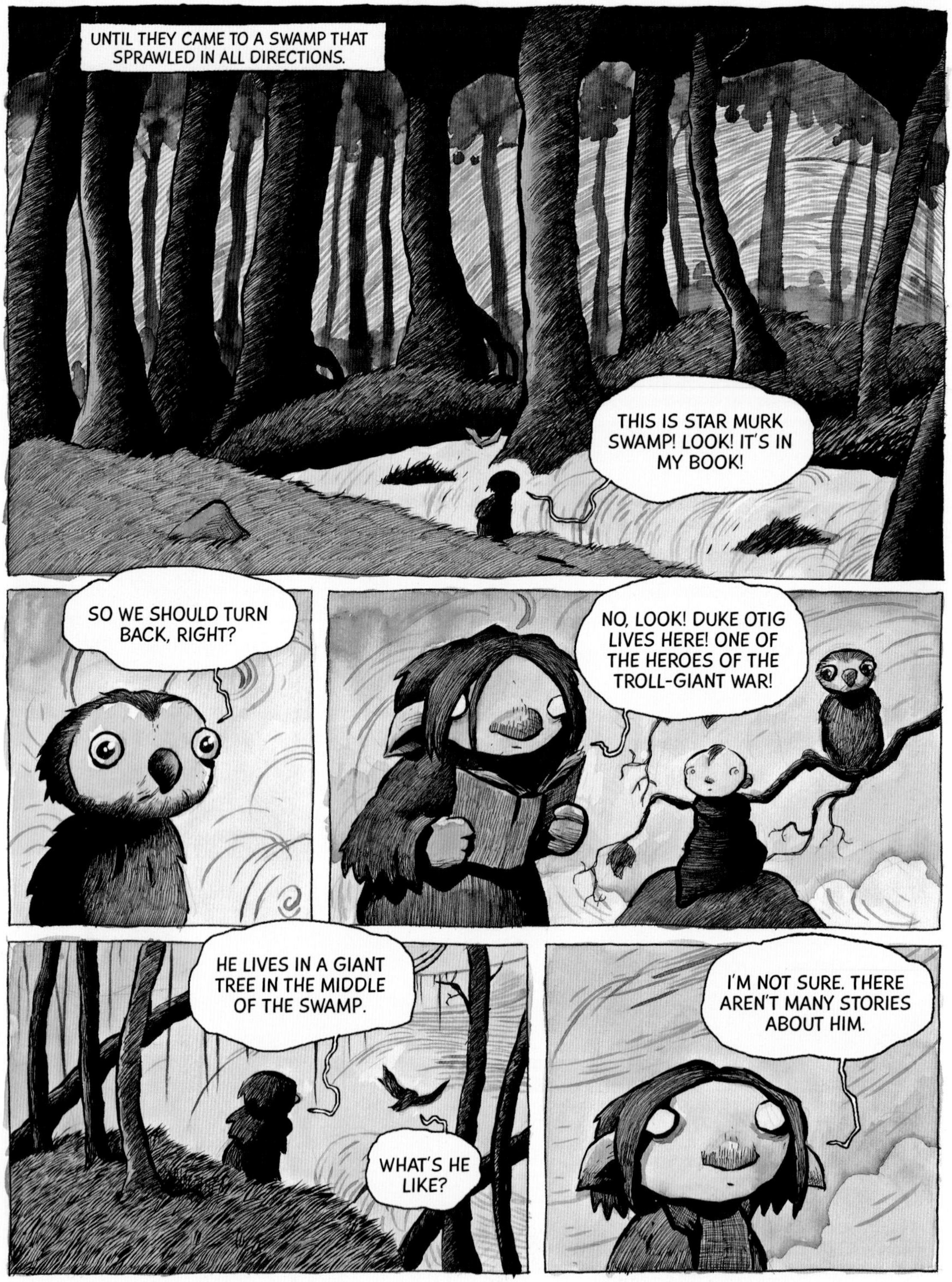
UNTIL THEY CAME TO A SWAMP THAT SPRAWLED IN ALL DIRECTIONS.
THIS IS STAR MURK SWAMP! LOOK! IT'S IN MY BOOK!
SO WE SHOULD TURN BACK, RIGHT?
NO, LOOK! DUKE OTIG LIVES HERE! ONE OF THE HEROES OF THE TROLL-GIANT WAR!
HE LIVES IN A GIANT TREE IN THE MIDDLE OF THE SWAMP.
WHAT'S HE LIKE?
I'M NOT SURE. THERE AREN'T MANY STORIES ABOUT HIM.

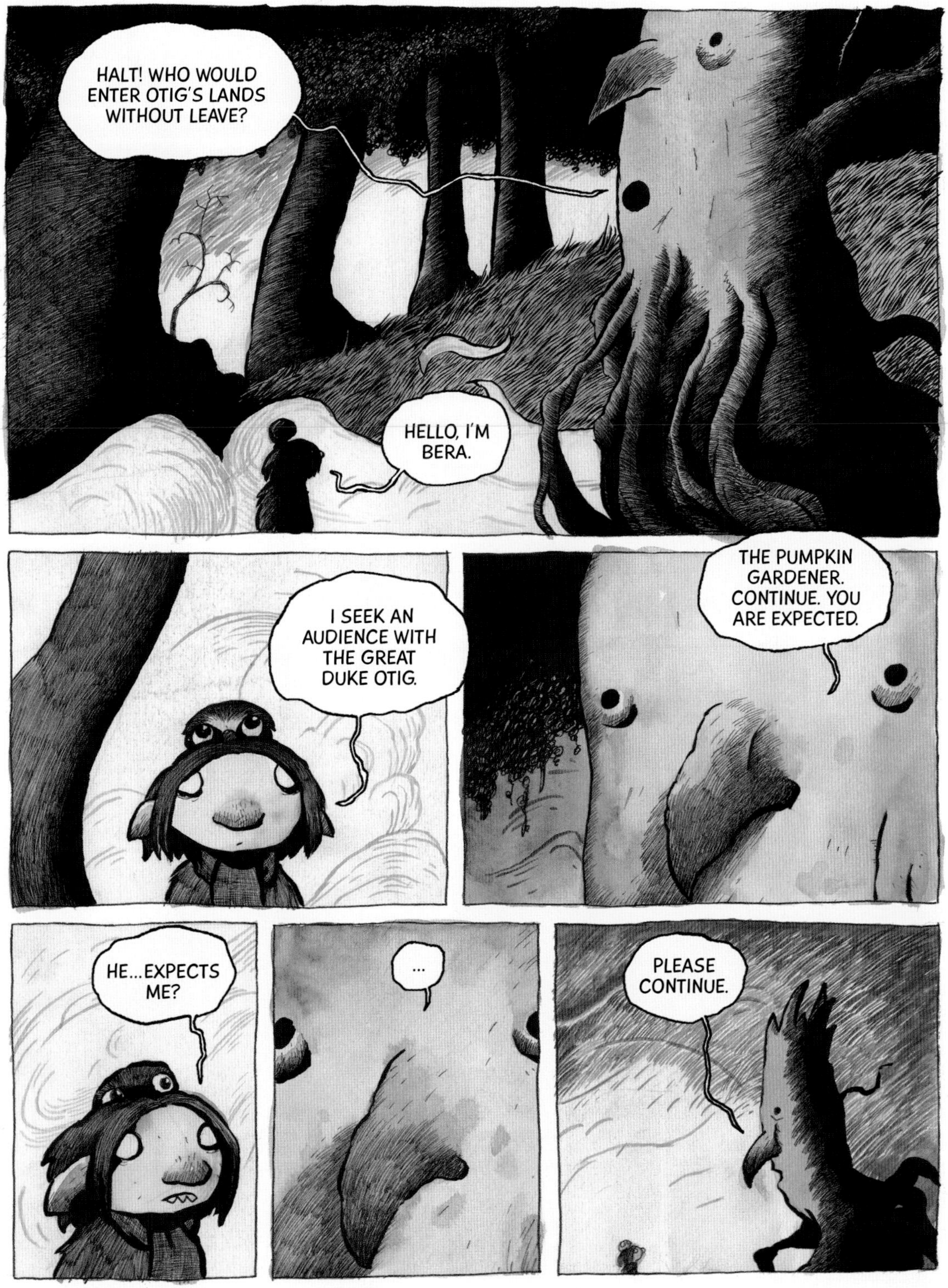

HALT! WHO WOULD ENTER OTIG'S LANDS WITHOUT LEAVE?
HELLO, I'M BERA.
I SEEK AN AUDIENCE WITH THE GREAT DUKE OTIG.
THE PUMPKIN GARDENER. CONTINUE. YOU ARE EXPECTED.
HE...EXPECTS ME?
...
PLEASE CONTINUE.

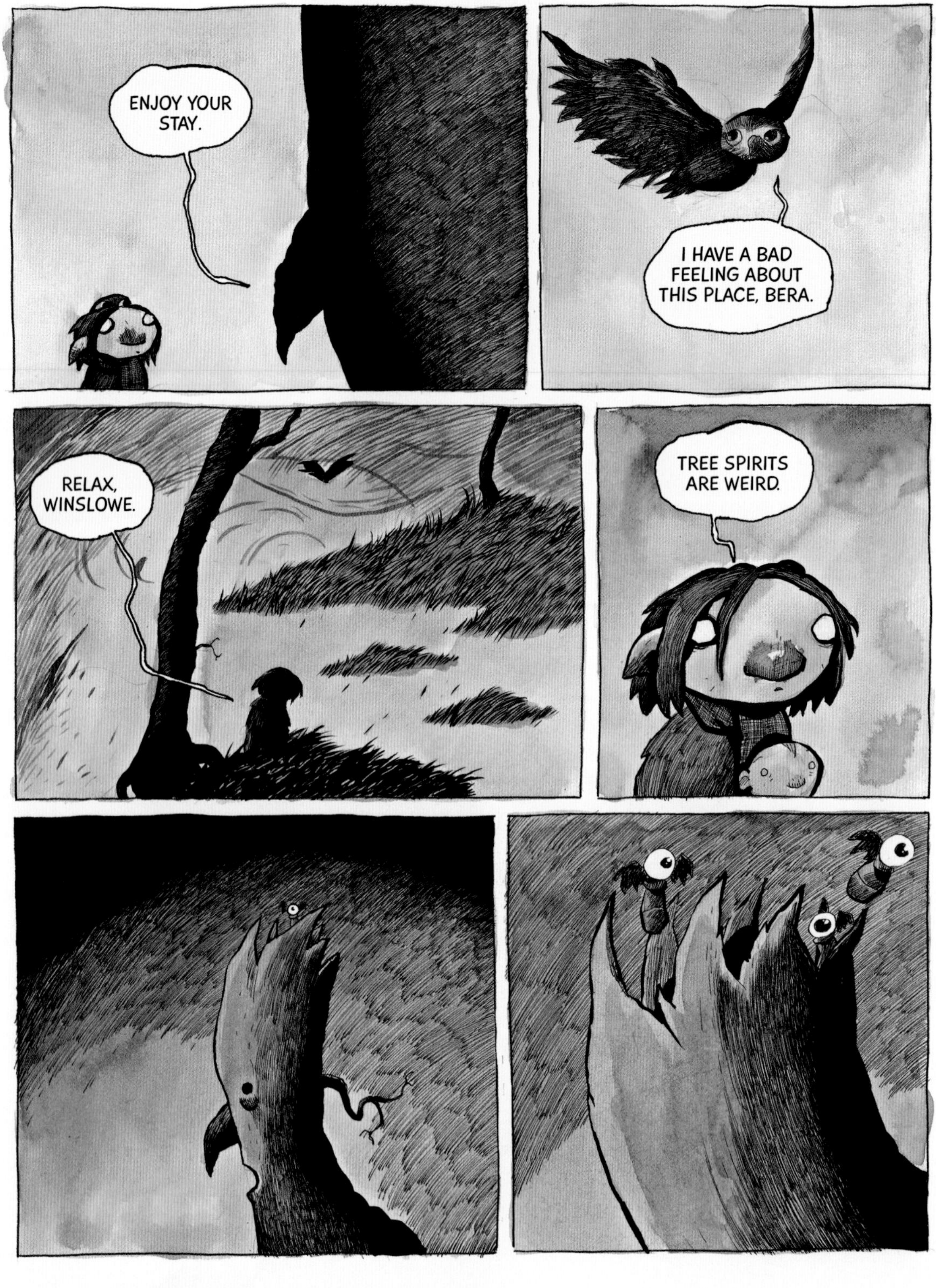
ENJOY YOUR STAY.
I HAVE A BAD FEELING ABOUT THIS PLACE, BERA.
RELAX, WINSLOWE.
TREE SPIRITS ARE WEIRD.

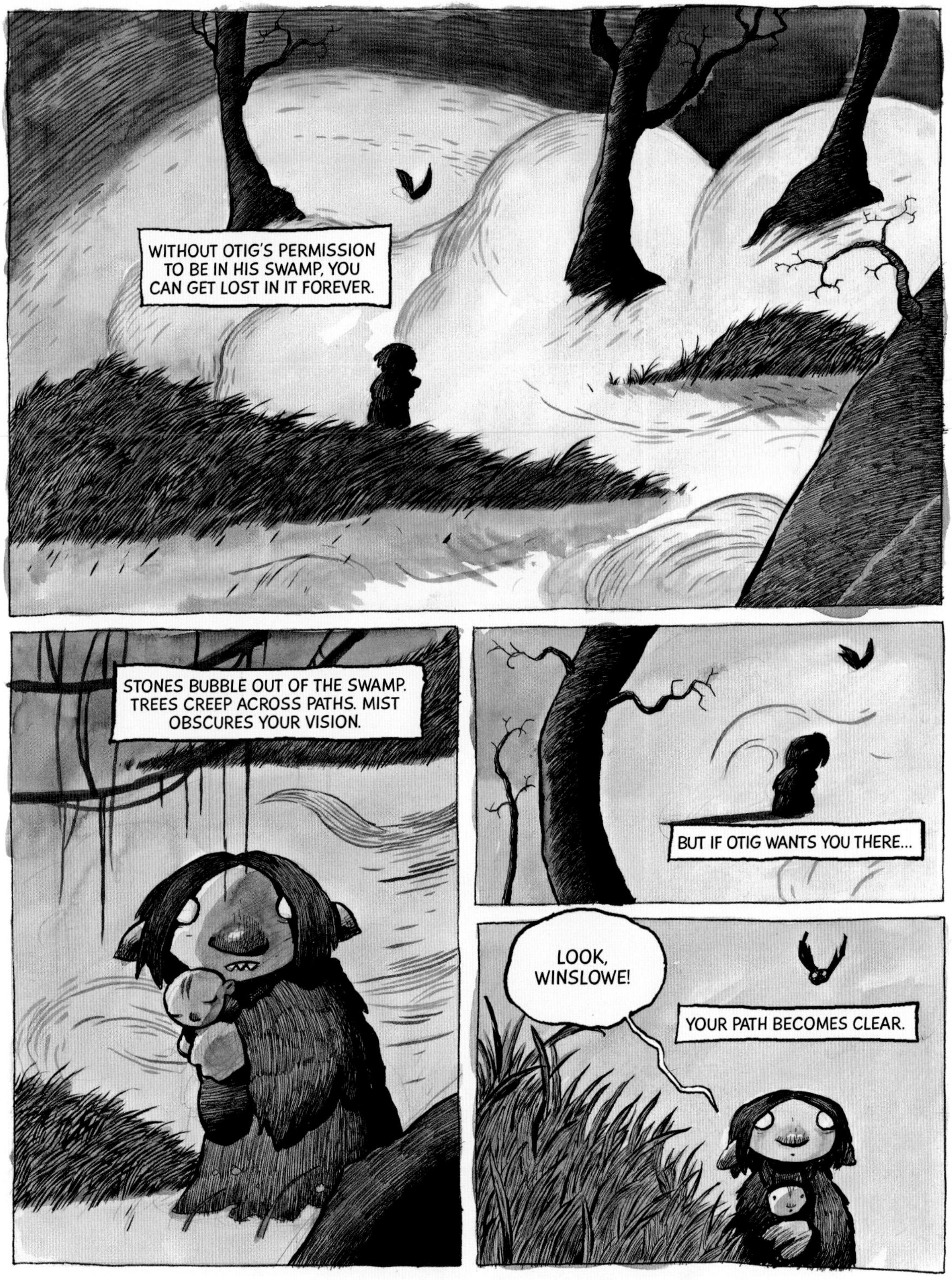
WITHOUT OTIG'S PERMISSION TO BE IN HIS SWAMP, YOU CAN GET LOST IN IT FOREVER.
STONES BUBBLE OUT OF THE SWAMP. TREES CREEP ACROSS PATHS. MIST OBSCURES YOUR VISION.
BUT IF OTIG WANTS YOU THERE...
LOOK, WINSLOWE!
YOUR PATH BECOMES CLEAR.

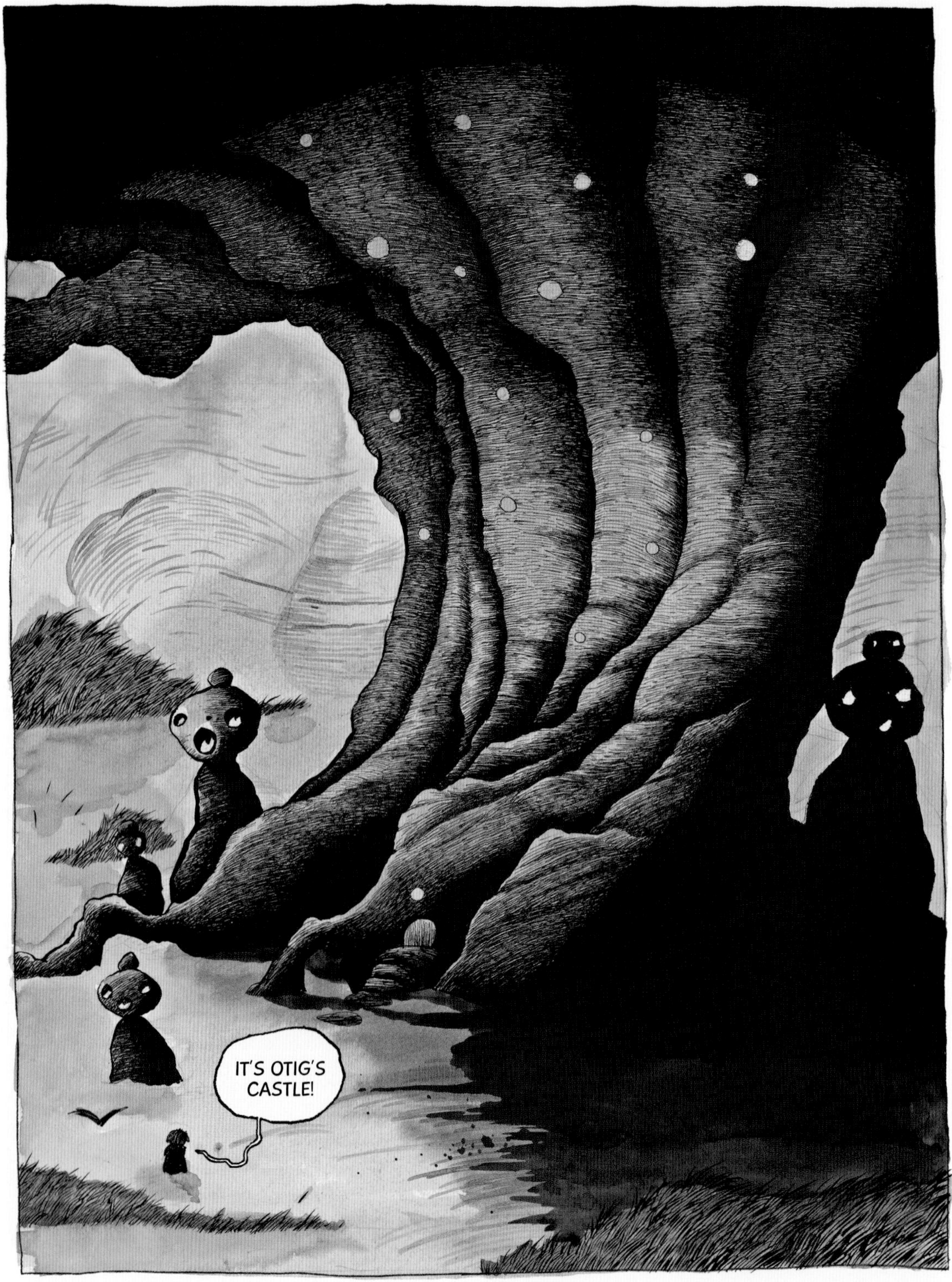
IT'S OTIG'S CASTLE!

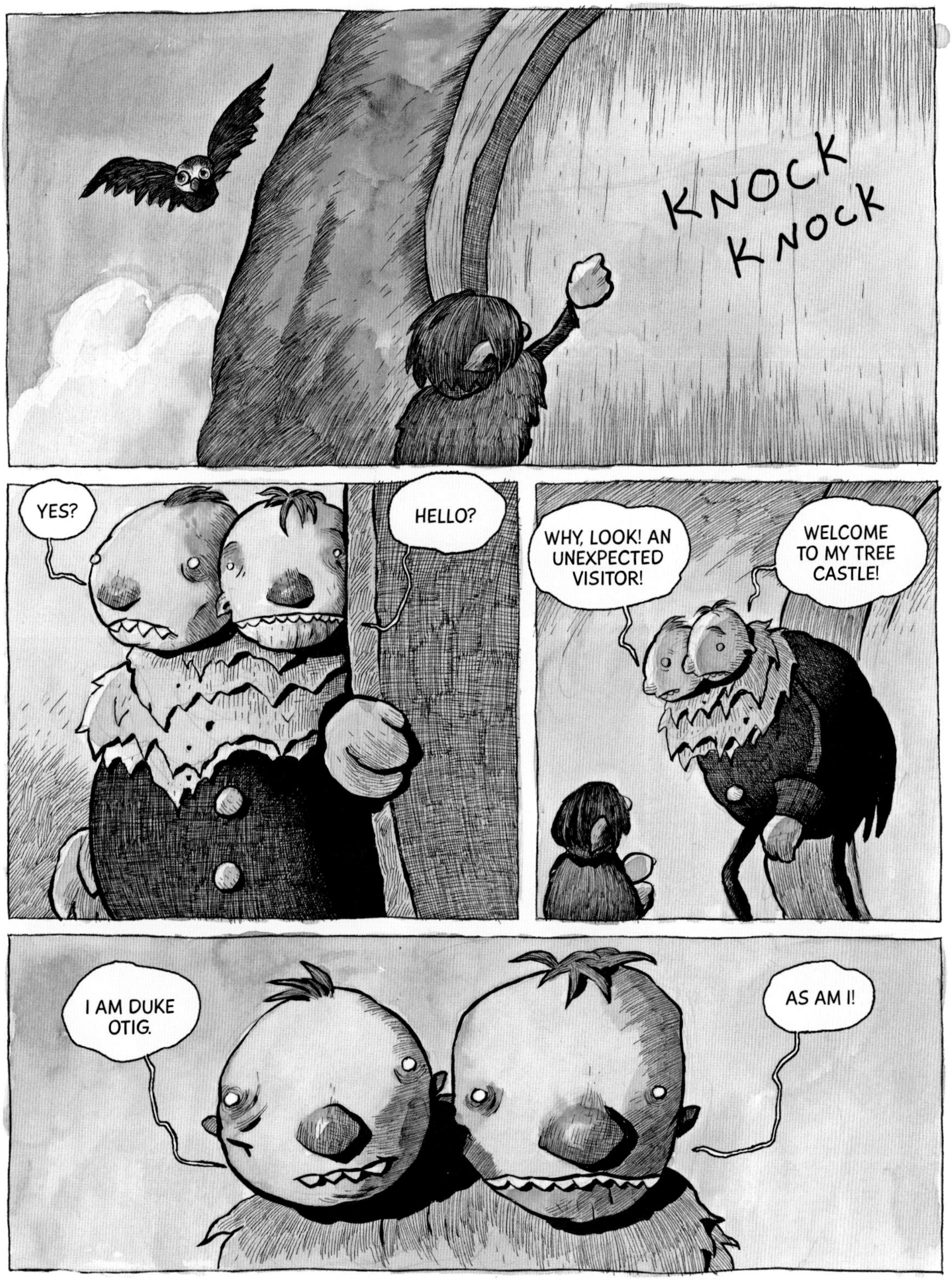
KNOCK
KNOCK
YES?
HELLO?
WHY, LOOK! AN UNEXPECTED VISITOR!
WELCOME TO MY TREE CASTLE!
I AM DUKE OTIG.
AS AM I!

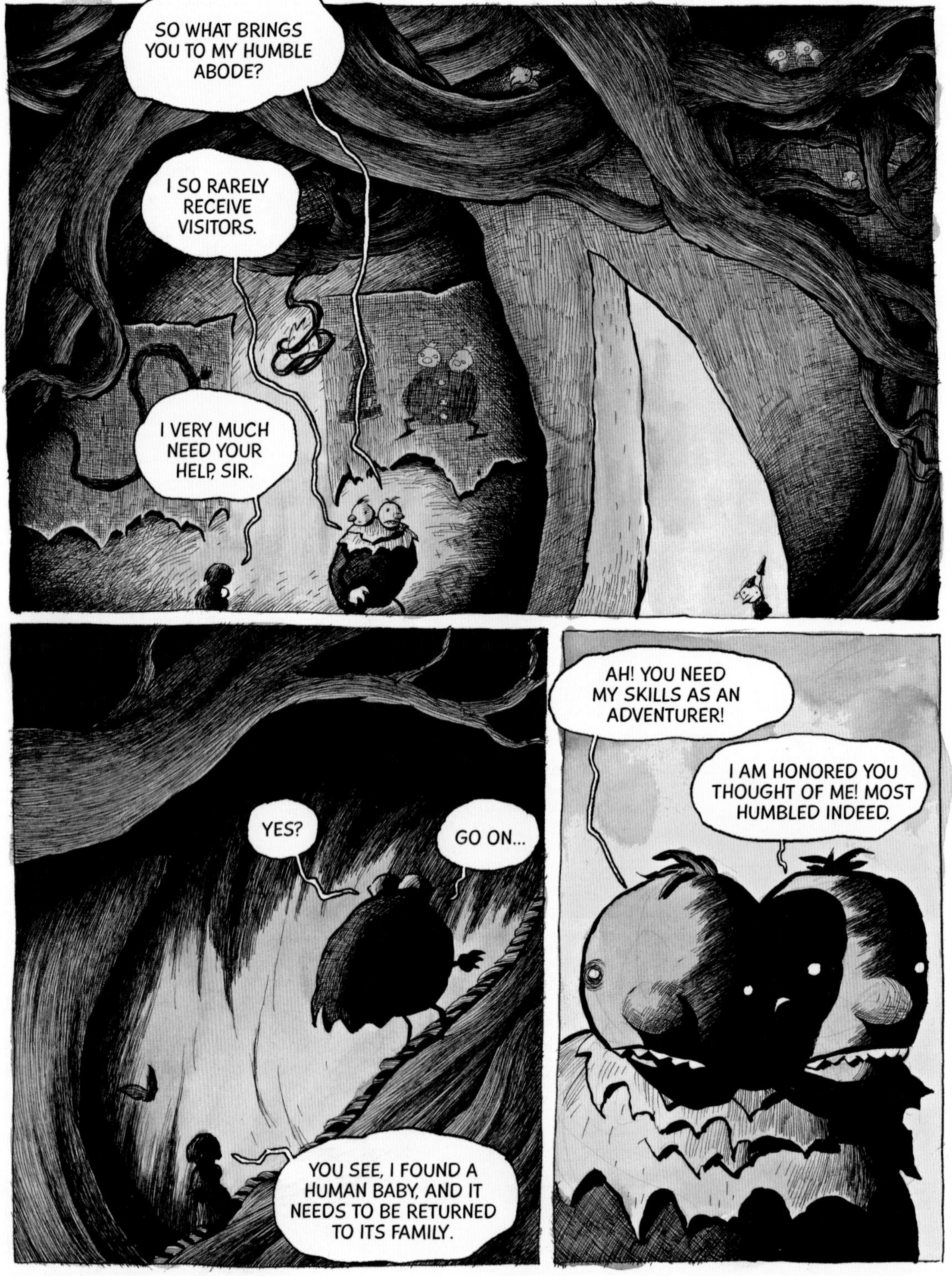
SO WHAT BRINGS YOU TO MY HUMBLE ABODE?
I SO RARELY RECEIVE VISITORS.
I VERY MUCH NEED YOUR HELP, SIR.
YES?
GO ON...
YOU SEE, I FOUND A HUMAN BABY, AND IT NEEDS TO BE RETURNED TO ITS FAMILY.
AH! YOU NEED MY SKILLS AS AN ADVENTURER!
I AM HONORED YOU THOUGHT OF ME! MOST HUMBLED INDEED.

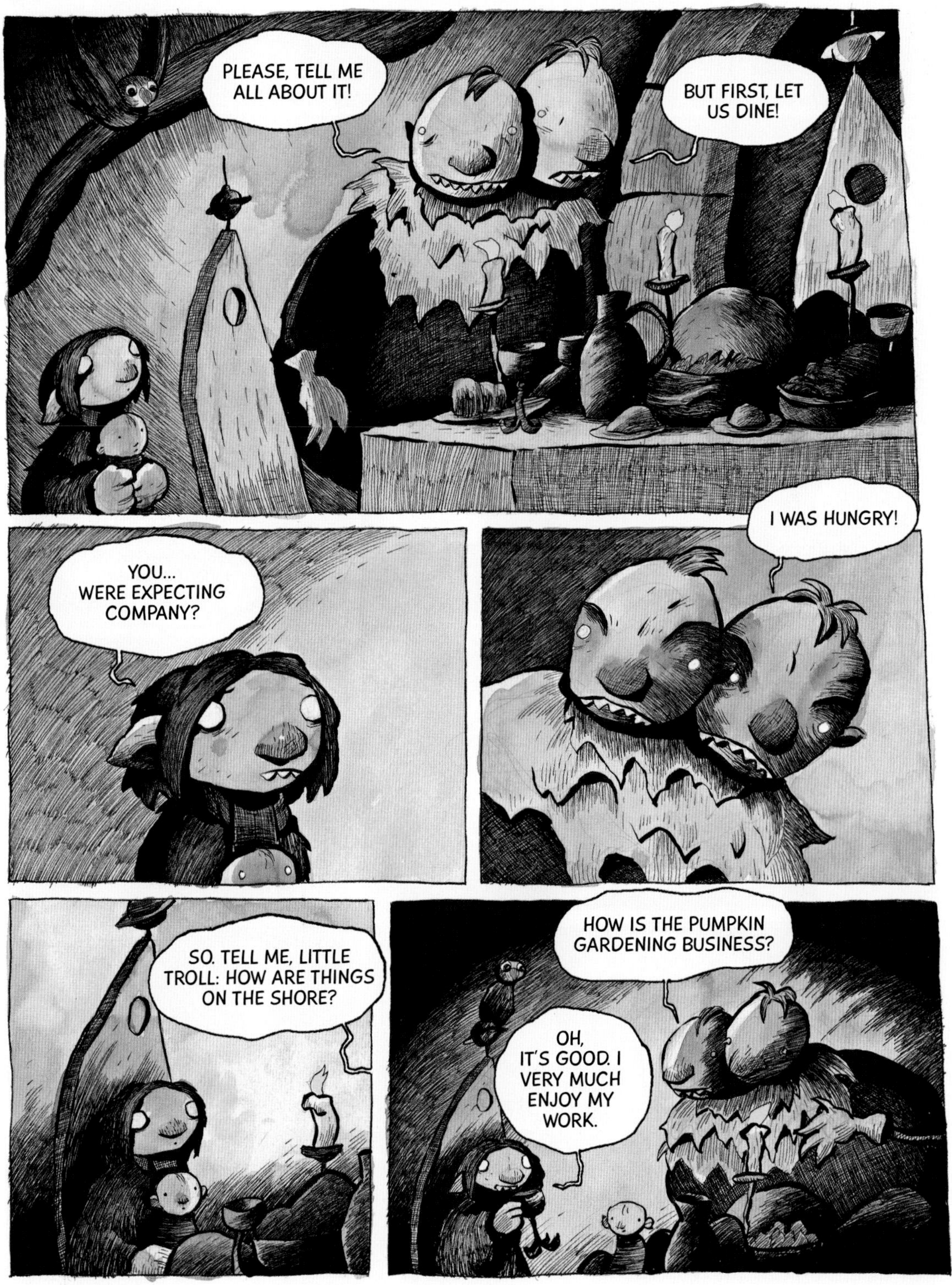
PLEASE, TELL ME ALL ABOUT IT!
BUT FIRST, LET US DINE!
YOU... WERE EXPECTING COMPANY?
I WAS HUNGRY!
SO. TELL ME, LITTLE TROLL: HOW ARE THINGS ON THE SHORE?
HOW IS THE PUMPKIN GARDENING BUSINESS?
OH, IT'S GOOD. I VERY MUCH ENJOY MY WORK.

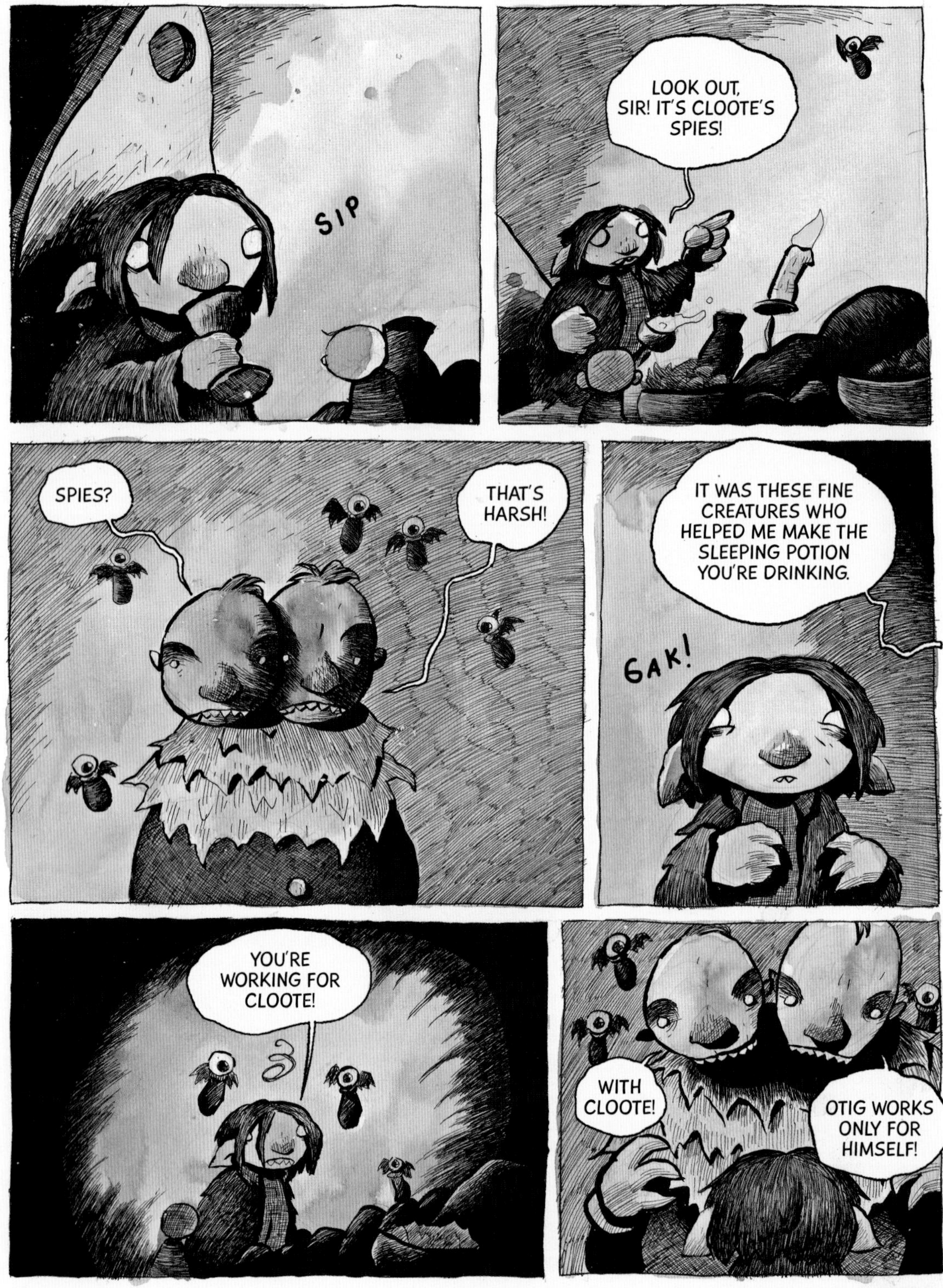
SIP
LOOK OUT, SIR! IT'S CLOOTE'S SPIES!
SPIES?
THAT'S HARSH!
IT WAS THESE FINE CREATURES WHO HELPED ME MAKE THE SLEEPING POTION YOU'RE DRINKING.
GAK!
YOU'RE WORKING FOR CLOOTE!
WITH CLOOTE!
OTIG WORKS ONLY FOR HIMSELF!

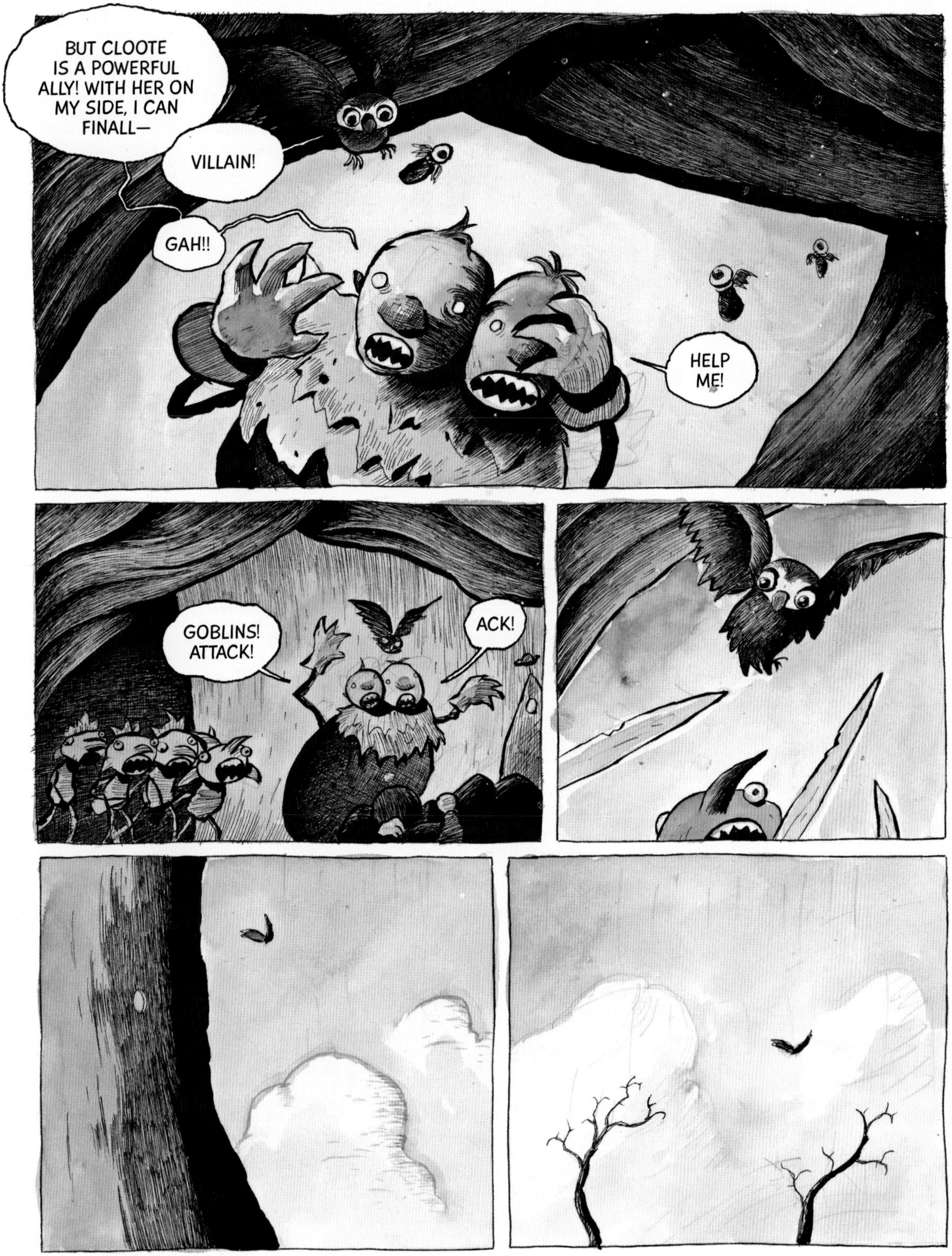
BUT CLOOTE IS A POWERFUL ALLY! WITH HER ON MY SIDE, I CAN FINALL—
VILLAIN!
GAH!!
HELP ME!
GOBLINS! ATTACK!
ACK!

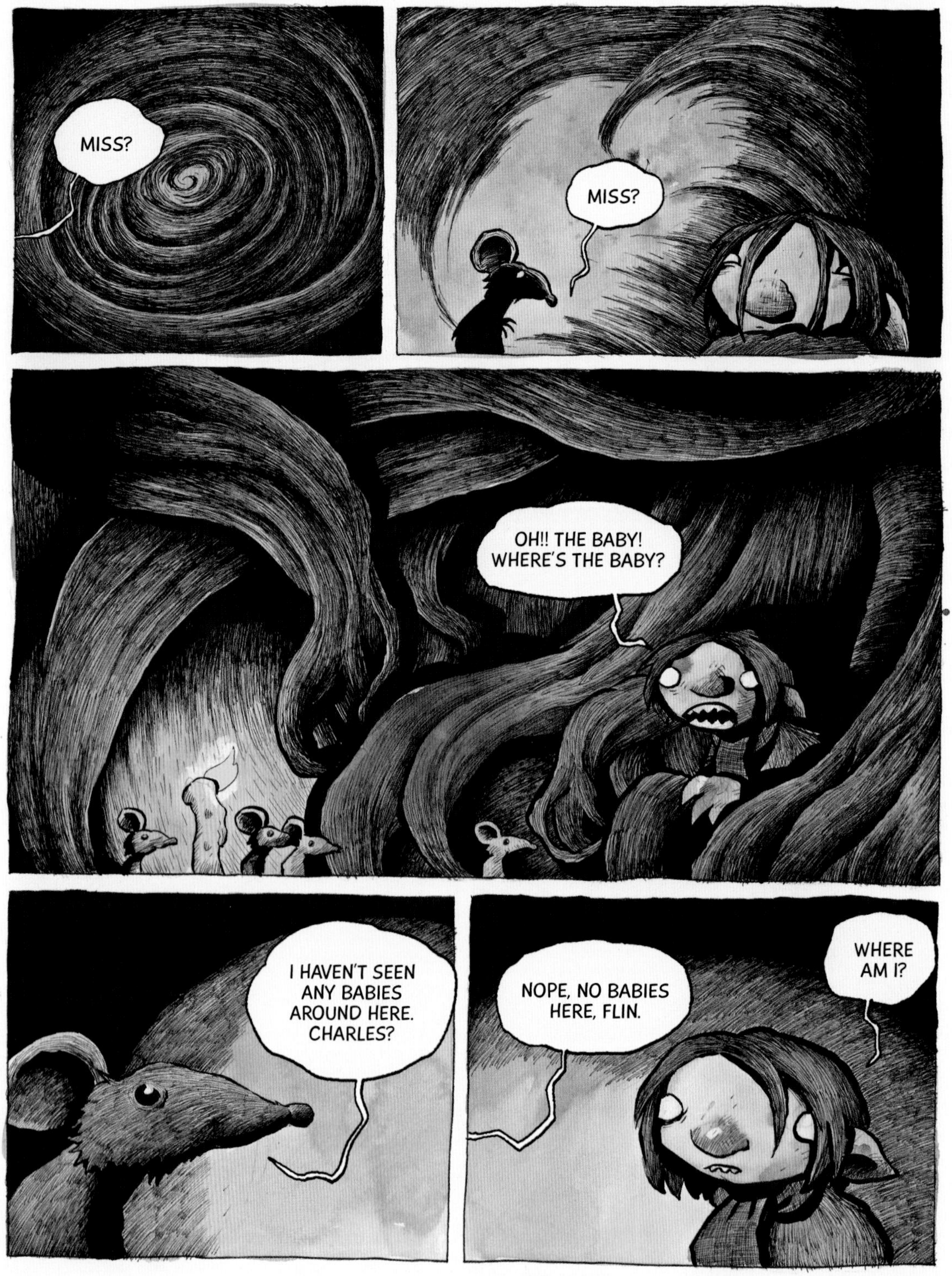
MISS?
MISS?
OH!! THE BABY! WHERE'S THE BABY?
I HAVEN'T SEEN ANY BABIES AROUND HERE. CHARLES?
NOPE, NO BABIES HERE, FLIN.
WHERE AM I?

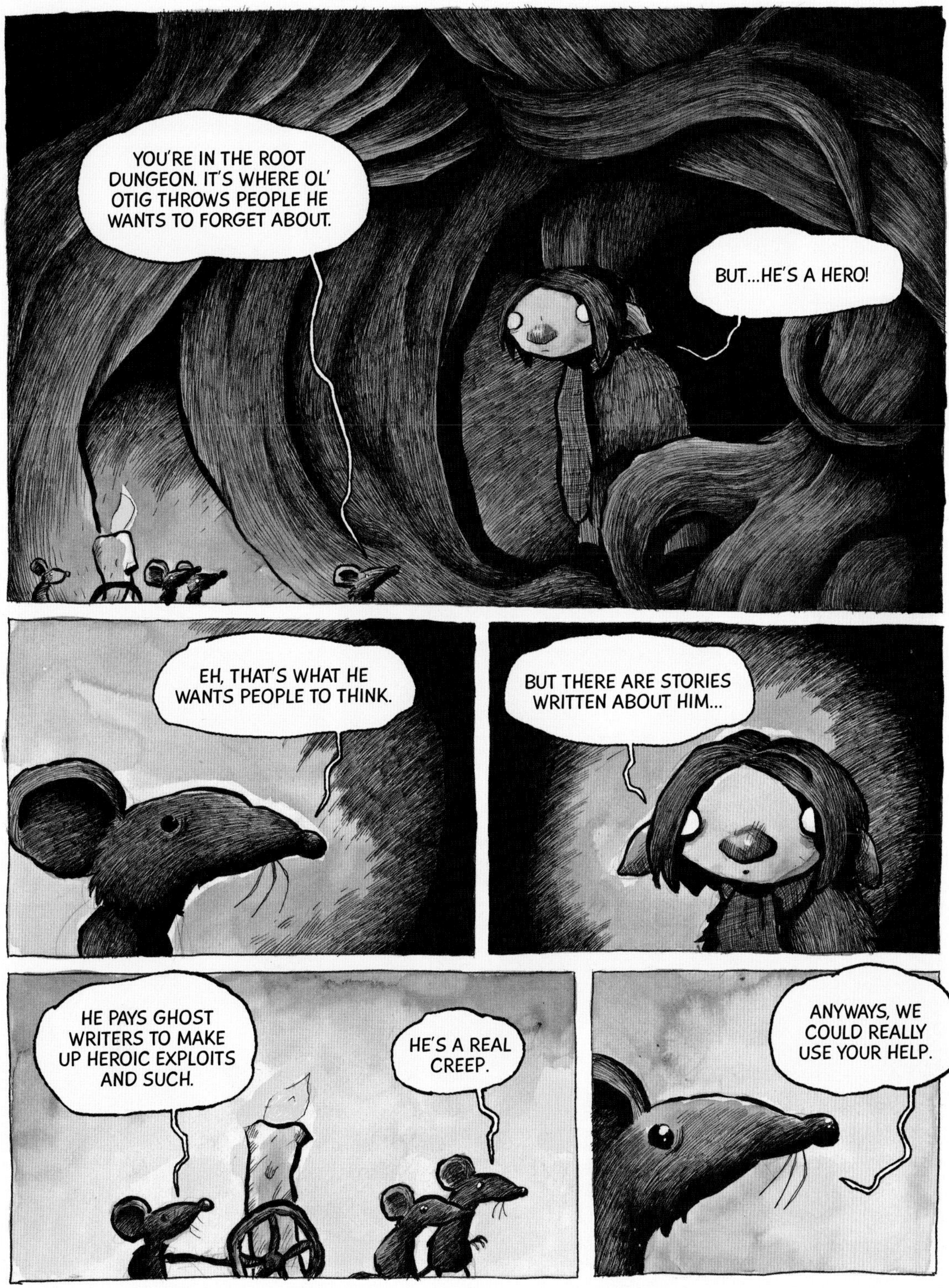
YOU'RE IN THE ROOT DUNGEON. IT'S WHERE OL' OTIG THROWS PEOPLE HE WANTS TO FORGET ABOUT.
BUT...HE'S A HERO!
EH, THAT'S WHAT HE WANTS PEOPLE TO THINK.
BUT THERE ARE STORIES WRITTEN ABOUT HIM...
HE PAYS GHOST WRITERS TO MAKE UP HEROIC EXPLOITS AND SUCH.
HE'S A REAL CREEP.
ANYWAYS, WE COULD REALLY USE YOUR HELP.

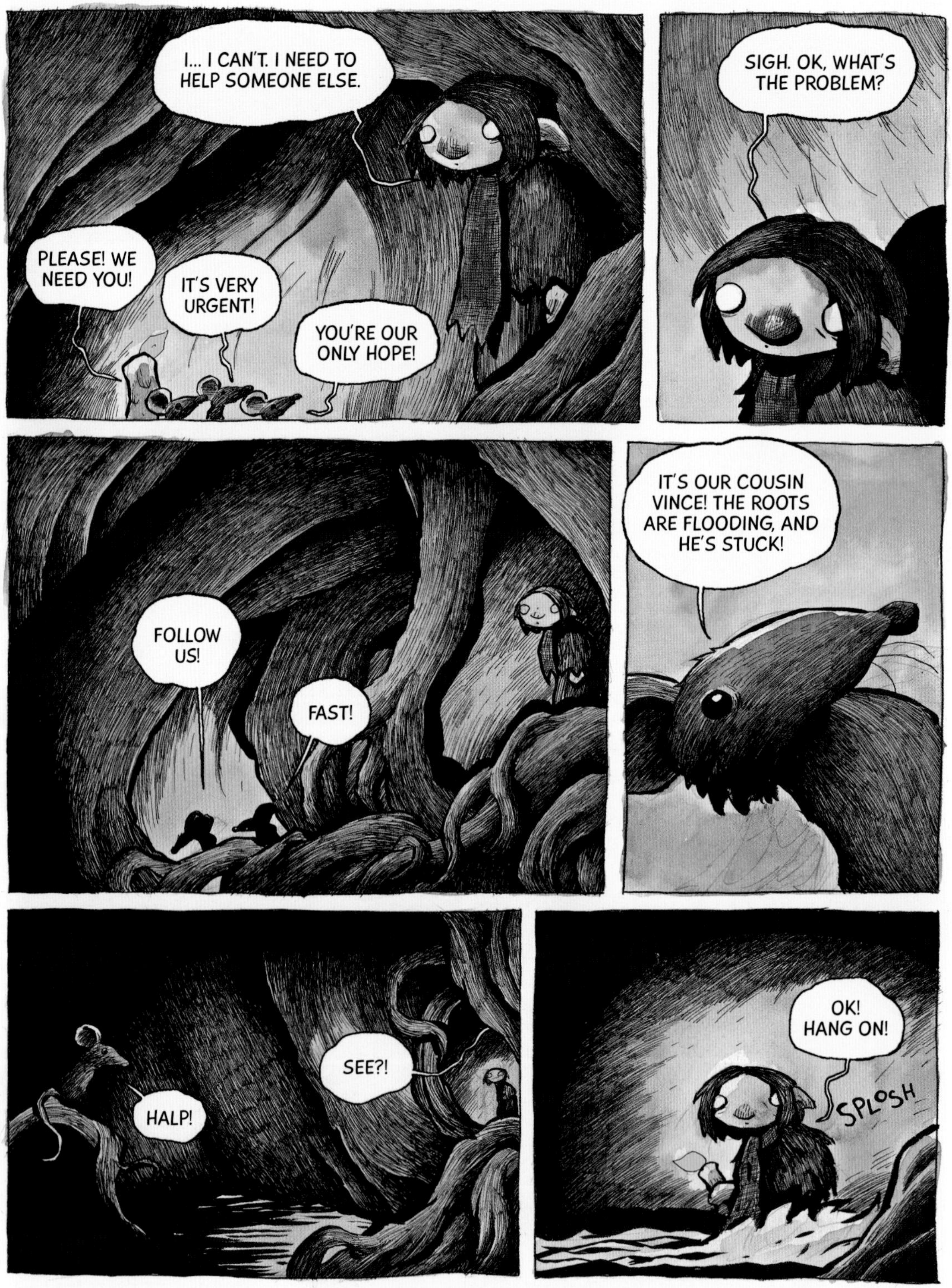
I... I CAN'T. I NEED TO HELP SOMEONE ELSE.
PLEASE! WE NEED YOU!
IT'S VERY URGENT!
YOU'RE OUR ONLY HOPE!
SIGH. OK, WHAT'S THE PROBLEM?
FOLLOW US!
FAST!
IT'S OUR COUSIN VINCE! THE ROOTS ARE FLOODING, AND HE'S STUCK!
HALP!
SEE?!
OK! HANG ON!
SPLOSH

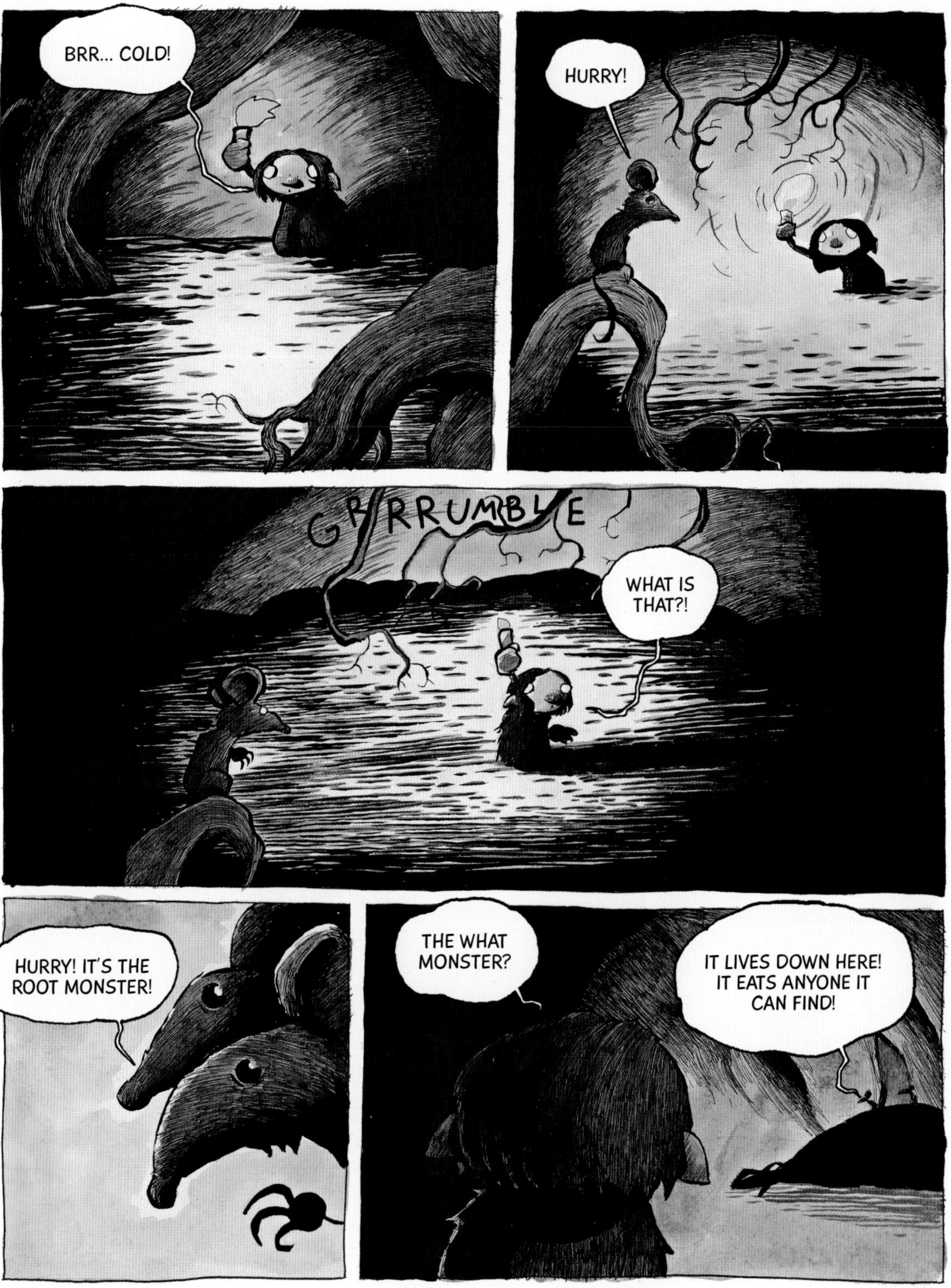
BRR... COLD!
HURRY!
GRRRUMBLE
WHAT IS THAT?!
HURRY! IT'S THE ROOT MONSTER!
THE WHAT MONSTER?
IT LIVES DOWN HERE! IT EATS ANYONE IT CAN FIND!

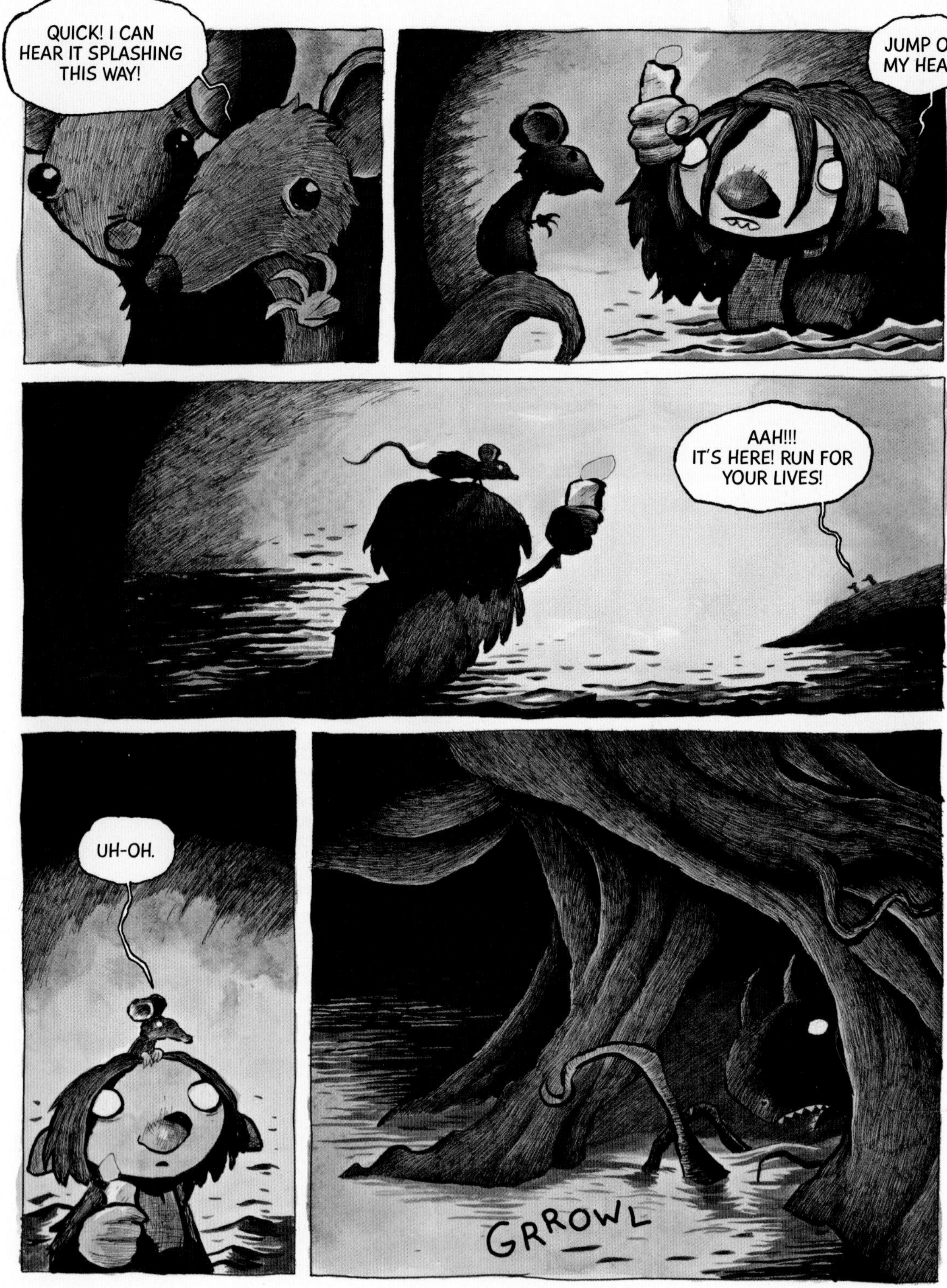
QUICK! I CAN HEAR IT SPLASHING THIS WAY!
JUMP ON MY HEAD.
AAH!!! IT'S HERE! RUN FOR YOUR LIVES!
UH-OH.
GRROWL

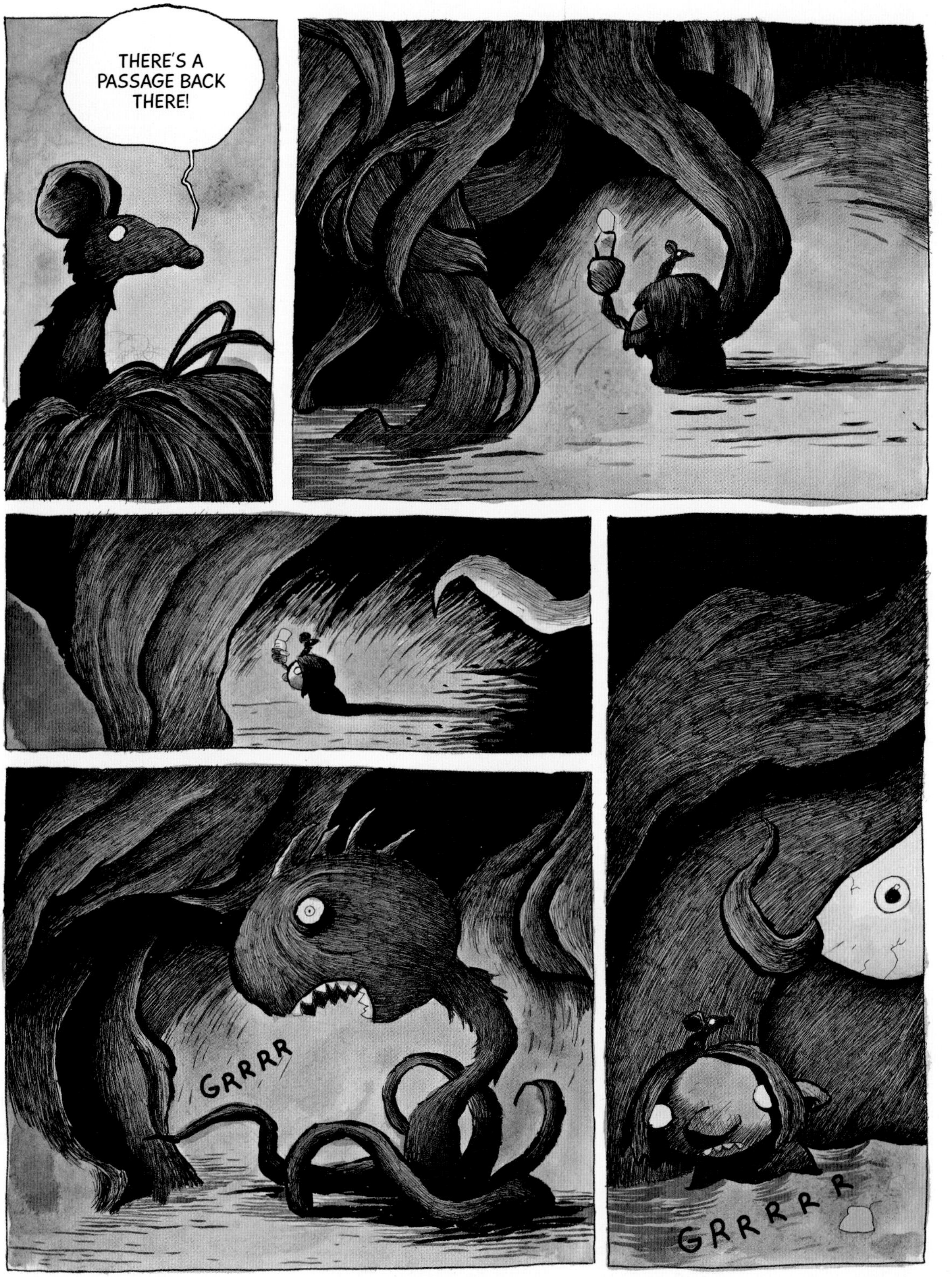
THERE'S A PASSAGE BACK THERE!
GRRRR
GRRRRR

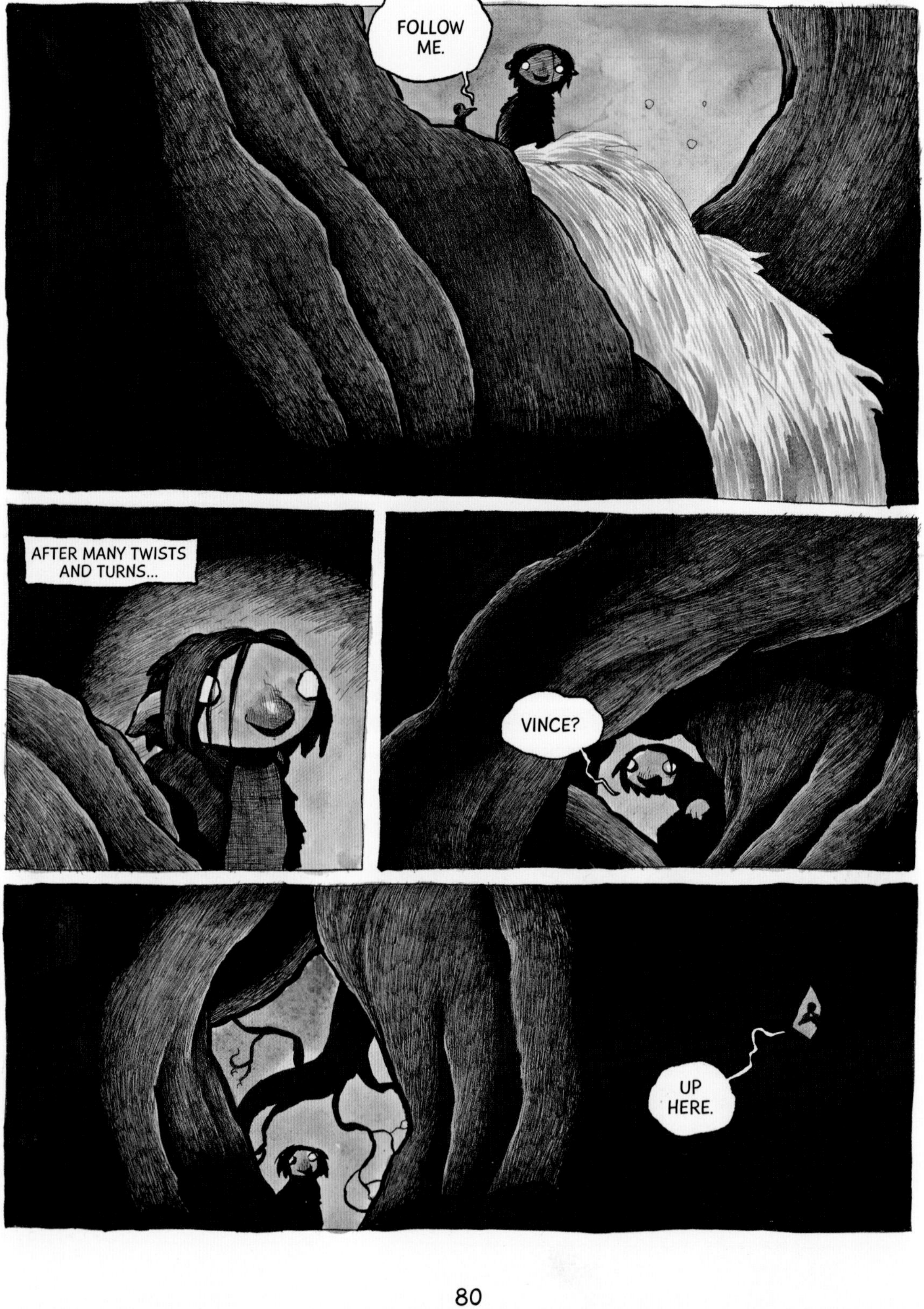
FOLLOW ME.
AFTER MANY TWISTS AND TURNS...
VINCE?
UP HERE.

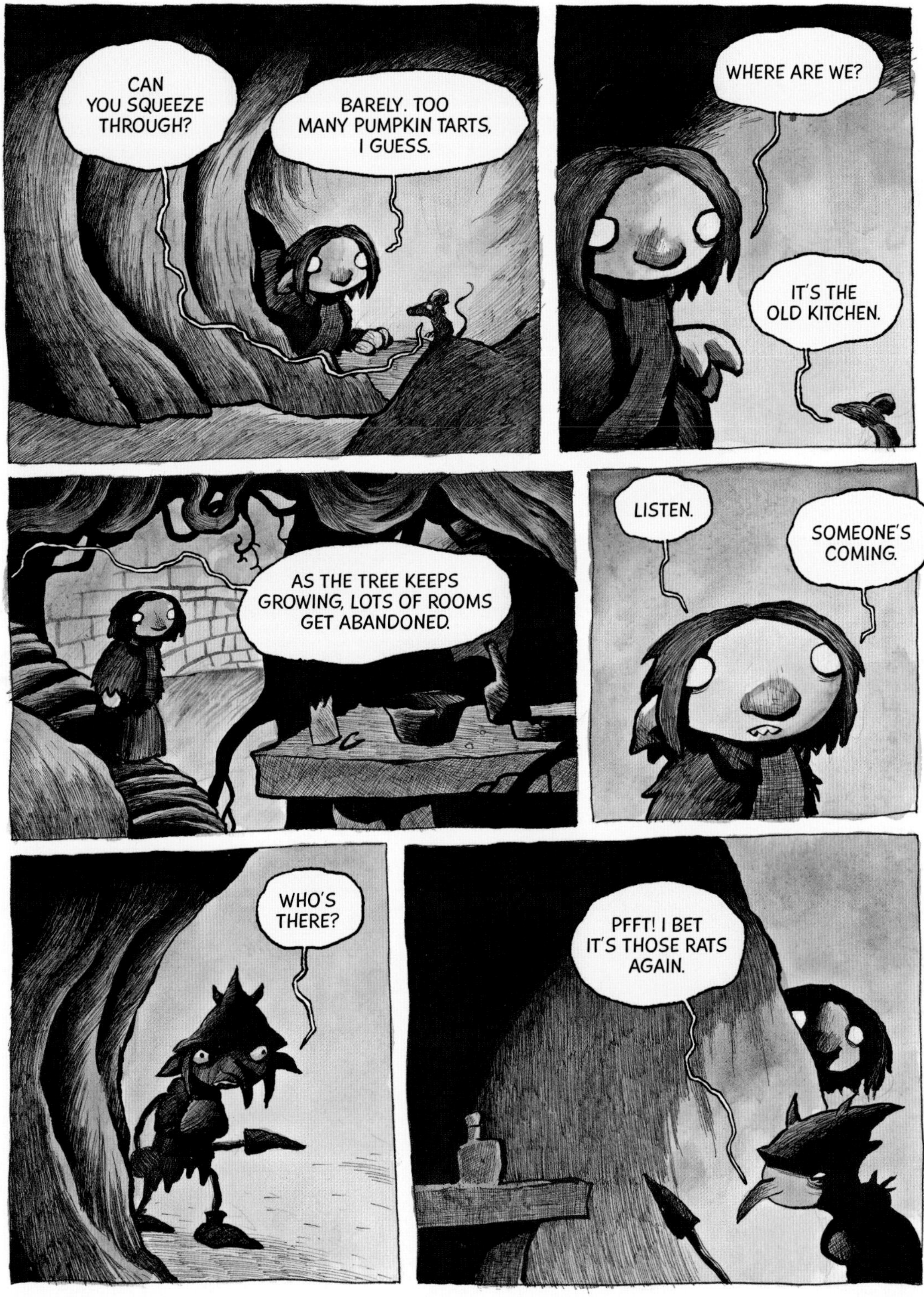
CAN YOU SQUEEZE THROUGH?
BARELY. TOO MANY PUMPKIN TARTS, I GUESS.
WHERE ARE WE?
IT'S THE OLD KITCHEN.
AS THE TREE KEEPS GROWING, LOTS OF ROOMS GET ABANDONED.
LISTEN.
SOMEONE'S COMING.
WHO'S THERE?
PFFT! I BET IT'S THOSE RATS AGAIN.

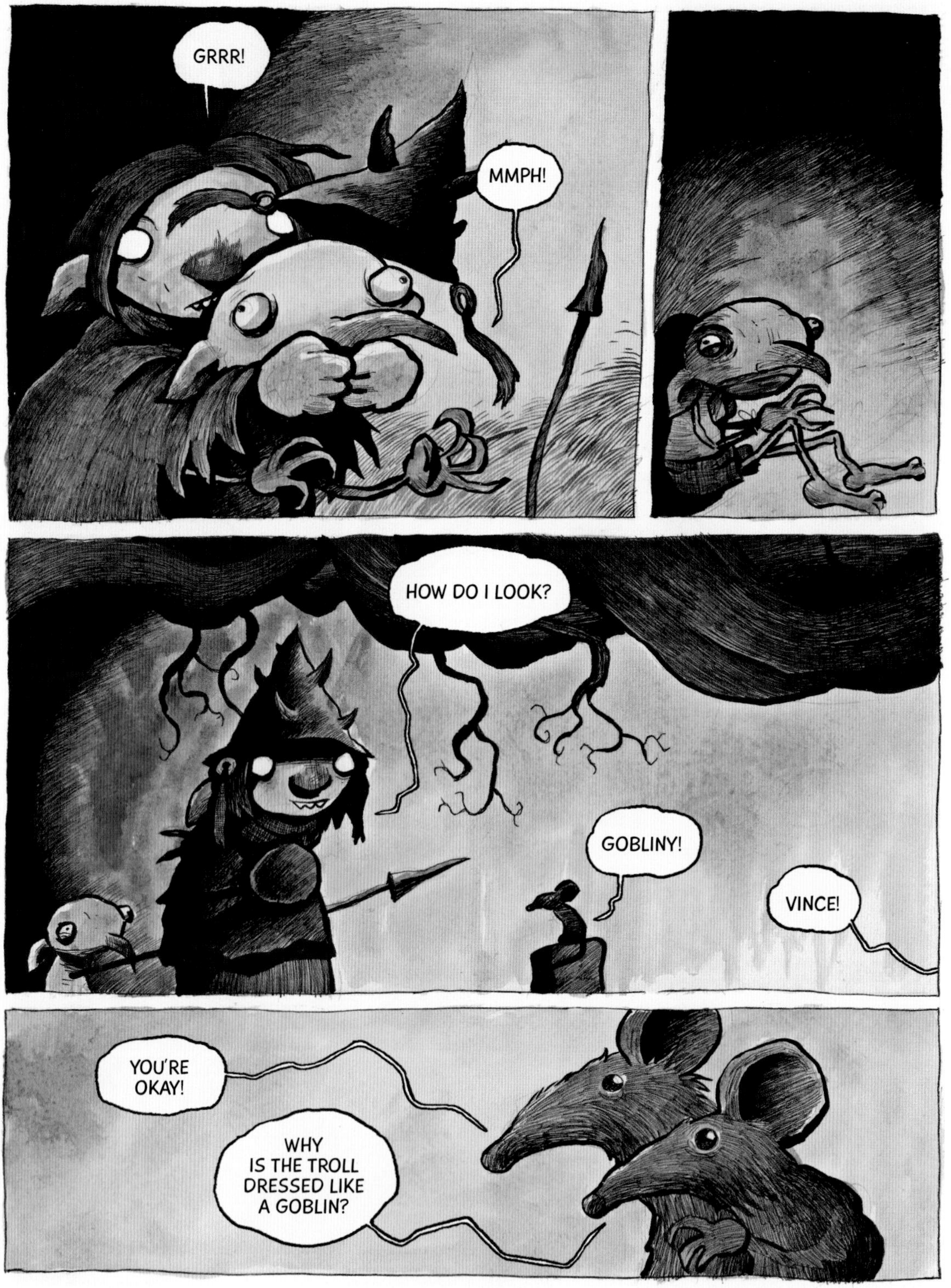
GRRR!
MMPH!
HOW DO I LOOK?
GOBLINY!
VINCE!
YOU'RE OKAY!
WHY IS THE TROLL DRESSED LIKE A GOBLIN?

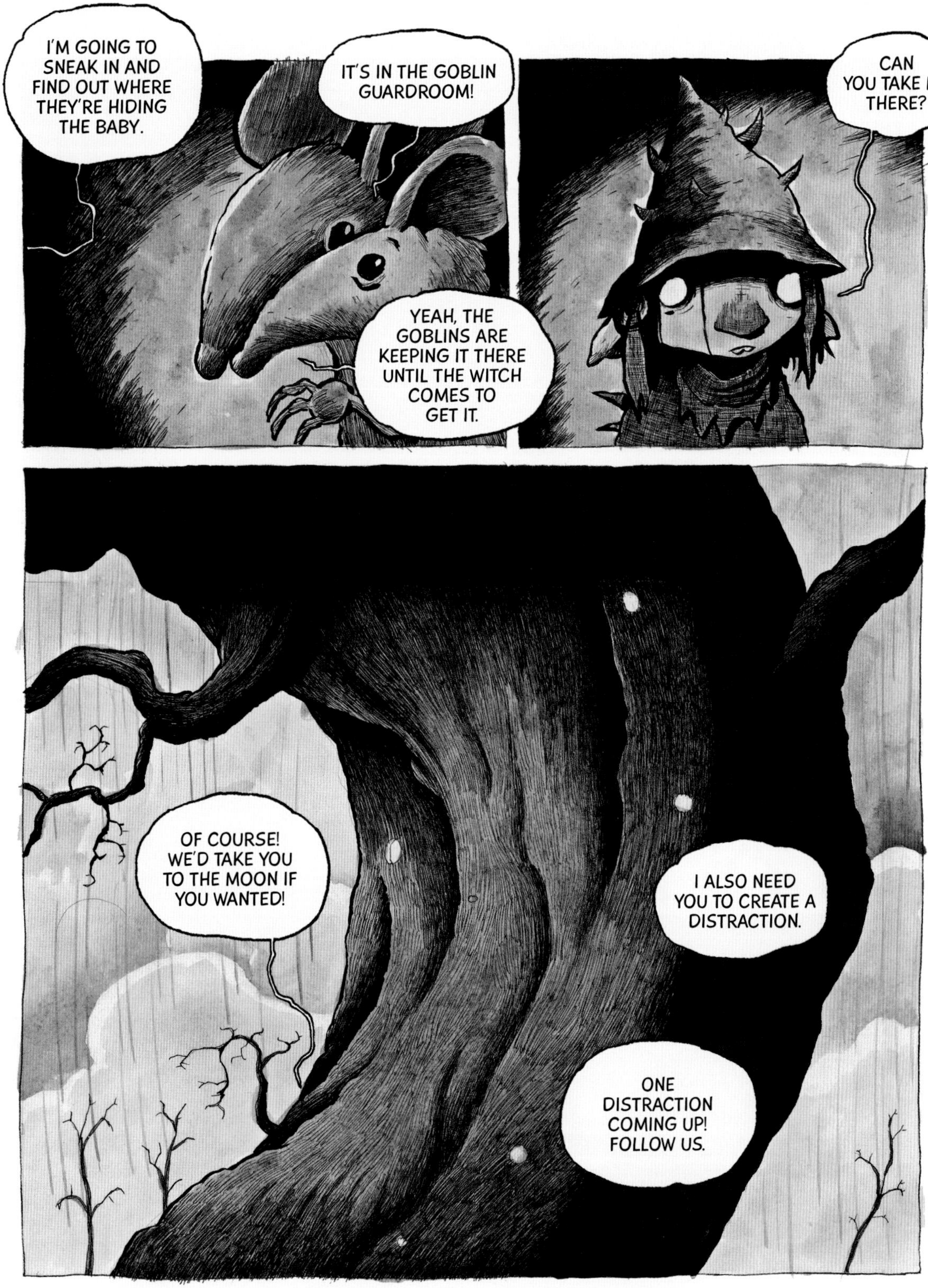
I'M GOING TO SNEAK IN AND FIND OUT WHERE THEY'RE HIDING THE BABY.
IT'S IN THE GOBLIN GUARDROOM!
YEAH, THE GOBLINS ARE KEEPING IT THERE UNTIL THE WITCH COMES TO GET IT.
CAN YOU TAKE ME THERE?
OF COURSE! WE'D TAKE YOU TO THE MOON IF YOU WANTED!
I ALSO NEED YOU TO CREATE A DISTRACTION.
ONE DISTRACTION COMING UP! FOLLOW US.

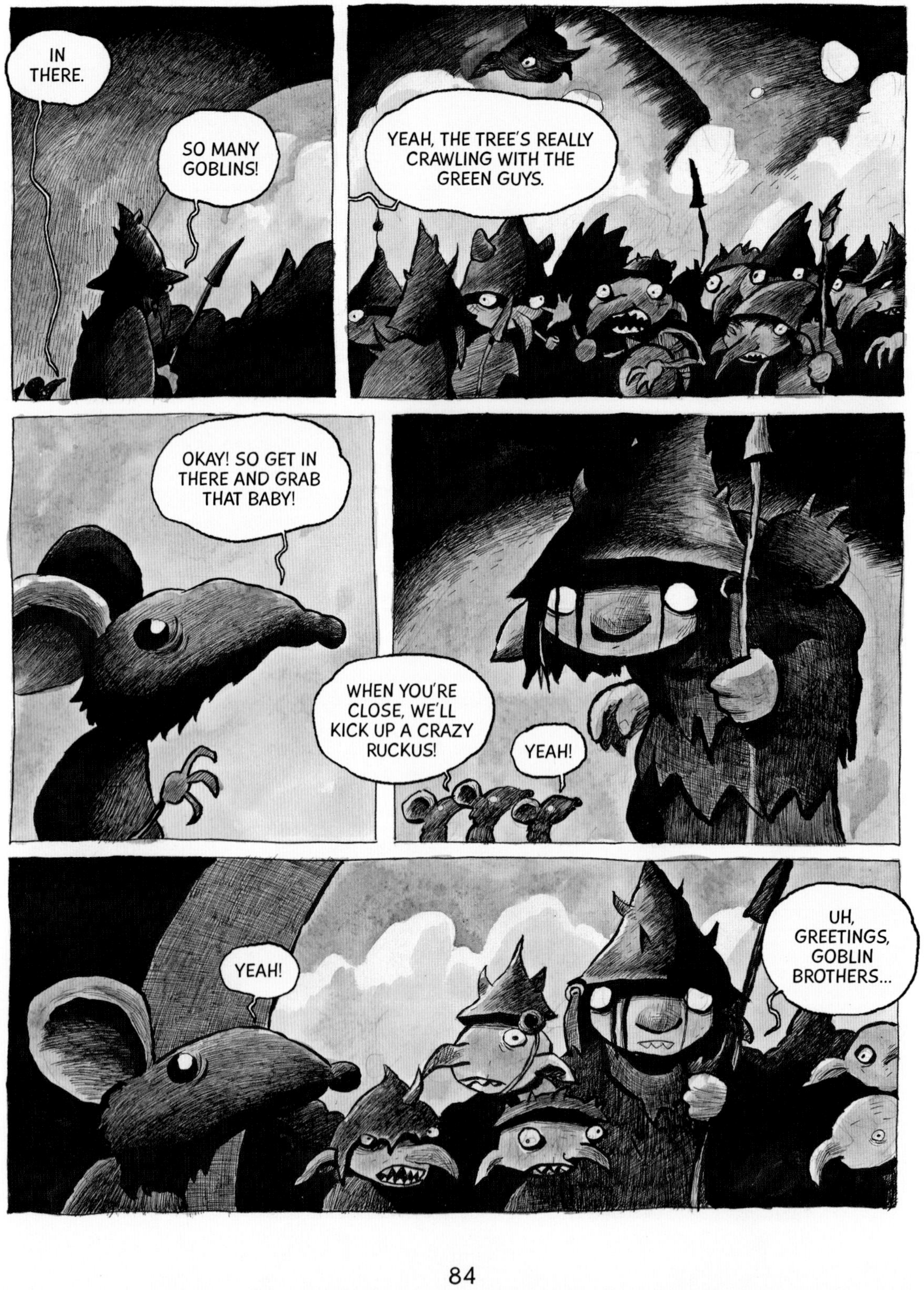
IN THERE.
SO MANY GOBLINS!
YEAH, THE TREE'S REALLY CRAWLING WITH THE GREEN GUYS.
OKAY! SO GET IN THERE AND GRAB THAT BABY!
WHEN YOU'RE CLOSE, WE'LL KICK UP A CRAZY RUCKUS!
YEAH!
YEAH!
UH, GREETINGS, GOBLIN BROTHERS...

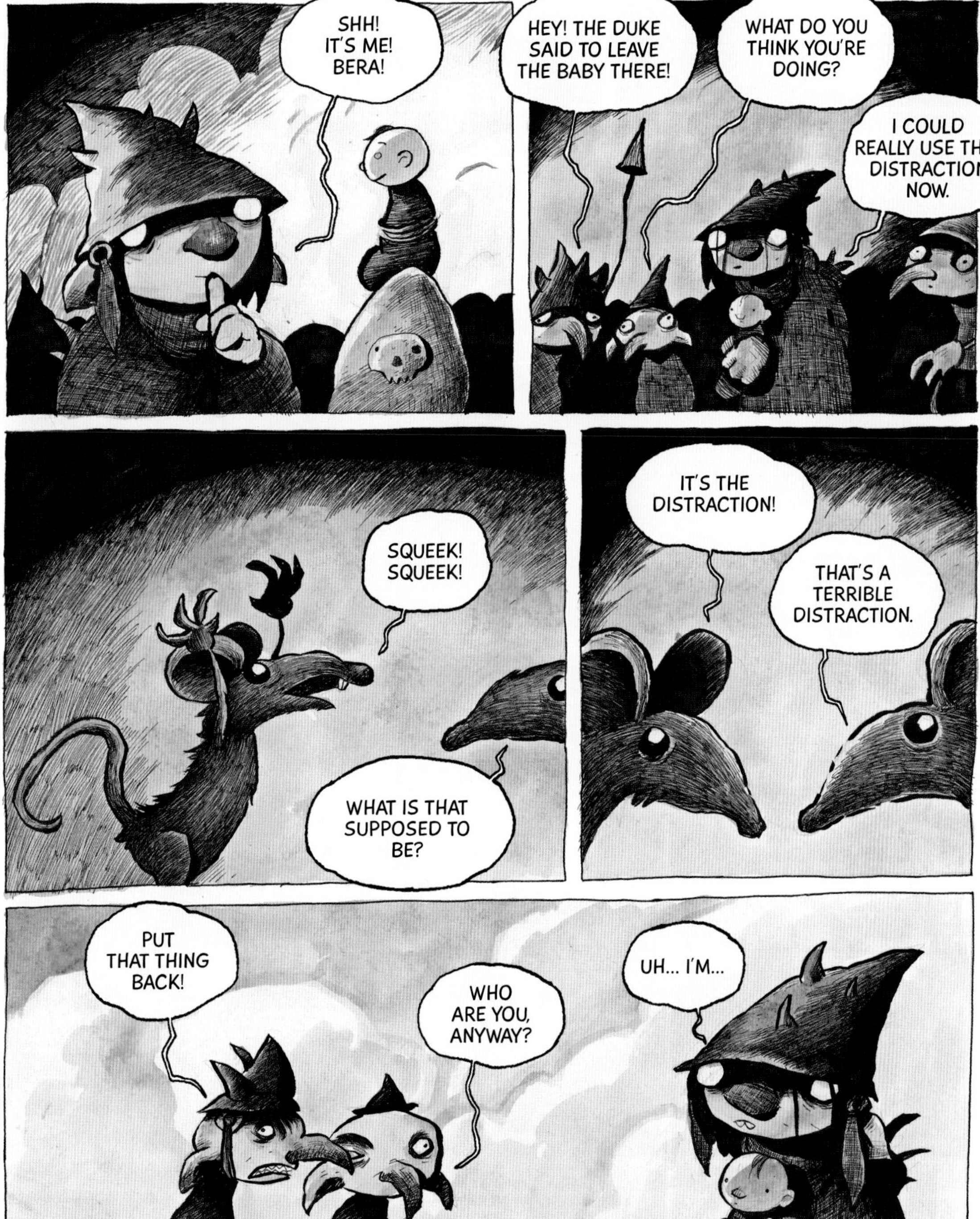
SHH! IT'S ME! BERA!
HEY! THE DUKE SAID TO LEAVE THE BABY THERE!
WHAT DO YOU THINK YOU'RE DOING?
I COULD REALLY USE THAT DISTRACTION NOW.
SQUEEK! SQUEEK!
WHAT IS THAT SUPPOSED TO BE?
IT'S THE DISTRACTION!
THAT'S A TERRIBLE DISTRACTION.
PUT THAT THING BACK!
WHO ARE YOU, ANYWAY?
UH... I'M...

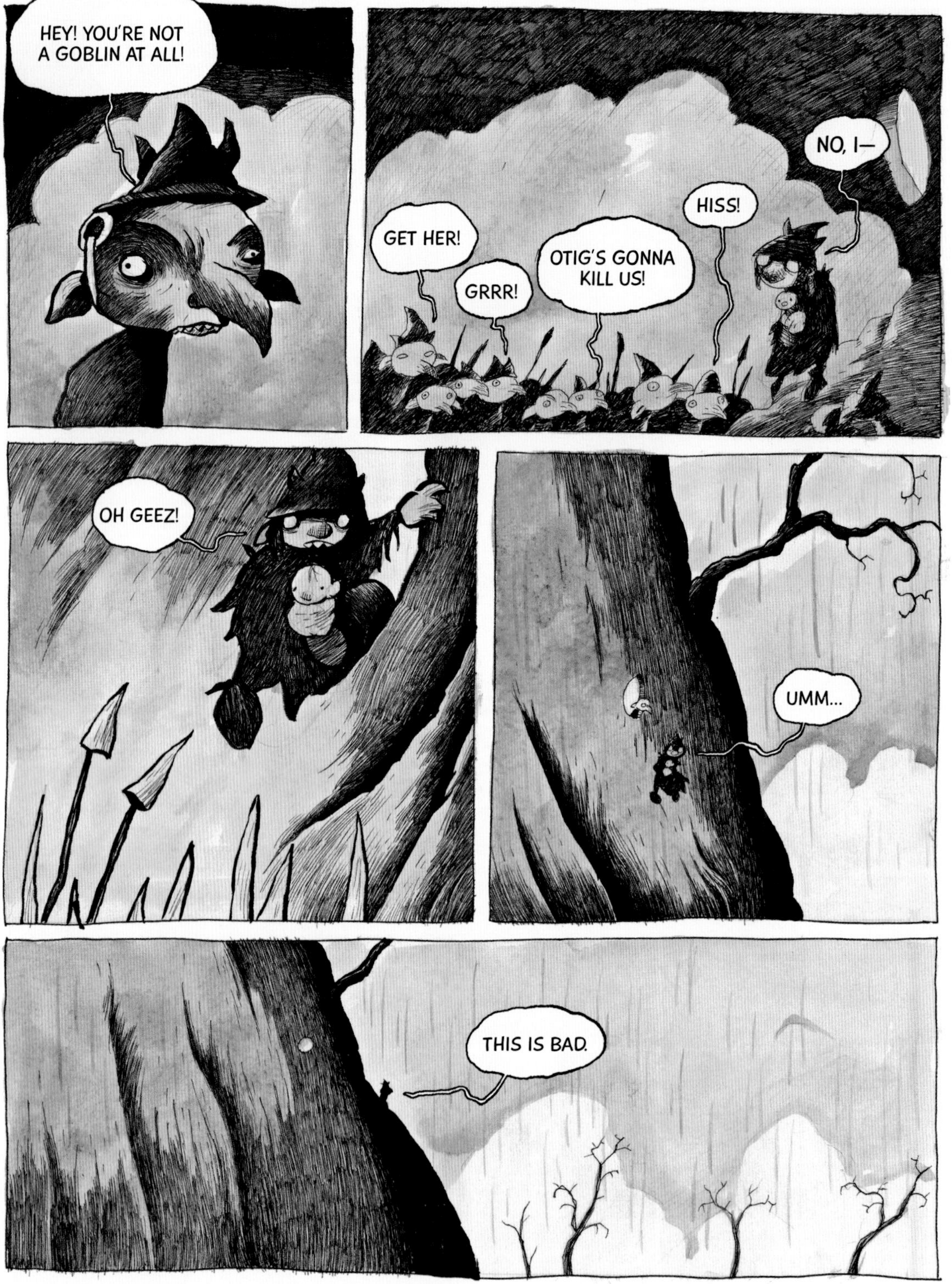
HEY! YOU'RE NOT A GOBLIN AT ALL!
GET HER!
GRRR!
OTIG'S GONNA KILL US!
HISS!
NO, I—
OH GEEZ!
UMM...
THIS IS BAD.

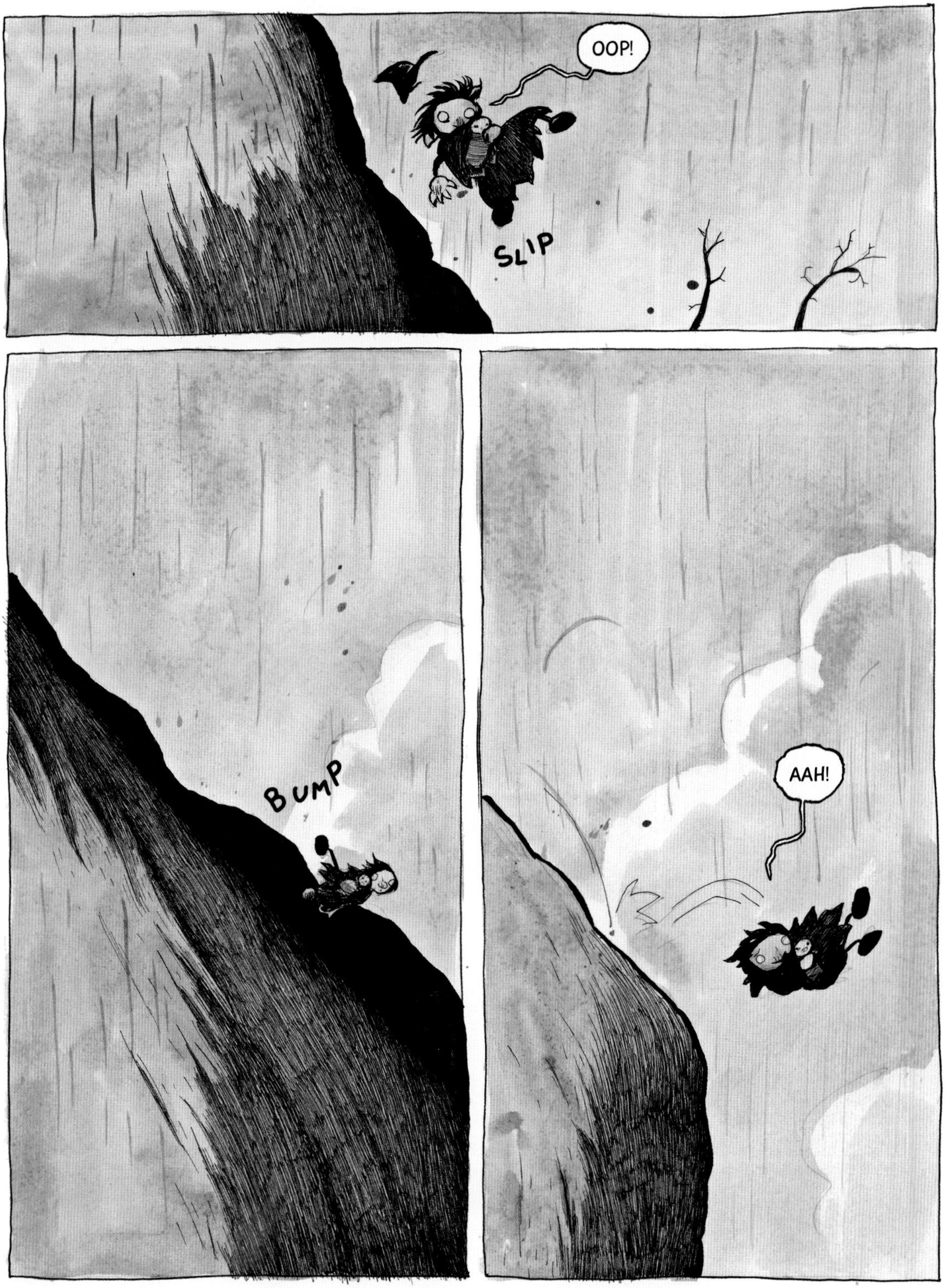
OOP!
SLIP
BUMP
AAH!

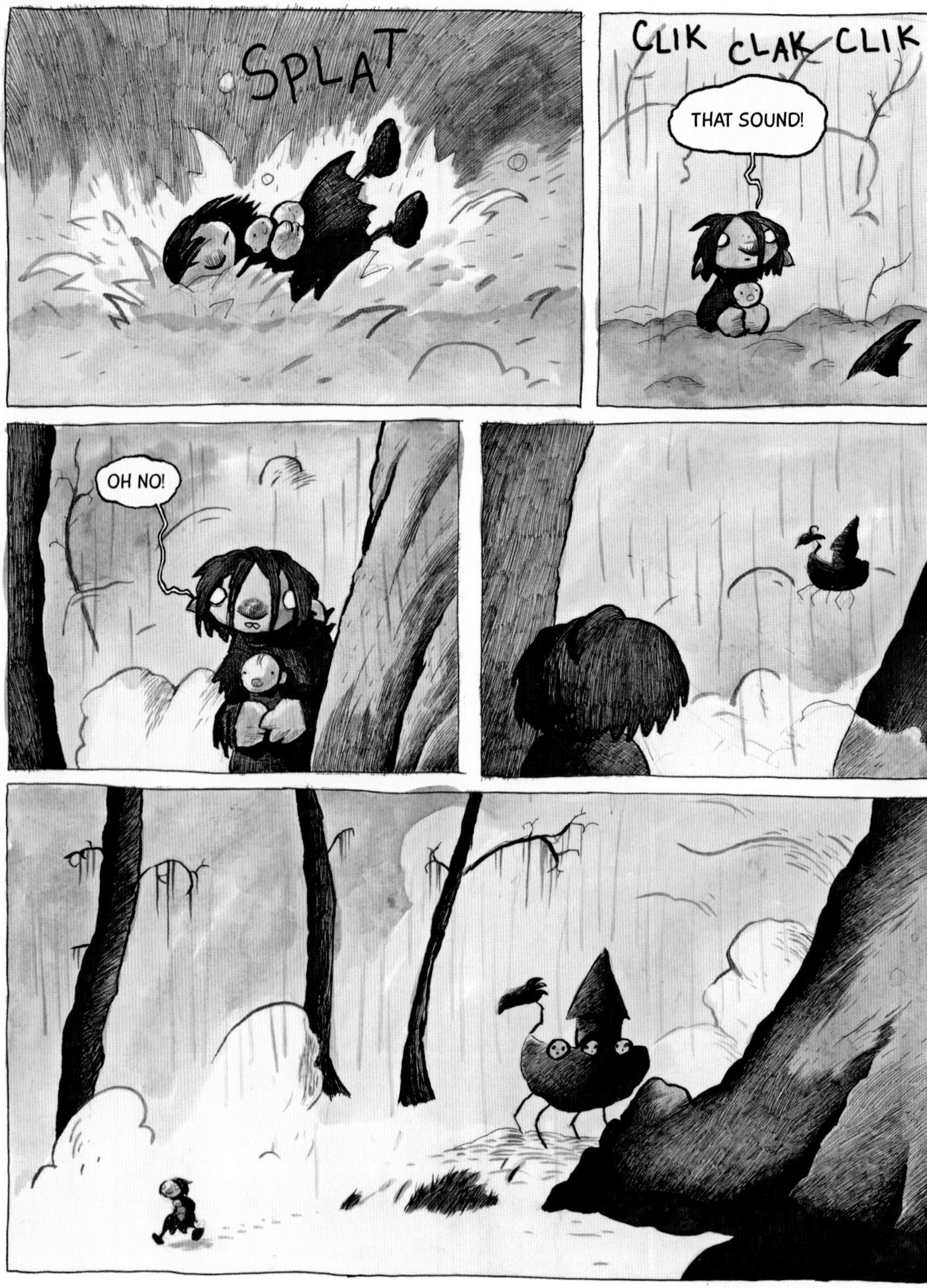
SPLAT
CLIK CLAK CLIK
THAT SOUND!
OH NO!

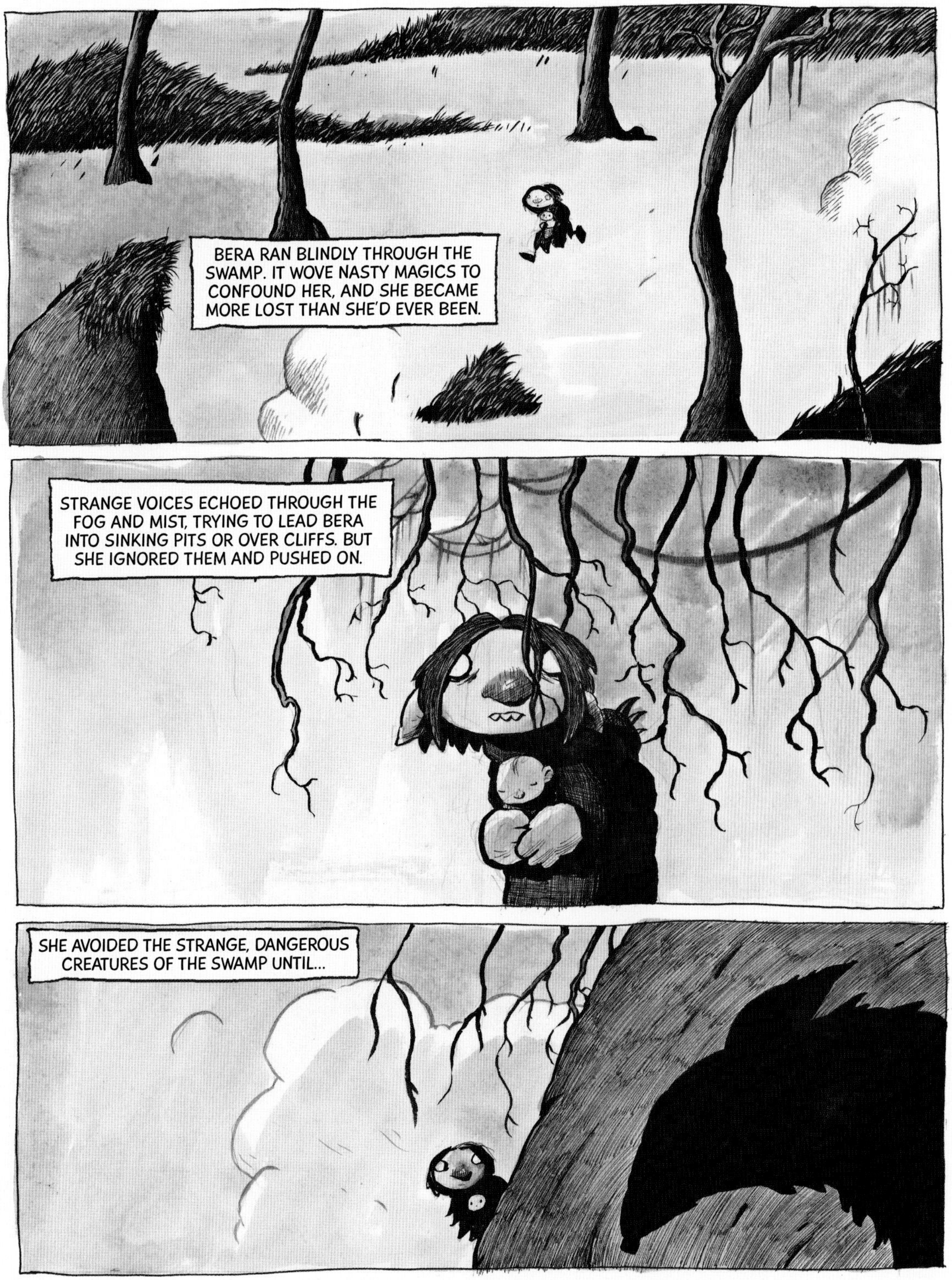
BERA RAN BLINDLY THROUGH THE SWAMP. IT WOVE NASTY MAGICS TO CONFOUND HER, AND SHE BECAME MORE LOST THAN SHE'D EVER BEEN.
STRANGE VOICES ECHOED THROUGH THE FOG AND MIST, TRYING TO LEAD BERA INTO SINKING PITS OR OVER CLIFFS. BUT SHE IGNORED THEM AND PUSHED ON.
SHE AVOIDED THE STRANGE, DANGEROUS CREATURES OF THE SWAMP UNTIL...

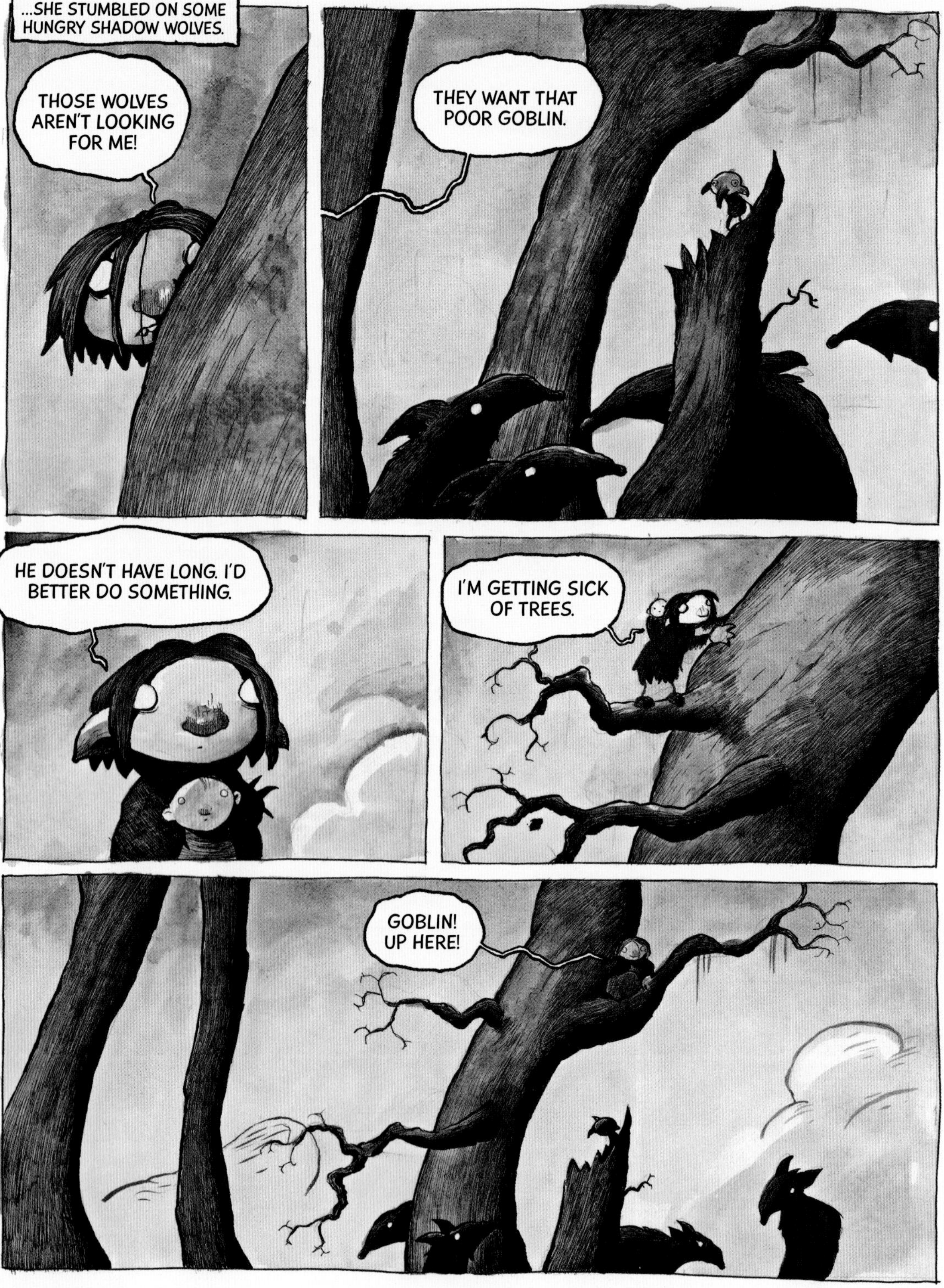
...SHE STUMBLED ON SOME HUNGRY SHADOW WOLVES.
THOSE WOLVES AREN'T LOOKING FOR ME!
THEY WANT THAT POOR GOBLIN.
HE DOESN'T HAVE LONG. I'D BETTER DO SOMETHING.
I'M GETTING SICK OF TREES.
GOBLIN! UP HERE!

IT IS UNWISE TO BARGE IN ON A WOLF'S DINNER, TROLL.

I BET IT IS! BUT IT CAN'T BE HELPED.

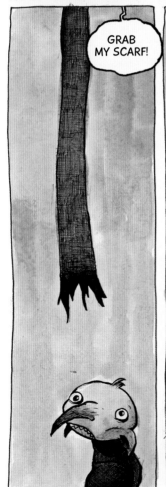

GRAB MY SCARF!

EEP!

SNAP

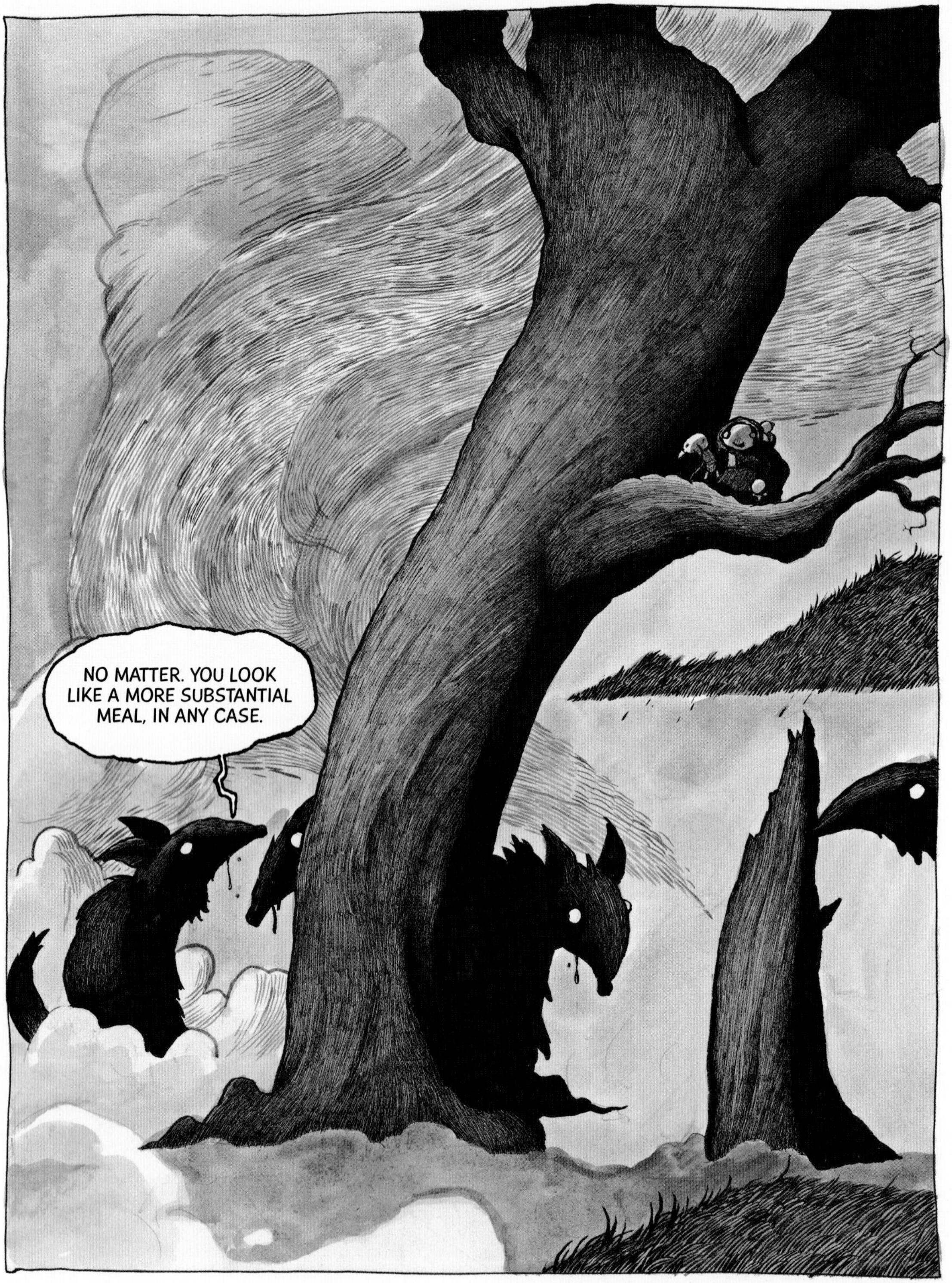
NO MATTER. YOU LOOK LIKE A MORE SUBSTANTIAL MEAL, IN ANY CASE.

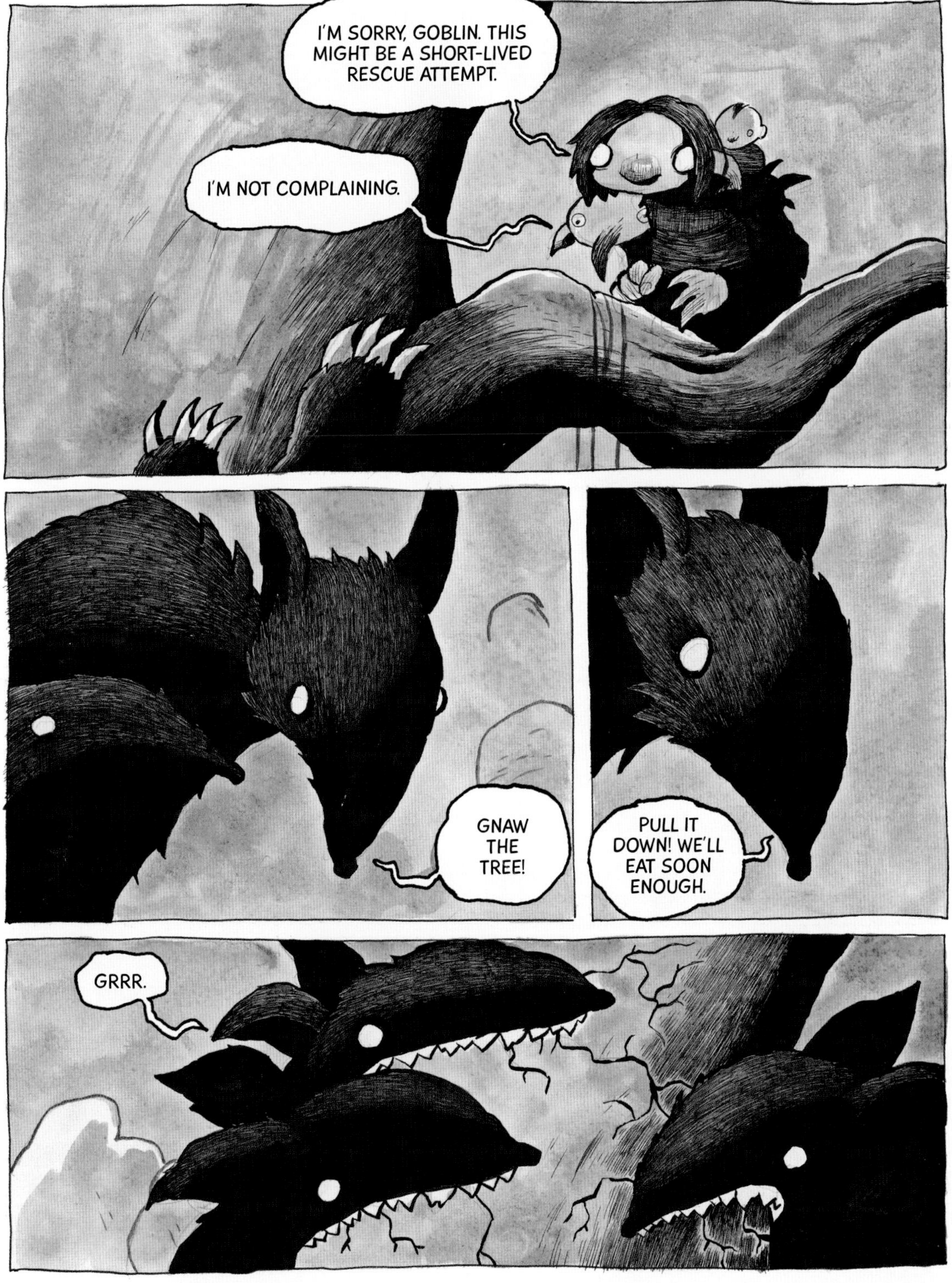
I'M SORRY, GOBLIN. THIS MIGHT BE A SHORT-LIVED RESCUE ATTEMPT.
I'M NOT COMPLAINING.
GNAW THE TREE!
PULL IT DOWN! WE'LL EAT SOON ENOUGH.
GRRR.

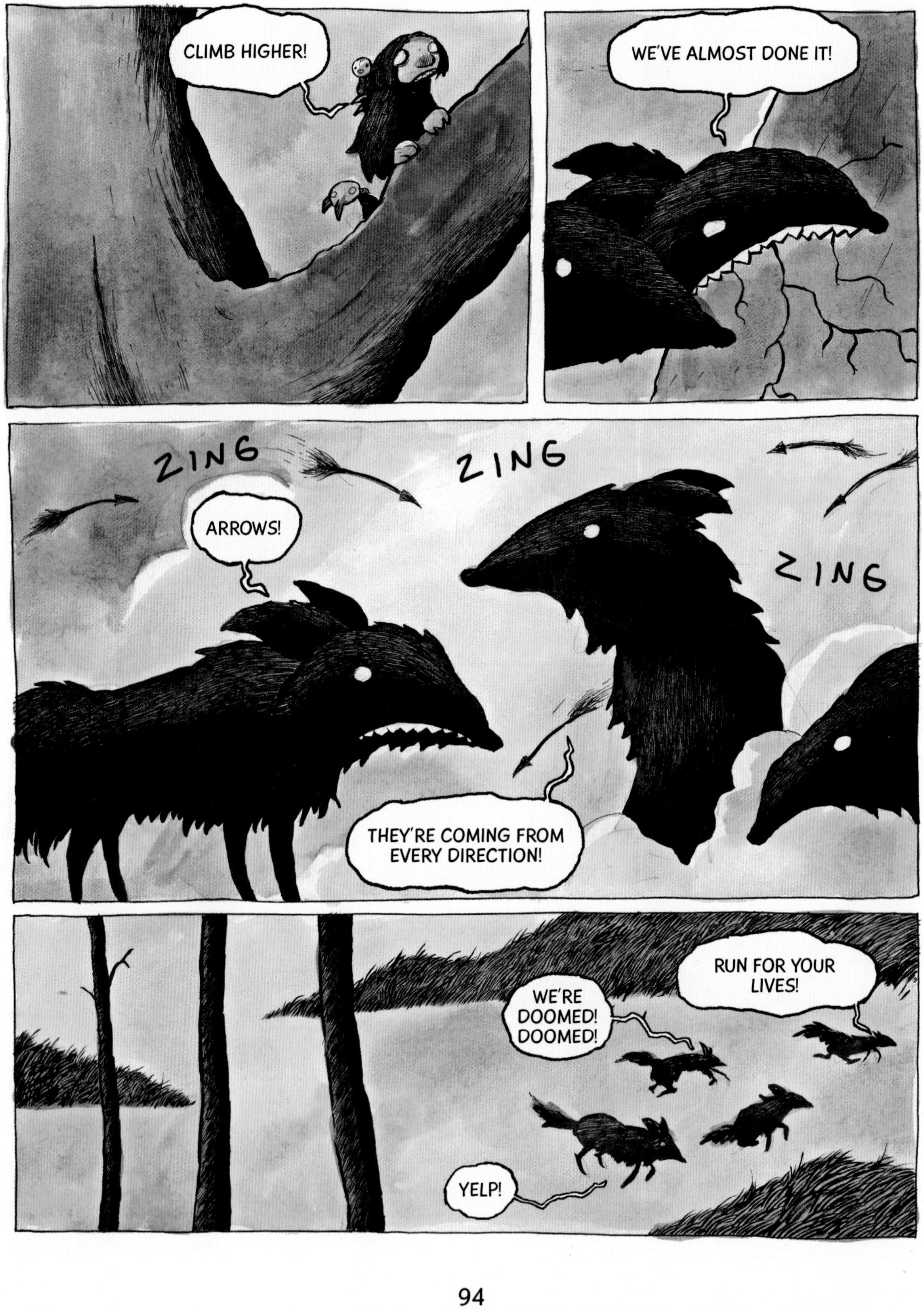
CLIMB HIGHER!
WE'VE ALMOST DONE IT!
ZING
ZING
ARROWS!
ZING
THEY'RE COMING FROM EVERY DIRECTION!
WE'RE DOOMED! DOOMED!
RUN FOR YOUR LIVES!
YELP!

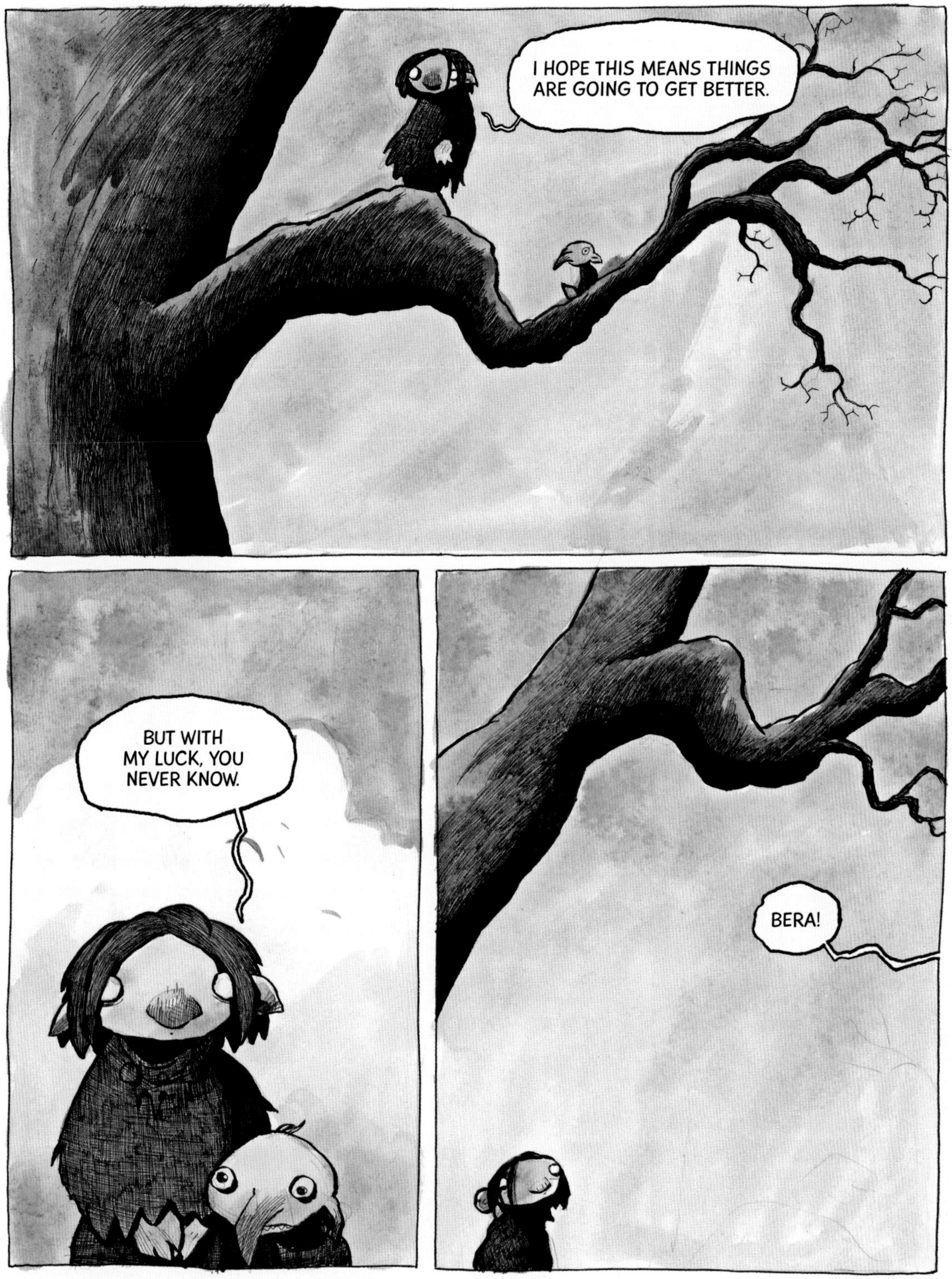
I HOPE THIS MEANS THINGS ARE GOING TO GET BETTER.
BUT WITH MY LUCK, YOU NEVER KNOW.
BERA!

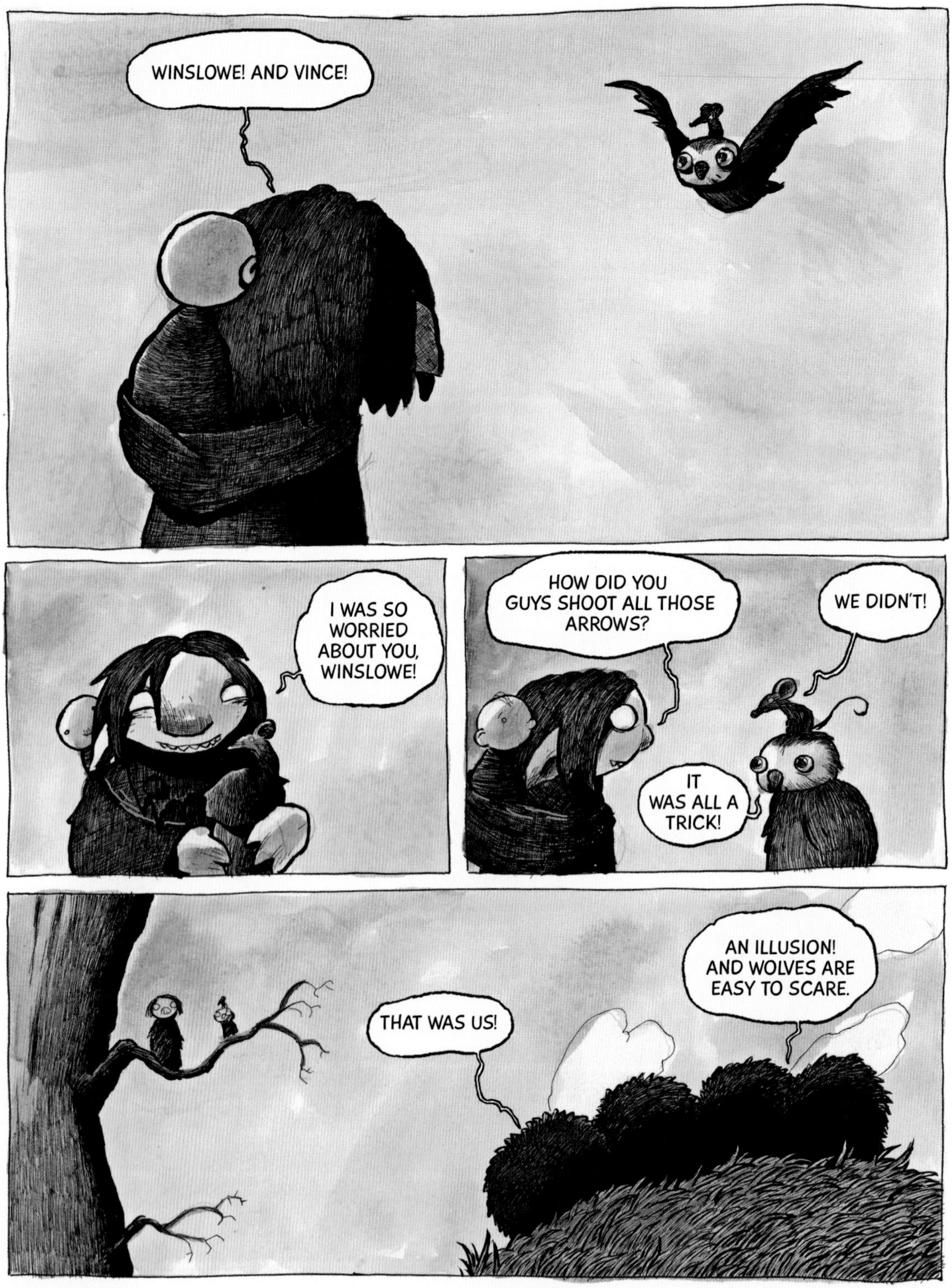
WINSLOWE! AND VINCE!
I WAS SO WORRIED ABOUT YOU, WINSLOWE!
HOW DID YOU GUYS SHOOT ALL THOSE ARROWS?
WE DIDN'T!
IT WAS ALL A TRICK!
THAT WAS US!
AN ILLUSION! AND WOLVES ARE EASY TO SCARE.

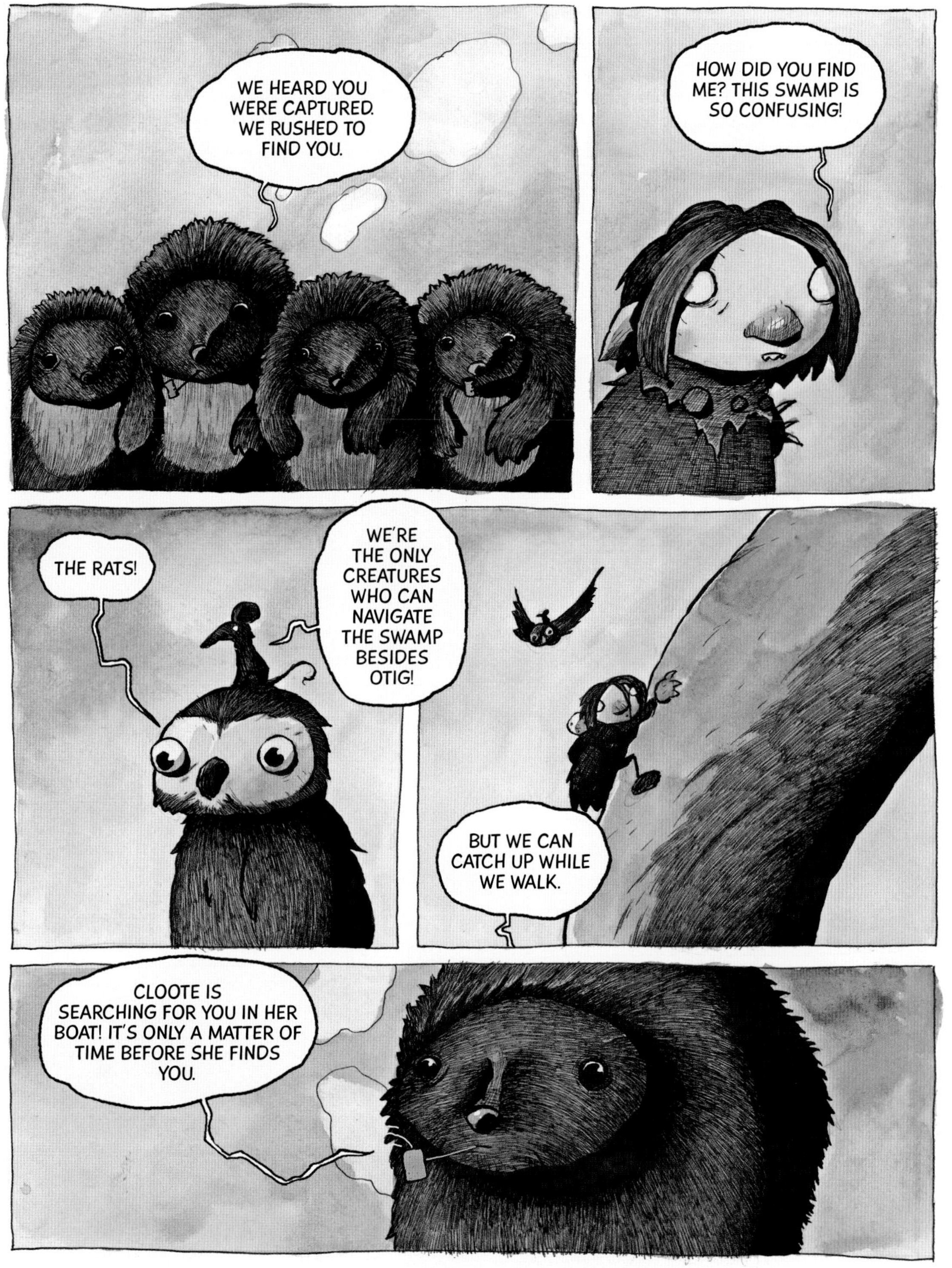
WE HEARD YOU WERE CAPTURED. WE RUSHED TO FIND YOU.
HOW DID YOU FIND ME? THIS SWAMP IS SO CONFUSING!
THE RATS!
WE'RE THE ONLY CREATURES WHO CAN NAVIGATE THE SWAMP BESIDES OTIG!
BUT WE CAN CATCH UP WHILE WE WALK.
CLOOTE IS SEARCHING FOR YOU IN HER BOAT! IT'S ONLY A MATTER OF TIME BEFORE SHE FINDS YOU.

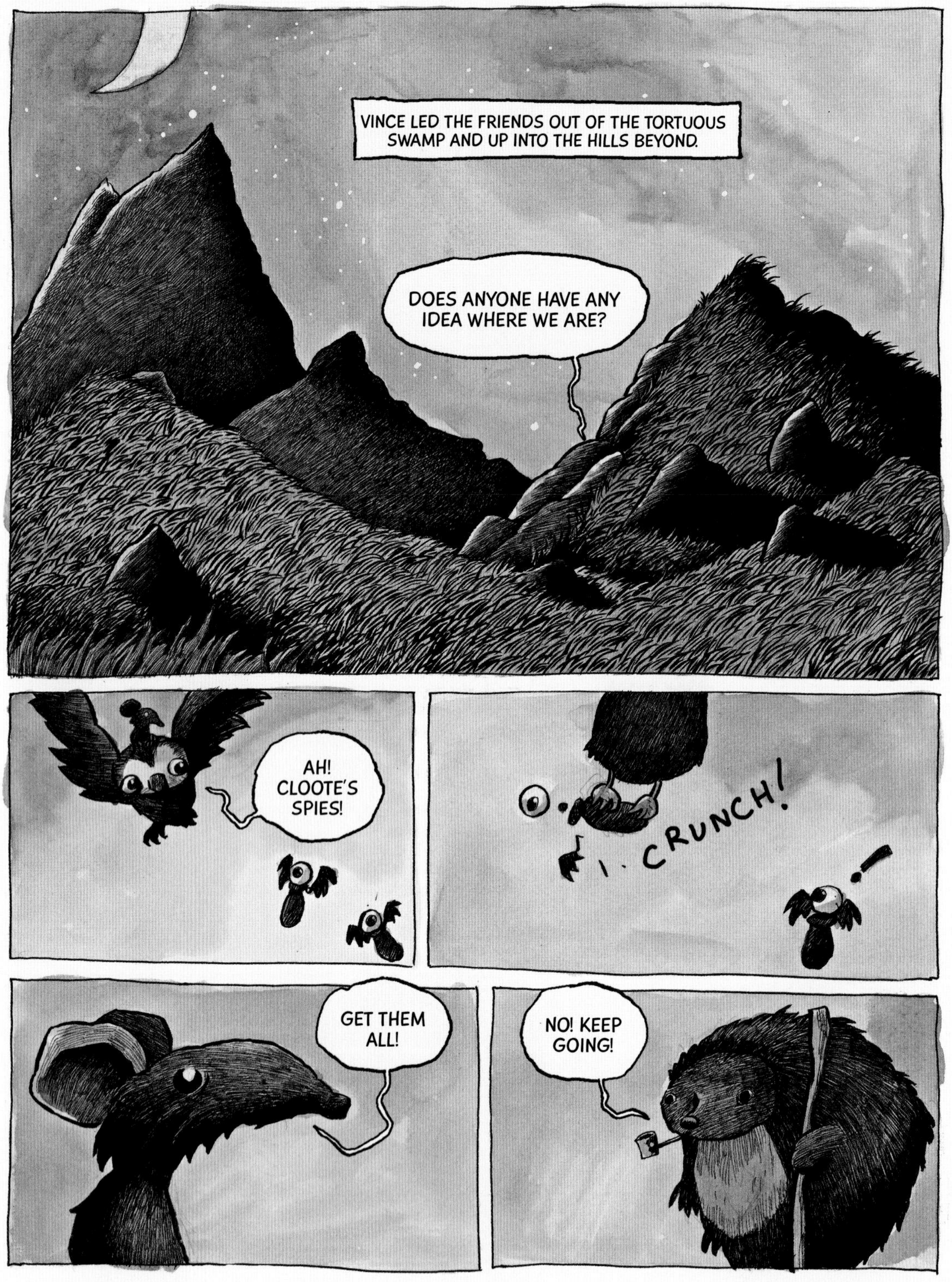
VINCE LED THE FRIENDS OUT OF THE TORTUOUS SWAMP AND UP INTO THE HILLS BEYOND.
DOES ANYONE HAVE ANY IDEA WHERE WE ARE?
AH! CLOOTE'S SPIES!
CRUNCH!
!
GET THEM ALL!
NO! KEEP GOING!

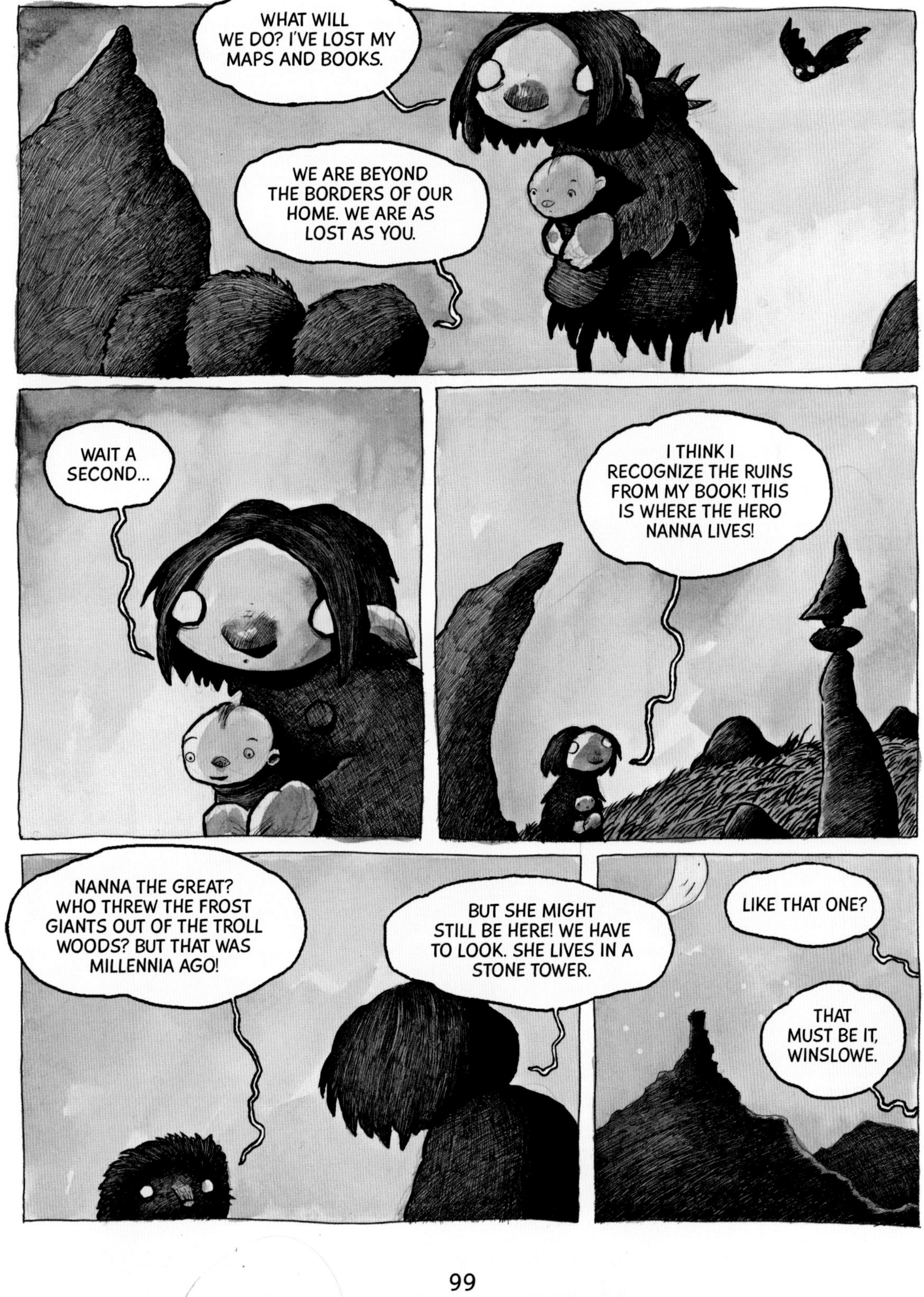
WHAT WILL WE DO? I'VE LOST MY MAPS AND BOOKS.
WE ARE BEYOND THE BORDERS OF OUR HOME. WE ARE AS LOST AS YOU.
WAIT A SECOND...
I THINK I RECOGNIZE THE RUINS FROM MY BOOK! THIS IS WHERE THE HERO NANNA LIVES!
NANNA THE GREAT? WHO THREW THE FROST GIANTS OUT OF THE TROLL WOODS? BUT THAT WAS MILLENNIA AGO!
BUT SHE MIGHT STILL BE HERE! WE HAVE TO LOOK. SHE LIVES IN A STONE TOWER.
LIKE THAT ONE?
THAT MUST BE IT, WINSLOWE.

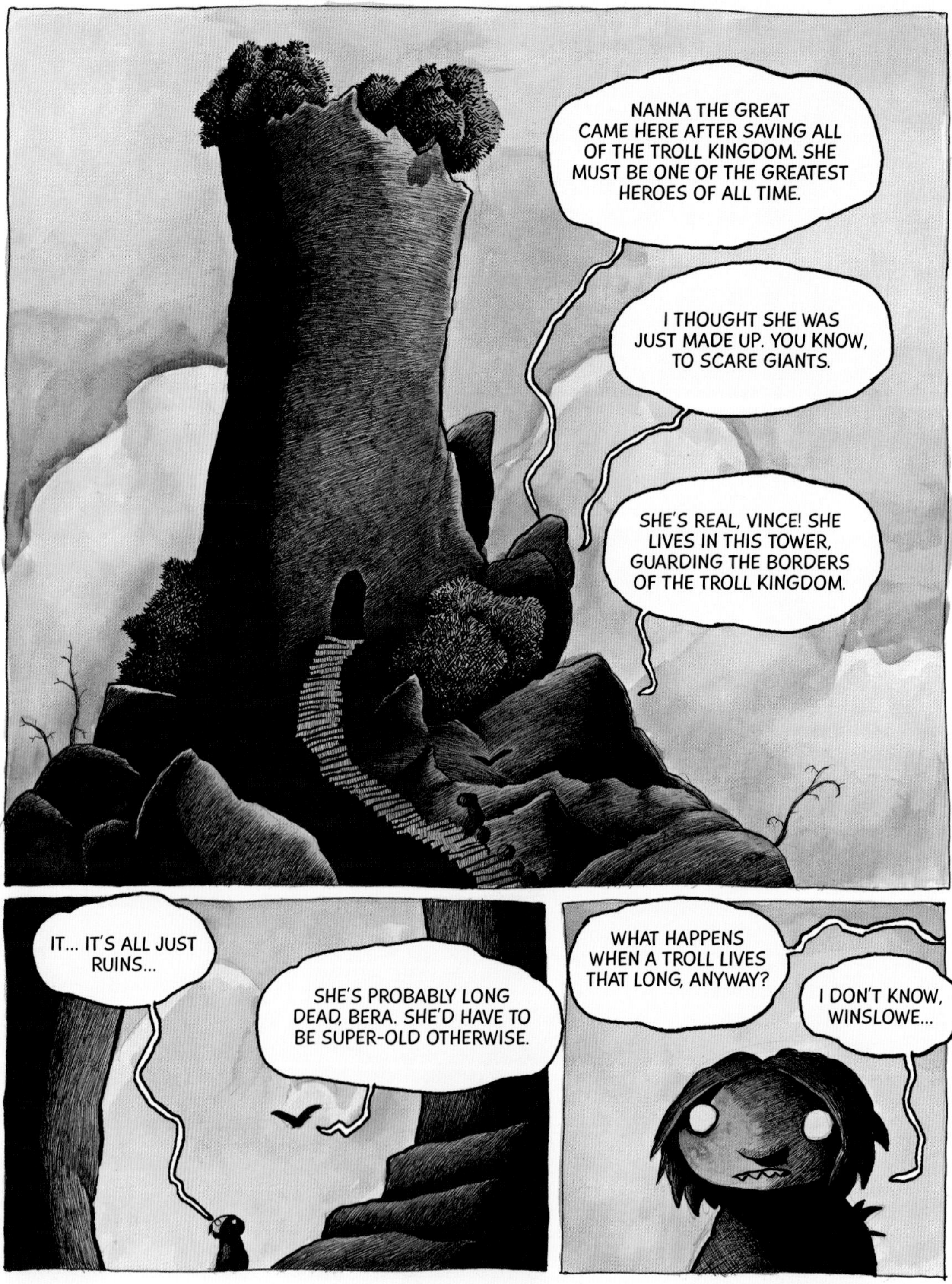
NANNA THE GREAT CAME HERE AFTER SAVING ALL OF THE TROLL KINGDOM. SHE MUST BE ONE OF THE GREATEST HEROES OF ALL TIME.
I THOUGHT SHE WAS JUST MADE UP. YOU KNOW, TO SCARE GIANTS.
SHE'S REAL, VINCE! SHE LIVES IN THIS TOWER, GUARDING THE BORDERS OF THE TROLL KINGDOM.
IT... IT'S ALL JUST RUINS...
SHE'S PROBABLY LONG DEAD, BERA. SHE'D HAVE TO BE SUPER-OLD OTHERWISE.
WHAT HAPPENS WHEN A TROLL LIVES THAT LONG, ANYWAY?
I DON'T KNOW, WINSLOWE...

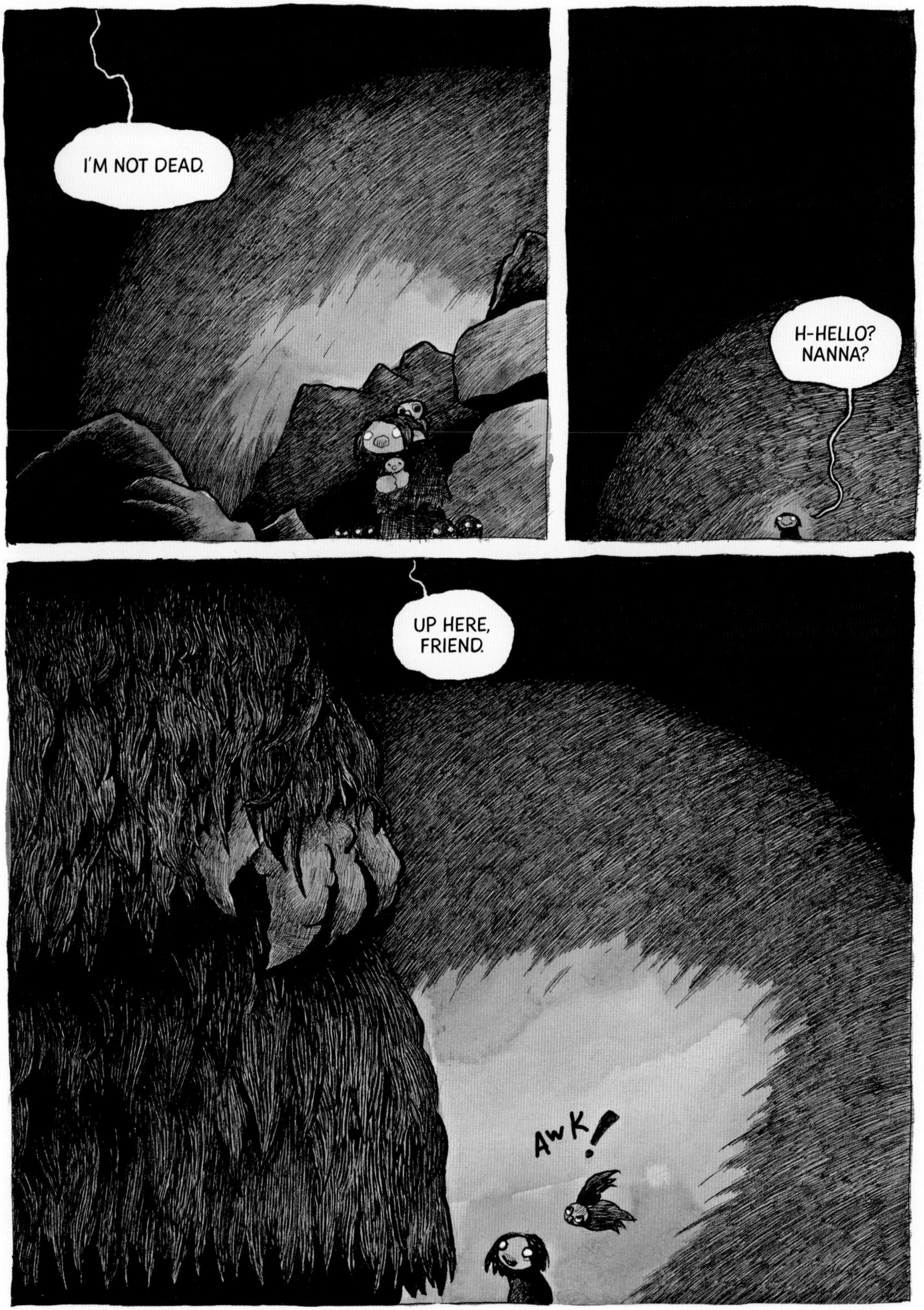
I'M NOT DEAD.
H-HELLO? NANNA?
UP HERE, FRIEND.
AWK!

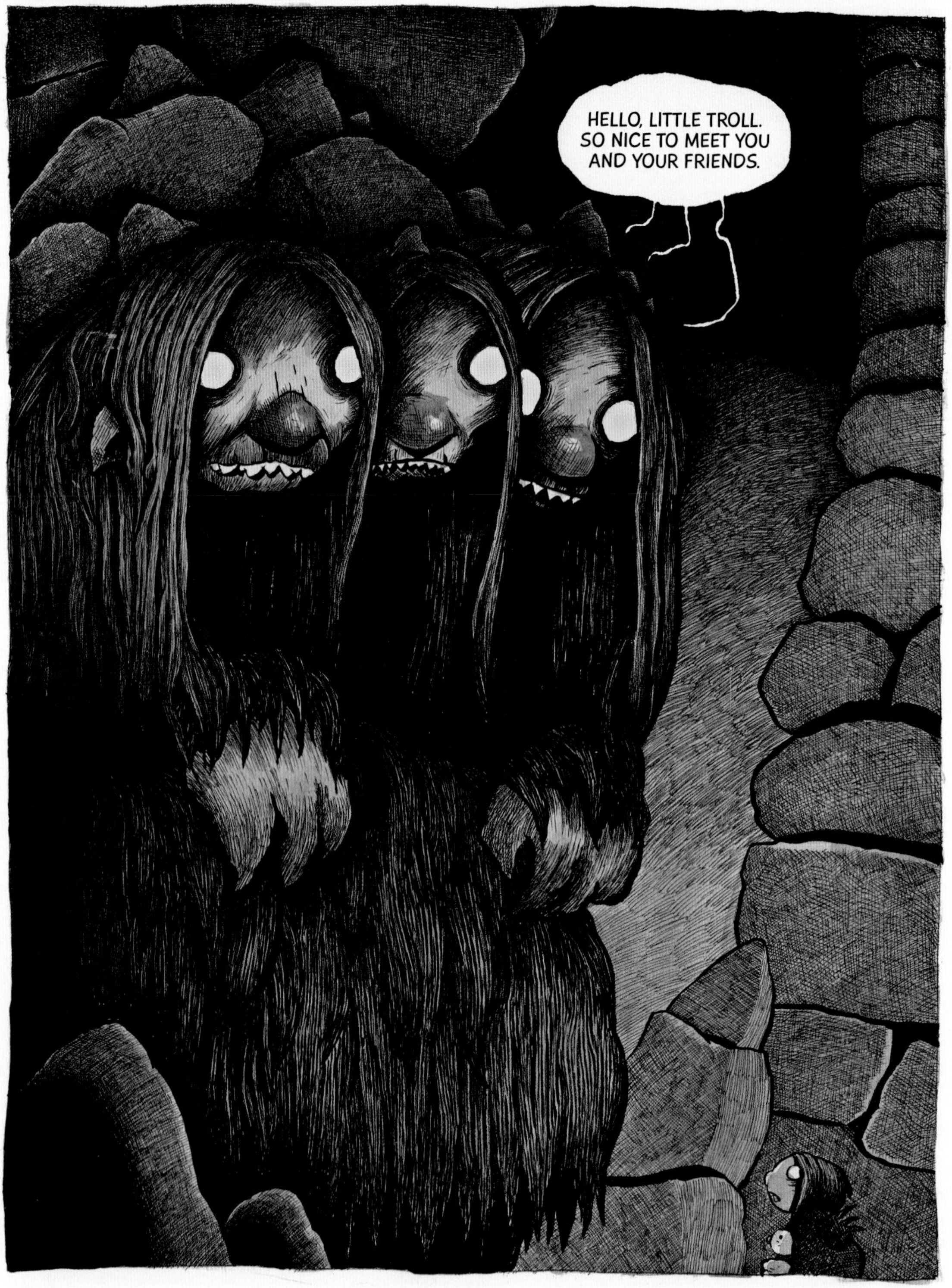
HELLO, LITTLE TROLL. SO NICE TO MEET YOU AND YOUR FRIENDS.

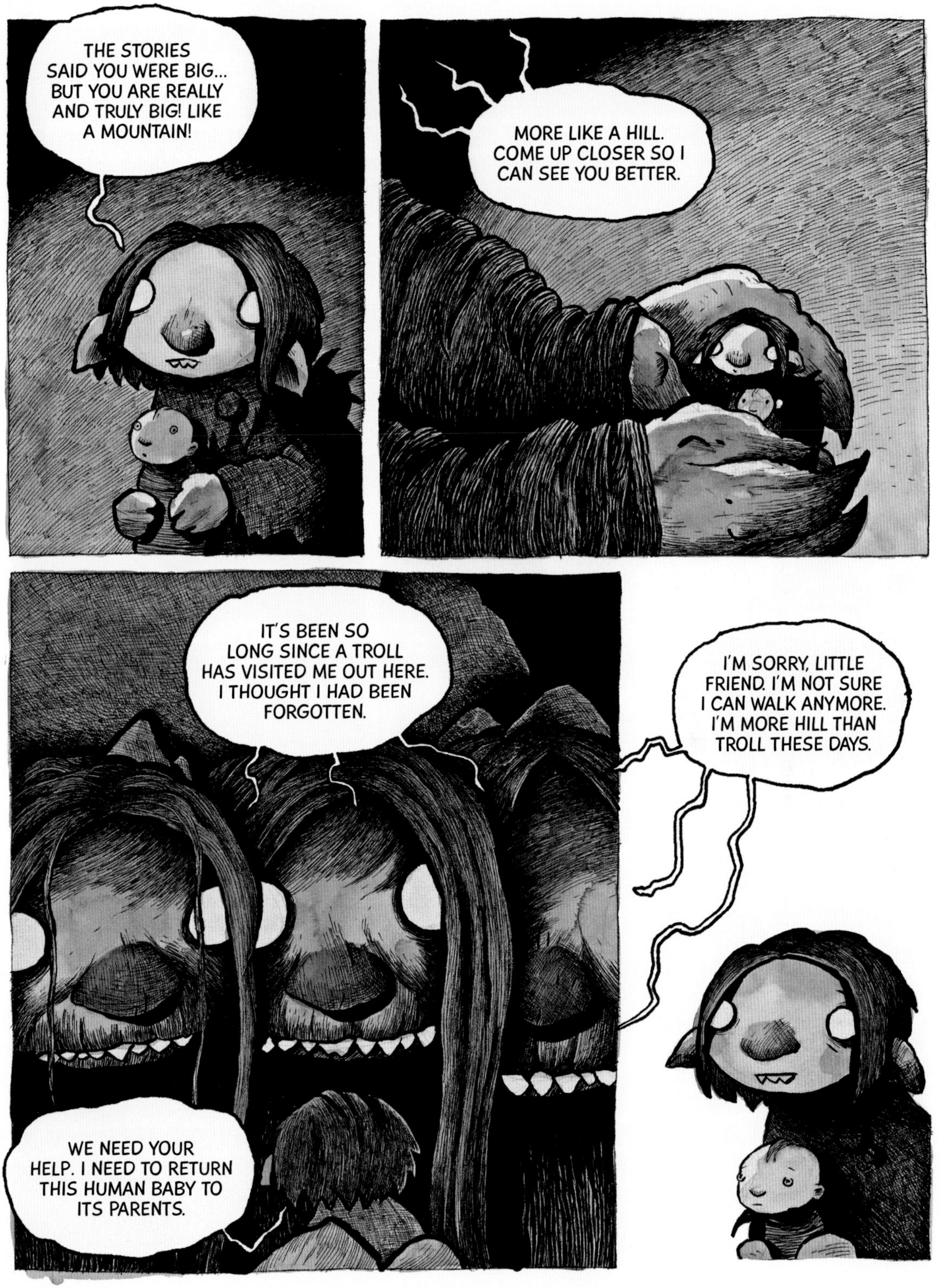
THE STORIES SAID YOU WERE BIG... BUT YOU ARE REALLY AND TRULY BIG! LIKE A MOUNTAIN!
MORE LIKE A HILL. COME UP CLOSER SO I CAN SEE YOU BETTER.
IT'S BEEN SO LONG SINCE A TROLL HAS VISITED ME OUT HERE. I THOUGHT I HAD BEEN FORGOTTEN.
I'M SORRY, LITTLE FRIEND. I'M NOT SURE I CAN WALK ANYMORE. I'M MORE HILL THAN TROLL THESE DAYS.
WE NEED YOUR HELP. I NEED TO RETURN THIS HUMAN BABY TO ITS PARENTS.

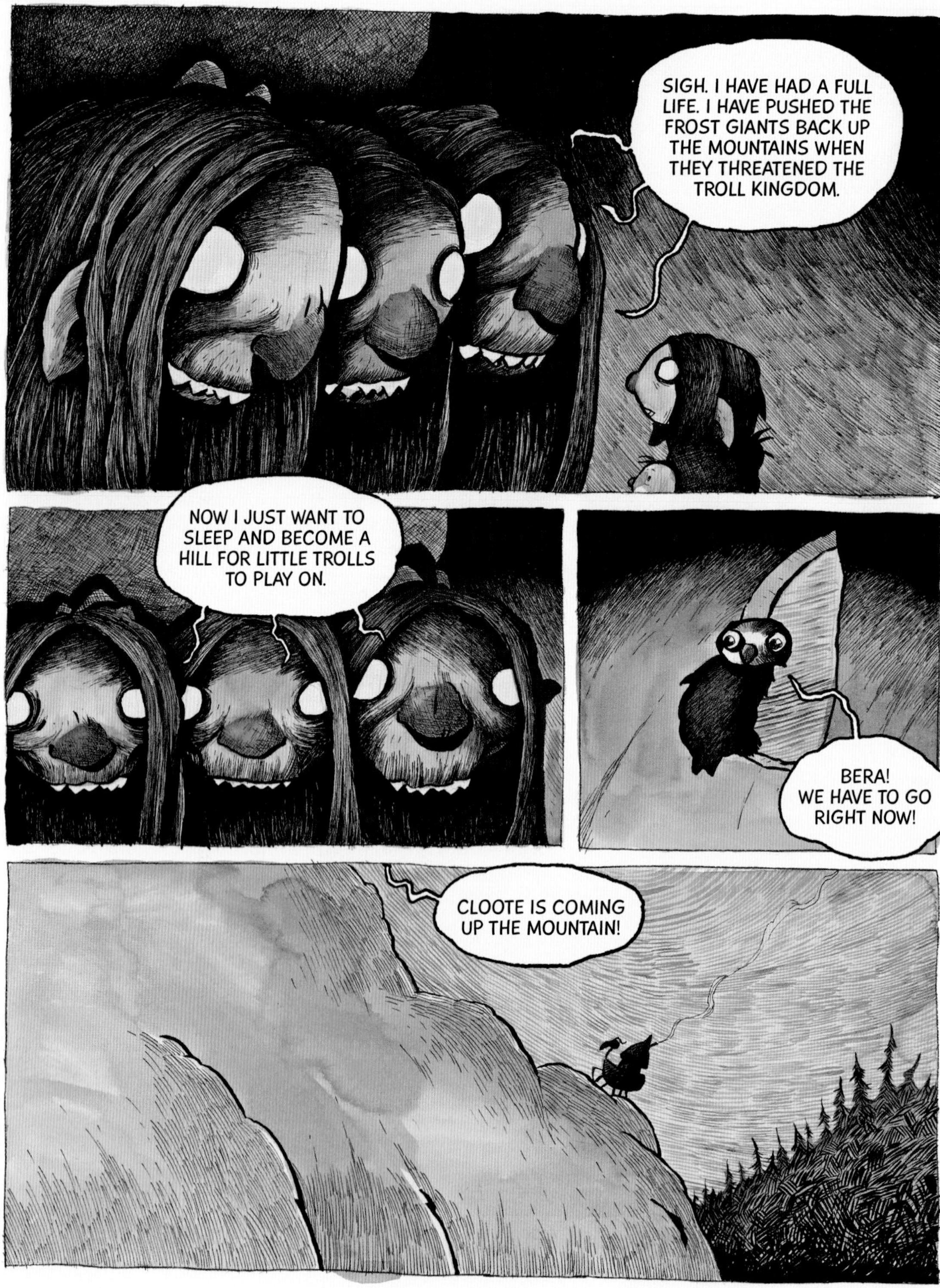
SIGH. I HAVE HAD A FULL LIFE. I HAVE PUSHED THE FROST GIANTS BACK UP THE MOUNTAINS WHEN THEY THREATENED THE TROLL KINGDOM.
NOW I JUST WANT TO SLEEP AND BECOME A HILL FOR LITTLE TROLLS TO PLAY ON.
BERA! WE HAVE TO GO RIGHT NOW!
CLOOTE IS COMING UP THE MOUNTAIN!

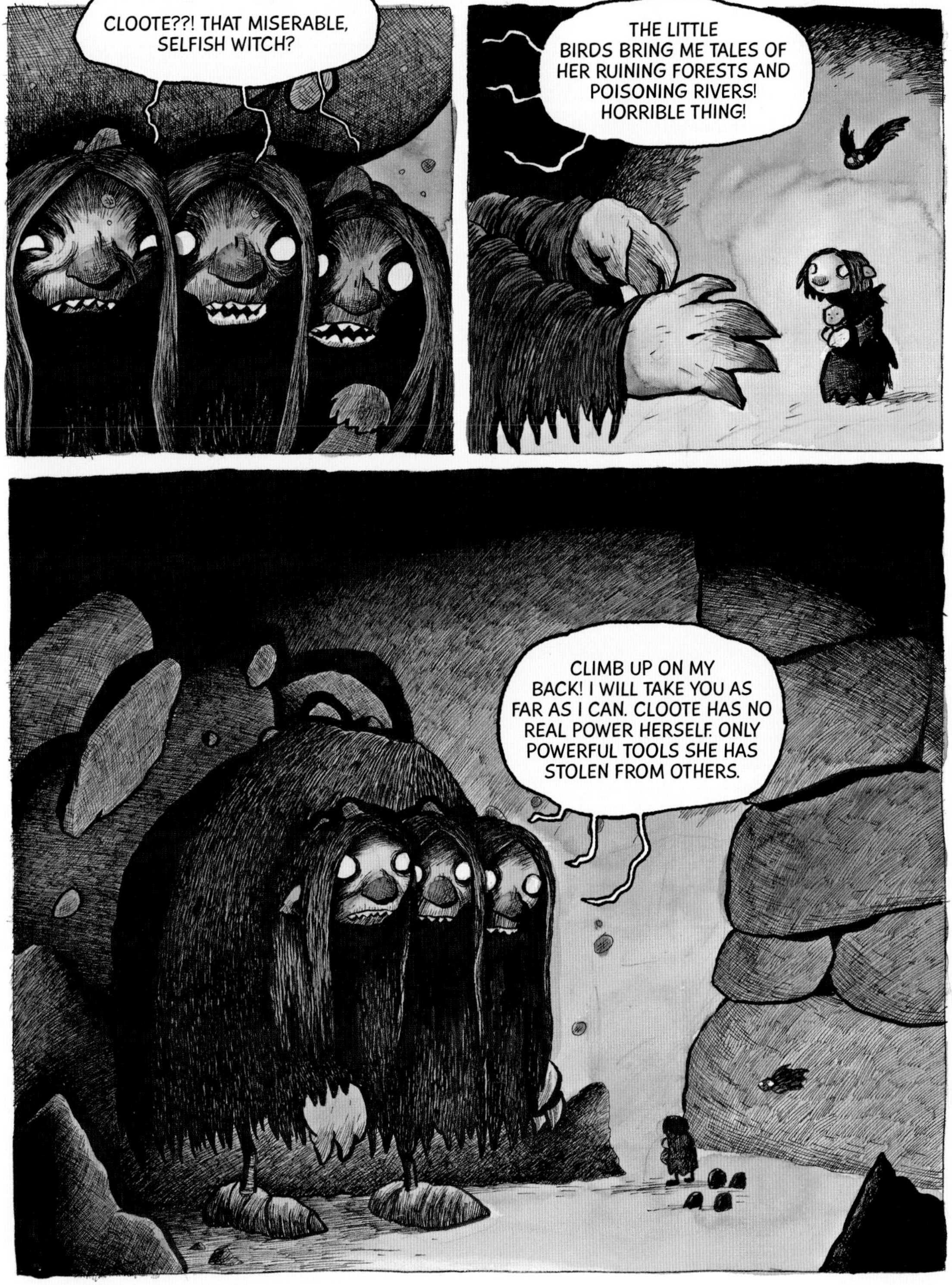
CLOOTE??! THAT MISERABLE, SELFISH WITCH?
THE LITTLE BIRDS BRING ME TALES OF HER RUINING FORESTS AND POISONING RIVERS! HORRIBLE THING!
CLIMB UP ON MY BACK! I WILL TAKE YOU AS FAR AS I CAN. CLOOTE HAS NO REAL POWER HERSELF. ONLY POWERFUL TOOLS SHE HAS STOLEN FROM OTHERS.

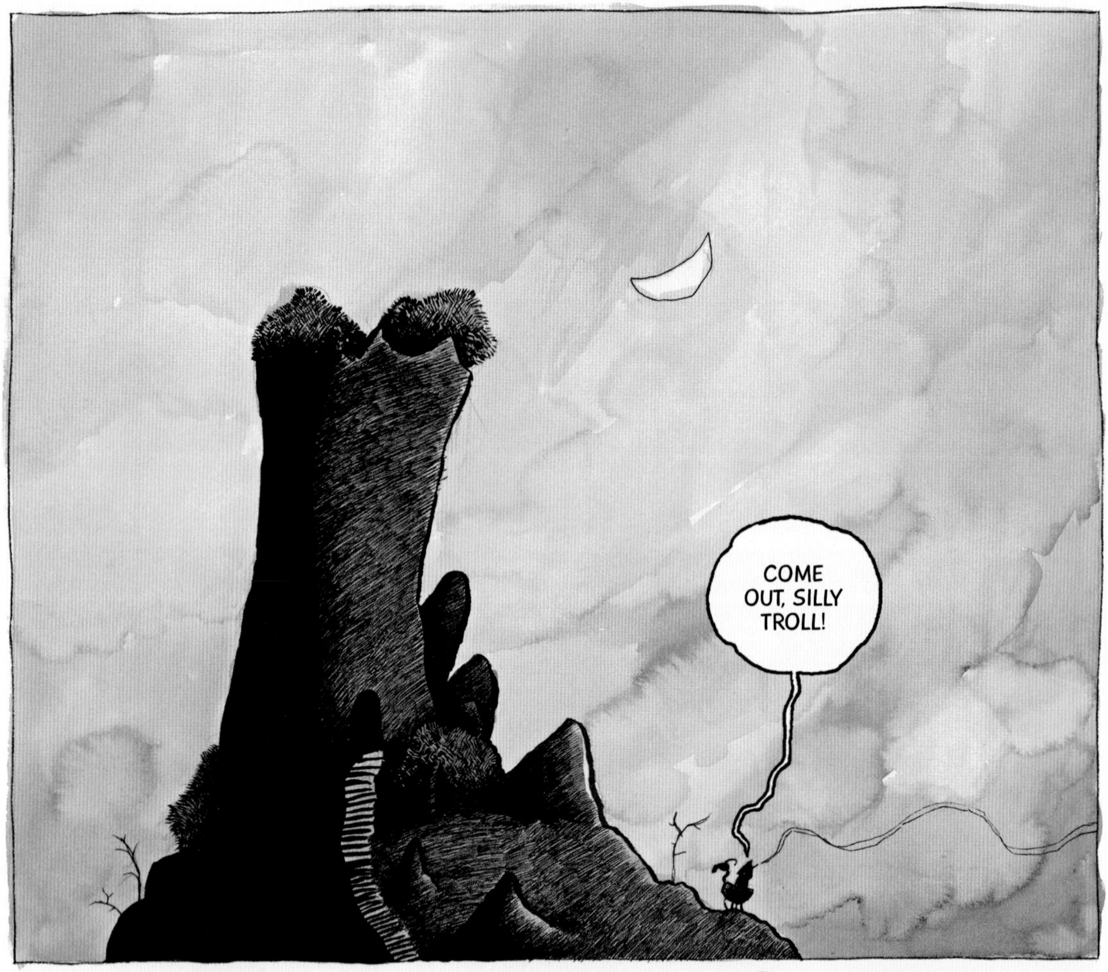
COME OUT, SILLY TROLL!

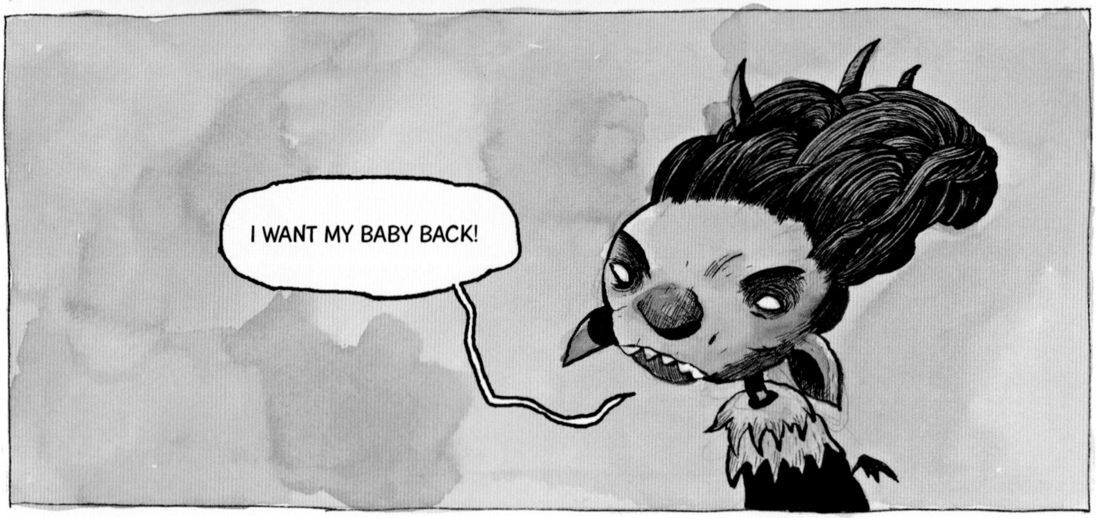
I WANT MY BABY BACK!

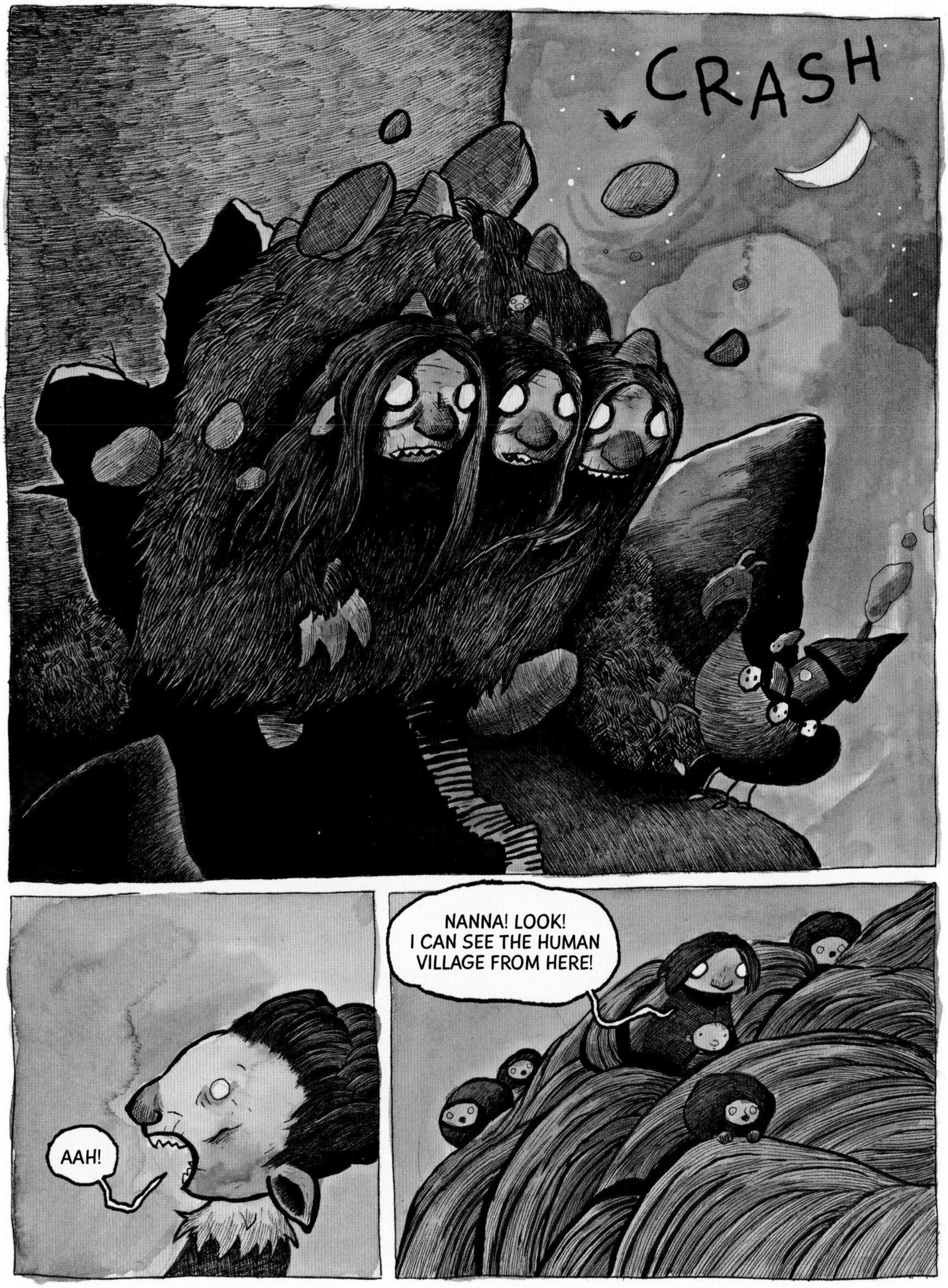
CRASH
AAH!
NANNA! LOOK! I CAN SEE THE HUMAN VILLAGE FROM HERE!

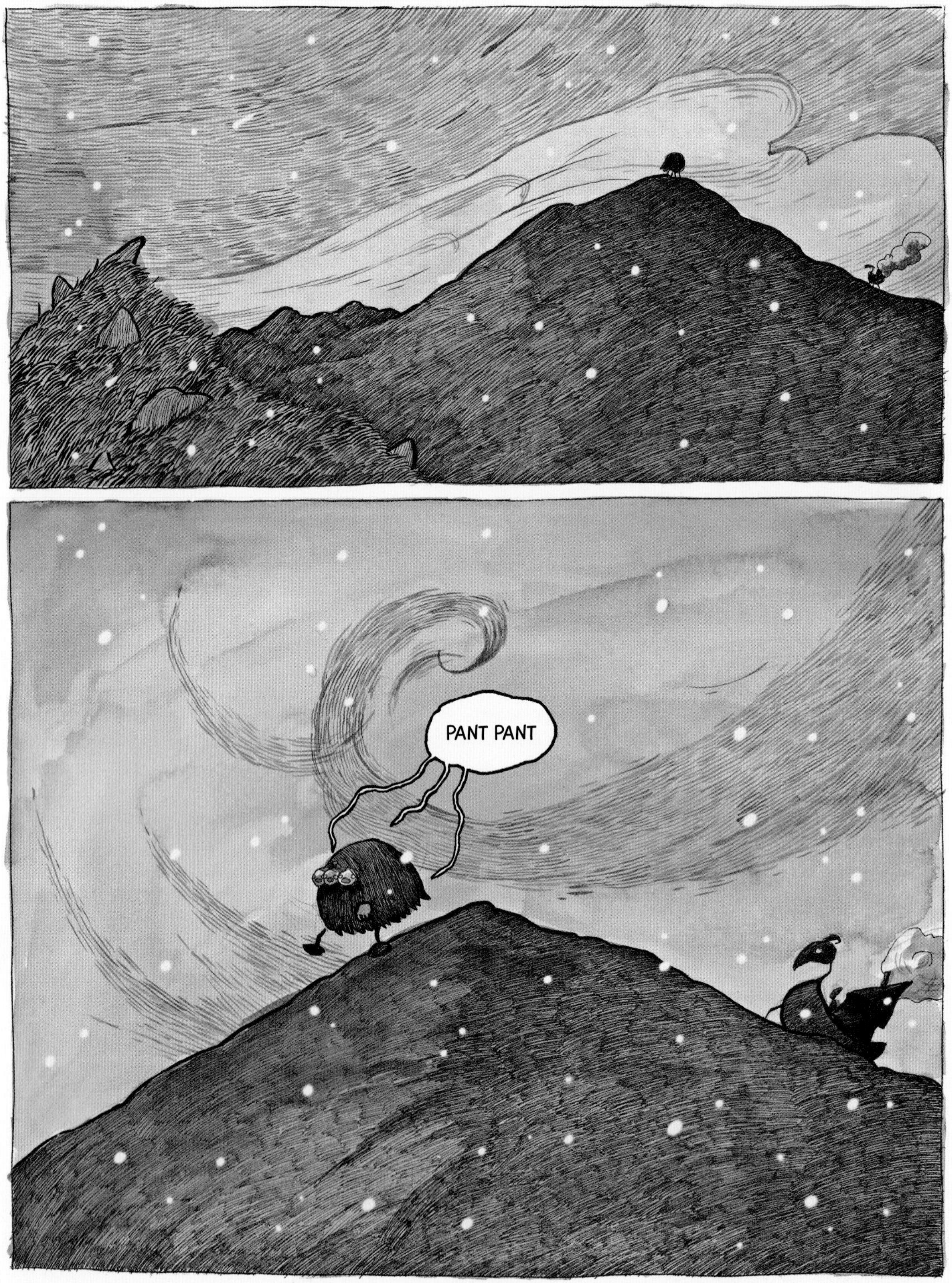
PANT PANT

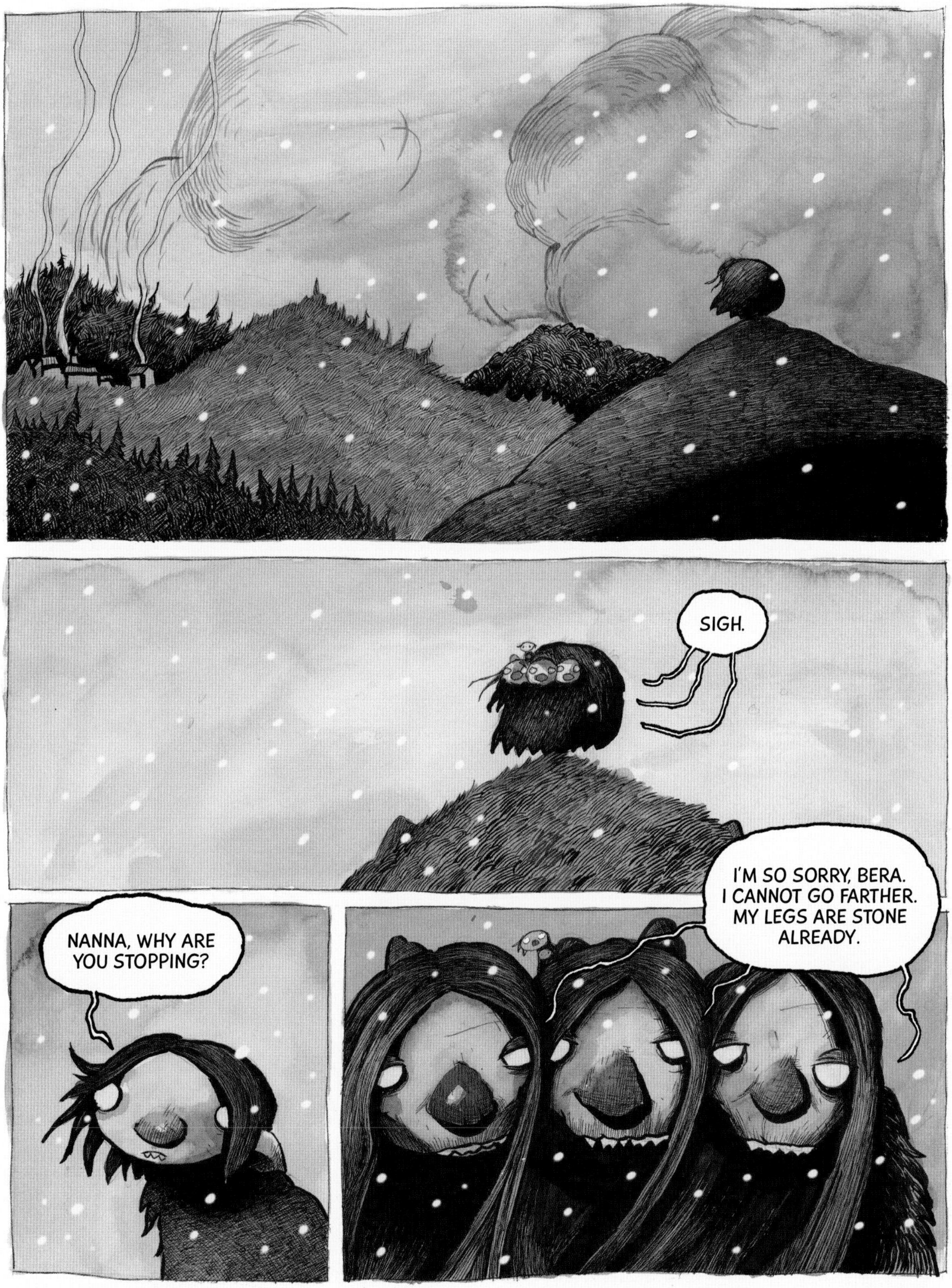
SIGH.
NANNA, WHY ARE YOU STOPPING?
I'M SO SORRY, BERA. I CANNOT GO FARTHER. MY LEGS ARE STONE ALREADY.

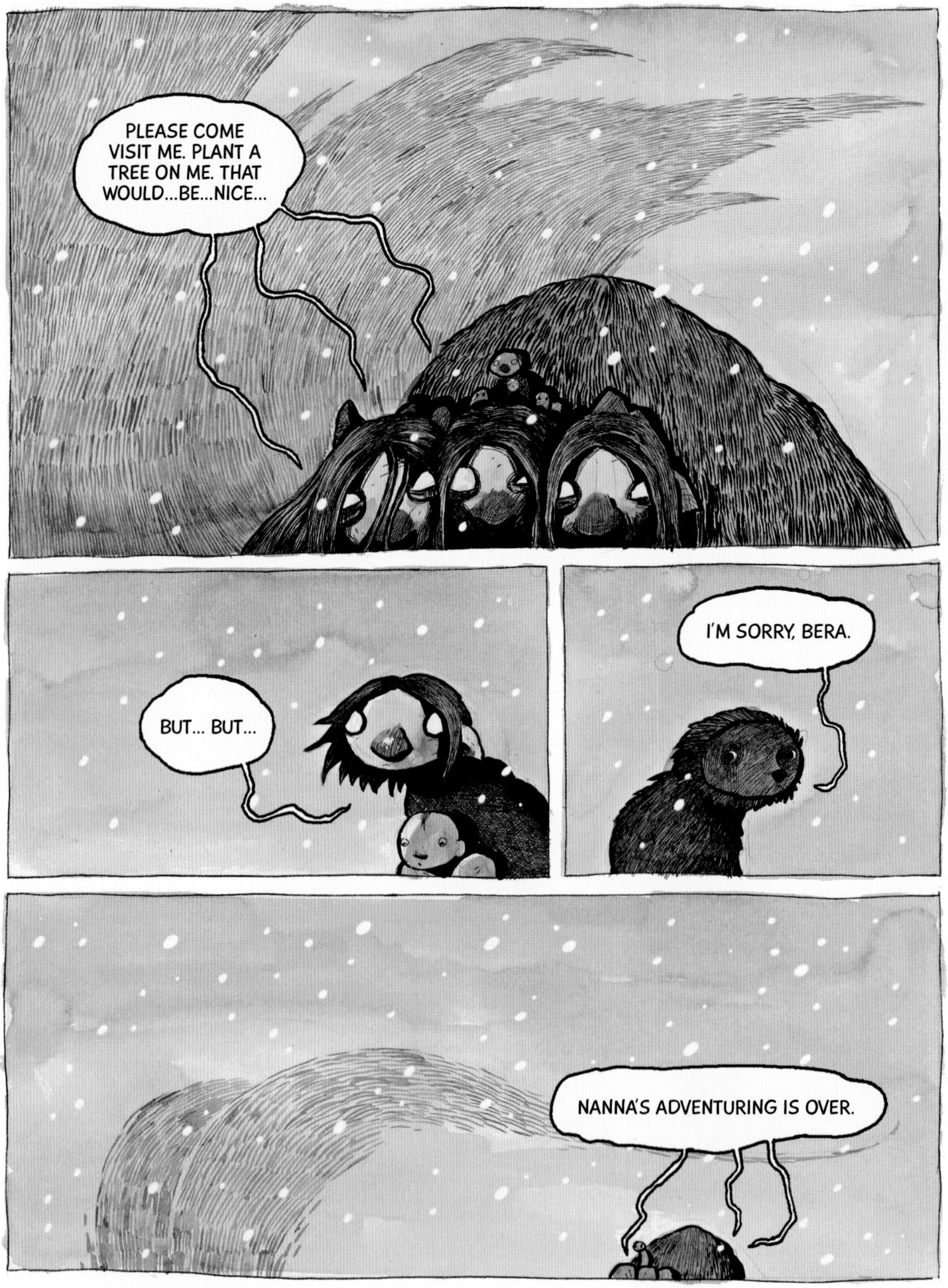
PLEASE COME VISIT ME. PLANT A TREE ON ME. THAT WOULD...BE...NICE...
BUT... BUT...
I'M SORRY, BERA.
NANNA'S ADVENTURING IS OVER.

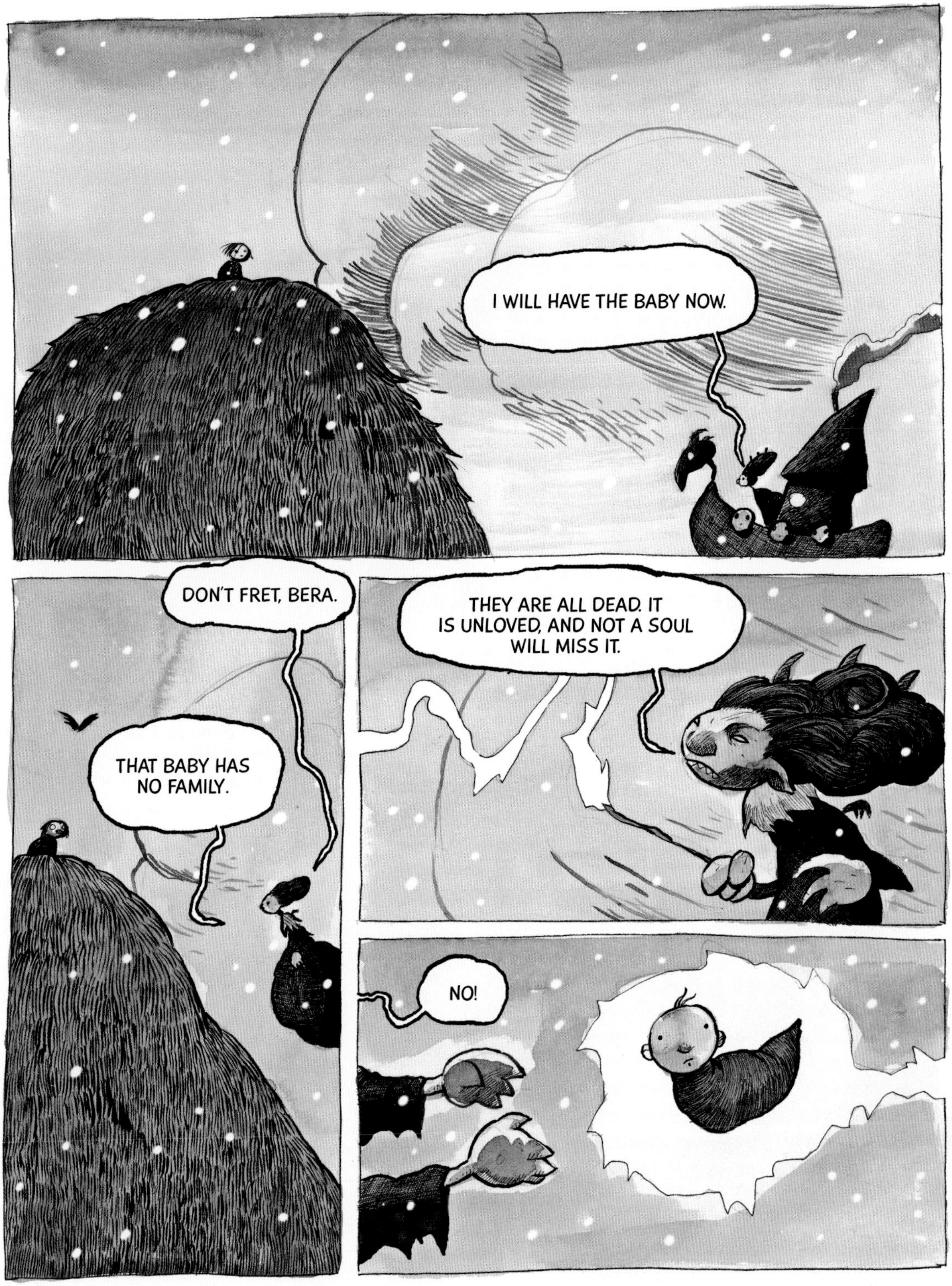
I WILL HAVE THE BABY NOW.
DON'T FRET, BERA.
THAT BABY HAS NO FAMILY.
THEY ARE ALL DEAD. IT IS UNLOVED, AND NOT A SOUL WILL MISS IT.
NO!

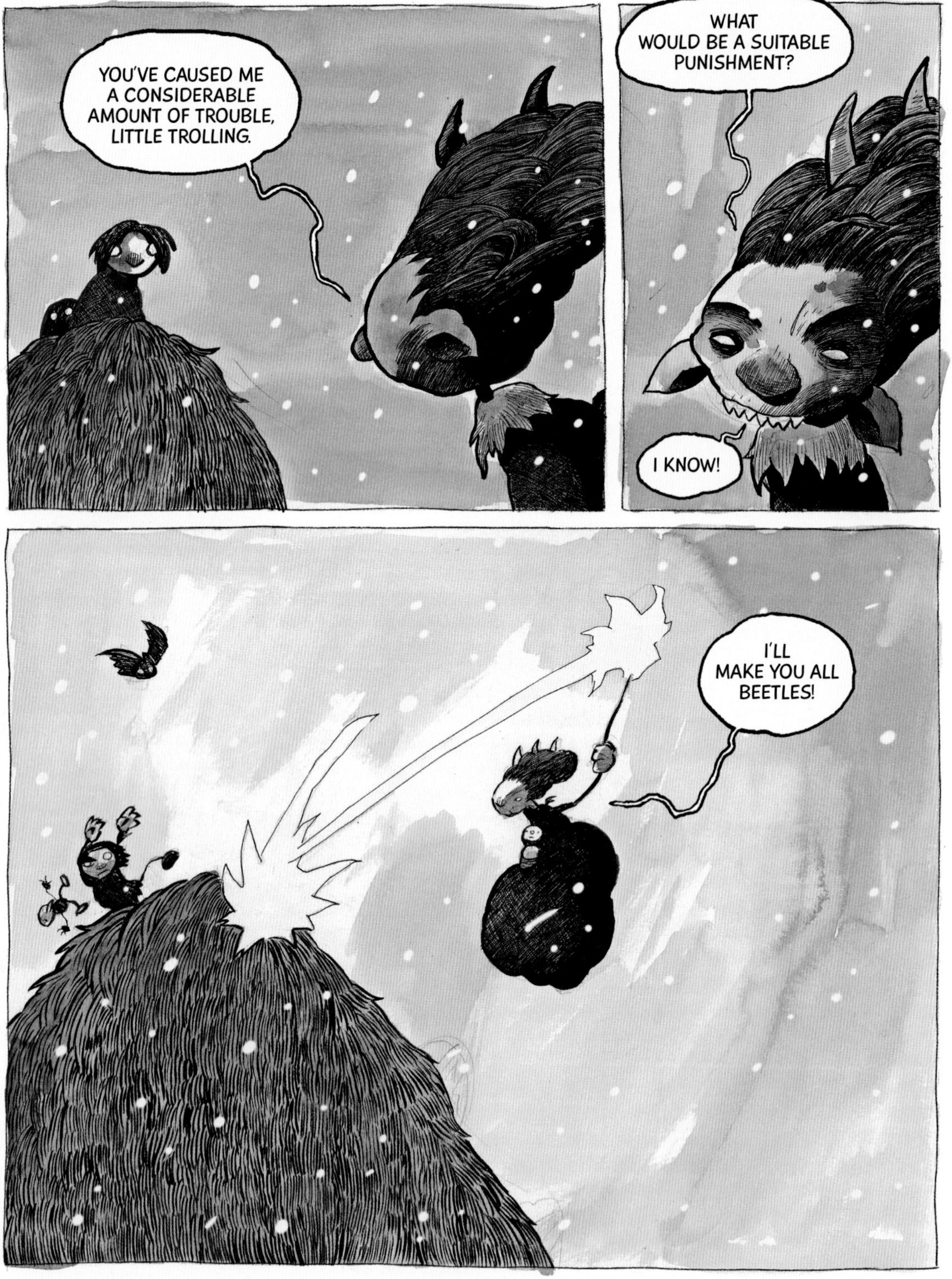
YOU'VE CAUSED ME A CONSIDERABLE AMOUNT OF TROUBLE, LITTLE TROLLING.
WHAT WOULD BE A SUITABLE PUNISHMENT?
I KNOW!
I'LL MAKE YOU ALL BEETLES!

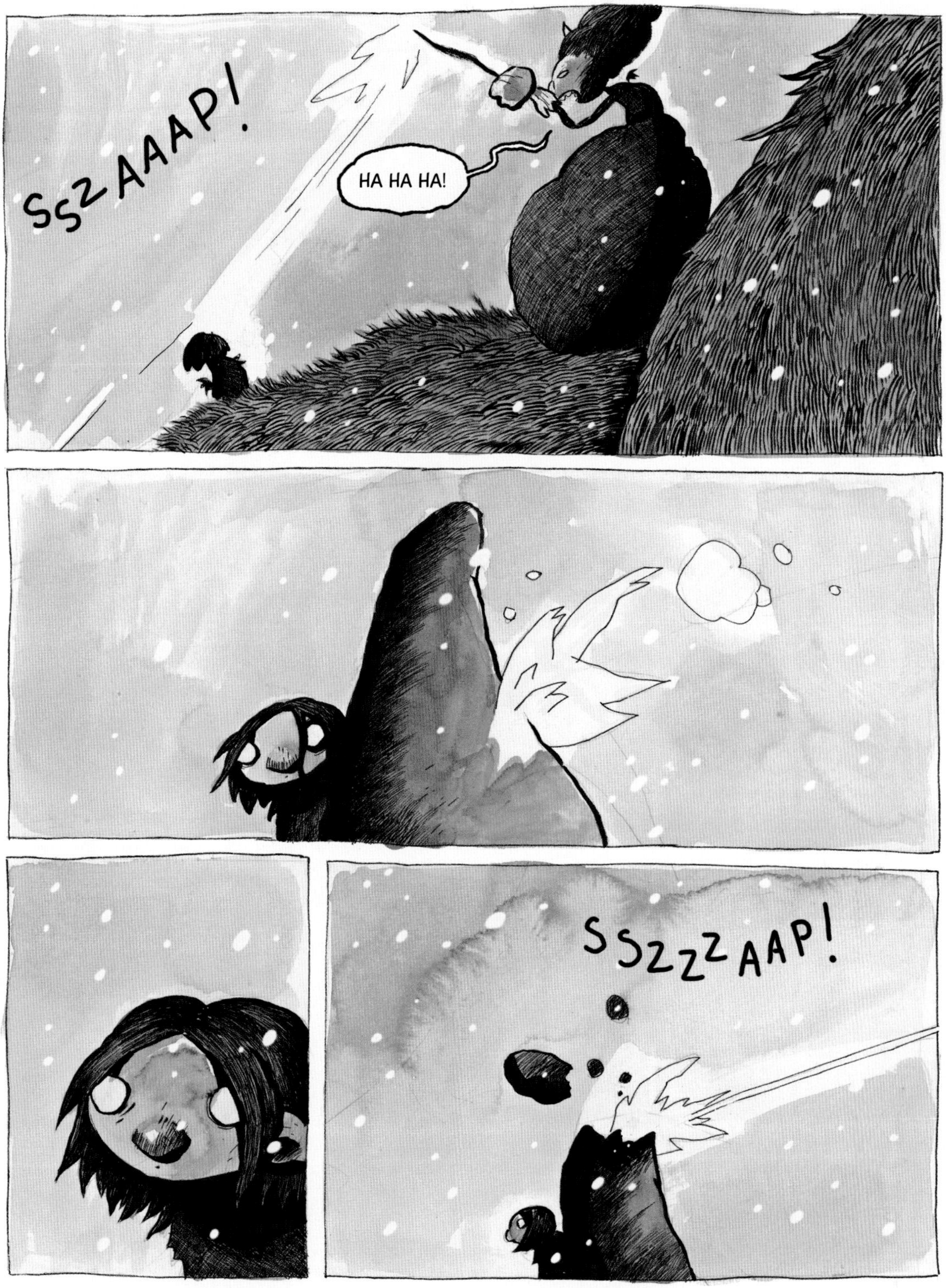
SSZAAAP!
HA HA HA!
SSZZZAAP!

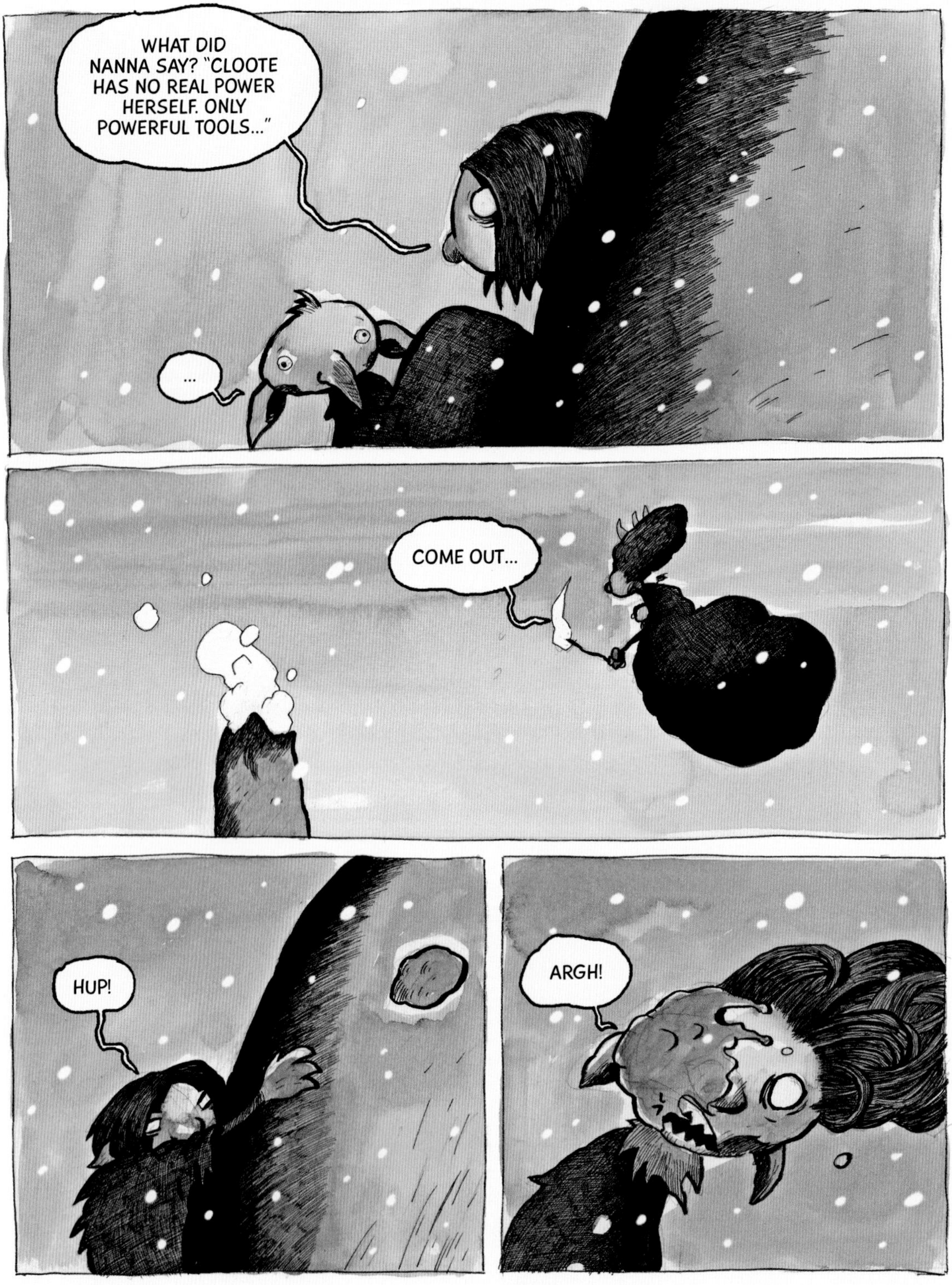
WHAT DID NANNA SAY? "CLOOTE HAS NO REAL POWER HERSELF. ONLY POWERFUL TOOLS..."
...
COME OUT...
HUP!
ARGH!

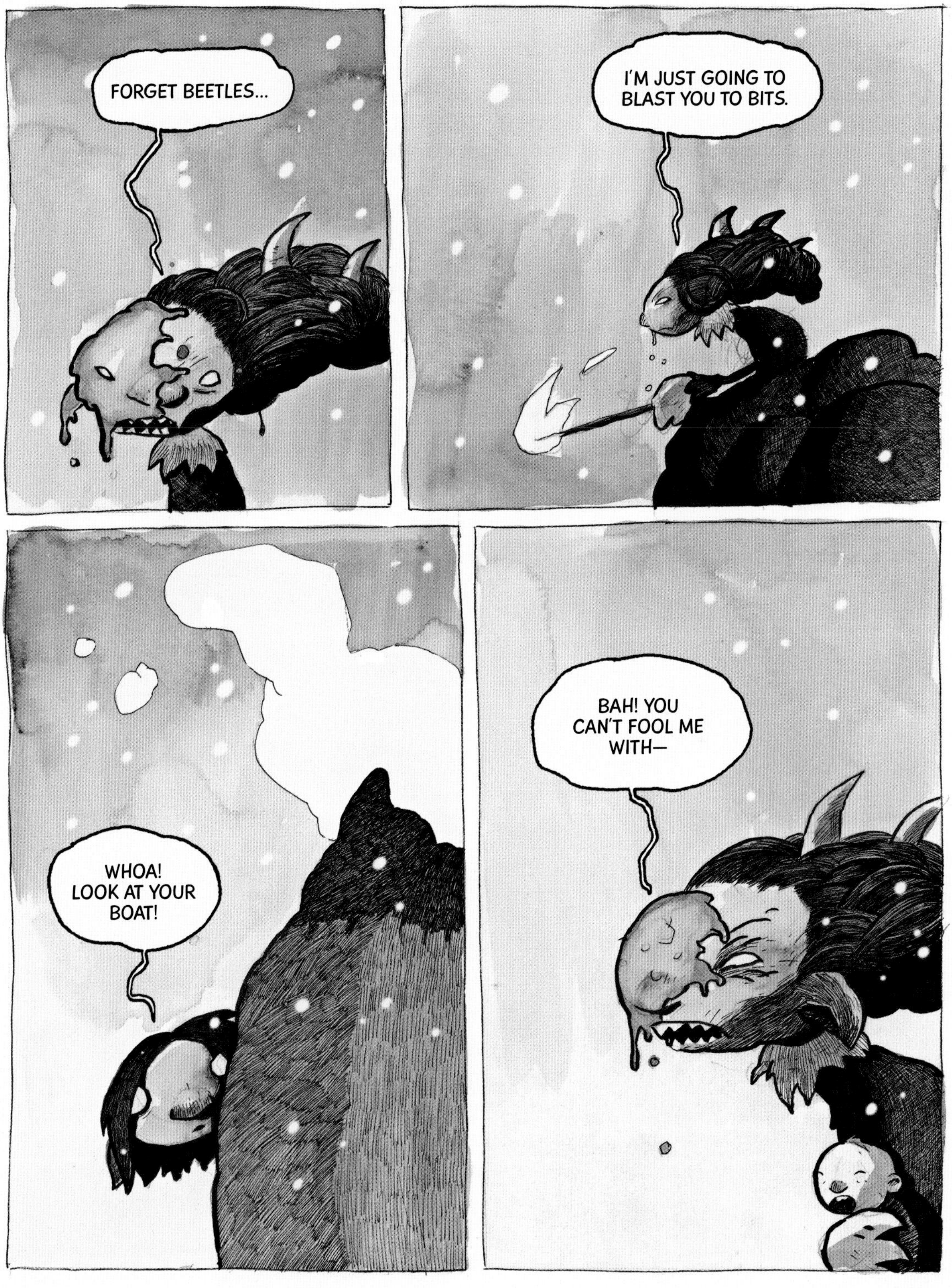
FORGET BEETLES...
I'M JUST GOING TO BLAST YOU TO BITS.
WHOA! LOOK AT YOUR BOAT!
BAH! YOU CAN'T FOOL ME WITH—

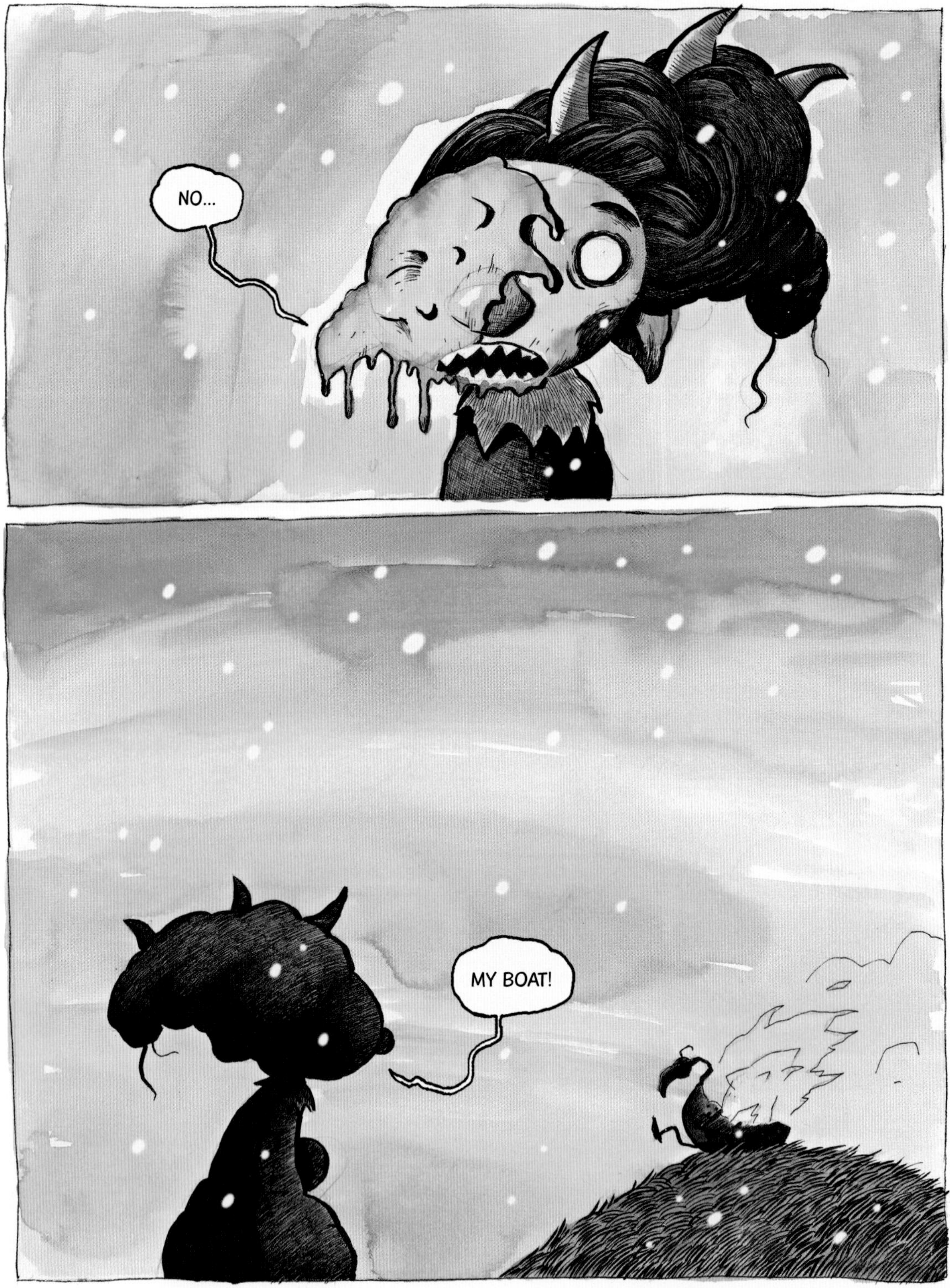
NO...
MY BOAT!

WHO DID THIS?
HA!
CHOMP!
AARGH!

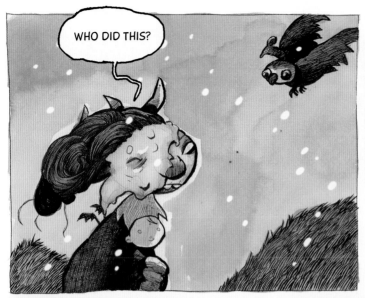

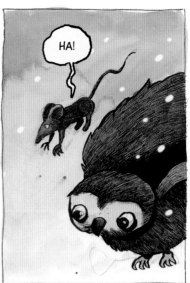

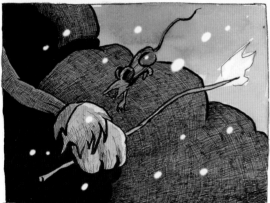

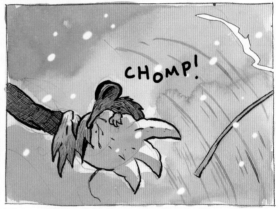

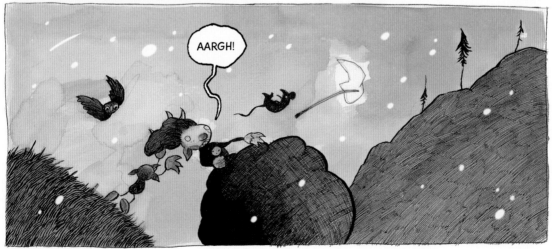

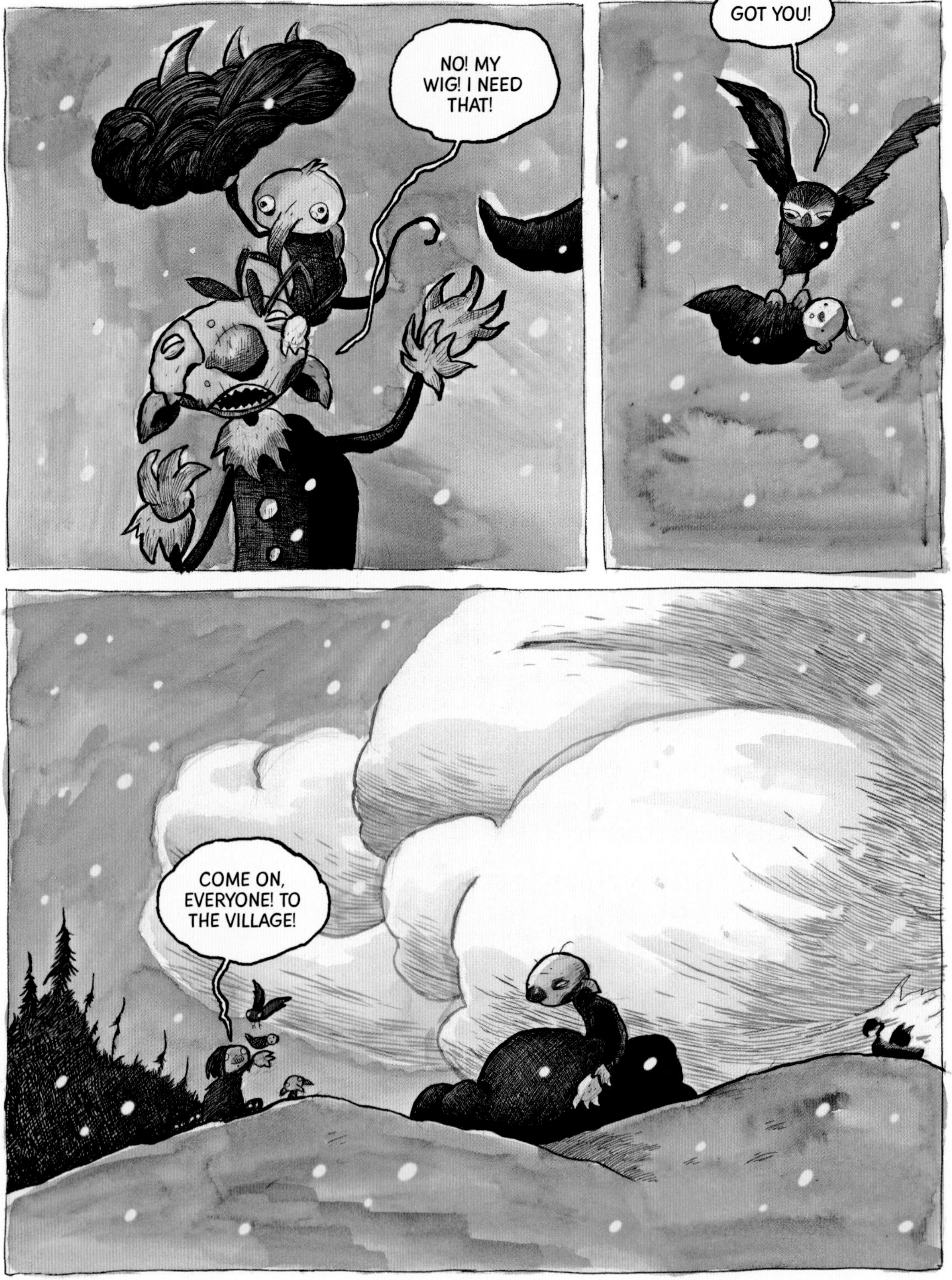
NO! MY WIG! I NEED THAT!
GOT YOU!
COME ON, EVERYONE! TO THE VILLAGE!

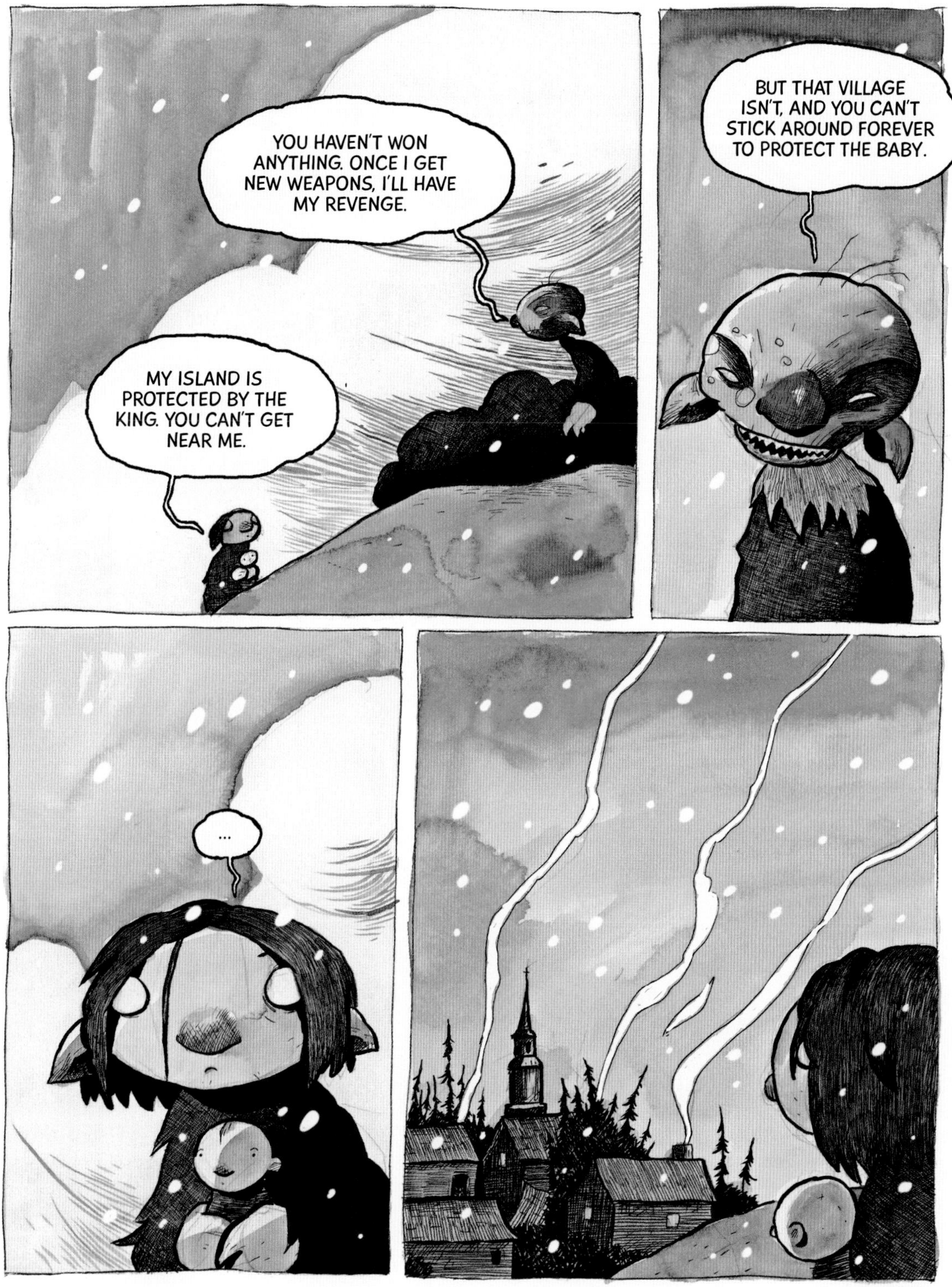
YOU HAVEN'T WON ANYTHING. ONCE I GET NEW WEAPONS, I'LL HAVE MY REVENGE.
MY ISLAND IS PROTECTED BY THE KING. YOU CAN'T GET NEAR ME.
BUT THAT VILLAGE ISN'T, AND YOU CAN'T STICK AROUND FOREVER TO PROTECT THE BABY.
...

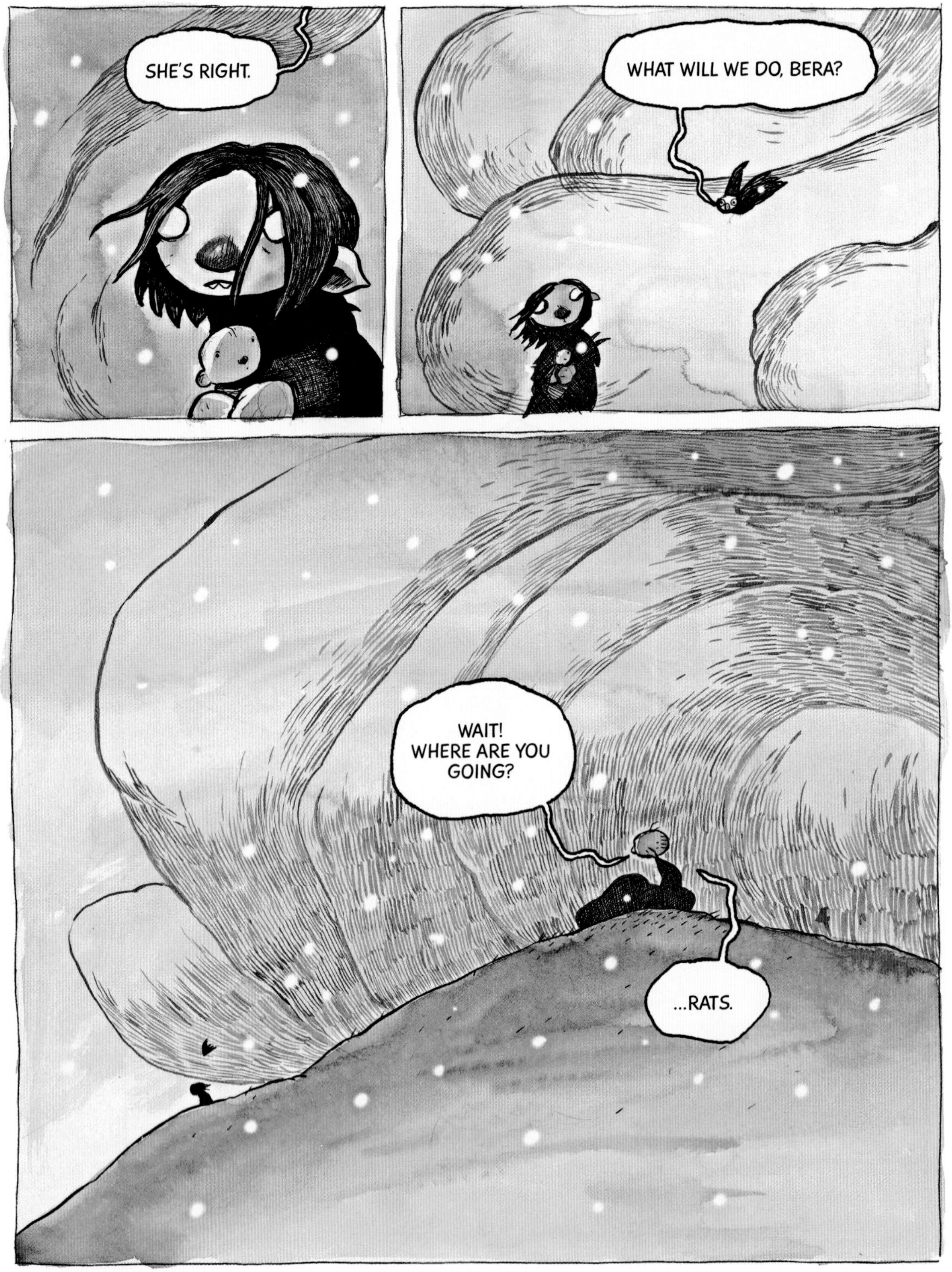
SHE'S RIGHT.
WHAT WILL WE DO, BERA?
WAIT! WHERE ARE YOU GOING?
...RATS.

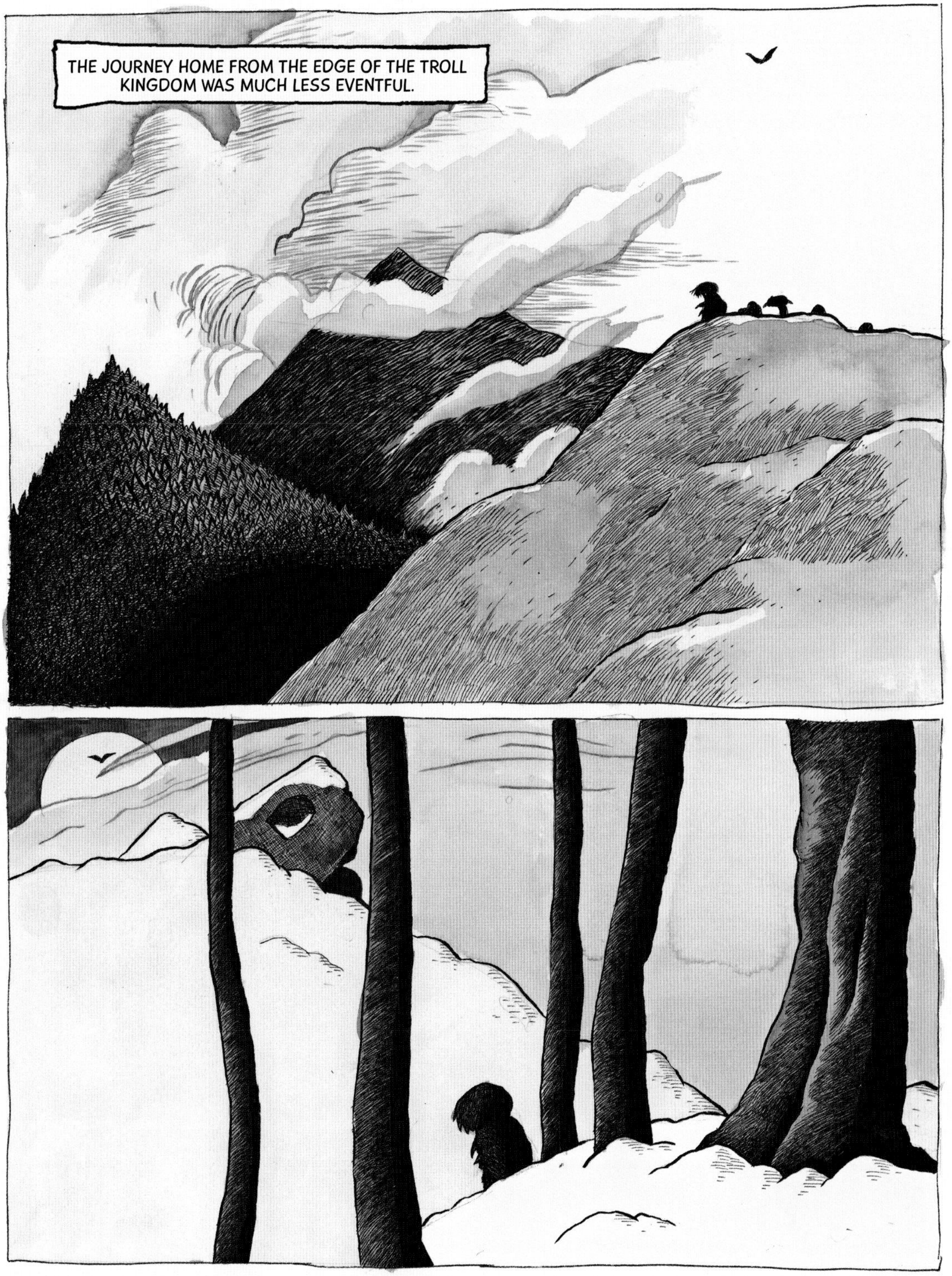
THE JOURNEY HOME FROM THE EDGE OF THE TROLL KINGDOM WAS MUCH LESS EVENTFUL.

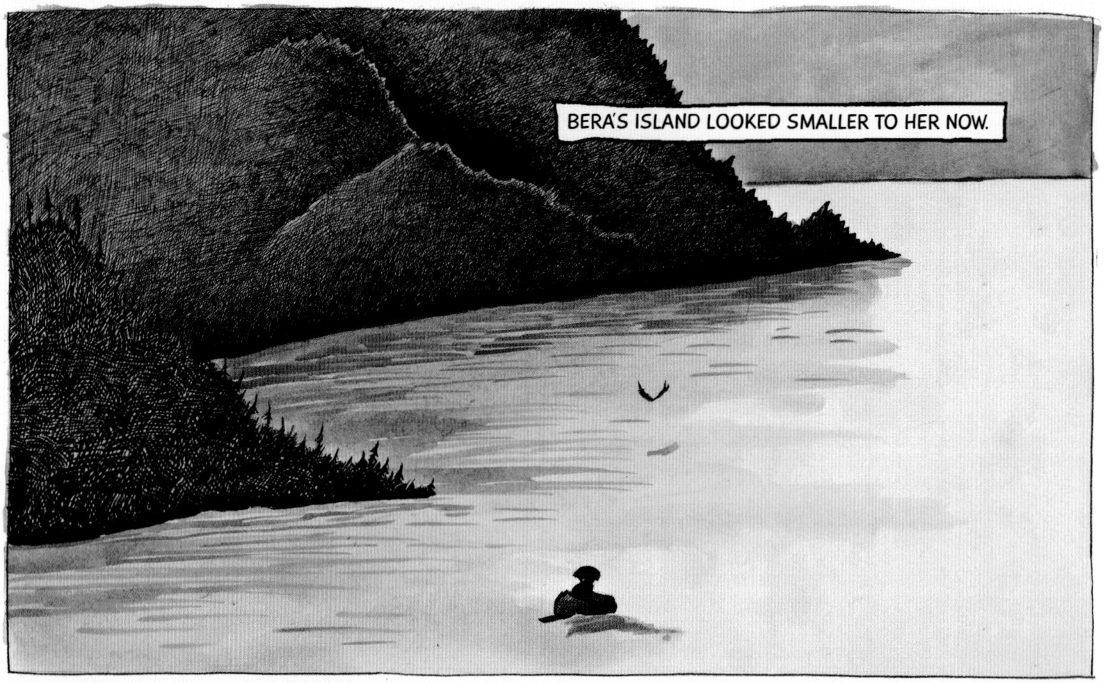
BERA'S ISLAND LOOKED SMALLER TO HER NOW.

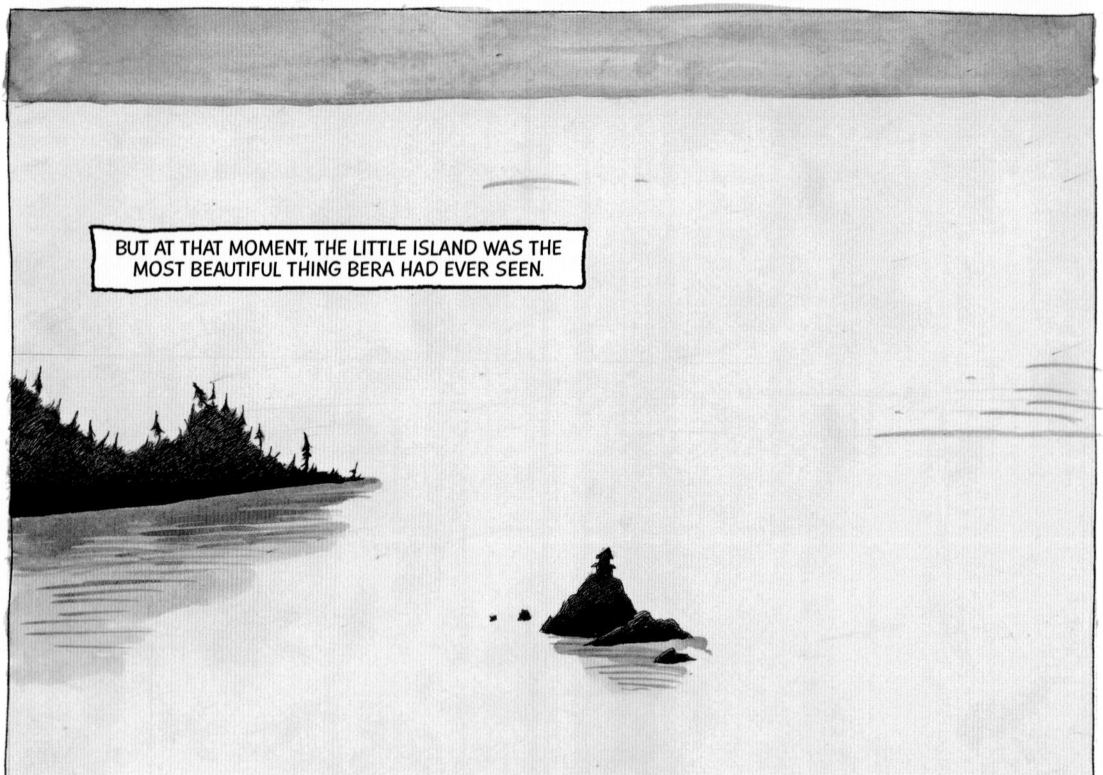
BUT AT THAT MOMENT, THE LITTLE ISLAND WAS THE MOST BEAUTIFUL THING BERA HAD EVER SEEN.

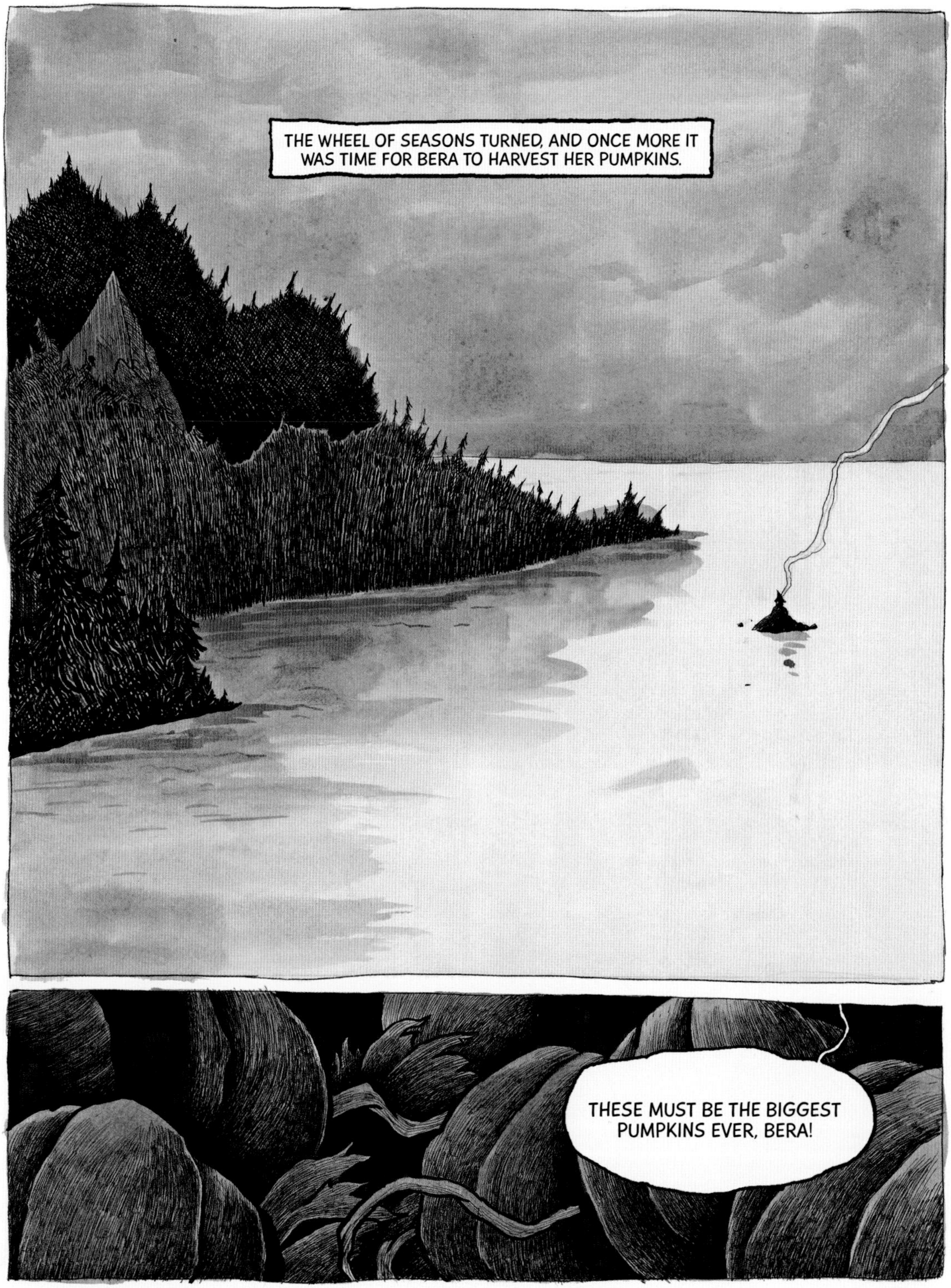
THE WHEEL OF SEASONS TURNED, AND ONCE MORE IT WAS TIME FOR BERA TO HARVEST HER PUMPKINS.
THESE MUST BE THE BIGGEST PUMPKINS EVER, BERA!

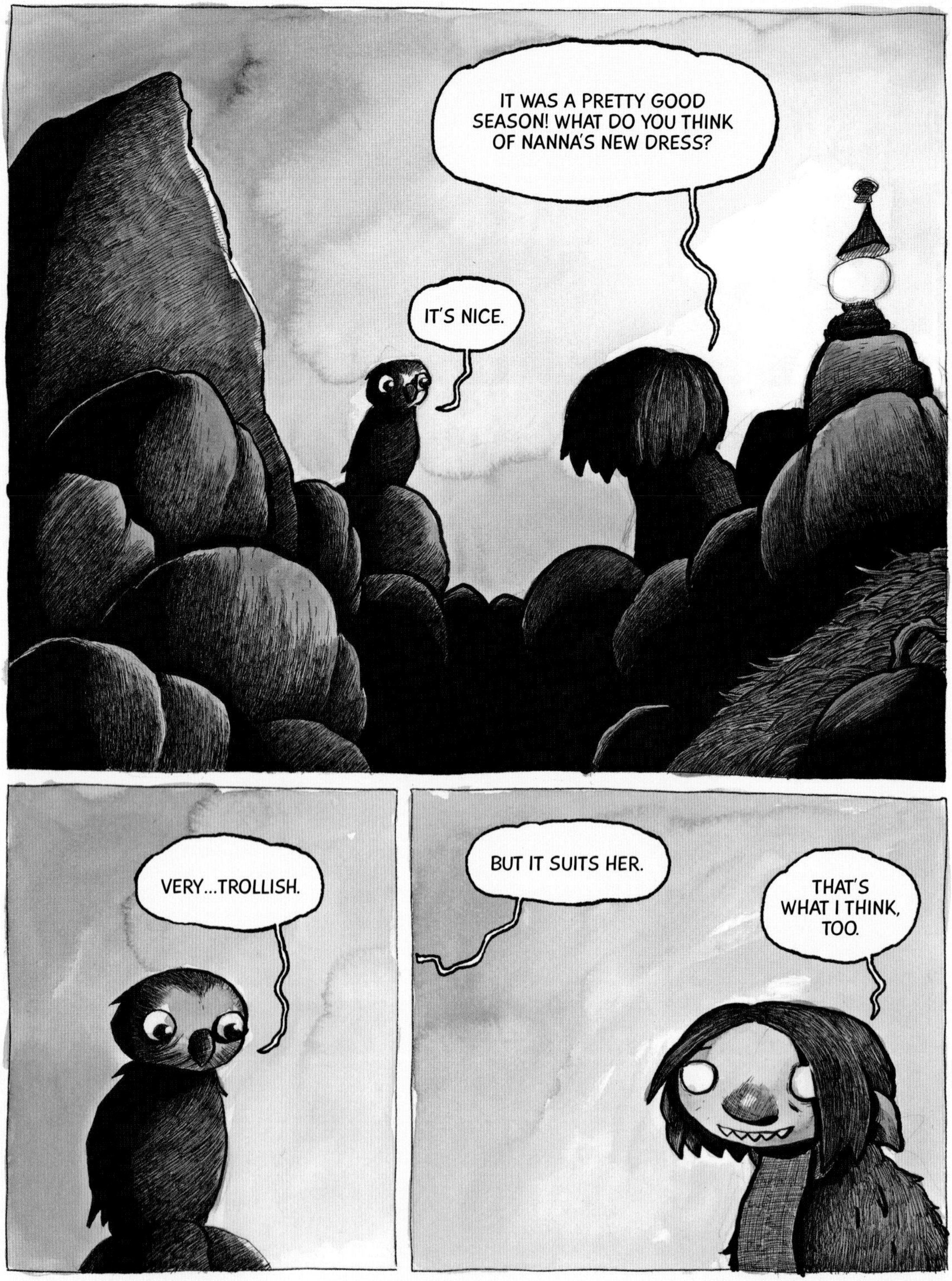
IT WAS A PRETTY GOOD SEASON! WHAT DO YOU THINK OF NANNA'S NEW DRESS?
IT'S NICE.
VERY...TROLLISH.
BUT IT SUITS HER.
THAT'S WHAT I THINK, TOO.

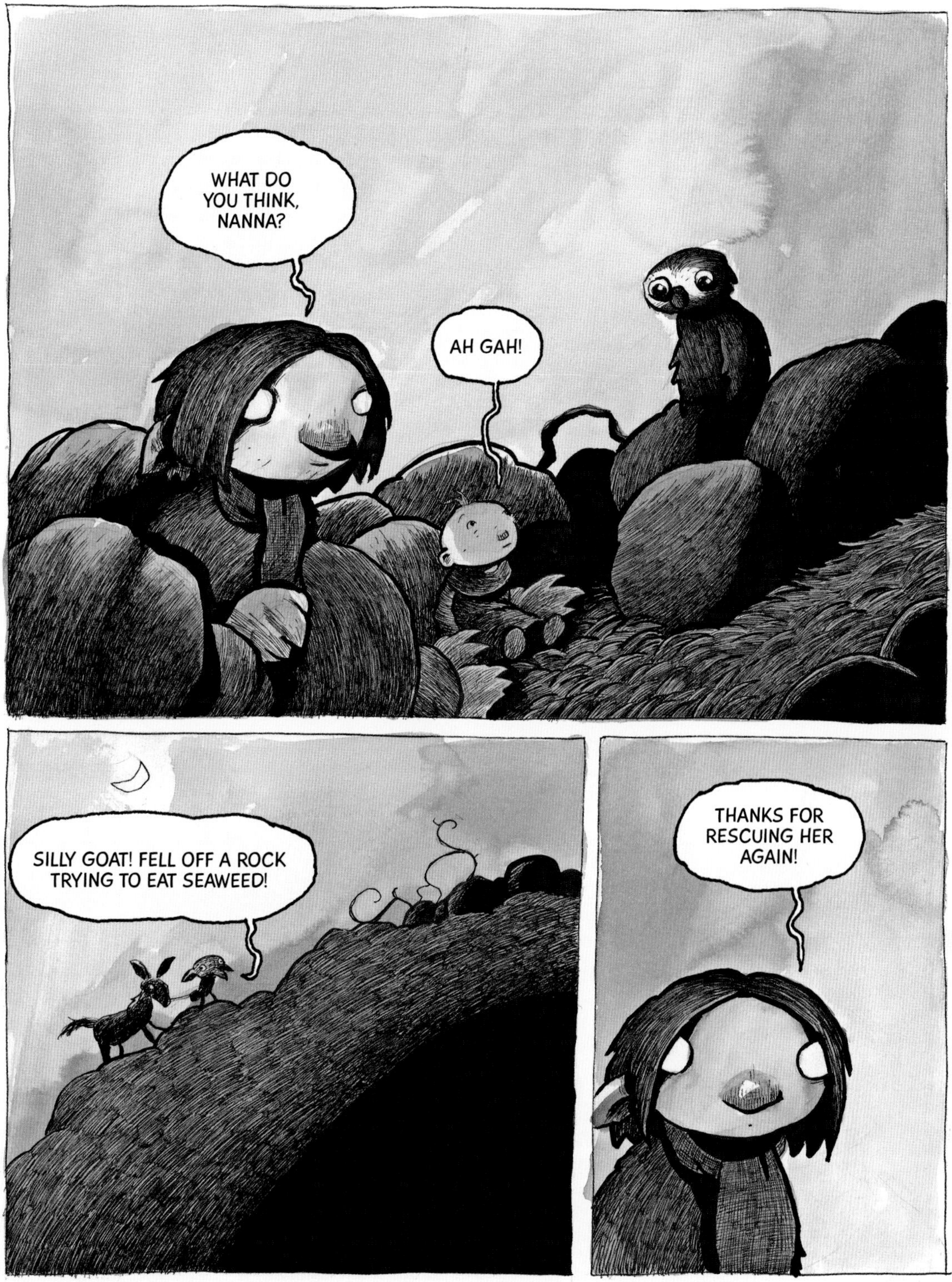
WHAT DO YOU THINK, NANNA?
AH GAH!
SILLY GOAT! FELL OFF A ROCK TRYING TO EAT SEAWEED!
THANKS FOR RESCUING HER AGAIN!

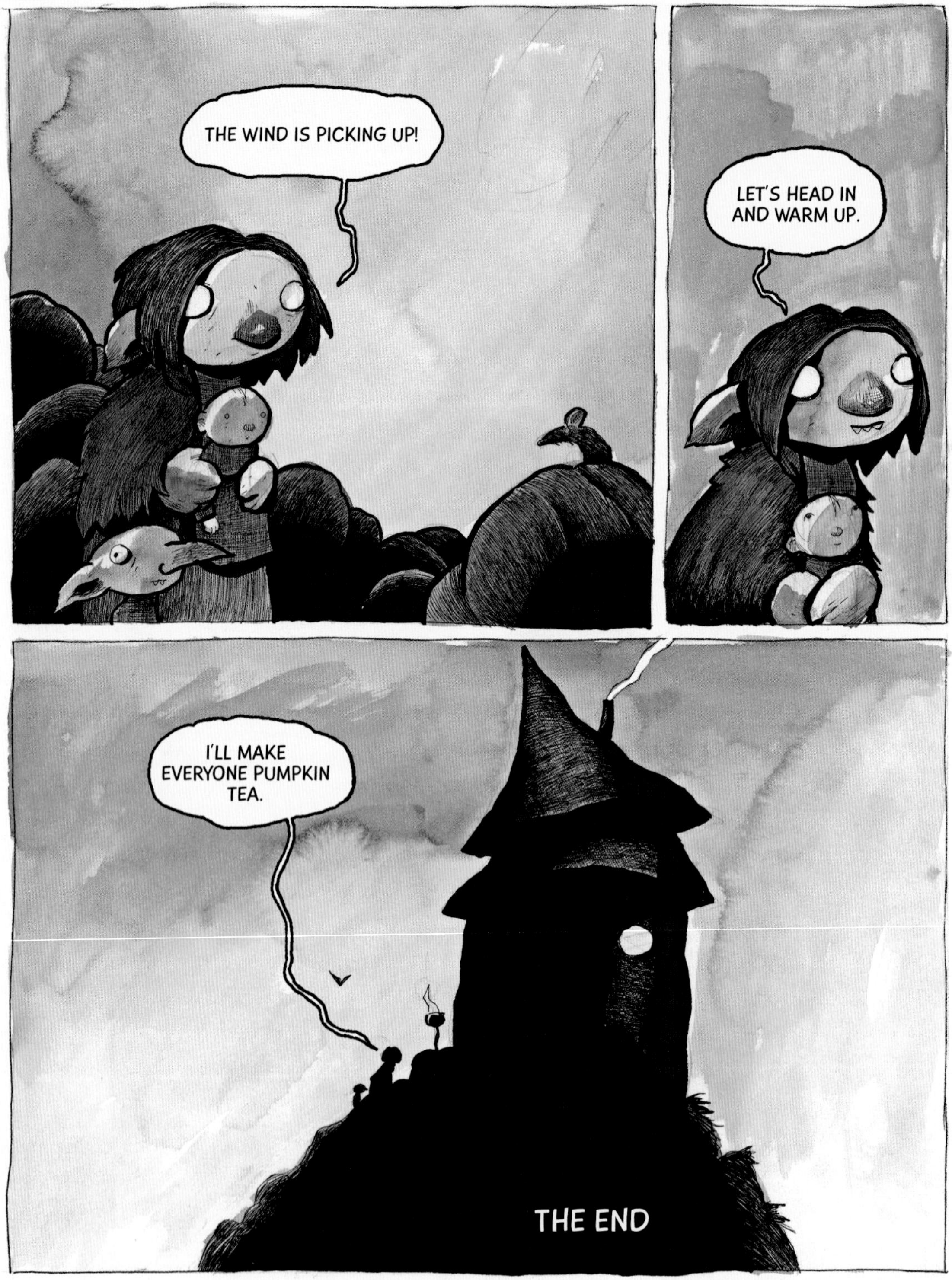
THE WIND IS PICKING UP!
LET'S HEAD IN AND WARM UP.
I'LL MAKE EVERYONE PUMPKIN TEA.
THE END